# THE HEART OF THE MATTER

---

## MORRIS BERMAN

ECHO POINT BOOKS & MEDIA, LLC
Brattleboro, Vermont

Two poems from C. P. CAVAFY: *Collected Poems*, Revised Edition
translated by Edmund Keeley and Philip Sherrard, ed. by George
Savidis. Translation copyright © 1975, 1992 by Edmund Keeley
and Philip Sherrard. Reprinted by permission of Princeton
University Press.

Published by Echo Point Books & Media
Brattleboro, Vermont
www.EchoPointBooks.com

Copyright © 2020 by Morris Berman
*The Heart of the Matter*
ISBN: 978-1-63561-931-7

Cover design by Kaitlyn Whitaker
Cover art: Beautiful old harbor with wooden fishing boat in Cefalu,
Sicily, Italy by Aleksander Todorvic, courtesy of Shutterstock

Author photograph by Azucena Guerra

## ALSO BY MORRIS BERMAN

*Social Change and Scientific Organization*

Trilogy on human consciousness:

*The Reenchantment of the World*

*Coming to Our Senses*

*Wandering God: A Study in Nomadic Spirituality*

Trilogy on the American empire:

*The Twilight of American Culture*

*Dark Ages America: The Final Phase of Empire*

*Why America Failed: The Roots of Imperial Decline*

*A Question of Values* (essays)

*Destiny* (fiction)

*Counting Blessings* (poetry)

*Spinning Straw Into Gold* (memoir)

*The Man Without Qualities* (fiction)

*Are We There Yet?* (essays)

*Neurotic Beauty: An Outsider Looks at Japan*

*Genio: The Story of Italian Genius*

# CONTENTS

# 1

## MURDER, HE WROTE

His name was Charles Calvert, but everybody called him CC. At age forty-four he was, due to an unexpected inheritance, very wealthy. He lived in a large house on a quiet, leafy street—a cul-de-sac, actually—with only one neighbor across the road. That neighbor, however, was *not* quiet, playing rock music at top volume from the second-floor balcony, morning noon and night. When CC asked him to lower the volume, he told him to fuck off. "It's my house," the guy told him. "I can do what I want." CC called the police about it, but the desk sergeant told him they were preoccupied with rapes, murders, and other real problems.

The house across the street had three occupants, all in their late twenties: the jerk, another guy, and a woman. What their relations were, CC had no idea. He guessed they were renters, and when he looked up the property register at city hall, the owners were listed as living in Cyprus. Good luck with that, he thought.

He began taking photos of "Mr. X," the obnoxious one, surreptitiously, with a telephoto lens, for about two weeks, before he hired two hit men for the job. He felt, like Nietzsche, that all of this was beyond good and evil. He had no reservations about what he was about to do: Mr. X had it coming. CC looked forward to pulling the trigger himself. Did this make him psychotic? He couldn't care less. Sometimes life needs a dash of psychosis, just for the flavor, he thought.

He also observed Mr. X's habits. Every day, around 2 p.m., he walked out of the cul-de-sac and down to the open road, half a mile away. Then he turned around and walked back. CC had one of the Scorsi brothers rent a van using a fake ID, and park it one street away. Around 1:30 p.m. on the appointed day, they brought the van around to the front of his house, and CC got in. The Scorsis owned a collection of guns they kept in a locked attaché case, and CC chose the one that most closely resembled his service revolver from his tour in Iraq, a Beretta M9 sidearm. It was a beautiful spring day, very quiet along the lane. Right on schedule, a few minutes before two o'clock, Mr. X stepped out of his front door and began walking toward the highway.

At about the midpoint, the van pulled up alongside of him and the Scorsi boys jumped out. Mr. X didn't have a moment to think. The Scorsis threw a blanket over him, and hit him over the head with a cosh to knock him out. Then they tossed him on the seat next to CC, got back in the front seats, and drove away. It couldn't have been smoother. CC figured they must have done this operation dozens of times.

They drove past the city limits and into the countryside. The landscape was a bit barren, with a few trees here and there. Slowly, Mr. X came to, and pulled the blanket off of his head. He stared at CC, bleary-eyed.

"Do you know who I am?" CC asked him.

"Guy across the street," mumbled Mr. X.

"Can you guess what's going to happen to you?" Mr. X shivered, said nothing. CC continued: "In less than half an hour, you're going to be dead. I'm going to put a bullet in your brain."

"You're gonna kill me for playing the music too loud?" Mr. X asked him.

"I also didn't appreciate the insults," said CC. "When someone is that rude and inconsiderate, death is often the only solution."

"How about you take me back home, and me and my girlfriend and my brother move out of the house and never return?"

"Not a bad suggestion," said CC, "but I expect you'd go to the cops instead. Besides, it will give me a lot of satisfaction to blow your brains out. You're a real asshole, and assholes deserve to die." By now, tears were streaming down Mr. X's face.

"Look," said Mr. X, "I'm really sorry about the music and being rude. Just let me go, and you'll never hear from me again."

"No can do, amigo," said CC. "Look, you only have one decision to make at this point: to die with dignity, or to die like a coward, begging for your life. Which is it going to be? Because *not* dying is not an option for you."

The van stopped in the middle of nowhere. The Scorsis opened the passenger side door, and pulled Mr. X out of the van, onto the ground. He was shivering once again. They handed the Beretta to CC. "Bombs away!" said one of them.

CC looked at Mr. X, lying on the ground. "Get up onto your knees," he told him. "Don't you wish now that you had been a better neighbor?"

"Look, this is crazy. I can't believe this is happening. All I did was—" The bullet pierced his head, and he fell over dead. The Scorsis got shovels out of the back of the van and proceeded to dig a grave. After about half an hour, the space was large enough, and they tossed Mr. X into it, without the blanket, and after removing his wallet. Then they covered him up with dirt, and patted it all down. The landscape looked placid once again. CC

3

carefully wiped off the gun with his handkerchief and gave it back to them, along with an envelope containing $10,000. "Burn the wallet," was all he said.

They drove back to the city in silence. The Scorsis dropped him off at the intersection of the highway and his street, and CC walked the half mile down the road to his house.

⸻

CC WAS AWAKENED the next morning by the sound of very loud music coming from across the street. He blinked and sat up. "What the hey?" He put on his bathrobe and walked out the front door, looking up at the balcony across the street.

"Hey!" he cried out at Mr. X's brother, who was standing on the balcony. "How about lowering the volume already?"

"What are you going to do, shoot me?" the X-brother shouted back at him. CC had to bite his tongue. Apparently the guy was not concerned that his brother hadn't returned last night. Maybe he stayed out a lot. CC went back into his house, dug up the piece of paper, hidden in a pepper mill, that had the Scorsis' phone number written on it. He dialed the number, and one of them answered.

"Same gig, different guy," was all he said. They buried the brother in a different location, about a mile away from Mr. X.

About ten days later Jean, the only person left in the house, knocked on his door. "I live across the street," she said; "may I come in?" He let her in, sat her down in the kitchen, offered her tea.

"What's your name?" she asked him. "I'm Jean. Look, I didn't come here for a tea party. I'm here because I have a feeling you killed Rudy and Jim, the guys I was living with."

"Why in the world would you say something like that?" CC asked her.

"Because they had no enemies except for you, who was angry about the loud music."

"So a neighbor plays loud music, and the logical response is to kill him? Seriously? Do I *look* like I'm insane? Besides," he went on, "where is your evidence? A feeling is not evidence. And who knows? The two of them might still turn up. Why assume they are dead?"

Jean sat there, shaking her head. "I just know you did it. I don't know how, but I just know it." She was quiet for a while. "Anyway, you're right: I can't prove anything." She started to cry; he got her a box of Kleenex. "I guess I'll just move out," she finally said.

"How about you stay, and I pay two-thirds of your rent? I don't want to take the chance on someone else moving in, and playing loud music. All I ask is that you keep the volume down."

"Don't worry," she replied; "I hardly want to wind up like Rudy and Jim." She got up and left.

CC rarely saw her after that; only on the first of the month, when he went over to her house to give her two-thirds of the rent. This went on for three months. The fourth time, she invited him in for coffee, much to his surprise. The truth was, he was attracted to Jean, but obviously could do nothing about it. She was his type: ample chest, broad bottom, and a pretty face, dotted with freckles. He wondered what this invitation could possibly be about.

"Did you really not kill Rudy and Jim?" she asked him directly. "Jean, I swear it: I never touched them. This is a crazy world, and people get snuffed out randomly these days, all the time. You read the papers, so you know what I'm talking about. Besides, as I already said, who kills people because of a volume knob?"

"There is a psychic in town who comes highly recommended. Would you be willing to meet with her?" she asked him.

"Hell, I'll even pay for her services," said CC. "But there's only one problem: whatever she says—guilty or not guilty—it can't be definitive. I read that some police departments employ psychics, and on average they are accurate only 75 percent of the time. That's a very big margin of error. So what's the point of doing this?"

"If she says not guilty, it'll put my mind at ease," she replied.

So they went to see the psychic, and the verdict was guilty. "You shot them and you buried them," she said to CC. "Where, exactly, did I bury them, then?" he asked her. "I'd like to take Jean and a shovel and see if we can't dig them up."

The psychic closed her eyes, and meditated for two minutes. "I don't know," she finally said. "Somewhere outside the city limits, but more than that I can't say. The message gets blurry."

For some strange reason, all of this created a kind of bond between CC and Jean, contrary to what either of them expected. They started to drop in on each other occasionally, until one day they made love. CC tells her he wants to have a relationship with her, but only on condition that she agree to believe him, that he didn't murder Rudy and Jim. Jean agrees, but the psychic's verdict continues to nag at her.

---

TWO YEARS GO BY. CC and Jean are by now very close. But then, CC does something inexplicable. He asks Jean a "hypothetical" question: "Say I really had killed Rudy and Jim. Would you be willing to overlook it and stay with me?"

Jean stares at him for a long moment. "Is this really hypothetical?" she asks him. "Of course, I'd go to the police. What do you *think* I'd do?"

"Jean, for the thousandth time, I didn't kill Jim and Rudy. I guess this 'hypothetical' was a big mistake. I suppose I was testing your love. The answer I was looking for was, 'I'd stay with you no matter what'. But I see now that this was a dumb move. I'm sorry. Forget I ever asked."

So the "test" backfired. Now, there was a strain in the relationship, a rift that couldn't seem to heal. CC starts to think about secretly dating outside the relationship. He meets a woman in a café, says he's a writer, and wants to try out a story he's been working on, on her. So he presents the whole scenario, and she says, "I'd leave the guy." CC says, "I wonder if most women would. I'm looking for a woman who would say, 'let's forget it; it's all in the past.'" The woman says, "Good luck with that. By the way: this 'story' sounds true; is it?" CC shakes his head. "No way," he tells her.

His next "subject" is Carla, a rather steamy redhead. She is very sexy, wears revealing clothes. He tells her the story, and she says she wouldn't leave the guy. "Wow!" says CC. "Why not?" Carla tells him, "If we had already been together for, say, a year or so, and the sex was really intense, I wouldn't be willing to throw it all away." "But the guy's a murderer," says CC. "He's also a nut job. He killed two guys over loud music!" Carla shrugs. "The truth is that I'm a sex addict, and if I don't get to have sex every day, eventually I go a bit loony. So the guy's past is of no concern to me if he can satisfy me. I have no other morality. Sorry to disappoint you."

CC is quiet, mulling it over. This he was not expecting. Carla says: "Most women tell you they'd leave, I'm guessing." She shakes her head. "Life is too short for principles. It may sound crazy to you, but what guides my life is pleasure. Not that I sleep with just anybody. I need to at least like the guy." Then she adds, out of the blue: "This 'story' is true, isn't it, and you're the killer. Am I right?" CC is left speechless. "N-not at all," he finally says. Carla winks at him. "Sure, baby. Listen, I'll be happy to go out with you, if you'd like."

And so their relationship began. Carla experienced violent orgasms, whimpering at the end. CC had to wear a T-shirt, so that she wouldn't leave scratch marks on his back. But CC began to understand why she wasn't bothered by his dark past: sex was religion to her. Fucking was her form of worship; orgasm was direct contact with God—transubstantiation. What's a little homicide next to that? was her way of thinking. But she was savvy: "I know you killed those two guys," she would say occasionally. CC would just shake his head.

And then the day came when the bodies were discovered. Jean went down to the police station when she heard the news, offering to identify the corpses. Of course, the bodies themselves hardly proved CC was the killer, but Jean knew it was so. What had the psychic said? Shot, and buried in the countryside. That was proof enough for her. She moved out the next day, and left the neighborhood completely. Shortly after, Carla moved in.

"You're lucky there's no evidence tying you to those murders," she said to CC. "I didn't kill them," he protested. "Yes you did," she said.

Sex aside, CC was not clear as to why he stayed with Carla. They didn't seem to have much in common. But there was something about her that was intuitively brilliant. She moved through the world like a cat, always knowing what to do next, always landing on her feet--the ultimate pragmatist. One day she said to him: "Why don't you write the whole thing up as a short story, and then get it published in one of those fiction magazines?"

He pondered this for a moment. Did the police read fiction magazines? If so, would he get traced? He had no interest in being a modern-day Raskolnikov. Carla broke into his train of thought. "Afraid it would expose you?" she asked.

"Carla, I didn't kill—" She looked at him sharply. "Of course you did, CC. You know it, I know it, and Jean—wherever that poor girl may be—knows it. And that psychic from years back knows it. Do you take me for a complete idiot? What's to lose in coming clean with me? I told you I would never go to the police, and what proof would I have if I did? Some half-assed short story? So cut the crap. Let's talk reality, for fuck's sake."

"It doesn't bother you that I murdered two guys in cold blood because they played loud music?"

"Why should it bother me? The fact is that you and I are both immoral. I've never pretended otherwise, and neither should you. Did it ever occur to you that that's what holds us together? We know each other inside and out. There's nothing more I want from a relationship. Is there more you want? If so, tell me right now."

CC sat there in silence, stunned. Slowly, he shook his head. "No," he said; "there's nothing more that I want."

"Right answer," said Carla. "Now listen to me: a short story is not proof of anything; you are completely safe. Plus, you'd have everybody thinking about sex, death, morality, psychosis, and all of that crap. A literary sensation, overnight. So why not give it a go?"

And there you have it.

## 2

## THE HEART OF THE MATTER

Alfredo was dreaming again, the same dream he kept having about once a month. In the dream he was in an art museum, like the Louvre, walking down a long corridor. On the wall was a series of objects—but not paintings, as one might expect. The frames contained ice cream cones, Jockey shorts, a ball peen hammer, a pail and shovel—etc. It was all random, and really, senseless; there was no connecting theme. The last frame contained a metal box, which Alfredo decided to steal. He walked out of the museum with the box; no one stopped him. He sat down on a bench in a nearby park, and opened the box. It contained an ancient Greek manuscript, which Alfredo recognized was by Plato; except that it had never been published. The word on the title page was *oi skiés:* The Shadows. At this point, Alfredo would wake up.

He looked around the room. Light was glowing around the curtains. If only I could stay asleep past this point, he thought, I might find out what the manuscript was about. But how to do that? He had decided to write a fictional biography of Plato in which the shadows on the wall of the cave were real, and the light of noetic illumination was the illusion. But he was unable to get beyond page two, and had to give it up.

Alfredo was lucky to have a girlfriend who believed in him. She was convinced that if he could crack the dream, great things would happen. She also believed in revelatory experiences—epiphanies—that occurred in everyday life, and pointed in the direction one was supposed to go. Dreams fell into this category; so did orgasms. Anything that was discontinuous with "regular" life.

Alfredo was a writer, and earned a large amount of royalties several years back for a novel based on Alice's theory of epiphanies. The book sold over a million copies. Like the Harry Potter books, it was a pitch for the reality of magic in daily life. Oprah, of course, loved it, and had Alfredo on her show. He thought she was a consummate jackass, but kept his mouth shut as his bank account continued to fill up. Meanwhile Alice, who was employed as an insurance adjuster, was working on a book called *Sexual Magic in Daily Life*. It was bound to be a best-seller, thought Alfredo, who was helping her with it. SMDL, as they called it, was actually a workbook for women; a lot of it came out of their own sex life, although how popular these exercises would be among the general female population was not clear. Alfredo himself had no complaints: after five years of the relationship, Alice was still full of surprises. One exercise had begun two weeks into the relationship: she wanted him to whisper in her ear, while they were having sex, that she was a whore, a slut, and that she would spread her legs for any stiff cock that came along. Alfredo imagined a lot of women would be turned off by this; in Alice's case, it pushed her over the edge into pure ecstasy. She never got tired of it.

As for his own writing, Alfredo was about six months into writer's block. He had no trouble working on SMDL with Alice, but he simply couldn't think about anything of interest for himself. His desk was littered with false starts. He kept hoping the Plato dream would unlock the door, but so far it was a dead end. He decided to call Alice at work, on one of those typical dead-end days. "Hi, hon; any epiphanies in the insurance business today?"

Alice laughed. "No, just a few scraped fenders."

"So nothing we can use in bed, then?" he teased her.

"Stop, you pervert; I'm getting all aroused."

"Yeah, right. How about I take you to lunch today?"

"I thought your royalties were dwindling down to zero," she said.

"True, but the zero point is probably a few months away, just yet. Anyway, nothing fancy. I feel like a pastrami sandwich at Jews Unlimited. And please don't tell me I *look* like a pastrami sandwich."

"No," she replied; "I was just wondering what possessed the owners to use that name for the store. Sort of like leading with the chin, don't you think?"

"I think they wanted to throw the local antisemites into a frenzy. Probably not a good idea, given recent events, but then they opened the place twenty years ago. Well, no rocks through the windows yet. Meet you there at one." They hung up.

---

ALFREDO HAD a secret relationship with an ex-girlfriend. There was no sex involved anymore; besides, Gina was married, and wasn't seeking to rekindle the flame; or so she said. But if Alice ever found out, there would be hell to pay. For Alice, as it turns out, was a jealous gal: she didn't want him to have relations of any kind with other women. And he didn't, except for Gina—who also didn't tell her husband about the secret relationship with Alfredo. So what were the two of them doing, anyway? About twice a month they would meet at her loft, talk about art and writing for a while, and then, fully dressed, lie on her bed and hold each other. Gina claimed that this enabled her to "soak up" his energy, and that after every session she found herself motivated to paint. Alfredo didn't get the connection, as her art was purely abstract; nor did the holding do anything special for his own creative energies. But he couldn't explain it: he needed these sessions. Five minutes of holding was like two hours of meditation. He always got up feeling at peace with the world. Alice would never understand this.

He dialed Gina's number. "This is Gina," she said, as she always did.

"Feel like being held?" he asked her.

"I was just thinking about that," she laughed. "Yes, come on over."

Alfredo took a taxi over to her studio, and she let him in. "Listen," he said, "I'm meeting Alice at one, so I don't have time to discuss art or writing. But let's do a thirty-minute holding."

"Wow!" said Gina; "this is new. What's going on with you?"

"This isn't about sex, Gina. I'm *lonely*, and I've only just begun to realize it. Oh, Alice is great, and also a great comfort. But I can't explain it. Despite that comfort, and despite great sex, I often feel all alone. Who would care about me if I died?"

"Well, *I* would, for one," she replied.

"I know, I know...It's just that I have this feeling of wanting my body to merge with another body, and I can't seem to get close enough to do that."

"But that's what you have with Alice sexually, no?"

"Yes and no. I mean sure, yes; but what I have in mind is somewhat crazy. I want our *skeletons* to fuse. Being inside her vagina is not enough. There's an existential gap, still and all. Do you ever feel that kind of loneliness?"

"Sure," she said; "all the time."

"What do you do about it?" he asked her.

"I paint."

They lay together for thirty minutes, this time, squeezing each other hard. Then Alfredo got up and left, without saying a word. Had he betrayed Alice? He hoped not.

---

ALFREDO GOT to Jews Unlimited a few minutes after one; Alice arrived shortly after.

"Why are your clothes all rumpled?" she asked him. "I fell asleep in them," he lied. The waiter came by. "Is it true there are no limits to Jews?" Alfredo asked him.

"Absolutely," replied the waiter. "We're poised to take over the world. Hadn't you heard? Check out the Protocols Special." Alfredo looked at the menu. Classic Jewish sense of humor: the Protocols Special was pastrami on rye with cole slaw and Russian dressing, along with a half-dill pickle. "That sounds good," he said.

"And for you, madame?"

"Ham on white bread," said Alice. "No, just kidding. I'll do the lox platter." The waiter bowed stiffly at the waist and departed. "But can he dance the *kozotsky*?" mused Alfredo.

"You do know that if you ever cheated on me, I'd actually kill you," said Alice.

"Whoa! Where is *this* coming from? I have no intention of cheating on you."

"Then what's with the rumpled clothes bit?" she said accusingly.

"Since when do rumpled clothes indicate cheating?" he asked her.

"You're right. I dunno, I'm a bit paranoid today, I guess. You just seem different somehow."

"Different how?"

"Hard to say. Like your mind is buzzing." Their food arrived at this point (mercifully, Alfredo thought), and they dropped the subject.

"So what's on deck for the next sexual exercise?" he asked her.

"For us, or for the book?" she replied.

"Is there a difference?" he countered. She ignored him. "I'm thinking of a chapter on loneliness," she said. Jesus, this gal is psychic, Alfredo thought to himself. He tried not to act startled. "How do you mean?" he asked her.

"Alf, what do you think real intimacy consists of? Because it's not necessarily sexual relations. What could be lonelier than being a hooker, or fucking one?"

"OK, you tell me. What does real intimacy consist of?"

"Being seen. Being recognized by another person. What you and I have, for example." Alfredo's mind wandered off. Did he have that with Gina? Would that be a kind of cheating? He wasn't sure.

"Alf?"

"Sorry, I was just thinking about it. Lots of philosophers have written that we can't really know ourselves, let alone another person."

"Maybe that's what your 'Shadows' dream is about," she offered.

"In what sense?"

"Well, I've said it before: if you could dream past your usual stopping point, and read the manuscript, maybe it would reveal the hidden you."

"What if there *is* no hidden me?" he replied. "What if the Buddhists are right, and the self is an illusion? I mean, just look at the items on this menu: the Protocols, the ZOG (Zionist Occupied Government), Maccabees' Delight, the Masada—it's like the Jews are trying to fashion an identity, prove they exist. Their attempt at being recognized."

"So you see?" she said. "It all comes down to recognition."

"But these are all jokes, don't you think?" he suggested.

"Jokes with a point, as Freud would have argued," Alice replied.

———

ALFREDO CALLED Gina the next day. "The other day wasn't enough?" she teased him.

"No, it's not about that. I want you to paint my portrait."

"Why?" she asked him.

"Alice wants me to get down to my hidden self. I have this 'Shadows' dream that almost does it, and then stops."

"But I'm an abstract painter. I don't do portraits. You know that."

"I want you to do an abstract portrait of me, then. I'm guessing something unexpected will show up."

"What the heck. Come on over."

Gina sat him down opposite her easel, on which she had placed a fresh canvas. "You sure you wanna do this?" she asked him.

"Gina," he said, "you know me inside and out, possibly even more than Alice. Just paint what comes to mind. Something is bound to float up from your unconscious."

It started with a golden orb, orange-yellow, in the shape of a swollen flame. The eyes were horizontal black slits; and behind the image, the ocean, stretching out to infinity. Blue-black streaks dotted the upper part of the canvas, sort of like Van Gogh's crows. It was finished in an hour. Alfredo got up, stood next to her, staring at the canvas. "It's as though my hair is on fire," he finally said.

"Anything else?" Gina asked him.

"Not really. What do *you* see?" Gina took a deep breath. "You aren't going to like it," she said. He looked at her, questioningly. "The 'magic' part of your life is over," she went on. "But what is going to happen is that you will be lionized as a spiritual leader — a guru to millions."

"Where do you see *that*?" he asked her.

"In the infinite ocean; and also in my mind's eye. This may be what your 'Shadows' dream is about. Your unconscious stops before your hidden self is revealed. Kind of a protective device."

"But I have no desire to be a guru to millions," he said.

"Your desires, and your historical role, are two different things," she replied. "And that role is to become a world religious leader."

"And what, pray tell, will be my message?"

"Ha! That everything people are doing with their lives is bullshit, and that they must stop it immediately."

"Well," he said sarcastically, "that should go over well."

"You'll be surprised," said Gina. "One other thing: you and I are going to become lovers once again. Alice and I will be the twin 'goddesses' at your side."

"Alice will kill me first," he told her. "Seriously. Actually, I think you've gone mental. All of this sounds like some deranged Bollywood scenario. In the meantime, let's hold off on the sex."

"I'm in no hurry," she said. "All of this will take about a year to play out."

"And what will be the name of this Alfredo cult?" he asked her.

"NoMoreBullshit.com"

"I love it," he declared. "Thank god none of this is true." Gina smiled, leaned over, and kissed him.

IF NOTHING ELSE, Gina had given him a lot to think about. How all of this was going to take place was a mystery. He certainly didn't intend to make any guru-type statements. But he raised the topic with Alice over dinner that night.

"Al, how does a guru become a guru?"

"You're thinking of taking it up when your money runs out?" she asked him. "I hear it's a lucrative business."

"No, seriously, Al: How does history go about selecting any particular individual for the role? Why Gandhi? Why St. Francis? Why MLK?"

"Something about being 'called', as far as I know. The person fulfills a deep particular need in a wide segment of the population. Don't you think?"

"So at this point in time," he said, "what might be a deep particular need on the part of the American people?"

"Janis Joplin said it was a Mercedes-Benz," she replied. "I'm guessing she was right."

"Not reality? Not authenticity?"

"Check out any major shopping mall on a Saturday afternoon," she countered. "That's about as authentic as it gets."

"Depressing thought," he replied. But if Gina was right, how could all those millions of people get off of buying crap and onto a meaningful life? And how could he possibly be an agent of that unlikely conversion? "There's gotta be a better way."

"See?" said Alice; "you're starting to sound like a guru already."

"Al, do you feel we are real with each other? That we truly know one another? It seems to me that a lot of our conversation consists of jokes and banter. As though we were avoiding something. I feel lonely, as a result."

Tears welled up in Alice's eyes. She was unable to speak. Finally, she stopped crying, and blew her nose. "What are we avoiding?"

"I don't know. But sometimes I feel the only time our relationship is real is when I'm inside you, and calling you a whore and a dirty little girl." Alice nodded, and cried some more.

"You really *could* be a guru," she said. "You go right to the heart of the matter. Alf, I *am* a dirty little girl. I've felt that for years. And you're the only person who knows my secret, which is why I'm afraid you'll leave me. It's that fear that keeps me joking around."

They were quiet for a while. Finally he said, "Alice, I'm not going to leave you. You may not know it, but you literally enable me to live. For me, *you* are 'the heart of the matter'." Alice cried some more, and then they made love—quietly, this time.

The Heart of the Matter, Alfredo mused to himself the next morning, over coffee. If I do intend to become a guru, that's what I should call the name of our movement. But what kind of movement? Most people were not looking for what was deep and true; they didn't want to get to The Heart of the Matter. They really did want to pass their lives in shopping malls, literally and metaphorically. They really did want a Mercedes-Benz. In effect, they wanted very little from life, without knowing that it was, indeed, very little. Gina couldn't be right, about him attracting millions as a spiritual leader. Thousands, maybe; perhaps only a few dozen, max.

So if this was going to be his new career, how was he supposed to make that happen? Put up a shingle that said "Spiritual Counseling"? He hadn't the faintest idea of where to begin. He understood that it had to be a movement of attraction, not promotion: people, no matter how few of them, had to *want* what he was offering. There could be no proseletyzing for the cause, so to speak. He decided to go with flyers, and put up about fifty of them in the neighborhood.

THE HEART OF THE MATTER
Are you drowning in bullshit?
Do you often feel empty, or lonely?
Would you like to change that?
[e-mail address]

For a few days, nothing happened, and then a few queries began to trickle in:

"Who are you, exactly?"

"Yes to all three: please send me some lit."

"This will cost a lot, won't it?"

Alfredo answered each of them:

"I'm a successful author, but this is a new direction for me. I'm interested in helping people find their authentic selves."

"We have no literature as yet, but I can meet with you for coffee and explain the concept, if you'd like."

"It's completely free, for now. If our organization grows, there may be some charges down the line, but only on a voluntary basis."

Alfredo met with all three of them, as a group, to explain what he had in mind. Since he didn't really know what he was doing, he asked Alice to help out. She decided to explain to them—two guys and a gal—the breakthrough they had in their relationship: how Alfredo had confronted her about avoidance, how she had cried, and how, after five years of living in "the shadows," they had both decided to turn to the light. Alfredo talked about Plato's Parable of the Cave, his own "Shadow" dream, and how he and Alice felt that their relationship was just beginning.

"Look," he told them, "this is not some secret, esoteric lore; it's out there in the open, if you know where to look. Reality vs. bullshit is the theme of Marcel Proust. It's in the art of Remedios Varo, the films of Federico Fellini, the story of St. Francis. It's a lesson that has been told again and again, and repeatedly ignored.

Or I should say, it remains invisible to nearly 100 percent of the population. They don't even know it exists. So the chances of Alice and I becoming the high priest and priestess of a cult with millions of followers and dollars are less than zero. Nor is it what we are after."

"What *are* you after?" asked one of the three.

"That's pretty easy," said Alfredo. "To make a few people happy. We don't want your money, and we don't want your adulation. If we can shift your lives from charade to reality, we will have done our job, and you never have to see us again."

"So then you're saints," said another one of the three.

"Saints of reality," Alice replied. "Saints of the obvious. It's a strange kind of sainthood, you have to admit."

"So what's the plan?" asked the last questioner. "What happens next?"

"You three meet once on your own, this week, and decide what you want to do," said Alice. "Then we all meet back here a week from today, and see where we're at." And with that, they split.

---

THE QUERIES CONTINUED to trickle in, and Alfredo began spending a lot of time online, answering questions. One week after the meeting with the "original three," as he liked to call them, they got together at the original café, which went by the name of The Unmuzzled Ox (1 Timothy 5:18). Brenda, a divorcee with a teenage son in college, was in her early forties. She was mildly attractive, with blond bangs and large brown eyes, but didn't dress or act in a flirtatious way.

David was about twenty-three. In the year since he graduated college, he lived with his parents and had no idea of what he wanted to do. His favorite film was *Laggies*, starring Keira

Knightley, about the so-called "failure to launch" syndrome. He referred to it a lot, in trying to explain his own situation.

Ralph, the third member of the group, was a bit of a surprise. At age fifty, he owned a chain of fast-food restaurants that had made him immensely wealthy. He was married, had very little in common with his wife, and felt empty and lonely much of the time. He said he wanted a new life, but didn't know how to get it.

The five of them — Alice had come along, once again — ordered their mochaccinos or whatever, and sat around a round table, tucked into a booth.

"OK," Alfredo began; "you guys met together this week on your own. Can someone tell me what you came up with?" Brenda was the first to speak. "We met for three hours," she said, "and bonded very closely. I feel like David could be another son. He invited me over to watch *Laggies* with him, and I met his parents, who were very warm and friendly. We actually met a second time, here in this café, to discuss the movie. It's pretty much on target as a study of a young woman who refuses to continue living out a false self, and who wants her definition or identity to come from inside her."

"Does she succeed?" Alfredo asked. "I've never seen the film."

"She falls in love," Brenda replied, "and gives up the long-term, staged relationship she had been stuck in. I can see why it would appeal to David. He too is floating until something real comes along, refusing to define himself by an external social concept."

"What about your son?" Alfredo asked her.

"Oh, I guess he's one of the lucky ones. Jeff is a kind of math prodigy. He also fell in love — with calculus — at age thirteen. He's now a senior at Caltech, at age sixteen, and just co-authored a paper with his thesis adviser. He dreams equations. We should all be so lucky."

Alice broke in at this point. "Is it the case, then, that

authenticity is about loving someone or something? Is that the formula?"

"I don't think there's a formula," said Ralph, "although I'm sure love could hardly hurt. But I want to follow up on what Brenda said about how we bonded. After our meeting, I felt close to her and David, like these were my kind of folks. You know, if you eavesdrop on American conversations—and I do it often, out of a kind of morbid fascination—you discover that they have no real content. They are about TV shows, or video games, or apps, or what various stars wore to the Oscars. They are never about what the three of us here, or the five of us, talk about. It's as though the American population consists of ghosts. What I want, instead, are real conversations with real people."

"Hopefully, you've come to the right place," Alfredo responded. "Sounds like all of you had a great week. So the question I now have is, Where do we go from here? I'm getting more and more mail queries. Do we invite the 'second wave' to a larger meeting? What do you think?"

"I'd like to meet more of 'my kind', so to speak," said Ralph. Everyone else agreed.

The next meeting had ten people in attendance, of all sizes, shapes, and ages. They pulled together two tables at The Unmuzzled Ox, and everybody introduced themselves. Alfredo opened the meeting.

"Let me welcome you all to The Heart of the Matter. We have here a first wave, consisting of Brenda, David, and Ralph, and then a second wave—the other five of you. Alice and I are the originators of this thing, whatever it is.

"Several of you have written me asking what is our agenda. Good question. It consists of only one thing: to help you shift from a phony life that you secretly hate, to an authentic life that you openly enjoy. We don't really have any plans beyond that. I have no idea if membership will swell to a million people, or stabilize at ten. Size is not the issue. And participation is completely free. You can make a donation if you like, but money is also not the issue. Each of you will have an opportunity to review your life with the group, and talk about what's bothering you—if you would like to do that. But we shall give you no advice. Empathic listening, Alice and I believe, is the most effective form of healing."

"How is this different from est, or Scientology?" one of the newbies asked.

"I already mentioned one thing," replied Alfredo; "no costs. Those organizations typically charge huge amounts of money for their services. They are also very authoritarian; I'm sure you've read about it. Not our style at all. In addition, we don't seek to recruit Tom Cruises or any Hollywood stars, and in fact would prefer they stay away. It's also the case that est and Scientology reinforce the worst tendencies of American society: money and power. Est, for example, promotes the whole ethos of American individualism, whereby you are responsible only for yourself. We believe, on the contrary, that you are your brother's keeper; that life is not about social or commercial success, or about self-aggrandizement. These types of organizations want you to succeed within the capitalist system, whereas we would like you to transcend that system; to leave it behind, to the extent that you can. Plus, we are not into manipulating your emotions, cultivating adulation, getting you to adopt a certain type of vocabulary, or following some overt or covert ideology. Does that answer your question?"

"Pretty much," he replied, "if you can pull it off. After all, we come here as Americans, which means our deepest psychology is manipulative, self-seeking, power-driven, narcissistic, and money-grubbing. I'm guessing that those of us here today are here because we reject that way of life, are sick of it. But if the organization gets any larger, the chances are that we'll attract a lot of folks for whom 'authenticity' is just another weapon in their egotistical arsenal—another gimmick, not an alternative way of life at all. Do you see what I'm saying?"

"I do," said Alfredo, "and I appreciate your concern. But The Heart of the Matter will not be engaged in teaching new techniques, or a new type of language. Our sessions will involve only public self-examination, in an effort for each person to work things out for themselves in their search for an authentic life. My hope is that the gamesters in our midst will quickly get bored with this, inasmuch as we are offering no tools for power, profit, or self-advancement."

Another newbie spoke up. "It might be helpful if we were to do a session right now, just so we can get a clear idea of how the organization functions. Would that be possible?"

"Of course," said Alfredo. "Would you like to try this yourself, or would you prefer someone else have a go at it?"

"I'll go," she said. Her name was Rachel; she was about twenty-six or twenty-seven, and very attractive: pretty face, and the body of a model. "OK, then," said Alfredo; "tell us what is inauthentic about your life, and what authenticity would look like, for you."

She sat up straight, took a deep breath. "My name is Rachel. I'm twenty-six years old, and I work as a paralegal in a large law firm. The inauthenticity in my life exists on two levels. First, I'm bored with my work. It's forty-plus hours a week, and it's just not interesting. The only advantage is the salary, which is quite large. The firm is wealthy; it is also very generous. I live by myself in an upscale apartment, I drive a Porsche, and I wear expensive clothes. Part of me wants to chuck it all, get a degree in child psychology, and work with little kids. I love little kids. That's the heart of the matter for me, but I've been with this company for four years now—ever since I graduated college—and I'm frankly addicted to all of these luxuries. I think about quitting, but I never do it. Everything you said in your flyer, Alfredo, applies to me: lonely, empty, my life is a charade, and so on."

Her voice cracked at this point; she looked sad, desolate. "I have no friends," she said; "I've never told any of this to anyone." She was quiet for a moment, sighing a bit. "The second level of inauthenticity is my sex life. Everywhere I go—at work, in bars, in restaurants, on the street—men hit on me. And it has nothing to do with dating, or trying to form a relationship. All they want is sex. Since I want a lot more than that, I don't have much of a romantic life, or even a social life. Women shy away from me; I guess they are intimidated by my looks, I dunno. So all in all, I'm completely alone in this world.

"I've also used my sexuality to get things out of men, which I'm not proud of. But it's pretty easy. Men will do anything if they think they might get into your pants. They'll buy me expensive gifts, or work on my car for free, or feed my cat if I'm out of town, and so on, all in the hope that I'll 'pay' them by putting out. And when I don't, they get pretty nasty, as though there was an unspoken agreement that sex was part of the deal.

"So in both areas of my life, I'm trapped. There's very little meaning in my life, very little sex or friendship, and certainly no love. I'm hoping I can find friends in this group, and maybe get some ideas as to how to change my life for the better, as well. Thank you for letting me speak."

Everyone was silent, taking in Rachel's naked honesty. She herself sat with her chin drooped on her chest. The ambient sounds of the café were fairly muted. Finally, Alice spoke up.

"Rachel, thank you for all that. There was a lot I could identify with from my past life, pre-Alfredo. In any case, I suggest we meet here again in a week, and if the group gets any larger, I'll write everyone regarding the change in venue. Meanwhile, I brought copies of one of my favorite paintings, by the Spanish artist Remedios Varo. It's called *Breaking the Vicious Circle*. It's a portrait of her surrounded by a chain or wire, which she has broken out of, symbolizing the move toward freedom. This freedom, I believe, is possible for Rachel and for all of us." Alice handed out the copies, and the group dispersed.

---

ALFREDO'S PHONE rang early the next morning, waking him up. It was Gina. He hadn't seen her for more than a month. "So the big guru is too important to stay in touch with his old friends," she said, not without a touch of anger.

"God, I'm sorry, dear. But you're right, the guru business has been taking up a ton of my time. I don't think I'm going to attract millions, but I think we're now up to fifteen."

"Alfredo, it hurts to be ignored, OK? Plus, I need to be held." He heard the pain in her voice. "You're right," he said; "I'll be over in just a little while."

They lay on her bed, holding each other for about ten minutes. Then, lying a bit apart, he filled her in on what had been going on in the "guru business," giving her as much detail as he could remember. "Wow," she said; "you've come a long way, baby. The Heart of the Matter, eh?" They were quiet for a while.

"Alf, she said, "I feel the need to be authentic with you. I really haven't been, and I don't feel good about it. You know, I rarely see Jacques these days. As an art dealer, he spends a lot of time in Paris. I married him because I thought he could promote my career, and he has. But it's not an authentic relationship, and we very rarely have sex anymore. I suspect, inasmuch as he is French, that he has a mistress over there. Which I don't really care about, except that it has left me high and dry. Alf, I need you to make love to me. Will you give me that relief? I'm terribly lonely."

"Gina, I can't do it. If Alice ever found out, it would break her heart, and she'd probably leave me. And if I don't tell her, it would mean our marriage was pretty inauthentic."

"Baby, it would only be once in a while. Alf, please: I'm lonely and I need to have sex with you." And so Alfredo gave in; he gave her what she needed. After, she sobbed like a baby, while he held her in his arms. "I love you," she repeated over and over.

"Alf, why did you leave me for Alice?" she asked him a bit later. "Wasn't the sex good enough? I did everything you wanted."

"We weren't really getting along," he replied. "You know that. I don't know why, but there was too much fighting. Maybe if you had been needier, like you are now, it would have worked. Alice was needy from the start, and that attracted me."

"Well, I agree; I'm pretty needy now, right? Does it turn you on? Be honest."

"Yes," he said; "it does. But I think we need to limit our times together to once a month, at the most. Leading a double, inauthentic life while I'm posing as the guru of authenticity is going to be a heavy burden to bear. I need you to understand this." She said she did. They held each other a little while longer, and then he got up, got dressed, and left.

Alfredo got home, poured himself a double Scotch, sat in his favorite armchair, and took a long drink. *What*, he said to himself, have I done? He just kept shaking his head. I've turned my life into a lie, he thought. Why couldn't I have just said no, and stuck to it?

But he knew the answer: dependency in women excited him. It was like that with his first serious partner, Joyce, when they were both freshmen in college. Joyce was attractive, but not to the degree that, say, that woman Rachel was; men were not constantly hitting on her. She sat down next to him in the library, made up some excuse to start talking to him. They walked over to the student union, had coffee; Joyce may have even alluded to being lonely. A couple of dates, and they wound up in her bed. They were together for a year after that.

That was the pattern; he had never deviated from it, except with Gina—which is probably why their relationship had failed. Now, years later, lonely and horny, Gina was practically a different woman, the kind he couldn't resist. But what to do? He would deliver on his promise to her of once a month, but emotionally speaking, he was a mess. An old story: the guru with the feet of clay. All he could do, he figured, was to just wait it out, and hope everything didn't blow up in his face.

At the next meeting, they were fifteen. The Unmuzzled Ox could no longer accommodate them, so they met in Alfredo's apartment, which was fairly large.

"So in a short time, we've grown from five to fifteen," Alfredo said to the group. "At this point, it's hard to predict what will happen, But let's go around and introduce ourselves, and then maybe one of you would like to do some self-exploration."

The person who volunteered this time was again a woman, Angie, who taught Latin at a private, rather posh, British-style prep school. She was in her late forties, fairly attractive, with long legs and a good figure. She wore pastel-red lipstick and gold loop earrings, but dressed modestly.

"My name is Angie," she began. "I'm forty-eight, teach high school Latin, and have a materially comfortable life. I actually like my job, or could like it; the problem is that my students have no interest in Latin or Roman history, and are in my classes only because it's a required subject at this particular school. I never had any great career ambitions, but I've wound up in a situation where I have to drag myself out of bed every morning. Authenticity for me would be to teach a small number of students who share my passion for the subject, but that's a rare thing in America today. I doubt it even exists. I have no interest in pursuing an entirely different career; the problem is that this one proved to be a disappointment, and it soaks up about sixty hours a week.

"The major disappointment for me, however, has been my love life. At twenty-two, I was looking forward to, or at least hoping for, marriage and children. It never happened, and I think it's partly my fault. My feminism got me to dislike men, to look down on them, and the guys I briefly dated were not stupid: they could pick up on my attitude quite easily. I had sex occasionally, but it was basically to relieve tension, not much more. Authenticity in this area of my life would mean having a partner, instead of masturbating myself to sleep every night. But I'm not optimistic: the men I'm attracted to are interested in much younger women. I feel like the train left the station, and I wasn't on it."

At this point Angie began to weep. Alfredo sat next to her, put his arm around her. "I know it sounds stupid, but this is not the life I signed up for. I feel like I flunked life, and that I have only myself to blame. I remember that song, 'I never promised you a rose garden'. OK, I realize that life is not necessarily fair, but knowing that doesn't really help me very much. I play tennis, have a couple of great girl friends, thank god, to do things with; but I can't shake the belief that I'm in the wrong life. I'm angry about it and am determined to fight my way out of this situation. But I don't know how; which is why your flyer caught my attention. I saw it and at first I thought, 'Oh no, not more New Age bullshit'. But then I talked with Alice on the phone for nearly an hour, and I heard such warmth in her voice that I was encouraged to come here, and to believe that I might be able to turn things around. Thank you, Alice; you are such a kind person."

"You're welcome," Alice told her. "Just know that I believe in you, and I believe that life has good things in store for you." Angie began crying again, and one by one each member of the group got up and hugged her.

"Wow!" exclaimed Alfredo; "that was a great session. Rachel, I've been meaning to ask you: did anything change for you over the past week?" She smiled broadly. "I think my self-exploration of last week paid off," she replied. "First, I got a bunch of college catalogues and looked into their child psych programs. Second, I met a guy! I went over to The Unmuzzled Ox after work one day this week, and began talking to him—Paul, his name is—about his work. He's a writer; he writes mystery novels. He's about ten years older than me, but I don't care. I could sense that he wasn't a player. Anyway, we're going out for dinner this Saturday."

The whole group applauded. Alice said, "You know, in order to change our narratives about our lives, we first need to recognize that we *have* a narrative. Most of us live in a kind of framework that is often negative, and which defines our reality. But it's possible to see that framework *as* a framework, and then to realize that other frameworks are possible. Rachel, last week you told us that you felt trapped. Do you still feel that?" Rachel shook her head. "I might be in the loooove framework," she quipped. Everybody laughed.

"OK, then," said Alice. "Next week, same time, same place." Everyone applauded again, and walked out into the street.

A week later, the group had grown to twenty. They could all fit into Alfredo's apartment, but only just. Alfredo figured he would have to see if they might be able to rent a hall in a nearby church, if this rate of growth continued.

"One thing I'd like to suggest to you," he began this week's session, "is cultivating a sense of humor about our lives. Sure, we are engaged in very serious work, but I think we need to hold it loosely, if you know what I mean; to relax. We don't want to become authenticity zealots. Flexible frameworks, not rigid ones."

"Angie," he said, turning to her, "any changes over the last week?"

"Nothing on the romance front, I'm sorry to say, but at work I posted a notice about starting a Roman history and language club, for those interested in exploring the subject more deeply. So far, one student signed up. Yea!"

"Good show," said Alfredo, and everyone applauded. "We need to hear from the men in the group. Any of you guys game to try?"

"I have a question, if that's OK," said David, one of the original three. "As most of you know, I'm floating, without any direction, like Keira Knightley in the movie *Laggies*. Her situation is resolved for her by accident, so to speak: her love for Craig suddenly emerges from nowhere. And in the case of Jeff, Brenda's son, he got his calling to mathematics very early, at age thirteen. Do these answers always fall from the sky? Am I supposed to just continue waiting?"

Alice responded. "David, we're not here to give advice, or supply answers. We're only here to listen. Why don't you try a self-exploration, and see what comes up?"

"OK." David sat up straight in his chair, and began. "My name is David, and I graduated college a year ago with a major in English lit. Since then, I've been living at home with my parents, trying to figure out what I want to do and not succeeding. I like English lit, but I don't want to be a professor, and I don't think I have the talent to be a writer. I don't really have anything to write about, anyway." He stopped, kind of lost in thought.

"When I try to think of what turns me on...it's puzzles. The only extracurricular thing I did in college was join the chess club, and the only course I took, outside of English lit, that I enjoyed was called Mathematics for Non-Math Majors, or something like that. I especially liked the unit on the history of infinity. I also enjoy doing crossword puzzles. As for chess, I became fascinated at one point with Bobby Fischer, and I worked through all of his games. But I can't imagine I could make a living out of chess, or crossword puzzles, or studying infinity." He stopped again, musing on the subject.

"Of course, I may be looking at it backwards, or upside down. I tend to block any inclination by saying that you can't make a living out of it. I mean, maybe the answer is just to plunge into whatever turns you on, and not worry, for the moment, if it can generate an income. Maybe I should just try it, chess or reading about the history of math, and see where it leads. I mean, obviously, I'm not getting anywhere now."

The room was quiet. Alfredo finally said, "Your self-exploration reminds me of something Federico Fellini once said, about embracing life with the openness of a child. He said if you do that, all good things will come your way.

"Anyway...our membership just took a quantum leap, up to thirty-three. We need a new meeting place. You all know the deli on First Avenue called Jews Unlimited, right? The owners are great people, and agreed to let us use their party room for our meetings, free of charge, as long as we don't meet on a weekend. So let's continue with our Thursday schedule, one week from today. You can all order food, if you want, but only after the meeting, not during it. Are we cool with this?"

"L'chaim!" someone called out. Alfredo laughed. "I guess that's a yes."

The Heart of the Matter continued to grow. Alice and Alfredo were forced to ask for donations so that they could rent a hall large enough to hold 250 people. Ralph, the fast-food magnate, stepped up and covered the entire cost for six months. This left about $1,000 in the "Heart" bank account, which everyone agreed should remain there in the event of future expenses. At the conclusion of one of these large meetings, Alfredo asked the group to think about future directions.

"Of course, our core activity is self-exploration; I think we need to keep on doing that. But I'm wondering, for example, if we couldn't print up a monthly newsletter, keeping us all abreast of members' progress. David is busy going for his Masters level in chess, and reading avidly in the history of mathematics. Rachel has been dating Paul for a month now, and is making plans to enter a university program in child psychology. Angie's Roman history club has grown to eight students—good work, Angie! Salvador has raised the money to visit his family in South America. And so on. All of these are great triumphs for the human spirit. So if any of you folks have expertise in layout and design, perhaps you could undertake the job, and we'll pay you for your time out of the Heart slush fund. Meanwhile, over the next week please think about what other projects we might consider doing. You all know what Cicero said, right?"

"No; what?" someone shouted.

"Dum spiro, spero," said Alfredo. "While I breathe, I hope," Angie yelled from the audience.

"Right on, Angie. Until next week."

---

IT WAS EVENING. Alfredo was at home, sitting in his favorite armchair, and drinking cognac. He felt it was time for him to take stock of what he was doing. First, the situation with Gina. Gina had managed to get him to increase their sexual encounters to twice a month. He had to admit that his need for her was starting to get much stronger. Why was that? he asked himself. Sex with Alice was still very satisfying, so why did he need to be making love to Gina? But he knew the answer: Gina's dependency had become very strong. Every time they made love, she would moan loudly at the climax, and often cry out, "I love you." It wasn't exactly an ego trip for him, some need for validation as a man. It went much deeper than that. Gina seemed to validate his very existence, whereas making love to Alice didn't have that quality to it. Gina was a repeat of Joyce, but in stereo, so to speak. The only reason he and Joyce broke up was that her family was having serious financial difficulties, and she had to drop out of school and go to work. For several months after she left town, he was something of a lost soul. Only his nascent writing career saved him.

It came back to the issue of recognition. Somehow, Gina's ecstasy translated into his brain as "To me, you are the most important person on earth." She wasn't jealous of Alice because she understood that the recognition she (Gina) provided Alfredo was much greater than Alice's. Alice was half-lover, half-friend, whereas to Gina, Alfredo was her entire reason for being. She would walk through fire for him. Alfredo was, of course, aware that if Alice ever found out about the affair, all hell would break loose, but he simply couldn't stop himself. All he could do was pray that she would never find out.

Second, the direction of The Heart of the Matter. Over time, an idea had been forming in his mind about the overthrow of capitalism. Not socialist revolution, which certainly was not going to happen in the United States, but a revolution of authenticity. To function, capitalism needed not only willing bodies but also willing minds. Everyone living within the system had to believe that it was good, just; that it fulfilled their deepest desires. The flaw in the system was that it precisely did *not* do this; it did *not* meet the individual's existential needs. So in order to get up in the morning, the individual had to pretend that it did; hence the deformation of the soul and the creation of a false self, for decades of one's life. What the Heart organization did was blow the whistle on all that; it *did* promise a rose garden, and for many members of the organization, it was working. But if it could work for millions of people, this could create a crisis for capitalism; it might amount to a revolution from within—a quiet revolution, so to speak. Every rejection of a false self, he reasoned, was a nail in the coffin of the capitalist system.

A comparison with communism was interesting. In the former USSR, the self had become "Leninized." This was the shell, the front, that everyone who wanted to survive had adopted. In that society, the breakthrough to the real self took the form of political dissent (dangerous) or poetry (also dangerous), The truth circulated in *samizdat*, underground publication. So you had Akhmatova, Mendelstam, Yevtushenko, Sakharov, Solzhenitsyn, and so on. In capitalist society, the citizens weren't Leninized; instead, they were monetized, moronized, and consumerized. They became, as Ralph had correctly stated, ghosts, but ghosts without even knowing it. Their lives were spiritually empty. It was not as rough as the communist system, but perhaps more insidious: Huxley rather than Orwell.

Of course, generating this revolution from within would be an uphill battle, to say the least. Alice was right: Americans had confused the good life with goods; they really *did* want a Mercedes-Benz, both literally and symbolically. They were worse than ghosts; they were fools. What, then, to quote Lenin, was to be done? The only thing that came to mind was proseletyzing, which Alfredo was opposed to on principle. His preferred m.o. was attraction, not promotion. But attraction as a political strategy would take eons. Change within his lifetime required stronger medicine. He decided to lay this out before the group, at the next meeting, but in the meantime he thought he would run it by his "girls."

Gina, as one might imagine, was enthusiastic, because this vision fulfilled her original prediction of Alfredo as a great spiritual leader. Proseletyzing for her was no obstacle; rather, it was the obvious solution. Sure, major promotion would probably bring in the "gamesters," as had been discussed at an early point, but this might be a small price to pay for a widespread conversion to real selves. And, they would have to avoid the est model, with all its accompanying drawbacks, such as turning authenticity into a commodity, or turning the project into an "American" program (success, wealth, individual achievement, etc.). So yes, lots of potholes down the road, but still worth a shot.

Alice was a lot more cautious. "If you want to compare the US and the USSR," she argued, "lots of Russians probably pursued private, true-self activities while paying lip-service to their false ones. The Roman empire functioned in a similar way, and capitalism is just as elastic. What I'm saying is that millions of Americans could follow The Heart of the Matter without it posing the slightest threat to the capitalist system. For many, capitalism is already just a giant con game, a game of Let's Pretend. Alf, I think you need to be a bit more realistic about the threat that Heart is going to pose to the American Way of Life. And frankly, the system's propaganda will always be greater than Heart's proseletyzing."

"Al, it's the word 'always' that I'm skeptical about. Historically speaking, no system is forever; and while there were a lot of factors at work in the fall of Rome, a big one was that its citizens simply stopped believing in it. This is what the shift to the true self does. Meanwhile, capitalism is already coming apart at the seams. The Heart program would just be contributing to that process."

They sat together at the breakfast table, holding hands. Alfredo was aware of how much he loved this woman. Jesus, if only I could shake my addiction to Gina, how much simpler life would be, he said to himself.

"I still think, by any estimate," countered Alice, "that you're talking about the very long term, whether you decide to proseletyze or not."

"You could be right," he told her. "I think we need to have this discussion with the group."

Which is what he suggested at the next meeting. About 250 people showed up. "I'm going to ask," he said to everybody there, "that we not do any self-exploration today, and instead debate the possibility of Heart having a widespread impact on the entire social and economic system. This may require more than one meeting, but let me lay out the issues Alice and I have been discussing, and see what you think." Alfredo proceeded to present the political dimensions of his concept over the next half hour, and the case for proseletyzing; Alice then took the microphone (which they now needed) and gave her reasons for being skeptical of it. At the conclusion of this, she and Alfredo turned it over for public discussion.

This proved to be intense. The members had very strong opinions, both pro and con. When someone finally suggested taking a vote on the matter, Alfredo intervened. "No vote," he said. "What we need is not, say, 130 to 120; that would leave too much dissatisfaction in the ranks. What we need is a platform that can obtain consensus, i.e. one that practically everyone can get behind. What I suggest is that you all form study groups this week, in which you hash it out, and then report back to the group as a whole next week. Is that agreed?"

Alfredo went to see Gina the next day, first to make love, and second to tell her how things went at the last meeting. But for once, she was not eager to get into bed. "Alf, I need to hear something from you before we have sex. I believe, with all my heart, that you love me. You never say it, but I'm sure it's true. I need you to start saying it. I know you'll think it's a betrayal of Alice, but the only betrayal going on is that she doesn't know that we're sleeping together, or that we even see each other. It's hardly impossible for a man to love two women, or for that matter, for a woman to love two men. But that *is* your situation, Alf; you *do* love two women, if in different ways. I'm not delivering any ultimatum here; I'm just asking you to come clean, and say what I already know."

"I love you," he blurted out. Gina hugged him. "Now I'm going to give you a good fucking, and I want you to say it when you come."

Later on, back home, he thought about it. What worried him was that Gina might be on a course to escalate things. First he has to declare his love; then he has to say he loves her more than Alice (never!); then he has to tell Alice about the affair (forget it!); and finally, he has to leave Alice for her (no fucking way!). But this could be paranoia on his part. It was possible that they had reached a plateau, and that Gina was satisfied with his crying "I love you" when he came. He certainly hoped so.

A week went by; the "blessed 250" met in the hall Alfreo had rented. It seemed like everyone was eager to speak. "Hearts!" Alfredo cried; "I love you. I think you already know this, but I decided that it was important for me to make it explicit." The group was on its feet. "We love you too, Alfie!" "Alfie and Alice forever!" "Nothing can stop a true Heart!" Etc.

"OK," he said. "I think we're ready to get beyond the mutual admiration society and start the discussion regarding the future of this organization. One by one, please come up to the mike and say what you have to say in five minutes or less."

So every possibility was heard and debated, but by 4 a.m. no consensus had been reached, and they decided to continue the discussion in a week's time. But by that time, the whole thing had gone viral. At the rented hall there were 250 people inside, and a mob of about 500 more outside. Alfredo hastily ordered outside speakers for the SRO crowd, and Alice took the mike.

"Hello, everyone, and welcome," she began. "Apparently the word is out. I'm going to circulate a sign-up sheet; just write down your e-mail address, and I'll contact you this week regarding our next meeting place. We are going to have to rent a larger hall, quite obviously. We ask that just for today, those of you standing outside be content to act as an audience, and listen to the discussion inside. Next week, when we are all seated in one place, we will welcome your participation. I really don't know what you have heard about our organization, but if you listen to the discussion today, it might give you some idea. In any case, thank you for coming."

Alfredo picked it up from there. "Following up on last week," he began, "have we reached a consensus on how we wish to proceed?" A man named Javier stood up. "I was intending to say that our group is in favor of proseletyzing, but given the attendance today, maybe promotion isn't necessary. Perhaps all we need is greater visibility: more flyers, a website, and spreading information by word of mouth. Attraction, in short."

"That's the consensus," someone shouted. "*Is* it?" Alfredo asked. There was a roar from the crowd. "OK, then; that's how we'll proceed. Listen, I'm going to need some help with this. Please talk to me afterwards if you want to be a paid volunteer. Also, if you feel moved to help us out financially, we won't stand in your way. (Laughter)

"So," he continued. "For those of you who are here for the first time, let me say that the Heart organization has only two goals. The first is to shift you out of a life of bullshit to one of authenticity. This is accomplished by public examination of your own individual situation, sessions we call self-exploration. We give no feedback or advice; you are encouraged to work out your destiny by yourself. Our success in this area has, quite frankly, been spectacular. A lot of people who were previously miserable are now enjoying meaningful lives.

"Our second, and more recent, goal is to erode and destroy the capitalist-consumerist system, which we believe is a major source of our misery. Our theory is that to survive, capitalism needs lots of false selves—deformed souls, in a word. As people shift to their true selves, the system won't be able to continue functioning. This may be a pipe dream, but what will happen to the system if we have 10 million converts? The whole thing could snowball, in other words. Nothing is as contagious as freedom. We should put that on a T-shirt. (Laughter)

"Finally, we are looking for people who are sincere about all this. If you are here for any other reason than the ones I just outlined, we ask that you not attend. This is America, a nation of hustlers; everyone is raised to find a trick, a gimmick, to use for their personal advantage. But we have no tricks; there is nothing in our way of operating that you can use in that way. Hence, if you are here to get a leg up, so to speak, you will surely disappointed. The goal of our members is not to become rich, or own a Mercedes-Benz. For those of you in that category, we ask that you leave, not put your address on our sign-up sheet, and thus not act as a negative influence on our own desire to live lives of integrity—un-American lives, in a word. I thank you."

And with that he, Alice, and about twelve paid volunteers swung into action. Thousands of dollars poured into the organization. Alfredo rented a large convention hall for the next four weeks; savvy computer types set up a website; and hundreds of flyers were printed up and posted all over the city. Alfredo and Alice were, much to their surprise, invited to present their ideas at a number of church meetings, and in radio interviews. The title of these programs was always the same: "If your goal in life is to own a Mercedes-Benz, do not attend or listen to this event." If the church or radio station objected, Alfredo and Alice simply cancelled the event.

One radio host, Bob Torres, took the bait, and began by asking them, "Maybe you could tell our listening audience why you have been using this particular title for your talks and interviews. By the way, I have a feeling that a large percentage of our audience is hungering for a Mercedes-Benz."

Alfredo and Alice laughed. "Well, Bob, you know the expression comes from a famous song by Janis Joplin. She was making fun of Americans, whose idea of the good life was having big houses and classy cars. Her point was that this type of life was empty, if not actually stupid."

"What's wrong with luxury?" asked Bob.

"What's wrong, Bob, is that it's all a con game. You get your Mercedes, you are excited about it for two weeks, after which it sort of becomes part of the background, and you're then searching for the next luxury item. There's no end to it because the hole in the American soul is really a bottomless pit. Plus, the car cannot and will not satisfy your real human needs."

"Which are?" asked Bob.

"Oh, Bob, everybody knows this: love, friendship, community, meaningful work, a deep sense of purpose beyond oneself, and so on. What capitalism does is take those things away from people and then say, 'Here are a bunch of toys to make you happy'. But it doesn't work, because these are substitute satisfactions."

"So how does The Heart of the Matter propose to solve that conundrum?"

"We encourage members to explore what their deepest desires are. The result is some stunning successes. A woman trapped in a meaningless high-paid corporate job drops out, and enrolls in a college program in child psychology. A young man who is living at home with his parents, just floating through life to no apparent purpose, winds up as a chess Master and is currently working on a book on the history of mathematics. The list is quite long by now, and none of these folks are so stupid as to believe that they need a Mercedes-Benz to make them happy."

"But what if someone tells you, 'But I really do want a Mercedes-Benz'? What do you say to them?"

"That's easy, " replied Alfredo. "I tell them, 'Don't let me get in your way. Knock yourself out.' "

"But isn't your goal to destroy capitalism?" asked Bob. "It seems to me that most Americans support capitalism and do want a Mercedes-Benz."

"Bob, " said Alfredo, "we don't imagine we can get the whole country unhooked from illusion. This is not a movement that can possibly attract very many people, most of whom live in some variety of Disneyland. What we're shooting for is only 10 percent of the population—a mere 33 million." He laughed.

"Piece of cake," Bob responded. (More laughter)

"Indeed," said Alfredo. "With 10 percent of the population on our side, we are certain to rock the foundations of the entire system."

"Well," Bob concluded, "you guys are completely crazy, but wonderful crazy. Thanks for coming on the show."

"OK if I send out a message to our listening audience?" asked Alfredo.

"Be my guest," said Bob.

"JOIN US!"

---

ALICE AND ALFREDO were in bed, making love. It lasted about a half hour. She's so good at this, he said to himself. Alice gasped when she came; then it was his turn. They lay there for a while, breathing quietly. A few minutes later she said, "I've got an idea for increasing Heart's visibility." Alfredo laughed. "Is this your idea of post-coital pillow talk?" he asked her. She sighed. "I wish I could be more romantic."

"OK, then; what's your idea?"

"We write a book called *The Heart of the Matter*. We talk about the history of the movement, our philosophy, our growth, and our successes. We include testimony from folks like Rachel and David. We provide a section on our political goals. Then, when the book becomes a best-seller, you return to the lecture circuit of years back, and take me with you. When it gets translated into forty languages, the two of us tour foreign countries. You become, in effect, an international spiritual leader."

Jesus, she really ought to get together with Gina, he thought. Nope, bad idea. "Not a bad idea," he told her. "Let's knock out an outline tomorrow. Right now I need to sleep."

Alice had by now quit her insurance job. The membership level had reached 10,000, with donations pouring in. The money could be used to pay her salary, as well as hire administrative staff and cover other expenses. She and Alfredo had managed to make it onto major TV shows, with titles such as "American Life Consists of Nonsense," and "David Brooks is a Jackass." (He had just written an article saying that despite his celebrity status and a $4 million apartment in New York, he was depressed. Duh!) Meetings and self-exploration continued every week; meanwhile, she and Alfredo put together *The Heart of the Matter* and sold it to Simon & Schuster for half a million dollars. They did do a lecture tour across America, at the end of which membership had swelled to over 900,000.

"What would you say is the secret of your success?" one TV host asked them on one occasion.

"It's that we really do go to the heart of the matter," said Alice. "The plain fact is that most Americans hate their lives and their jobs. They tell themselves everything is OK, but on some level they know it's not—typically at three in the morning, when they can't sleep. The great majority will remain victims of the system, confusing the good life with goods, believing that wealth and fame are attainable, and will make them happy. What we offer the interested few—by now nearly a million members—is to spring the trap for them, and help them shift to a modest lifestyle that is meaningful and satisfying. We are not magicians, of course, but given the power of the American Dream, we're actually doing pretty well. It's our ultimate goal to force a crisis in capitalism by getting enough Americans off the consumerist merry-go-round. Capitalism depends on people feeling empty and trying to fill the Void with tons of garbage. The Heart organization teaches them how to fill the Void with things that matter, so that the garbage becomes unnecessary. If we can get enough Americans to make that shift, capitalism will not be able to sustain itself."

With a membership of nearly a million, of course, meetings had to move to the Internet. But in addition, Heart groups were springing up everywhere across the country, so that self-exploration exercises could continue. In the meantime, the US government and the Power Elite began to perceive a threat, and began talking about the Heart organization as "communist inspired." (You'd think these people could find a new theme, but no...) "If we are," Alfredo retorted, "then it's the communism of Jesus. Look what he says about rich people, after all."

And then, the crucial event occurred: an attempt was made on Alfredo's life. It turned out that the month before this, Alice insisted on hiring a bodyguard for him, and it was this individual who took the bullet—and died. John Walters was an ex-police officer and a family man, with a wife and three kids. But the *pièce de résistance* was the identity of the would-be assassin: an FBI agent. Yes, the US government had actually tried to bump off a much-beloved spiritual leader, a man that many were hailing as the "new Gandhi."

Of course, the whole thing became a major scandal. Funeral services were held in DC for Sgt. Walters; Senate hearings were initiated regarding exactly who, in the government, had ordered the hit. (Did it go all the way to the top?) Alice and Alfredo were on practically every TV and radio interview show in the land. He was extremely effective in telling the American people that this event proved that their government was truly evil, and that it was their birthright to dump the system and pursue a different way of life. "You may say that I'm a dreamer," he told his audiences, "but I'm not the only one."

And he wasn't. In the wake of all of these horrific revelations, Heart membership hit the 3 million mark. Bob Torres had the two of them back on his radio program. "Well, you guys: when you were on this show several months ago, I said that you were crazy. I now have to eat my words. It looks like you and your followers may be the only sane ones in the bunch. It also looks like the FBI is, first of all, a collection of thugs, and that in their infinite wisdom, they did you a big favor."

"They did," said Alfredo, "but I have to say to you and all our listeners that I mourn the death of John Walters, who took a bullet for me. He admired the Heart organization; secretly, I think he was one of us. He was an *ex*-cop, you should know; he quit the force and was studying for the ministry, which is where his heart, his true self, always was."

"That's quite a story," said Bob. "But where to now, Alfredo? Some version of Occupy Wall Street?"

"No, Bob; not our style. They didn't want to change the system, they just wanted to redistribute the wealth. And in the end, they really didn't accomplish anything, as far as I can see. Of course, even with 3 million members, the Heart organization cannot bring capitalism to a standstill. As I told you last time, we need at least 10 percent of the country to do that. But if we do manage to go from 3 million to 33 million, corporate America is going to start to feel the pinch. I'm actually hoping some of those folks will join us — and not as spies and infiltrators — but I suppose that's a long shot, at least for now."

"OK, then," said Bob; "time will tell. In the meantime, a big thank you to Alfredo and Alice for helping Americans find their true selves. May they grow and prosper!"

When Alfredo got home that afternoon, there was a message from Gina in his e-mail (a risky undertaking, he thought). "I told you so," she wrote. "Meanwhile, Little Gina needs watering." Alfredo wrote back, "Saturday, 2 p.m.," then deleted the messages. When Saturday rolled around, after lunch, Alfredo told Alice he was going to go out for a while, "to clear my head," and took a taxi over to Gina's studio.

"Hail the survivor!" she greeted him, "the conquering hero. I'm guessing that fame has rendered your penis very stiff." He laughed. "We'll see," he replied.

"So what's next on the Heart agenda, Great Guru of the Western Hemisphere?" she asked him, after they finished making love.

"I suppose I should turn my gaze toward the East," he said. "Our book has now been translated into Chinese and Japanese."

"Alf, I just want to put your mind at ease about something, in case you were worried. I'm very happy with our present arrangement. I don't intend to press you for more, except to say that I'd like to see you more often. I have a lot of love in my heart for Alice these days, for taking care of you and promoting the cause. If I made this whole thing possible, so did she. I feel like we are sisters, in a way."

"That means a lot to me," he told her. "How is your artwork coming along, by the way?"

"Funny you should ask. I've been going like a house afire, ever since you told me you loved me. I send my finished canvases over to Jacques, and he sends me large checks in return. He's even arranged a one-woman show for me in Paris, and then in New York, and the *New Yorker* is intending to review it. Who could ask for more? The only thing I need more of is Alfredo-love."

"I'm happy for you, babe; really happy. As for the other thing, I'll see what I can do."

He returned home glowing. "Looks like you really cleared your head," Alice remarked. "Yeah, I guess you could say that," Alfredo replied. "Meanwhile," she went on, "I've booked you into

Madison Square Garden for December 20. The title of your lecture is "No One Needs More *Tchotchkes*."

"So now I'm Jewish?" Alfredo quipped. "Well," she countered, "at least you're circumcised. It's a start."

They had breakfast the next morning at Jews Unlimited. Myron Cohen, one of the owners, was ecstatic. "Hey, don't forget where you got your start, boychik," he said to Alfredo. "I'm thinking of quitting my synagogue and joining the Heart organization."

"Nah," Alfredo replied, "stay in shul and keep turning out those fabulous matzoh balls. By the way, Myron, what exactly are *tchotchkes*?"

"Knick knacks," Myron told him. "Like the kind of crap people buy as Christmas gifts for friends and relatives. Stuff you never really need."

"Ha!" said Alfredo. "On December 20 I'm giving a talk at Madison Square Garden called 'No One Needs More *Tchotchkes*'. Our goal is to crack Christmas, render it a consumer flop. Think I have a chance?"

"No," said Myron. He lowered his voice, and furtively looked around. "Alfredo, you know I admire you tremendously. Your message is right on, and you went from a handful of people in my party room to 3 million. Not too shabby, boychik. But you may have reached your limit, and 3 million people living authentic lives are not enough to do the job. Americans are clueless, Alf; they live in a fog of complete ignorance. The truth is that most of them not only want a Mercedes-Benz; they also want their shitty lives. What you are engaged in is a crusade of epic proportions. I don't think you can win."

"God," said Alfredo; "I may have to order an extra matzoh ball."

"It's on me, kid," said Myron. "Today, it's all on me. I love you guys." Back home, Alfredo and Alice set to work preparing a computer program for the December 20 lecture, consisting of photographs of Christmas tinsel and aisles and aisles of *tchotchkes* in stores. The opening photo was of a sign that said, in block capitals, DO YOU REALLY NEED ALL THIS DRECK?

"We need some humor in all of this," Alice remarked. "I mean, we can't just browbeat them as consumer morons for forty-five minutes. How's that gonna work?"

"How about some Jewish American Princess jokes?" Alfredo suggested.

"Too politically incorrect," Alice replied.

"Cartoons of people stuffing themselves with *tchotchkes*, until they explode?"

"Better."

"Cartoons of people drowning in an ocean of *tchotchkes*?"

"Also good."

And so they kept working at it, trying to mask the sting of the message in a flurry of jokes. Alice was keen to see if consumer buying would be off this year.

And so it was—so significantly that it was newsworthy. Alfredo got interviewed on TV, once again, plugging the message: "If you're a victim of the system, you think that junk is going to make you happy. To find a better way of life, join the Heart organization." Two days later, they were nearing 4 million. It got to the point that TV crews were showing up at Alfredo's apartment to interview him. With wry wit, he turned the tables on them. "Are you happy with your life as it is? Do you enjoy what you're doing? Instead of examining the Heart organization, why don't you chuck all this foolishness and join us?" The reporters were nonplussed.

AND THEN THE next disaster struck, although it was not of a political nature: Gina and Alice ran into each other in a large downtown department store. Alice was taking pictures of *tchotchkes*; Gina was buying art supplies.

"My God," said Alice; "how long has it been?"

"Five years at least," said Gina. "How have you been? Let's have lunch at their lunch counter." The two of them sat down and ordered tuna sandwiches and coffee. "Well," said Gina, "Alfredo is clearly in a different place these days than he was five years ago. They're calling him the 'new Gandhi'."

It was purely on impulse, as if it came out of nowhere. "Gina," Alice asked her, "are you sleeping with Alfredo?" Gina turned beet red, and gulped a few times. "I—I—"

"I guess that's a yes," said Alice. "For how long now?"

"Oh, Alice, I'm so sorry, really. After Alfredo left me for you, we didn't see each other for three years. And then—my fault—I called him and asked if we couldn't be friends, with no sexual involvement. My marriage had never been more than a business arrangement; I was terribly lonely. Alfredo and I began meeting at my studio once a month, just to talk"—she left out the part about the holding—"and we had so much to talk about. I don't know what he thought about it, but I didn't think I was taking anything away from you, not really. And then a few months ago, I realized I was in love with him, and I asked him to sleep with me. He resisted for a while, said he couldn't betray you and so on; but finally he gave in. We've had sex only a few times; believe me, he's quite happy with you sexually. He hasn't said anything specific about your relations, but I can tell it's true. The point is, I'm not a threat; and if you want us to stop, I will. I'd actually like for you and me to be friends, that is if you don't hate me. But please don't cut Alfredo out of my life, Alice; he means too much to me." She stopped, exhausted.

Alice took a while to absorb it all. "I feel like killing him," she finally said. "Look, you're right: our sex life is spectacular. Why, then, would he need someone on the side?"

"Because I'm not just someone. Alf and I were together for a long time. We have a long history together, one that includes a deep friendship. Sure, he loved you more five years ago, and that's why he left me. But neither of us, it turns out, could just shuck off the past. Do you think the three of us could form some sort of trio, but with Alf and me not having sexual relations any more?"

Alice sighed. "Jesus, what a mess. Honestly, I'm not angry at you. I understand your loneliness, and I understand your connection to Alfredo. But the image of him lying between your legs—it's like a dagger in my heart. Is he planning to reverse history, and leave me for you, now?"

"Never," said Gina. "Forget the sexual images, if you can. To Alfredo, you are Number One. I guarantee it. As for him and me, it was not a question of him just having a little extra on the side. As I said, the whole thing emerged from our history."

"That almost makes it worse," Alice replied. "I don't know what to do."

"Do you intend to leave him?" Gina asked her.

"No way. At this point I really hate him, but I also love him. Has Alfredo been the love of your life?" Gina nodded. "Well," Alice went on, "same for me. Maybe your idea of a trio is the only solution, especially if you two stop sleeping together. I just don't know." Their coffee had grown cold; their tuna sandwiches remained untouched. "I can't face fish right now," said Alice. "I've got to get out of here. Give me your e-mail address, and I'll let you know what's happening, if I can work through the hurt."

Alice took a taxi over to Alfredo's apartment; by the time she arrived, her face was swollen from crying. "Al, what happened?" Alfredo asked her, when she came through the door.

"Nothing much, except that I ran into your girlfriend."

"You mean—"

"Yes. She told me you had been sleeping with her for several months now. My cunt wasn't enough for you? Plus she gave me an earful about how much she loved you. Is it mutual?"

"Al, the truth is that I love both of you, but you are Number One. If you want me to end it with Gina, I will. Absolutely."

"Hmm!" said Alice. "Funny, she offered to do the same thing. The two of you are quite chivalrous. Listen, I need a couple of days off, just to put myself back together and decide what I wanna do. We can't let this domestic disaster threaten the Heart organization, and you have that Christmas lecture coming up. I just need some time to think." So she left, and returned to her own apartment.

All quiet on the Western front. Each of them retreated into their own cocoons, trying to sort out their emotions. It was something like this:

Gina: Can I really give up sleeping with Alf? I'm not sure I can.

Alice: I'm not going to leave him. But then, what can I do? Can I tolerate a triangle with him and Gina, if they agree to stop sleeping together? I'm not sure I can.

Alfredo: I can't imagine life without either of them, sexually speaking. I could promise Alice that I won't have sex with Gina any more, but I doubt I could stick to it. But if I don't make that promise, I'm scared that Alice will leave me.

All three of them, in short, were stuck.

Meanwhile, December 19 arrived. Alice phoned Alfredo. "We need to do a run-through of tomorrow's lecture," she said. "The equipment is at your apartment, so I'll come over to you. Have you written your speech?" "No, I just have a few notecards. They'll have to do," he said.

And then December 20 arrived. Alfredo walked up to the microphone. The crowd was on its feet; the applause was deafening, went on for twenty minutes. Finally, everybody sat down.

"Thank you," said Alfredo. "The applause is really for yourselves, for seeing through the capitalist-consumerist con game and saying, 'No thanks'. My friends, we can break this system; we just have to act with one mind and one heart. (Roar of applause) People write me and ask if I'm selling success. I write back: 'Yes—success of the heart'. The Heart organization has no agenda up its sleeve to enable you to be successful in a capitalist system. In fact, most of the people we have helped are probably worse off, financially speaking, now than before they came to us. Those of you who are here to pick up tips on how to better game the system—well, you're in the wrong place.

"Today's message—that you need more *tchotchkes* in your life like you need a hole in the head—is the same message Alice and I have been repeating for over a year now: things, objects, won't make you happy. Once you see through the system, it becomes possible to reject it and opt for spiritual and emotional wealth, as opposed to the shabby form of wealth that the system offers you. Let me show it to you."

At this point Alfred clicked on the computer cable and ran through the photos he and Alice had prepared. Most of them were funny, satirizing people gorging on *tchotchkes*. "Do you think these people are happy? And if not, it's important to understand why not. I ask you to think about this over the next few days, and if you can really get it—that junk will not fill your soul—don't spend a penny on stuff for your family and friends. Instead, offer them love, warmth, and companionship—your presence rather than your presents. (Laughter)

"But this will have larger repercussions than your household. To end the misery of people living under capitalism, it will be necessary to end capitalism. And here is how we are going to do it: we are going to stop buying superfluous crap, and start meeting our real needs instead—the needs of the heart. If this movement gets large enough, it will break capitalism in two. So scared of this are the powers that be, that they sent an FBI agent—a thug—to rub me out. I may not be alive a year from now, for all I know, but all of us here can do a lot in that year and beyond to bring the system down. I ask you to start today: don't buy anything for Christmas. Love goes a lot further than toys. Thank you."

A standing ovation, once again. Alfredo hugged Alice, who had been sitting on the stage, and the two of them walked out, hand in hand.

---

CHRISTMAS CAME AND WENT; THE "TRIO" did not contact each other during that time. Finally, Alice unloaded a bombshell. "Alf, I don't believe you will be able to resist having sex with Gina, no matter what you promise. I know you and I have had a great sex life, for nearly six years now, and I want it to continue. But I'm convinced that you're getting something from Gina that you are not getting from me. I don't know what it is, but I believe it's true. And that means that if I want to keep the relationship with you, which I do, I'm going to have to let you continue sleeping with her.

"The problem is that the imagination is scarier than reality. Not being present when the two of you make love leads me to imagine fantastic sex that I could never live up to. So what I am willing to agree to is this: you can continue to sleep with Gina, but only when I'm present."

Alfredo stared at her like he had been hit on the head with a 2 x 4. "You're shitting me," was all he could say.

"It's called a *ménage*, Alf. The three of us would hardly be the first trio to do it."

Alfredo couldn't catch his breath. He just sat there, shaking his head. Alice went on. "Some other conditions. First, I want us to buy a house and live together. You and I are both doing fairly well these days, and Gina, I suspect, is rolling in dough from art sales, and has nothing to spend it on. So the three of us can afford to give up our apartments and buy a house.

"Second: no making love on the sly. If you want to fuck Gina, you have to include me. If you want to fuck me, you have to include Gina."

"Third: I want our threesome to extend to the management of the Heart organization. Gina has to paint a bit less, and devote some of her time to the project, and to our goals. What do you say?"

"I'm in," said Alfredo.

"OK, then. I'm going to drop in on Gina, tell her our decision, and ask if she agrees to our conditions. If so, I'll ask her to come over tonight and fuck you, while I watch. I simply have to know the source of her hold over you."

"I doubt that will work," said Alfredo. "With you present, I'm sure we'll both be very inhibited."

"Maybe, but I'm guessing that will change over time. We've got to start somewhere. And I'll tell you this, sweetheart: whatever she's giving you, I'm convinced I can give you as well. Now I'm going over to her place."

Alfredo sat there, trying to take it all in. "Overwhelmed" didn't come close to what he was feeling. I'll be damned, he finally said to himself.

An hour later, the phone rang; it was Alice. "She's in," she told him. "She agrees to all our conditions, and intends to begin house-hunting tomorrow morning. We'll be over at your apartment in half an hour. Go take a shower."

Alfredo felt like he was in a dream, or a movie. He took a shower, then fixed himself a Scotch. The doorbell rang, and the two women entered. Gina flew into his arms. "I'm so happy, Alf. I owe you and Alice more than I can say."

The next steps were a bit awkward; all of them were new to this. So they played, they laughed, they explored, and they came. Thus began their *ménage à trois*.

———

GINA DID MANAGE to find them a house, and they soon settled in. It would be the new headquarters of the Heart organization, as well their center for sexual exploration. Alfredo remembered that line from Fellini, that if you approached the world openly, with the wonder of a child, all good things would come your way. Bravo, Maestro!

Meanwhile, with Heart membership still growing, it was time to launch a new campaign. It was Gina's idea. The slogan would be LOVE, NOT "FILLER", and members would picket department stores and shopping malls with signs, while the three leaders would give lectures and interviews on the meaning of the slogan.

Before they could launch the campaign, however, another bolt came out of the blue. A very successful theater director, Mort Fineberg, decided he wanted to stage a musical called *Tchotchkes!* At this point, he explained to Alfredo, Alice, and Gina, he had nothing written, and very little idea of what the plot would consist of. "I need a team like Rodgers and Hart," he said, "but they have yet to show up. However, the theme of the show is going to be that the first *tchotchke* was the Golden Calf, and that from that point on, everyone, Jews and Gentiles alike became addicted to *tchotchkes*. I envision a scene at the end where everyone is vomiting *tchotchkes* into the Red Sea." Alfredo broke out into a fit of laughter. "Honestly, Mort," he said, "this sounds almost as bad as *Springtime for Hitler*."

"And look how well that did," Mort shot back. (But only in fiction, thought Alfredo.) "I want this play to hover between the hilarious and the grotesque. What do you say?"

"It's gross," said Gina. "I love it. I'll be happy to design and paint the sets for you." Mort nodded his appreciation; he knew of her work.

"And Alf and I can beat the bushes for writers and composers," added Alice. "We'll let you know what we find."

"I'll have a contract sent out to all three of you within the next few days," he replied. "Now you'll have to excuse me, as I'm expecting the delivery of a case of Manischewitz any moment now. Just kidding!" Back at the house, Alfredo said to the gals, "Look, we don't have any musical talent, but maybe we can write the script ourselves. What do you think?"

They managed it in three days. It had to be one of the stupidest plays ever written. After an initial scene in the desert, worshipping the Golden Calf, the Israelites are suddenly transported to Wal-Mart's, where they undergo a frenzy of *tchotchke*-buying. Christ makes an appearance, telling them that all of these trinkets will not fill their souls, but they pelt him with *tchotchkes*. Then they burst into a chorus of "I Love My Tchotchkes." After a number of misbegotten adventures with *tchotchkes*, they are back in the Middle East, vomiting *tchotchkes* into the Red Sea. The final song is called "If Only I Had Known."

"God," declared Alfredo, "this really is a piece of dreck." He e-mailed it to Mort, and waited for his reaction. It came two dalys later: WORST PIECE OF CRAP I EVER READ. I LOVED IT. FULL STEAM AHEAD. And so, once the composers were hired to provide the songs, the play was done, and appeared on Broadway four months later.

The response was rather schizophrenic. The critics hated it, calling it "utter drivel" and "rancid kasha varnishkes." But the public loved it. The play was sold out a year in advance. Once again, Heart membership spiked, now up to 7 million. Street theater popped up all over the country, with ordinary people dancing, singing the songs, and imitating the closing vomit scene. Consumer sales continued to drop nationwide. Gina and Alice decided it was time for another rally in Madison Square Garden, to assess the state of the organization and also to launch the LOVE, NOT "FILLER" campaign. As before, Alfredo took to the mike, while Gina and Alice sat on the stage.

"I'm still alive," he began. (Roar from the crowd) "We are now 7 million strong, and consumer sales in the US are seriously down. Attacks on us—in Congress, the press, on Wall Street, from the White House, and from major corporations—are getting increasingly hysterical. These folks are *scared*, my friends; their whole world is based on all of us being good little consumers, and we're not playing the game. As our lives become real, their phony lives go down the drain. They are cowards, whereas we are the most courageous people on earth. (Long applause)

"A word of caution. We are dedicated to the cause, but we are not zealots. Word reached me that one of our members went to a Wal-Mart store in Philadelphia and peed on the merchandise. (Laughter) While I agree with the sentiment, this sort of fanaticism gives us a bad name. I am going to suggest something tamer, as a next step in our drive to save Americans from consumer fetishism. This is a campaign devised by Gina here (he points to her; she waves), which she calls LOVE, NOT "FILLER". All of you, of course, know what this means. We are going to deliver thousands of signs bearing this slogan to Heart offices across the country, and ask that you pick up some of them and picket Wal-Mart, Target, shopping malls—the works. Politely approach would-be-consumers in the parking lots, and explain to them the meaning of the slogan. Tell them the difference between love and 'filler,' and point out that recreational shopping is a spiritual dead end. But please, no coercion and no urine. (Laughter) Our m.o. is attraction, not promotion. We are strong, we are growing, and if the FBI doesn't kill us off, we shall break capitalism apart within the next two years." (Wild applause)

And so the organization continued growing, crowds were lining up for *Tchotchkes!*, picketers took to the stores and shopping malls, and consumer sales continued to drop. Meanwhile, back at the ranch, Alice's research into the secret of Gina's attraction continued unabated, but she was unable to crack the code. "Does it matter?" Alfredo asked her. "All of us are enjoying the sex, so why bother with all this?"

"I'm convinced that you enjoy her sexually more than me," said Alice, "and I need to know why." Gina gave Alfredo a look, and he nodded. "OK, Alice, I'm going to tell you. But it could create problems for us. It could make things worse. Are you sure this is what you want?" Alice nodded. "OK, then, here goes. Alfredo has a particular sexual psychology. He is excited by women who are needy. When he and I were dating, it didn't work out very well. I had, if not strength, then the appearance of it, and so we were constantly fighting. Then you came along, and Alfredo sensed a great need in you for love and sex. So he dumped me and got involved with you, with whom he almost never fought, I'm guessing. That was a real blow to my self-esteem, and over time, I began to drop the phony shell of strength and allow myself, with the help of a therapist, to experience my dependency, my vulnerability. Three years later, as I already told you, I contacted Alfredo and suggested friendship, no sex. Because of our long history, he was open to it. But then I fell in love with him, and had no time to play-act the strong, independent woman any more. The rest is history.

"Alice, you *are* a strong woman, and I am not. Please don't deny it; it's really true. Part of me wishes I could be more like you. And Alf adores your body; I'm sure you know that. But he experiences mine more intensely, because of my need. So there you have it. I hope I haven't hurt you."

Alice was thunderstruck. She said nothing, for a while. Finally she said, "so the only way I can deliver the same pleasure that you do is by becoming needier than I presently am, is that it?"

"I'm sorry," said Gina. "That seems to be the case. But don't think for a minute that Alf doesn't love your body."

"Well," said Alice, "I am who I am, and you are who you are, and Alf is who he is, so I guess I'm just stuck. What a bummer. This is the worst news I've had in the last ten years."

"I do love you, Alice," said Alfredo, "and I do enjoy making love to you." She shook her head. "It's not enough," she told him.

It all cast a pall over their sex life. Alice didn't want to do it very much any more, and she lost the desire to watch Gina and Alfredo do it. She became morose, and neither Gina nor Alfredo could shake her out of it. "I'm just a second-class lay," she would say. None of them knew where this was heading. Except that over time, in a paradoxical way, her depression did render her needier. She was willing to make love to Alfredo only privately, without Gina in the room. Alfredo was very gentle with her, and one day told her that she was, in fact, becoming more exciting to him. It took three or four months, but her depression began to lift, without rendering her less needy. Slowly, things seemed to be back on track, except that she was not willing to make love as a threesome. "I need you to stroke my sexual ego," she said to Alfredo. "I really need to know that I'm a good enough woman for you." And in fact, Alfredo felt a great kindness toward her, and out of that kindness a renewed sexuality was born. Somehow, they had weathered a very threatening storm.

On the "work" front, Alfredo decided to call a meeting at his home base, Jews Unlimited. It would be on a first-come, first-served basis. Members brought sleeping bags and camped out the night before. When the doors opened, they all rushed in. When

#35 was reached, the doors were closed. Speakers were once again set up outside. Alfredo took the mike and addressed the crowd.

"Thank you all for coming. Sometimes I worry that our success could go to my head, so I wanted to come home, so to speak, and work with two or three of you on self-exploration. You all know of the success we've had; much of it seems hard to believe. But the core of this program is the conversion from false to true self, and that depends on self-exploration. So if there's anyone who would like to do some work, please come forward."

A man of about sixty stood up. "Alfredo, I hope this isn't out of line, but so many spiritual leaders are corrupt that a lot of questions have been circulating about you. Will you permit me to ask them?"

"What's your name, sir?"

"Phil. Phil Ackroyd."

"Sure, Phil. Go ahead."

"Are you living with two women, the ones who now appear with you on stage?"

"Yes I am, Phil," he replied. "Look, we all know about the Zen masters and yoga teachers who sleep with their female disciples. It's practically the norm, sad to say. This isn't like that. I haven't slept with a single member of the group. Gina was my girlfriend many years ago; then Alice came along, and I felt she would be a better partner for me. I didn't think much more about it until three years ago, when Gina contacted me, and I began hanging out with her on a strictly friendship basis. But slowly, it became clear to me that I was in love with her, as well as with Alice. The upshot was that we all agreed to live together, and we are quite happy with the arrangement. So please don't think this was some sort of frivolous ego trip, or sexual exploitation. The fates gave me two loves; that's just how it turned out."

"What about the money in the Heart organization treasury? Is that disappearing into your personal expense account?"

"Actually," Alfredo replied, "the three of us are putting cash *in*, rather than the reverse. Gina is a very successful artist, and has donated much of her income to the organization. Sales of *The Heart of the Matter* have generated a lot of royalties for Alice and myself; most of that goes into the treasury as well. In a word, my hands, and my conscience, are clean."

"OK, just one more question," said Phil. "How is your ego these days? Do you really believe you are the new Gandhi?"

"No, Phil; of course not. I can't help what the media says. But like Gandhi, I'm a follower on the path of the true self. The man had no pretense; he was just what he was. My inspiration is encapsulated in one of his most famous sayings: 'People ask me what my message is. I have no message. My life is my message.'"

"Those were honest answers, Alfredo," said Phil. "Thank you."

"OK. If no one has any other questions, would someone like to do some self-exploration?" A man in his late thirties stood up. "I'll go," he said. "My name is Bill. Actually, I'm a bit afraid of doing this, because I feel like a fraud, being here. What I mean is, I'm one of those folks who wants a Mercedes-Benz, among other luxury goods. And the desire feels real to me, not some sort of substitute satisfaction.

"I feel like I'm a very odd duck. I have occasional short-term relations with women, but I'm not interested in anything serious. I don't have any close friends, and am rather estranged from my family. But as a loner, I don't really feel lonely. My focus has been on becoming rich, and that feels like my true self. I know it sounds crazy. Anyway, an opportunity recently came up that could earn me millions of dollars. If I accept it, and if it goes off as planned, I could own a Hollywood-style mansion, hire servants, buy a Benz, or a Porsche, and spend time on the French Riviera.

The payoff, in other words, is huge. But there's only one drawback: the assignment is possibly illegal. *How* illegal, I'm not sure. But I do know that it's not 100 percent kosher, and if the thing backfires, I could be in for a whole lot of litigation that might not go my way. I have four days to decide whether or not to take the gig, and right now I'm unable to make up my mind.

"I do wish I fit into the Heart organization, and felt so fulfilled inside that none of this would appeal to me. But as I've listened to the stories of those who have downsized, I say to myself, 'That's not me'. The truth is that I want the high life—wealth and all that goes with it. The only thing holding me back with regard to this assignment is that I might wind up in jail. If there were no legal risks, I wouldn't hesitate to do it. I guess I don't really belong here, but I felt the need to be honest, expose myself. You know, some time ago I was reading a biography of St. Francis, and the comment of one wise old pope was, 'Not everybody can be St. Francis.' That line stuck with me. I'm not a saint; I wasn't cut out for the essentials that the Heart organization is always talking about. My only beef with capitalism is that it has not yet delivered the goods for me personally. Thank you all for listening."

"Thank you, Bill," Alfredo responded; "a very honest self-exploration. I suspect you've given us a lot to think about. Yes, Angie?"

"I for one am very glad Bill shared what he did. I worry sometimes that the Heart organization is relying too much on the false consciousness argument. Who is to decide what's false and what's true? If the man or woman in the street tells us that their deepest desire is a big house and a Rolls Royce, I can't see that it makes much sense for us to insist that all of that is substitute satisfaction, or the result of being brainwashed by the system. After all, our own outlook on the world could also be accused of brainwashing."

"Good point," said Alfredo. "Anyone else want to speak to this issue?" Nobody said anything. Finally Angie said, "I don't want to monopolize the session, but if no one minds, I'd like to do a self-exploration. Just a short one, I hope."

"Go for it," said Alfredo.

"Well, the last time I did this exercise, I talked about how I had a negative attitude toward men, and as a result was not asked out very much, and was worried that I would never have a serious relationship. That self-exploration somehow blew my circuits open, and in a short time I began to have a number of dates. The guy I'm currently seeing must have a lot of patience, because I haven't let him do anything more than kiss me. But a few days ago he asked me to go away with him for the weekend, and I felt if I said no, that would end the relationship. So I said yes, but that, to my mind, means sex; and I find I'm really afraid of it. When I imagine having sex with him, even though I know he's a nice guy, everything about it involves surrender, as far as I can see. The woman is naked; she lies on her back, with her knees drawn up; she spreads her legs; the man enters her, and eventually ejaculates. He conquers her, in short; she submits to him. I know I must sound like a teenager, but the whole thing frightens me. I could cancel the weekend, but that's the coward's way out; and as I said, I think he would then break off the relationship.

"I asked one of my girlfriends about it, one who has been involved with a man for two years now, and she said that the reality was a version of 'she stoops to conquer'. She told me it was a kind of optical illusion; that her boyfriend was dependent on her surrendering to him. 'If anyone is the victor here,' she said, 'it's me. And he knows it.' She also suggested something that I think is quite smart, if I can muster the nerve to do it: talk to the guy about it, before setting out on the trip, and be completely honest about my fears. I think that's what I'll do. I can't be going off on this trip in a state of anxiety. Thank you all for listening."

"Great session, Angie," said Alfredo. "You'll have to tell us how it turns out. OK, folks, that's all the time we have. Thanks for coming, and Godspeed."

───────

WHEN HEART MEMBERSHIP hit 15 million, signs of a crisis began to show up in the American economy. In the previous six months, consumer spending, nationwide, had dropped off by nearly 30 percent, and the corporations were up in arms. Lots of people were also quitting their jobs, retreating to the countryside to make jam and cultivate vegetable gardens. The government decided that Heart was more of a threat to the US than ISIS—which was probably true —and declared it to be a terrorist organization. The Army began to break up Heart meetings with nightsticks and tear gas. Alfredo lodged more than a dozen lawsuits against the government, and called for a rally on the Smithsonian Mall. Of course they were denied a permit; 2 million people showed up anyway. Happily, the Heart organization brought their own loudspeaker equipment. Signs saying LOVE, NOT "FILLER" dotted the landscape.

"Let me tell you a story," Alfredo began, "about a society in China of some years ago known as the Falun Gong. It followed a gentle, yogic type of practice and was similar to Taoism in its philosophy. In particular, it encouraged its members to rely on their own inner voice as their authority, and not on anything else. Well, the Chinese government was not having it, inasmuch as they wanted the people to rely on them—i.e., their false selves—rather than their true ones. They cracked down on the organization, and even tortured its members. This is surely one of the darkest, and most shameful, chapters in modern Chinese history, and it speaks volumes about the Chinese government.

"While the US government is not yet torturing members of the Heart organization for pretty much the same 'crime', it is clear that it is benevolent toward its citizens so long as they obey an external authority called consumerism. Once such citizens switch their allegiance to an internal authority, namely the true self, and such switch starts to have an economic impact—which it has—then we get labeled as communists and terrorists, and become fair game for the organized terror of the state, as exercised by the Army in recent weeks.

"Since Heart is a nonviolent organization, the only weapons at our disposal are lawsuits and counter-propaganda. One wonders how long the courts will remain fair and impartial; only time will tell. I have a number of interviews lined up with the mainstream media, outlets that have been friendly to us in the past, but there is no telling if they will have the courage not to cancel on me. I hope so, because this will give us the opportunity to tell our side of the story. Again, time will tell.

"What I am here to tell all of you today amounts to two things: first, recognize that the US is showing its true colors, namely, that it is a government of gangsters. Its outer benevolent face is a sham. Underneath that face is raw violence, always ready to reveal itself if things don't go its way. Remember that the man who tried to kill me was an FBI agent, and that he was never brought to trial. He walks the streets a free man, even after murdering John Walters; and I wouldn't be surprised if he were dispatched to kill again. So my first point, then, is that we are living under a thug regime.

"My second point is to urge you to continue on the path of the true self. Hold your Heart meetings in secret, if necessary, and keep refusing to consume superfluous trash. After all, what can the government do? March 15 million of its citizens into Wal-Mart or wherever and order them to buy stuff at gunpoint? That would surely be the end of the nation as we know it. So take heart, dear Hearts; this is a battle we are going to win. And to the police and military personnel in our midst, I have only this to say: JOIN US!"

The roar from the crowd was enormous, and the Army was simply not able to disperse it. After a few minutes, Alice and Gina stepped up to the microphone. Alice: "Just a message to the women in our audience: most of you are in charge of domestic buying for your families. Buy only what's necessary. Give your kids love, friends, and time in nature. Don't fill their lives with video games and cell phones. Tell your husband that the family doesn't need a new car every two years. This is the revolution that will force an evil system to crash." (Roar from the crowd)

Gina: "Most of you know that I am an artist. I say to you, enroll in art courses, dance classes, theater productions, literature classes—the stuff that feeds your soul. The one thing you don't need in your lives is more *tchotchkes*. (Cheers from the crowd) One other thing: Why did the Chinese government persecute Falon Gong? Why is the US government now persecuting the Hearts? When someone who is living out of a false self comes into contact with someone who is living out of a true self, the reaction is typically one of anger. The false-self person understands that he or she has sold out, that they are unhappy, so they are jealous of the person who is living a real and happy life. I'm not a religious person, but what do you think the crucifixion was all about? (Applause from the crowd for five minutes) If the soldiers of the US Army had the courage to wake up, to enter into real life, they would have no interest in violently breaking up our meetings. No: they would be *participating* in our meetings. Unfortunately, this is not going to happen any time soon. I could say to the police and military personnel here today, 'You don't have to be bitter and angry for the rest of your lives'. But this would only terrify them, and in that sense, we *are* a terrorist organization. ("You tell 'em, sweetheart," etc.) In the meantime, please follow Alfredo's advice. Meet secretly, connect with other Hearts, and consume only as much as is absolutely necessary. The Army will continue to defend the State, but eventually there will be no State to defend. (Applause) Maybe then, they will join us."

The roar of the crowd was exceded 120 decibels. No one wanted to leave, but eventually they began to float out of the Mall. It was, as Alice said to Gina and Alfredo later on that evening, a triumph for the forces of Good.

———

THE NEXT DAY was a quiet one, and over breakfast, Gina and Alice decided to propose something to Alfredo, something they had been thinking about for a while. "Alf," said Gina, "you know that Alice and I love you beyond all rational limits, right?"

Uh-oh, he thought; what's *this* about?

"In the spirit of that love," she went on, "Alice and I want to go off birth control. We want you to impregnate both of us, hopefully a day or two apart. The kids will be the same age, and grow up as siblings. What do you say?"

Alfredo was completely caught off guard. This one he didn't see coming. "Before I answer that," he replied, "I have a question for Alice. This may or may not be relevant to the issue of pregnancy, but I need to know the answer. Alice, do you still feel sexually inferior to Gina?" Alice got red in the face. "That's a question for *you* to answer, Alf," she replied, somewhat angrily. "Do you still enjoy Gina more?"

"If there is a difference," he told her, "it is by now very slight. I have felt your neediness grow over time, and with it my level of excitement also increased. I think we should return to our original arrangement, of the three of us making love together. Especially if I am going to impregnate the two of you, I think it should be a group activity. It would mean we are becoming a real family."

Alice's anger cooled off somewhat. "You always know the

right thing to say Alf; I'll give you that. Honestly, sometimes I'm angry that I love you so much."

Gina laughed. "Ain't it the truth! So, Alf: you're OK with having kids?" "I am," he replied, "and I think we should begin with that today. Now, in fact. But I have a question for the two of you: Who gets the first load of sperm? Much as I'd like to, I can't be inside the two of you at once."

"Alice does," said Gina. "I want her to have the honors. I'll get the second load later on today." Nine months passed; the children were born a week apart. Alice had a girl—Rose—and Gina had a boy—Jack.

Meanwhile, the US government was in full attack mode on the Hearts, and the Hearts were in full rebellion against the government. The rate of consumer purchasing fell another 15 percent, driving the business community half crazy. Oppression fueled the resistance: exact figures were not available, but membership may have risen to 20 million. Secret meetings multiplied, despite the presence of government infiltrators. As in the days of the Solidarity movement in Poland, unmarked Heart vans cruised the streets, blasting out the Heart message on loudspeakers. And much to everybody's amazement, the Supreme Court ruled in favor of the Heart organization, and ordered the government to pay the latter $2.5 billion in damages. One of the judges was even overheard to say, "Fuck the government." Things also eased up on the interview scene, with Alfredo now giving talks entitled "Government by Thugs," and "Life in a Gangster State." Bob Torres was especially eager to have Alfredo back, along with Alice and Gina, who sat with their babies in their laps.

"It's great to see you again," Bob began, "especially with the new additions. I guess there has been an amazing turn of events. What do you guys make of it all? I mean, you told me you were going to overthrow the system, and now you seem to be doing it."

"Bob," said Alfredo, "the three of us are just historical agents.

We tapped into an important vein in American consciousness, namely that people just can't take the horse manure anymore. They want *real* lives, not the latest app, for God's sakes. Our slogan, LOVE, NOT "FILLER", has apparently hit home with lots of people." The conversation continued in this vein for about an hour, after which the Alfredo family returned home. Several hours later came the announcement on the radio: the president had shot himself in the Oval Office. ("Good!" exclaimed Gina.) Bob Torres was immediately on the phone.

"Alf," said Bob, "I want you back on the show tomorrow. We need the Heart commentary on this extraordinary event." Alfredo showed up the next day at the appointed time. "Alfredo," said Bob, to start off the interview, "millions of people are tuned into this show, and everyone wants to know what the Heart organization has to say about the president's suicide. Let me put it to you directly: Did the president kill himself as a consequence of the success of your movement?"

"Indirectly," Alfredo replied, "I would have to say yes. Or at least, I certainly think it's possible. The conflict between the true and false self that the Heart organization puts before the individual can generate an existential strain that is intolerable. The person knows he or she is on the wrong path, that their life is a mistake, but they just can't seem to make the leap from the fake to the real. It does take a certain strength of character to do it, and it's clear to me that the late president didn't have that strength. I apologize for speaking ill of the dead, but I always regarded him as a very weak man. All that bluster, all that strutting around with his chest puffed out, was there to cover up a scared little boy. It's possible that the Heart victory forced a crisis upon him that was more than he could handle, and that he saw suicide as the only way out. But I take no joy in his death, Bob. The truth is that capitalism, and the whole American system, is a mechanism for generating millions of false selves. The vice president, who has now been sworn in as president, is just such a person, if a bit less flagrant about it. So we just replaced one false self with another."

"Would you consider running for the office yourself?" Bob asked him. "Oh, Bob," he replied, "I have no interest in power, and I'm sure I'd make a very bad president in any case. Look, from the beginning of the Heart movement, my principal goal was to make people happy. That's what I'm going to continue doing."

"What do you see happening for the United States, then?" said Bob.

"It needs to be reconstituted on a whole new basis. You can call it utopian, but what we've had up to this point is what C. Wright Mills called 'crackpot realism'. The reign of crackpot realism, I'm guessing, is coming to an end." The two men stood up and hugged one another, and Alfredo walked off the stage.

"Why *not* run for president?" Alice and Gina said angrily, when he walked in the door. "Why the hell not?"

"Ah, you girls. Spiritual leaders should not try to be political leaders; it's not a good combination. I prefer to just stay on the path of eroding capitalism from the inside. We're doing a pretty good job of it, wouldn't you say?"

"OK," said Alice, "we can table that discussion for now. But I'm telling you, Alf, I very much want to fuck a president, and I'm certain Gina does as well."

"Can you settle with fucking a spiritual leader, for the time being?" he asked them. Both, it turned out, were amenable to the suggestion.

---

HEART *TCHOTCHKES* STARTED APPEARING in department stores, souvenir shops, and online. T-shirts sported the LOVE, NOT "FILLER" slogan; coffee mugs were emblazoned with LIVE

YOUR TRUE SELF. Alfredo asked a major TV network to give him a three-minute spot to address the issue.

"Good evening to all of you who are listening," he began. "The philosopher Herbert Marcuse once wrote that capitalism was so flexible, it could absorb anything, even its opposite. I fear that's what's now happening to the Heart movement. You know, the government was quite stupid, bringing in the Army to crush us; it only made us stronger. The business community is much more intelligent: this recent surge of Heart trinkets is threatening to undermine the movement, and I want to share my concerns with you. What they are effectively generating is a counter-movement, which we might call the pseudo-true self. This is known as cooptation. Americans who want to change without changing, who want to shift from a false to a true self but don't have the guts to do it, can now just buy a T-shirt or mug that says I'M LIVING THE TRUTH, or whatever, rendering the whole thing pointless.

"I certainly can't stop Madison Avenue from designing these *tchotchkes*, or the department stores from selling them. The only thing I *can* do, thanks to the generosity of network television, is ask you to reject all of these trinkets, and do the real work of spiritual conversion rather than the phony work. The world doesn't need more *tchotchkes*, and it especially does not need pseudo-true self ones. I thank you for hearing me out."

Alfredo left the studio and walked out onto the street. An elderly man was standing next to a pushcart, calling out, "Get your hot Heart *tchotchkes* here! Hot Heart *tchotchkes*, only three for $10." Alfredo had a great urge to vomit on the cart, but he took a deep breath and walked the other way. He passed a large souvenir shop; in the window were T-shirts that said things like DON'T LET YOUR LIFE BE ABOUT CRAP, and SAY NO TO TCHOTCHKES. Take me now, O Lord, he said to himself.

The Alfredo family met in the living room the next day, to have lunch and assess the Heart situation. Alice had hired

Eleanor, a full-time nanny and live-in cook, to work for them. They paid her generously, and also made sure this was work she really loved. She was twenty-eight, and very good looking.

"You had to go and hire a hottie," Gina upbraided her. "How long before Alfredo starts shtupping her, girl?"

"I also met her boyfriend," Alice replied. "He's gorgeous. I might wanna start shtupping him myself. OK, just kidding. The point is, I think he's giving Eleanor all the sexual satisfaction she needs."

"Except," said Gina, "that all women are aroused by charisma. They love getting their hands on guru-cock. Just look at you and me, for God's sakes."

"Guru-cock? You sure have a way with words, my dear. OK, I'll have a talk with her about it. If we suspect any funny business is going on, we'll fire her curvy ass. Meanwhile, have you ever thought about how much of human life is about sex?"

"Gee, do ya think?" said Gina. Eleanor, in any case, practically dressed like a nun. She made them omelettes and salad, and opened a bottle of white wine. They ate slowly. "So we managed to knock off a president!" exclaimed Gina. "That's practically what you said to Bob Torres, Alf. Who's next? The head of Goldman Sachs?"

"Let's leave the shmuck to his billions, for now. Meanwhile, Heart needs a new strategic campaign, and we need to think about what it might be."

"Why don't we just rest on our laurels for a while?" suggested Alice. "Especially in the wake of the president's suicide. Maybe it's time to lay low."

"Here's my suggestion," said Alfredo. "Mother's Day will soon be upon us. How about the two of you appearing on TV, holding up Rose and Jack, and saying things like 'Love, not iPods'?"

"How long before that line appears on a T-shirt?" Alice remarked. "Six hours?"

"Al, we can't control the whole world. I just think we need to focus on parents and children for a while. I'm also thinking of asking Myron Cohen to appear on the Bob Torres Show with me, where we discuss the concept of slow eating, and savoring one's food. We'll close the show with me looking into the camera and saying, 'Hearts know what counts'."

"Another T-shirt," said Alice. "I dunno, it sounds cheesy. I suggest we stick to the Mother's Day theme for now. Lots of public lectures by me and Gina, in addition to the TV spots. We can also do some gigs a month later, with you, for Father's Day."

"Gigs?" said Alfredo. "Alice, you're turning into a wheeler-dealer."

"Yeah, it turns out that that's my true self," she countered.

"OK, enough of that," said Alfredo. "As for Mother's Day, I think it's a good plan. I'll have Arnie (the Heart general manager) set it up. Now I need a nap." Oddly enough, the three of them just slept.

The Mother's Day Initiative, or MDI, as they took to calling it, was another success. Mothers really did get the message that they needed to get their kids off of screens and into public parks. Lots of TV talk shows discussed the matter, with women calling in to say how much more sane and relaxed their children were, now that their cell phones and video games were taken away from them. In the month following Mother's Day, sales of electronic toys dropped off 44 percent. Americans were becoming happier, but the economy was tanking. A public outcry ensued, demanding that Alfredo appear on TV and explain his vision of a post-capitalist society.

"But I'm not a politician," he told the networks, "and I'm not a presidential candidate." "No matter," they replied. "If anyone has answers, it's you. Besides, you got us into this mess, so you should be thinking about how to get us out of it." He figured they were right. Alfredo appeared at prime time on Thursday night. All the networks covered it; nothing else was on TV. The title of his talk was "A Political Message from a Non-Candidate."

"My fellow countrymen, and women," he began, "let me start by saying that I do not intend to become a presidential candidate. Believe me, nothing could interest me less. The Heart organization has only two goals, which I believe are related: to make people happy, and to destroy the regime of capitalism. We have had some modest success in both areas, as you know, but it must be said that even before Heart came on the scene, the capitalist system was imploding. It has feet of clay; it's demise is only a matter of time.

"Of course, the specter of the end of capitalism inevitably raises the specter of communism. Since the government thinks that you all are a collection of morons, it seeks to scare you by telling you that the post-capitalist regime will take away your cars and your TV sets. Nothing of the sort is going to happen, although I would love it if you would all voluntarily ditch that stuff. But that's just me, and I'm here to discuss larger issues.

"Here's the point: there are more alternatives to capitalism than just communism. A post-capitalist society hardly has to be some version of the former Soviet Union. It was a cruel and tyrannical society, and its failure was inevitable. As for the nonsocialist alternatives to capitalism, the powers that be keep information about those possibilities well hidden, because if they can get you to believe that the choice is between Wall Street and the gulags, they know you are going to choose Wall Street. In fact, both of these choices are about the perpetuation of the false self. So I'm here to tell you, first, that you are not morons, and second, that the nonsocialist alternatives to capitalism are based on the the true self. In short, a better life is available to us all.

"What alternatives, then? Five great thinkers come to mind, and they all had similar ideas. Two of them were British social reformers, whose lives were deeply immersed in the world of art:

John Ruskin and William Morris. The third was a man who took his major inspiration from Ruskin, and a lifelong hero of mine: Mahatma Gandhi. One motto that guided his life was, 'The earth has enough for everyone's need, but not for everyone's greed'. Let Madison Avenue put *that* on a T-shirt, eh? The fourth was an American, Ernest "Chick" Callenbach, the author of a very famous book called *Ecotopia,* and the fifth, also an American, was Lewis Mumford, the author of many books critiquing the American Way of Life and exploring alternative possibilities. All five of these men were opposed to large corporations and large-scale industrialization. They were in favor of local crafts, decentralization, community life, and work that fulfilled the needs of the soul. In favor of the true self, in other words, not the false one.

"Of course, all five of them lost the battle. Gandhi's vision was sidetracked by Nehru's; Ruskin and Morris were pushed aside by the British industrial revolution, and Callenbach and Mumford by the American corporate machine. Yet who had the last laugh? India is today immersed in misery, and industrialization has nearly managed to destroy the planet. The disparity in England between rich and poor is severe, and America is perched on the edge of an abyss. All of this could have been avoided if we had chosen the path these men campaigned for, the path of the true self. Instead, we ridiculed them, labeled them 'quaint' and 'utopian'. At this point, it may be too late to do anything about our situation; I really don't know. But I would suggest, at the very least, to start having serious discussions about these alternatives, and proposing legislation in the direction of implementing them.

"As I said, I'm not a politician and I'm not running for office. But what I will do, want to do, is make myself available for those discussions, and to be an adviser on that legislation. I see people running around in T-shirts with my face on it. Please, my friends, take them off and burn them. This is the road to nowhere, I'm telling you. Instead, join a Heart group, do a self-exploration, and discuss how your group can help institute a regime based on the five men I've referred to. Worshipping me can only sidetrack the process. I cannot be your new false self.

"Let me conclude by saying that I am convinced that the capitalist reign of oppression is over, and that a much happier future might be possible. It all depends on us.

"Thank you."

The lecture plunged the country into turmoil, but it was a good turmoil. Books on or by Ruskin, Morris, Gandhi, Callenbach, and Mumford flew off the shelves. Heart rallies occurred throughout the land. The great break came when the head of the Joint Chiefs of Staff, Butler Smedley, held a press conference announcing his resignation. "What has the American military done," he declared, "but increase misery around the globe for the sake of a wealthy few? I don't intend to worship Alfredo, but I do intend to offer my services to him as a peace consultant, if he would be interested." Of course, Alfredo took him up on his offer, and the two of them toured the country together, helping to set up cooperatives à la Ruskin et al. Myron Cohen saw to it that platters of chopped liver were delivered to every destination at which they arrived, to be distributed en masse.

Another development that occurred was secession. Various parts of the country declared their independence from Washington, saying that they were free to pursue their true selves: Vermont, Upper California, the Pacific Northwest, and the South. Texas announced that it was rejoining Mexico, adding that it should never have left. When the dust settled, there was very little left of the United States, and very few mourned its passing. Several of the new states printed currency with the faces of Alfredo, Alice, and Gina on it. No mention of "In God We Trust," however; just "Your True Self Is Your Destiny."

Alfredo made a final appearance on the Bob Torres Show,

flanked by Butler Smedley and Myron Cohen. It was actually a pretty boring show. The four of them sat around eating corned beef and pastrami sandwiches; conversation ran along the lines of "Would you pass me the mustard?" and "God, these matzoh balls are terrific!"

"I told you the Jews would take over the world," said Myron. "Hand me that bottle of Manischewitz, will you?"

# 3

---

# MOONIES

It was a small announcement in the newspaper: the techno-billionaire, Melon Tusk, was offering rides to the moon for $250,000. It would take three days to get there; passengers would camp out for three days, and then they would all return. Flights would take place only if there were a minimum of seven people (plus Tusk and a physician), and the cut-off point was twelve. Those interested were asked to meet at the Crater Café on Friday at 7 p.m.

Six people showed up, four men and two women. So this particular flight had not met its quota, but Mr. Tusk would place another ad the following week. They all ordered drinks; what he wanted to do was find out who they were and why they wanted to go to the moon. "Let's start with the lady on my left," he said.

"My name is Sheila Bowers," she began. "I'm a retired schoolteacher, and quite honestly, I've led a pretty dull life. I haven't even been to Europe. The day before Mr. Tusk's notice appeared, I was thinking I would die without having really done anything at all. So I thought I'd come tonight and see what it was all about, see if this was something I might wanna do."

"Thank you, Sheila," said Tusk. "And on your left we have—"

"Frank Farmer," said a man of about sixty. "I guess my situation is rather similar. I spent my life making money, but I never really did anything interesting. Of course, the lunar surface doesn't look especially interesting; I suppose I should spend two weeks in Paris instead, at far less expense. But then the moon seems so exotic..." His voice trailed off.

"I'm Marjorie Wright," the person next in line said, after waiting a bit for Frank to continue. "My own purpose is political. I always regarded the moon landing of 1969 as a terrible mistake, an artefact of the Cold War that made no sense, given the cost and the needs of people right here on earth. I'd just like to go up there and see what all the fuss was about. How was it 'one giant leap for mankind'? I see it as a giant leap *backwards* for mankind."

"OK," said Tusk; "great to have a dissenting opinion. And you, young man?"

"I'm Cranston Flake," he said, "twenty-two years old. Obviously, I can't afford this myself, but after I graduated college, my parents decided to give me this trip as a graduation present. I'm actually quite pumped about it. I mean: the moon! Wow!"

The next person said: "I'm Blaine Cogswell, about to turn forty. I unexpectedly got rich from a startup company, and last year I decided to retire; or semi-retire, I guess. Truth is, I don't know what to do with myself. I guess you can put me down as just curious."

Finally, the last person spoke up. "I'm Hank Carter, fifty-one years old. I'm a mountaineer. Two years ago, I climbed Everest. What else is there? I figure after the moon, I might take a shot at Mars."

"Well," said Tusk, "we seem to have a real mixture of ages and motives. Personally, I think it's good; it should lead to some lively discussions. I'm going to place another ad, to see if we can't attract one more person, and I'll get back to all of you when we do. Just give me your cards, or write your e-mail address on a napkin. In the meantime, let me suggest that the six of you meet one more time together, without me, to get to know one another and see what you think about this whole adventure. Thanks again for coming. I have a feeling we'll be lunar-bound sometime within the next two weeks." He got up and left.

The six "Moonies," as they decided to call themselves, made small talk for a little while longer, then agreed to meet again at the same place on Monday evening. As they were leaving, Hank took Blaine aside. "Has anyone ever had sex on the moon?" he asked him, only half joking.

Blaine laughed. "I guess we'd have to call it a moonfuck," he replied. "How about a T-shirt?" Hank went on: I GOT LAID IN THE SEA OF TRANQUILITY. "You could probably charge $50 a pop for that," Blaine told him.

---

SO THE MOONIES reconvened on Monday evening. "Marjorie," said Hank, "I'm curious about your criticism of the 1969 moon landing. Maybe you could say more about it."

"Glad to," she replied. "You know, practically my entire life was lived under the shadow of the Cold War. Someone once wrote, after 1991, that if you were nostalgic about the Cold War, then you didn't live through it. Anyway, since that time, I've done a lot of reading about it. You can string together a whole series of events, basically amounting to American aggression, from 1946 to 1989. Much of it was barbaric, like what we did in Iran, Guatemala, Chile, and Viet Nam; a lot of it was symbolic, like the Khrushchev-Nixon kitchen debate, or the Fischer-Spassky chess match. These were political footballs, and the moon landing was surely the biggest one of all. How does landing on the moon prove American superiority, except in a narrow technological sense? What it did was manage to distract the American people from the real problems going on at home. You could say they got moonfucked, if you'll pardon my French." Hank and Blaine shot each other a knowing look.

"Wow!" said Hank; "a lot to think about; although given your strong feelings on the subject, I'm not clear on why you want to make this journey. I mean, all you're going to see is a rather bland lunar surface. Surely there are better ways to spend $250,000, at least for you."

"Honestly, Hank, I wish I had a good answer for you. Truth is, I'm not sure myself. Obviously, I can't undo the Cold War, and repeating the moon landing fifty years later is certainly not going to do the trick. But it's a symbolic journey for me, in some way. To me, the Cold War was theater, a big joke played on the American people, who were unable to see through it. And I too was caught up in it, reading *Darkness at Noon*, hearing about the murder of Patrice Lumumba, watching Khrushchev pounding the desk at the UN with his shoe, and always living under a nuclear shadow. And then the marching and demonstrations against a phony war being waged by war criminals—Viet Nam. I feel I got robbed of my real life."

"I guess it depends on your definition of 'real'," Frank Farmer interjected. "I spent my whole life accumulating wealth, and now that I've succeeded, I look back and also see it as theater. It certainly seemed real enough at the time, all that wheeling and dealing, but what single person could possible need a billion dollars? It's nothing more than a number in a bank account, a digital reality. Meanwhile, all of my human interactions amounted to nothing more than hustling, manipulation. At the insistence of my minister, I recently read a book called *I and Thou*, by some Jewish scholar, and realized that I hadn't had a single genuine relationship in my entire life. As far as this moon trip goes, I'm as confused as Marjorie as to why I'm doing it. And Blaine, you also seem unclear as to your motives as well, no?"

Blaine sighed. "Guilty as charged. You know, if the six of us passed on the trip, and pooled our money, think of what we could do with $1.5 million. Open homeless shelters, set up soup kitchens, save the eyesight of a little kid, going blind, whose parents can't afford the operation—you name it."

They were all quiet for a while. "I never thought of it that way," Cranston finally said. "I just saw the space race as a great expansion of human capabilities. Heroic, in other words. It's amazing, what human beings can do."

"You know," Frank put in, "Tusk is a guy who fully and sincerely believes that any problems we have as a nation can be solved by technology. The moon landing of '69 was, for me, a kind of confirmation of that way of thinking. But when you realize how much worse things are now than they were fifty years ago, it tends to undermine that belief. The author of *I and Thou* barely refers to technology. His own belief is that our problems can only be solved by the human heart, not the human brain. Perhaps *that* would be the 'giant leap for mankind', what do you think?"

"No criticism intended here," responded Blaine, "but it sounds like you got religion, Frank."

"Yeah," said Frank; "I wonder. Maybe *I and Thou* was the wrong book to read on the verge of a trip to the moon. Although, getting to know you guys in a real way, over the course of nine days, could be an opportunity all its own."

"Hell," said Hank, "we could accomplish the same thing by going on a camping trip." Everybody laughed.

"I think we could all use another drink," said Blaine. "This round will be on me." They all took a breather, refreshed their drinks, and sat there for a while, taking it all in.

"Just for the fun of it," said Sheila, "let's brainstorm what we might do together if we decided not to go to the moon. Any ideas?"

"Would this be a kind of bucket list?" Cranston asked her. "I guess so, in a way," Sheila replied; "except this would be a group project, not an individual one."

"We could assemble an arsenal and attack the White House," suggested Marjorie. "Except that really *would* be kicking the bucket," she added. (Chuckles all around) "Or maybe assemble a time machine, go back to 1945, and do things differently this time around," she went on.

"I like that," said Frank. "Why don't we put it to Tusk? After all, he has infinite faith in technology."

And so they did. The six of them wrote him a group e-mail, that went as follows:

"Dear Mr. Tusk,

"We enjoyed meeting with you the other day. All of us have been great admirers of you for some time now, and share your faith in the power of technology. Regarding the moon voyage, however, our collective feeling is, Been there/Done that. Of course it was a great challenge and adventure in 1969; fifty years later it seems rather tame — tourist stuff. $250,000 is a lot to spend on a cliché, we've been thinking. As a result, we have something else in mind. Let us lay this out for you, to give you some time to think it over, and perhaps then we can all meet again at the Crater and get your views on the matter.

"It has been pointed out by a number of historians and scientists that science fiction often anticipates reality. Did you know, for example, that television was predicted in exact detail in a French sci-fi novel of 1894? Similarly, there have been a number of sci-fi novels (H.G. Wells, for example) that describe a time machine, i.e. a device that would enable one to go backwards and forwards in time. Now *that* would be no small accomplishment, and a project worthy of your talents. Or so we all believe.

"Marjorie thought of the idea in connection with her feelings regarding the Cold War. What if we could go back to 1945 and see to it that the Cold War never happened? How much better a world that would have been! We could start by canceling the dropping of atomic bombs on Hiroshima and Nagasaki, for example. This would, of course, require an additional technology, of a 'Manchurian Candidate' variety, namely getting into President Truman's head and having him decide that the use of such a weapon would be the ultimate war crime, to be avoided at all costs. Since we now have the historical record of the 'Iron Curtain' speech, the CIA coups of the 1950s, Viet Nam, Chile, Reagan's military buildup and so on, the 'Manchurian' technology could be used to head all of that off at the pass, so to speak.

"What do you think? Is any of this do-able?"

[Six signatures]

Tusk's reply:

"Thank you for your letter, and your innovative ideas. I'm hoping we might also be able to get inside Stalin's head, inasmuch as I've never been a big fan of brutal dictators. Please meet me at the Crater this Friday at 7 p.m.

"Yours very sincerely,

"Melon Tusk"

Friday rolled around; the entire group arrived early, brimming with anticipation. Tusk came in at 7:10. He ordered a double Scotch at the bar, and then joined them at their table.

"Actually," he began, "your message is probably the most important one I've received in the last ten years. It may surprise you to know that I have been working on a time machine for the last seven years, and have almost got it perfected. What I failed to think about, however, was the *purpose* of the damn thing. Let's say we push ahead to 2095. What would we then do? Look around, take notes? If, for example, we discovered an earth that was virtually uninhabitable, do we then return to the present day and become Cassandras or Chicken Littles? But today's scientists are saying exactly the same thing about global warming and resource depletion, and no one is paying any attention to them; so why would they pay any attention to us? 'We've just come back from the future, and can tell you it doesn't look very good'? We'd be dismissed as kooks.

"Similarly with going back to the past. Say we go back to 1945, and warn people, again, that we've returned from the future, and that we can give them a rundown of all the shit that's about to hit the fan in the next seventy-five years. Again, we would come off as raving lunatics.

"However, suppose we had the 'Manchurian Candidate' technology you spoke about. In both cases—1945 or 2095—we would be able to get into people's heads, like Truman's, as you suggested —and cause them to think, say, and do very different things. Now that would be a whole different ball game. But until we have this 'Manchurian' technology, there really is no point in doing any time travel. And right now, the closest thing we have to that is hypnosis, which is a rather hit-or-miss technique. I can start working on this technology tomorrow morning, but what if it takes me two or three years to perfect? You see the problem."

They were all silent for a while, digesting Tusk's "oration."

"But time is really irrelevant here, isn't it?" asked Hank, finally. "Let's say it does take three years: So we do the experiment *then*. What's the difference when we do it? And if it is of any help, if any of us can offer you our resources, financial or otherwise, I bet most of us would be willing to pitch in." At this, everybody around the table nodded.

"Jesus," said Tusk, "you guys are bowling me over. I offer you a lame, overpriced trip to the moon, and you come back with an idea that could stand history on its head. Yes, imagine eliminating Hiroshima, Viet Nam, Iraq, and every other disaster of the last seventy-five years. To quote Jerry Lee Lewis, 'Great Balls of Fire!'"

"Mr. Tusk," said Marjorie, "why don't we break for a week, during which time we all read up on the technology of hypnosis? Then we meet back here next Friday, and share what we've found." Tusk looked around the table. "Is everybody in? Moon voyage out, hypnosis research in?" Six people nodded their heads. "See you all in a week," he said.

———

So, THEY MET again in a week. Tusk announced, "I apologize, I couldn't find the time to do any hypnosis research, so I'm going to have to rely on you guys. Marjorie, inasmuch as you are probably the most invested in this project, why don't you tell us what you turned up?"

"I'm afraid the news isn't good," she said. "There is a lot of disagreement as to what the phenomenon actually is. In the film, *The Manchurian Candidate*, it's portrayed as a trance state that is induced by a psychological trigger, a trigger that was planted in the subject's mind weeks or months beforehand. Many experts disagree that it is an altered state, but the real problem is getting the individual to submit to being hypnotized. The US military investigated the possibilities in the sixties, and in 1966 issued a classified report—now unclassified—that concluded that hypnosis was not feasible for military purposes. It's a technical problem: you would first have to kidnap your subject, which means you would be trying to obtain compliance from a resistant source under hostile circumstances. They concluded that this simply could not be done.

"I mean, say we traveled back to July of 1945, our goal being to get the president not to drop the bomb on Hiroshima. If we try to kidnap him, it's likely that the Secret Service would shoot us. If, however, we could actually pull it off, then what? If he is resistant to being hypnotized, which he would be, it just wouldn't work. It looks like this whole thing is dead in the water."

"You know," said Frank, "it's vague in my memory, because I saw it several years ago, but I seem to recall a movie in which some military personnel were kidnapped, and then had a tiny computer chip implanted in their skins while under heavy sedation. The individual could then be operated like a marionette. There was no need to hypnotize them, or obtain compliance."

"There's still the problem of kidnapping the president," observed Hank. "It's not clear to me how we would be able to pull that off."

"Hmm," said Sheila. "Could the chip be put in his drink, or food, and then be made to lodge somewhere in his body? If so, we wouldn't have to kidnap him. We would just have to bribe the White House cook. What do you think, Mr. Tusk?"

"Well," replied Tusk, "this is a technology I've never explored. I have no idea if it's feasible. You'd have to give me some time to figure it out. But quite honestly, the whole thing is getting extremely convoluted. First, I have to invent a computer chip that we can monitor, and that if taken orally stays lodged in the body. Then, I have to finish up work on the time machine, and we have to set the dial for July 1945. Then, having arrived in Washington at that time, we somehow sneak our way into the White House and bribe the chef to drop the chip into Truman's beer, or whatever. If this scenario were taking place in a novel, who would believe it?"

"Hang on a minute," said Hank. "Maybe this doesn't have to involve the president. When was the Trinity test, in New Mexico?"

"July 16, 1945, at Alamogordo" said Marjorie.

"Jesus, Marjorie," said Hank; "you really know your stuff. OK, suppose we arrive in June with our computers. We have access to a technology that Oppenheimer and his crew did not. There's no getting onto the base at Los Alamos, but would there be a way of fucking up their operation at a distance, like with a GPS, so that the Trinity test was a complete failure? That would not only derail Hiroshima; it could also derail the entire Cold War. With Trinity in his back pocket, Truman was able to dictate to the Russians how everything was going to play out. This effectively launched the arms race. Without Trinity, he'd be forced to negotiate rather than dictate."

"That," said Musk, "is do-able. Or at least, I think it is. Listen, I'm going to put everything aside for a week and concentrate exclusively on that. Blaine: your startup company: Was it in computers and hi-tech?"

"Indeed it was," Blaine replied; "Cogswell Systems. I still have controlling shares in the company."

"So you could deploy a research team to work with me?" Tusk asked him.

"Would be my pleasure," said Blaine.

"Hot damn!" exclaimed Tusk. "We are going to undo Hiroshima and roll back the Cold War!" Marjorie was beaming from ear to ear. "It's always military solutions with the Americans," she said. "Don't negotiate; just drop bombs. Well we, the Moonies, are going to upend all of that. We'll show those fuckers."

It actually took Musk and the Cogswell team three weeks, working around the clock, to get the technology right. The final test was causing a two-minute blackout across New York City from their base in Yonkers, twenty miles away. Once that was perfected, they turned to the time machine. Getting that to be operable took another month, after which the Moonies met once again at the Crater Café.

"Quite frankly," said Tusk, "I can't believe this is happening. You guys are something else. Here I was, offering the public boring moon flights, and you guys come along and remind me what technology is for."

"Which is what?" asked Cranston.

"Extending into new frontiers," Tusk replied, "rather than recycling old ones. A toast: to new frontiers!"

"Hear! Hear!"

"Clear your calendars," he told them; "we touch down in June 1945 in a week."

———

THE TIME MACHINE didn't go with the group; it just transferred them all to a different moment in time. They suddenly found themselves on the street in Yonkers, where Tusk had his last base of operations. What he had brought with him was several computers and a suitcase crammed with $100 bills, so that they could buy contemporary clothing, and whatever else they might need. It was obviously important not to stand out. The next task was to take the bus to New York, and then the train to Albuquerque. Tusk wanted to get as close to Los Alamos as possible, so they picked Eespañola, eighteen miles away, and booked themselves into a hotel. (What the locals thought of this was never recorded.) It was mid-June; they had a month to sabotage the Manhattan Project. Tusk set up his computers with the super-GPS built in, and directed them toward the lab at Los Alamos. What he saw was a tremendous amount of excitement. For the scientists involved, the context of the project was irrelevant. Originally, the bomb was going to be used against the Nazis. When it became clear that the Germans had no nuclear weapons project going on, they turned their attention to the Japanese. The target could have been Antarctica, for all they cared. And if, as the top brass admitted, the point of it all was to send a message to the Russians, these scientists were fine with that as well. The whole thing was completely amoral for them; their focus was on the project, which they frequently described as "technologically sweet." Tusk was appalled by this, but he recognized a lot of his own attitudes in it, and it bothered him.

His computer systems, in any case, were not able to affect the nuclear materials being handled, but he was able, as in the Yonkers test, to disrupt the electrical grid. Since the work could not proceed without a functioning grid, the scientists at Los Alamos had to shift their attention from the bomb to repairing the grid, which took a day and a half to fix. Tusk let them get on with their nuclear research for several days, then disrupted the grid once again. As July 16 approached, he did this with increasing frequency. The Potsdam Conference with the Russians was scheduled for July 17-August 2; when it arrived, and the Trinity test had not taken place, Truman had no ace up his sleeve, and had to negotiate with the Russians rather than dictate to them. There never was an atomic bomb; nothing got dropped on Hiroshima; and no nuclear arms race between the US and the USSR ever took place.

Indeed, when the Moonies returned to 2019, they found a radically changed world. America and Russia were allies. The Soviet Union had not collapsed in 1989, and no one had ever heard of Ronald Reagan, or Richard Nixon, or John Foster Dulles. Adlai Stevenson had been elected president in 1952 and 1956; the decade had been one of peace, and good will at home and abroad. No Iran, Guatemala, or clandestine destruction of "enemies." No Viet Nam, and no Chile. In both Russia and America, money was being spent on health, education, and welfare, rather than on military buildup. The rapaciousness and anxiety that had characterized the social atmosphere of the previous 2019 was gone. The Moonies could hardly believe what they were seeing. Singlehandedly, they had derailed the Cold War, and had created a more benevolent world.

There had also been no moon landing in 1969, because there was no Cold War to require symbolic gestures. (Marjorie was overjoyed. Tusk's moon voyages were now nonexistent.) Fischer did defeat Spassky at Reykjavik, after which the two of them conducted a three-year world tour together, teaching children of all countries how to play chess.

The Moonies reconvened, with Tusk, at the Crater Café, which was now called the Green Earth Coffee House. "Well," said Hank, "that was quite a caper. And just look around: no one in this café knows about the horrible world that could have been."

"What shall we tackle next?" asked Frank. "Hitler? Stalin?"

"God almighty," Sheila interjected; "I need a rest. How many worlds can we straighten out in a week?"

"You know," said Frank, "in some ways, we went from an I-It world to an I-Thou world. Without the Cold War and its attendant nuclear anxiety, people are more willing to relate to one another on a real, heart-to-heart basis. And I'll tell you something else," he went on; "James Joyce once wrote that history was a nightmare from which he was trying to awaken. Well, we did that, folks. You remember that discussion we had, ages ago, about reality? The Cold War, in my opinion, was the theater, the fake reality—the nightmare. Now, we are living in the world we should have had all along."

"Amen, amen," chanted the others. They ordered another round of drinks.

"Reagan really was a terrible asshole, wasn't he?" said Marjorie.

# 4

## THE CHICKEN FARMER

It was in the late 1970s that I was living with my then girlfriend in San Francisco, in a two-bedroom apartment near Russian Hill that had a view of the Golden Gate Bridge. Looking back on it now, the rent was absurd: $275 a month. I'm guessing it now goes for $5,000 or $6,000, mínimum. In any case, my girlfriend and I finally split up, after four years. She didn't want the apartment, and left for parts unknown. I had to place an ad for a roommate. The folks who came through: I tell you, it was like Zoo Parade. One person was stranger than the next. In one case, the potential renter rejected the place because he said he couldn't live without hardwood floors. I could have written a short story about it all, really.

Finally, a "normal" guy came by, a stockbroker in his early twenties, very good looking, and with a sense of humor. I didn't know, at the time, that Clive was an alcoholic, and I was fairly ignorant of what alcoholic behavior entailed. But all that came later. I told him he could move in.

There was one aspect of his life that I was a bit jealous of; it was certainly foreign to my own experience. Clive worked in the financial district, and he told me that from Monday to Thursday, all the brokers slaved away at their computers, putting in very long hours. But at about 3 p.m. on Friday, it was like a switch was turned on (or off). All of the young people in the firm would troop down, en masse, to the bar across the street, with the express purpose of getting drunk and laid. I guess it was the reward for a hard, nerve-wracking week. First, everyone got so blottoed that they could barely see the wall. Then, the women would file into the men's bathroom, pull up (or remove) their skirts, drop their panties, and get fucked—either standing up or bent over. Apparently, they had little interest in who was pounding them. Clive certainly didn't care: a typical afternoon, he told me, involved four girls in a row, all of whom he barely knew. Of course, this could have been nothing more than macho bragging, but as he told it, it seemed real enough. Saturday morning he would wake up in our apartment with a ferocious hangover, having only a vague memory that he had gotten laid a lot the day before. It's really a pity that the penis doesn't have a memory.

You'd think a stud like that would be happy with his sex life, but he wasn't. It was the oddest thing: once in a while I would start dating someone, which occasionally led to her sleeping over. This drove Clive into a fit of jealousy. I just didn't get it. The guy was drowning in pussy, but got upset if I got a bit once in a while. He would then act out, usually a few days later, by bringing home some girl and fucking her on the living room floor, so that I could hear her screams. It was puzzling: I was not in any sexual competition with him, but there he was, trying to prove that he could nail the gals as well as I could. I never asked him what the deal was; it was obviously a sore subject with him.

Over time, I managed to figure it out. The Friday afternoon orgies notwithstanding, Clive was a romantic. His jealousy of me was not sexual; it was that he could see that in the case of my (very occasional) girlfriends, I was more or less involved with them, and he wanted that for himself. The likelihood of finding that in the bathroom of a bar with drunk, anonymous coworkers was vanishingly small, and it grated on him. It was also, I realized, even larger than that. Clive was drifting; he was searching for meaning, and he wasn't finding it. His Catholic faith was not delivering the goods, and he was smart enough to realize that the stockbrokering life, with its mindless and endless pursuit of money, was pretty shallow. Where, then, to turn?

I was in my mid-thirties, and I guess Clive saw me as older and wiser (terrible mistake), because he began to pour his heart out about his religious doubts, his sexual misadventures, and above all—his work. It turned out that at an earlier point in his life, he had apprenticed to be a carpenter, and had worked solo on some fairly complicated projects, like constructing a bar and rec room for some rich guy in his home town. He showed me pictures of his work; it looked pretty impressive.

"I dunno," he said; "I guess I got sidetracked. Carpentry is very exacting work, and the pay is OK, but nothing to write home about. Then a friend of mine was getting into the brokering business, and pulled me in along with him. I never really hit the big bucks down in the District—a number of guys were making millions—but it was way ahead of a carpenter's income. Two years later, I'm sort of floating along. I don't really know why I'm doing anything."

I should say something about my own life at the time. I survived by doing glorified secretarial work—for private individuals and, for a while, at the University of California Medical School (UCSF). I was deep into Buddhism, meditating every day at the San Francisco Zen Center, and writing a book about Buddhism for the modern age. From Clive's point of view, I was a total oddball, and he often wanted to talk about what I was doing, or what I was thinking. So I talked to him about *maya*—illusion—and how, according to Buddhism, most people were sleepwalking through their lives. They never figured out who they were, and in a sense were little more than vegetables. Clive was fascinated by all of this; he may have wondered if he too was a vegetable.

The whole thing came to a head when very suddenly, out of the blue, Clive quit his job, went over to the bar across the street (it was not a Friday), got roaring drunk, and took the bus back to Russian Hill. He sat at the back of the bus, screaming at the top of his lungs, "You're all vegetables! You are sleepwalking through your lives! Your lives amount to nothing! You're vegetables!" Why the bus driver didn't eject him from the bus I never understood, but I'm guessing Clive's accusation hit home with a number of people. Maybe with most of them, if Buddhism is right about human beings. In any case, his life became more erratic after that. There were several more women loudly getting laid on our living room floor; Clive also took to coming home drunk at 3 a.m., singing opera at the top of his lungs. After about a month or so of this, I had had it, and asked him to leave.

I got a new roommate; I never saw Clive again. He called me once, asking me how to register to vote, but that was the only contact we had after he left.

Years went by. I was living in a different city, and one day I cruised by a newsstand, and began leafing through a popular American journal. Looking down the table of contents, I saw an article called "Motorcyclists: A Photographic Essay." It was a series of pictures, sort of like *Playboy* centerfolds, of various men striking poses with their Harleys or whatever. Except for the very first photo: there, staring out at me from the page, was Clive. The look in his eyes was not proud or aggressive; it had a faint air of being puzzled. He didn't look particularly happy. He was standing next to his cycle, surrounded by chickens, and the caption read, "Clive Jenkins is a chicken farmer in Nebraska."

"Oh no," I said, almost aloud. "Oh no. Did *I* do this?" As I said, I hadn't known much about alcoholism way back then; I didn't even know there was an organization called Alcoholics Anonymous, to which I could have steered him. So what happened in the interim? I had become a minor author on the "spiritual" lecture circuit, talking about Buddhism; Clive had become a somewhat doubtful chicken farmer. Apparently I had, with my interest in Buddhism, given him a bridge to nowhere. For it's not enough to realize that you're a vegetable; you also have to figure out how to undo that, and *not* be a vegetable. I knew (or thought I knew) how to do this for myself, but that was where my knowledge ended. As the Buddhists say, you can't live out someone else's karma for them; that's their responsibility.

Nevertheless, I felt guilty. My Buddhism suddenly seemed only theoretical. But perhaps I was being unfair: Who's to say if writing books and lecturing is more meaningful, or worthwhile, than raising chickens? Most of us enjoy egg dishes and chicken salad, after all, and surely the world contains its fair share of happy chicken farmers. But the ambiguous look in Clive's eyes told me he believed that in terms of his own life, he had missed the boat. Shit. I did this, I thought. I "infected" the guy, couldn't really help him deal with the whole phenomenon of self-transparency, and apparently, ruined his life.

I thought of contacting Clive, but I realized I didn't know what to say. Should we talk about motorcycles, or chickenfeed? I had no idea. But somewhere out there in the great American Midwest is a guy on a motorcycle, raising chickens, and wondering what the hell happened.

I ask myself the same thing.

5
———

# THE WIRE CAGE EXPERIMENT

As a salesman of the *Encyclopaedia Britannica*, George Walraven enjoyed his job, but in the digital age he was fighting an uphill battle. He liked going door-to-door, talking to people about their lives, and the importance of being well-informed. But most of them didn't want to buy the encyclopedia, because they said they could get whatever information they needed online. George immediately pointed out that *Britannica* had an online paywall. This pitch worked some of the time, but mostly not. Still, he loved the job and didn't want to give it up.

In terms of developing new sales strategies, George was inspired by an episode of *Friends*, in which an encyclopedia salesman comes to Joey Tribbiani's apartment and tries to sell him a set of encyclopedias. He asks Joey if he ever feels out of it, sitting around with his friends, who are discussing something he knows nothing about. Joey admits this is a frequent occurrence, but says he just can't afford to buy these books. So the salesman asks him how much cash he has on him at the moment; it turns out to be $50. "For $50," he tells Joey, "I can sell you a single volume. What letter would you prefer?" For some reason, Joey picks V. Then follows a rather amusing scene in which Joey, sitting around with the Friends, keeps trying to steer the conversation to subjects such as Volcanos, Viet Nam, Vivasection, and other V's.

George loved that episode, and it gave him an idea. In these days of economic hardship, he reasoned, most people simply can't shell out $1,200 for the entire set. But like the salesman on *Friends*, he could probably get them to buy a single volume. Once he had sold all of the volumes, from A to Z, he figured he might be able to throw an "encyclopedia party," in which each person in attendance represented one letter of the alphabet. And then what? Some kind of party games? He wasn't sure. But he was convinced there was an angle here, one that would enable him to sell more books.

George's wife, a rather attractive blond ten years his junior, was keen on the whole idea, even thinking that if George could sell two sets of A to Z, it might be possible to organize a public competition between the two teams and run it on network TV. It took a few months to make this happen, but finally the show took place: "From A to Z: The War of the Books." Prizes ran from $1,000 to $10,000. First up were the 2 A's. Each person had a buzzer; George's job was to name an A entry, and the person who buzzed first then had to explain the item, say what it was. The two A's were a housewife from Cincinnati, and an insurance salesman from Topeka. The winner would be the first to give ten correct answers.

"What is the *Aeneid*?" George asked them. Brittany, the housewife, was quick on the draw. "Long poem by Virgil providing a foundation myth for Roman civilization," she said. "Right you are!" exclaimed George. "Next, what is abalone?" Lorenzo, the insurance salesman, pressed the buzzer and declared, "A type of processed meat." The audience was convulsed with laughter. "No," said George; "you're thinking of baloney, which would be a B question. Brittany?" "A type of sea snail, or mollusc," she responded. "OK," said George; "the score is now 2 to 0."

George proceeded to run through Aardvark, Aeolian harp, All Hallows Eve, and so on, until Brittany was the victor with a score of 10-5, racking up winnings of $1,000 (so far). The audience applauded, and she and Lorenzo retired from the stage. The B's were up next, but before that contest could take place, someone in the audience stood up. "Is this game rigged?" he called out.

"Wha?" George exclaimed. "Of course not." "Abalone is processed meat?" said the man. "Are you shitting me? Remember the show *Twenty-One*, the big scandal? Contestants were fed the correct answers, including Charles Van Doren, a professor at Columbia. People will do anything for money."

"Sir," said George, "you need to sit down. This game is not rigged, and you are completely out of order."

"But that denial is exactly what that earlier generation of execs at NBC said!" he cried. At this point, Security was called in, but the man had apparently come with a bucket of rotten vegetables, which he skillfully deployed against the officers. Somehow, this triggered a mob psychology response, with people choosing up sides: rigged or not rigged. A total melee ensued. Out of nowhere, a man in a Tarzan outfit swung through on a rope, and a woman thrust a Boston cream pie in George's face. "Criminals!" she screamed. "Thugs!"

All hell broke loose. The mob was able to overwhelm the Security guards, in some cases banging their heads against the floor. People picked up on the cry of "Criminals!" and "Thugs!", tore up the seats of the studio, attacked the contestants, and threw volumes of the encyclopedia at each other. The madness lasted for over an hour, at which point everyone stopped, as if on cue, dusted themselves off, and left the building.

"This may not have been such a good idea," George said to his wife, through gobs of Boston cream pie.

Of course, most of the melee was caught by various people on their cell phones, and the footage was used on the late-night news report. The anchor said something like, "A riot was unexpectedly triggered this evening at the opening of an NBC quiz show called 'From A to Z' by a defrocked priest, the Rev. Pierson J. Flanksteak. Rev. Flanksteak, without any evidence, accused the network of rigging the show, which resulted in an outbreak of mob violence. The audience went wild, and the riot went on for over an hour. When later questioned by the police as to why he made the accusation, Rev. Flanksteak said he was out to demonstrate Freud's theory that civilization was but a thin veneer over a massive 'iceberg' of barbarism."

"From A to Z" was subsequently cancelled; instead, all of the networks hosted panel discussions of Freud's theory, what had happened, whether Flanksteak (now sitting in jail) was a lunatic or a genius, and so on. It was all hot air; most of the TV audience, and the media, correctly concluded that these "experts" were fools. George quit his job with *Britannica* and went on to write a best-selling book, *From A to Z: The Riot at NBC*. The promotional flyer contained the following passages:

"The Rev. Flanksteak set out to validate Freud's notion that civilization was a shaky cover on top of raw, irrational emotions. He had no evidence that the program was rigged, and in fact, it wasn't. What he actually demonstrated was that the public can be made to go crazy by the use of certain charged words—'rigged' being one of them. 'Post-modern' is another. My own theory is that Americans are badly squeezed by the inexorable disintegration of their way of life, such that when these words are uttered, huge amounts of energy are suddenly released. This is important information for us to have about the fragile condition of the American people. Flanksteak now sits in jail, whereas I think he more correctly deserves to receive the Presidential Medal of Honor.

"I don't think, as a nation, that we can afford to be conducting our daily affairs while sitting on a kind of semantic volcano. What I propose is that we set up controlled experiments on the release of energy. I have consulted with Senator Riggins about this, and we are going to arrange for such an experiment two weeks from today. For this, we need 1,000 volunteers. Interested parties should sign up at the NBC studios as soon as possible."

The signup sheets filled up very quickly. NBC constructed a huge wire cage to house the participants. On the appointed day, they were all frisked for weapons and then locked inside the cage. George stood outside of it with a megaphone. "Is everyone ready?" he called out. "Ready!" came the response. "OK," he said; "here goes:"

## FEMINISM!

The people inside the cage went nuts. They began to scream, tear their hair, bite each other, and beat each other up. Many got down on all fours and barked like dogs. It went on for thirty-five minutes, until they ran out of steam. Exhausted, most of them were lying on the floor. Some were bleeding.

"Well done," George called out on the megaphone. "Now let's try another phrase:"

## POLITICALLY INCORRECT!

Again, this set off a massive reaction of rage and violence, but since most of these folks were rather tired from the first round, it lasted only twenty minutes this time.

# RACISM!
# MUSLIMS!
# ISRAEL!
# DIVERSITY!

George bombarded them with these charged words until there wasn't a person left standing. The medical teams and ambulances that were parked outside now hauled most of the mangled participants off to local hospitals, where hundreds of them spent a week or more in recovery.

As would be expected, George was in high demand on the TV talk shows. The typical first question he was met with was, "Given the disaster of the wire cage experiment, what do you plan to do next?" George's answer was always the same:

"Bob [or Freddie, or Chrystal], this was no disaster. As a pilot project, it was a great success. It revealed the depths of negative energy stored in the American psyche—energy we are going to have to drain, if this country has any future. You know, we are constantly hearing about the need to 'get America back on track'. Well, this is how to do it. Think of it as draining the pus of an infection. If a bunch of words can push the American public right over the edge, then it's safe to say that we are dealing with a whole lotta pus—metaphorical pus, infecting the body politic. Myself, I'm looking forward to Wire Cage Experiment No. 2."

And the rest is history. As the "pus" was drained from the American people, a certain (limited) restoration of sanity settled over the land. "I think it's safe to say," George finally announced, "that we have made America great again."

# 6

## HOW ARE YOU DOING?

It was a daily routine with Ralph, walking over to the supermarket in his neighborhood, only four blocks away. For one thing, it used up some of his time (he was retired), and secondly, it allowed him to have fresh food every day. He had no interest in shopping once a week, stocking up on supplies; that would deprive him of both benefits. The store was staffed by teenagers; he guessed they were paid minimum wage. Like most Americans their age, they lacked any affect: they had no interest in their work or in their customers. Perhaps that was to be expected; except that the kids in other countries he had visited seemed to be a lot more animated. Or just, animated.

Every time he checked out, the cashier would say "How are you doing?" to him in a flat monotone. He would invariably say "Fine," give her the money, take his change and his bag of groceries, and leave the store. But one day, on a whim, he decided to alter his response, just to see if the girl was even present, mentally speaking. "Oh, as good as can be expected," he ventured. The cashier gave him the faintest of nods, and as usual he took his groceries and left the store. The next day, he replied:

"About the same as the earth." She looked up, gave him a blank stare. For the third day, he tried: "Not so good; my mother just died." In response she looked at him—a first, really—said nothing, and handed him his groceries. Day Four: "Not very well; I may have to kill myself." Her response was the same as it had been on Day Three.

It also seemed to him that these kids were very different from himself and his friends when he was their age. Fifty years ago—or even twenty? He wasn't sure—American youth still had some life to them, some spark. You could banter with cashiers, or even strike up some innocuous conversation. All of that was apparently the behavior of a bygone era, as though one were reminiscing about the Middle Ages.

Could it be the result of 9/11? he wondered. Somehow, after that event, the country seemed to be drifting. There didn't seem to be any purpose to anything. But he doubted that this sea change could be ascribed to any one cause. It seemed more "global," somehow, as though a heavy fog had drifted in from the coast, and settled across the land as a kind of oppressive presence. Ralph remembered that the writer Don DeLillo had predicted something of the sort in the eighties: he had called it a "toxic event." And now, the fog had made its way into the American soul, especially the souls of the young people. Indeed, the supermarket girl actually seemed drugged.

He wondered what might happen if he were to escalate his answers. Like, "I think I'm going to vomit," or "A bit sad; I just beat my dog to death," or even, "This is a really shitty job, isn't it?" He was sure that "I could really use a blowjob" would get a rise out of her, but that was obviously not a good idea.

And then a possible angle occurred to him. On Day Five, in response to "How are you doing?", Ralph gave it a go. "You know," he said to her, "I'm a writer" (not true), "and I'm currently writing a book about your generation—is it Y or Z now? I seem to have lost track. Do you think I could meet with you and your friends after work, and sort of interview you all? I'll be glad to buy you guys dinner."

Somewhere, from deep inside the fog, something stirred. The girl's eyes flickered. "Uh, say what?" she finally said. Ralph repeated the offer. "It would help me a lot," he added.

"You couldn't use our real names," she said to him. He shrugged. "Not a problem."

"OK," she said, "I'll ask the others, see what they say about it. Come by tomorrow after six." "Will do," he replied. He left the market, rather amazed that they had had an actual conversation.

When Ralph returned the next day, there were five of them standing by the door. "So," he said; "dinner?" Joanna, his usual cashier, indicated that there was a steak-and-burger place a few blocks away, so they started walking in that direction. When they got there, they took a booth, and gave the waiter their orders. There was a round of Cokes; Ralph asked for a Bud Lite.

"The first thing you should know," Joanna told him, "is that we are actually an informal group. We've been together for about two years now; we call ourselves the Half Brains."

"Strange moniker," said Ralph. "How did you ever come up with that?"

"That's the second thing you should know," Joanna replied. "You may be wasting your time, because we aren't your typical high school seniors. If you are trying to get a bead on Gen Z, or whatever we are, it would make more sense for you to go over to our high school and sit in on a few classes. That would be reality. The Half Brains are anything but reality, at least within that context. We decided to call ourselves that because it was obvious to us that our fellow students didn't have half a brain. All they do is play video games, and their conversations are absurd. They know nothing at all—literally. And that's OK with them. The five of us, at least, have half a brain. What's your name, by the way?"

"Ralph," he said. "Ralph Ramírez."

"Oh, wow! You're Latino?"

"My father was," said Ralph. "What are your names?"

"For now," Joanna told him, "we prefer to use code names. I'm Medulla." The other kids, two boys and two girls, went around the table. "Hippocampus," said the first boy; "you can call me Hip." "Cerebellum," said the second boy. "Frontal Lobe," said the girl sitting to the left of Joanna/Medulla. "Stem," said the second girl.

Ralph smiled broadly; these kids were too much. "Jesus, you guys are a real trip. Certainly more than half a brain, that's for sure." That sort of broke the ice. "So you're a writer," said Hip. "What have you written?"

"I haven't," Ralph admitted. "This would be my first book. The truth is, at sixty-five I feel old, out of touch. I don't find people my age very interesting, to be honest. I want to know what young people today are all about. Which is why I wanted to talk to you guys."

"As I told you, Ralph," said Joanna, "you're talking to the wrong students. We're just not representative.

"OK, so tell me about that. How did you guys find each other, and why did you decide to form a group?"

Frontal Lobe, a slender brunette with dark brown eyes, chose to field that one. "It happened two years ago, in English class," she said. "Most of the teachers are duds, but Ms. Olivetti was actually kinda cool. She did something rather daring, assigned *The Catcher in the Rye* to the class. Us five loved it; the other kids didn't understand it, and thought the book was stupid. While we identified with Holden Caulfield, the others hated him, regarded him as a nerd, a jerk. The five of us thought *they* were the jerks. Ms. Olivetti wound up teaching the book to us alone, letting the morons get on with their video games and cell phones. She actually said some things to us that probably could have gotten her fired: that the other students were like the ones Holden encountered, and that it would probably be an uphill struggle for us, because most Americans were like that—clueless and ignorant. As a result, she said, we would be hated and isolated, and we needed to get used to it. 'Why don't the five of you form a sort of club?' she added, at the end of her little speech. And so we did. But she was absolutely right about being rejected by the others."

They were quiet for a while, taking it in. Finally Ralph turned to Joanna. "I have to say, Medulla, I'm really confused. Every time I went through your cashier line, I couldn't get much more than a grunt out of you. I actually wondered if you were retarded. Now I discover that you guys are bright and articulate. Did you just dislike me, or what?"

"Oh, no," said Joanna; "nothing like that. Being emotionally flat is just protective coloration—you know, the way some insects do it, as a way of hiding, of not being disturbed? None of us is particularly keen on cashiering, or having meaningless conversations with customers, so we just play dumb. It makes the job a lot easier."

"Well," said Ralph, "you sure fooled me. But tell me something else. This might be a hard one to answer, but I really would like to know what you guys think. Why are you so different from the other students in the school? How did that happen? I mean, there must be an explanation for this."

Cerebellum, a tall, thin boy with wavy hair, spoke up. "I think it may have to do a lot with TV. My parents never had one, and they regarded most of the programs as dumb. They bought me books from a pretty early age, and read to me every night before I went to sleep. But this made me a kind of freak, because none of the kids I knew read books. Everything was TVs and screens. I remember once making a reference to George Washington, and

everyone stared at me. They had no idea who he was. Being a
Half Brain has really saved my life."

"Is that the experience of the rest of you?" Ralph asked them.

"In my case," said Joanna, "I really can't say. Up to about
fourteen there was nothing on my mind beyond boys and lip
gloss. I was dating the captain of the football team, a very good
looking guy, and one day he said to me, 'In a couple of years'—he
was sixteen—'I hope to be driving a Porsche.' And then I asked
him if he had any other goals, and he said, 'Just to kill a lot of
Arabs'. It was at that moment that a light kinda went off in my
head. I asked myself, 'So what are *your* goals?' And it surely
couldn't be to be dating a guy who was obviously a moron, good
looks or not. I broke up with him a week later. My parents said
"Good!', and began to talk to me—this at age fourteen—about the
American Dream and US foreign policy. And so, I became a
freak. Then I studied *Catcher in the Rye* with Ms. Olivetti, and I
discovered that I was a female version of Holden Caulfield. As for
Ms. Olivetti, she once said to me, 'Stay under the radar, kid, and
you'll be all right.' That's one reason I don't do much more than
grunt at customers who come through my cashier line. It's what
we all do."

Ralph nodded. "Sure, I get it," he said. "But where do you see
Half Brain headed? What are *its* goals?"

The five of them looked at each other. Finally, Frontal Lobe
said, "We haven't thought that far ahead. Some of us have
individual goals, but as for group goals...I mean, we're not
thinking in terms of changing society, or even changing other
people. I suppose we just wanna stay out of harm's way."

"With all due respect to Ms. Olivetti," said Ralph, "isn't flying
below the radar a rather limited goal? Wouldn't it be great to live
in a world where the ratios were reversed? Where the number of
Holden Caulfields was very high, and the number of morons was
very low?"

Hip spoke up at this point. "Ralph, that just ain't gonna happen. I think you know that. But what I personally envision for Half Brain is a spiritual goal. I spent much of this year reading about magic: you know, alchemy, Carl Jung, that sort of thing. What's missing from the lives of the anti-Caulfields is a sense of mystery, enchantment. Their idea of sex is these stupid hookups, or oral sex parties. Last year I dated a college freshman—or I suppose, freshwoman—for a few months, and for me, the sex became about loving the whole world; which is how I felt. When I wasn't reading Jung, I was reading poetry—and, thanks to her, writing it. This is what people need in their lives, not video games."

"Why did the relationship end?" Ralph asked him. Hip looked sad, looked away. "She got pregnant," he replied, "and had an abortion. After that, the fire kinda died down." He looked like he was about to cry. "I'm really sorry," said Ralph. Things were quiet for a moment. Finally Ralph asked:

"What do you guys think of what Hip said? Should Half Brain pursue a spiritual goal? Should it try to reenchant the world, or at least, your world? Medulla—can you tell me your real name?"

"Joanna."

"Joanna, why not try this as an experiment? Tomorrow, when you are cashiering, instead of playing dead, pick one out of every five people and give them a compliment. Like, 'I like your dress'. Maybe all of you could do that, and then meet here again after work, and talk about what happened. How about it?"

"I'm in," said Cerebellum. "Me too," said Frontal Lobe. They all agreed to it. Another round of sodas, and they got up and left.

---

RALPH LAY in bed that night, unable to sleep. His mind was

racing, almost feverish. He was excited about having met these kids, and about what they discussed. He wondered how the "experiment" would turn out.

So the second meeting took place the next day, again at six o'clock. Ralph brought a volume of poetry with him. "I'm looking forward to hearing how your day went," he began. "But first, I'd like to read you a poem, and I'd like for each of you to tell me what it means to you. OK?" Everybody nodded. "This is called 'God's Grandeur'. It was written by a English poet named Gerard Manley Hopkins in 1877."

"The world is charged with the grandeur of God.
It will flame out, like shining from shook foil;
It gathers to a greatness, like the ooze of oil
Crushed. Why do men then now not reck his rod?
Generations have trod, have trod, have trod;
And all is seared with trade; bleared, smeared with toil;
And wears man's smudge and shares man's smell: the soil
Is bare now, nor can foot feel, being shod.

And for all this, nature is never spent;
There lives the dearest freshness deep down things;
And though the last lights off the black West went
Oh, morning, at the brown brink eastward, springs —
Because the Holy Ghost over the bent
World broods with warm breast and with ah! bright wings."

Frontal Lobe burst into tears. She sobbed for a full five minutes. Finally Ralph asked her, "Do you know why you are crying?" The others passed her some Kleenex. Frontal blew her nose and nodded. "I'm Amy," she said. "It's the line about the lights in the West going out. We aren't stupid, the five of us. We know our way of life is ending. We've talked about it a lot. It's why we all went numb, checked out. Because we saw it, and we knew there was nothing we could do about it."

"Does the author believe there is nothing we can do about it?" Ralph asked her.

"No," said Amy; "he's obviously Catholic, believes the Holy Ghost is the answer. I don't believe that."

"Suppose for 'Holy Ghost' we substituted 'magic', or 'enchantment', or 'spirituality', Ralph suggested.

"How would that work?" she asked.

"How did your day go, Amy? Any events out of the ordinary?" Amy nodded, started crying again. "I did what you said. An old lady came through, and I said to her, 'I like your dress'. She dropped her grocery bag and hugged me very tightly. She said, 'Oh my dear, I'm so lonely. Nobody talks to me. In America, old folks are treated like dirt, like they don't exist. Would you come to my house for tea sometime? I live right nearby.' I took down her address, told her I would."

"You're a great person, Amy," said Ralph. "You touched her soul. And you didn't need the Holy Ghost to do it, either." "I'll tell you this," she said; "I'm finished with 'Have a nice day'." The others chuckled, and nodded in agreement.

"Anybody else?" said Ralph.

Stem spoke up. "I'm Aline," she said. "A guy came through wearing a U of Connecticut sweat shirt, and I asked him if he really went to UConn. He lit up like a Christmas tree. Then I asked him what he was studying, and he said Semitic languages—Hebrew and Arabic. 'Any particular reason?' I asked him. He said he wanted to be a peace negotiator in the Middle East. 'Heroic work', I told him. The Christmas tree got even brighter. He was on cloud nine when he left the store."

"So you also touched a soul," said Joanna.

"What is it we all want?" Ralph asked them. They were silent.

"To be seen," he went on; "to be validated, valued, recognized. Am I right?"

"Maybe also to be loved," said Hip. "When someone values you, in a way they are saying that they love you."

"Where do you guys want to go from here?" Ralph asked them. "The Half Brains can be anything they want. Or almost anything."

"Ralph," Joanna replied, "I want you to be our new Ms. Olivetti. I want you to meet with us once a week, and teach us things, like the Hopkins poem. Or give us tasks to do, like talking to people in the store. Am I right, guys?"

Enthusiastic assent. "OK, then," said Ralph; "here's this week's homework assignment. Make a list of all the things you love, and write down why you love them. See you next week."

———————

THE THIRD MEETING rolled around pretty quickly. They all had their lists, and were eager to share. Why couldn't American education be like this? Ralph wondered. "Aline," he said; "you go first."

"Things I love," she began. "Being close to someone; the Half Brains; my dog, Pepper; a long hot shower; masturbating."

"Wow!" said Ralph; "that was pretty courageous. What do you think all of those things have in common?"

"I thought about that," she replied. "I think it's that all of these things allow me to forget myself. When I'm playing with Pepper, it's like he's the only thing in the world."

"Anything you might add to that list?" Ralph asked her.

"Baseball," she said. "I'd like to hit a home run."

"OK," said Ralph; "your assignment for this week is to think how you might make that happen. Hip, you're up next."

"Making love," he began; "Chinese food; playing tennis; the

Half Brains; getting a haircut from Joanna—she's really good at it." (Everybody laughed.) "I'd also like to write—something, anything."

"OK," Ralph told him; "your assignment is to write the first chapter of a book about the Half Brains: why they exist, and why you think it's important that they exist."

And so they went around the table, talking about their loves and their dreams. Ralph suggested that their next meeting take place in a Chinese restaurant (he continued to foot the bill), and everybody agreed. Hip was ecstatic.

Are these kids my family now? Ralph asked himself when he got home. Isn't this pathetic, or even pathological? I have no family left, or close friends, so I latch onto a bunch of high school kids. Who probably value—love?—me, which feels very good. Am I regressing to adolescence? Well, fuck it: if I am, who is it hurting?

Oddly enough, the Half Brains raised that very issue with him at the next get-together. "Ralph," Hip asked him, "what's in it for you, this thing? I mean, it's clear what's in it for us. But all of us are wondering why you are hanging out with a bunch of teenagers. I know, you said you wanted to learn about today's youth. But has you know, we are hardly 'today's youth'. So what are you really up to?"

"I'm not sure I know myself," Ralph responded. "Clearly, if I had wanted to learn about mainstream teenagers, the ones who hate Holden Caulfield, I could have visited a few classrooms. But after that first meeting we had, I realized that I was a lot more interested in learning about you all—the misfits. And after that, I really saw no reason to stop. Would you like me to stop? Because if you guys want that, I can just disappear. No hard feelings."

"We don't want you to stop, Ralph," said Hip; "we're all

happy that you're tutoring us, so to speak. We're just not clear as to where you are coming from, why you really wanna do this."

"Well, for one thing," Ralph replied, "it's fun."

"Are you married?" Hip asked him. "Do you have family, friends?"

"No, nobody," said Ralph. "So maybe this is a hedge against loneliness. I'm telling you, I really don't know."

"OK," said Hip; "sorry for the third degree."

"Not a problem. Moving right along…Aline, take me out to the ball game." (Laughter)

"Sure," she replied. "I approached the gym teacher and asked him if he'd be willing to start and coach a girls' baseball team. He said he'd think about it."

"Hip," said Ralph; "how's the book coming along?"

"It's not," said Hip. "I just couldn't get into it. I wrote a poem instead."

"Could we hear it?" said Ralph. Hip took a notebook out of his book bag. "It's about my ex-girlfriend, the one I told you about. It's called 'I Miss You'."

"Letting go of love
when you have no choice
is a little like dying without morphine.
And then you realize—though you knew it before, of course—
that the closeness was not about sex
but about being able to take care of someone
without a thought for yourself.
'Our goal is not to make something happen,'
goes an old Gestalt saying;
'It's to see what actually does happen.'

I found out."

"How beautiful," said Joanna, almost in a whisper. Amy got up and hugged him.

"Thank you, Hip," said Ralph; "forget about prose. Poetry is clearly your strong suit. To write from the heart like that is no easy thing. For next week, I'd like each of you to bring in your favorite poem, read it to us, and explain why you like it."

And so it went, week in and week out, until the high school got wind of it, and Ms. Squashlife, the principal, phoned Ralph and asked him to come in. (How she managed to get his phone number Ralph never found out.) She was a large, badly dressed, seriously overweight woman; anger hovered over her like a swarm of bees.

"Mr. Ramírez," she began, "word has it that you have set up some kind of alternative school. Is this correct?"

"Not an alternative, Ms. Squashlife; I prefer to think of it as supplemental."

"And why would you think that American high school students would be in need of supplementary classes?"

"It was their idea, Ms. Squashlife," Ralph replied. "They apparently felt the need to explore issues that they said didn't get raised in their regular classes. This especially after Ms. Olivetti left the school." Ms. Squashlife stiffened a bit. "Ms. Olivetti was let go, Mr. Ramírez. She was teaching a lot of material that didn't fall within curriculum guidelines."

"I guess that must have been the material these kids wanted to explore," Ralph suggested.

"Do you have credentials in the field of education, Mr. Ramírez? My sources tell me that your own field is, or was, chemical engineering. In what way are you qualified to conduct high school classes?"

"Sources, or informants? It sounds like you've been conducting a kind of spying operation. In any case, these meetings with the students are not classes. I'm hardly grading them, or handing out diplomas. We just meet once a week to talk about things we are interested in, nothing more. As far as I know, this does not constitute illegal activity, if that's what you are implying."

"True," she responded, "there is nothing illegal about what you are doing, although an older gentleman hanging out with teenagers would strike anyone as being very peculiar. Myself, as an educator, I find it a bit unethical."

"How so, Ms. Squashlife? I fail to understand your reasoning in this matter. Perhaps you could enlighten me as to how what I am doing constitutes unethical behavior."

"Well," she began, and then started stuttering. "I mean—well —it's just that—" She turned red in the face, and started coughing. "Water?" said Ralph. She began waving her arms, signaling no. She looked like a large boiled lobster. Ralph got up and left. At the next Half Brains meeting, he reported the conversation to the group.

"She's a douche bag," said Cerebellum (Jack). "Most of the fat she carries is between her ears."

"I can't believe they fired Ms. Olivetti," exclaimed Amy. "The one good teacher they had. Although the art teacher is pretty good too. Ms. Novak."

"Well," said Ralph, "we can keep meeting, but I suggest we move the venue around, just to prevent Ms. Squashlife or any of her assistants from trying to crash the party, or spy on us. I have an uneasy feeling that we haven't heard the last of her. She's obviously threatened by what we are doing."

"Sure," Joanna interjected. "Because it's real education, not bullshit. That's what got Ms. Olivetti fired—she wanted to talk about real things, real life."

"OK, gang," said Ralph; "your assignment for next week: research obesity online and write one page analyzing why Ms. Squashlife is eighty pounds overweight."

"Groovy!" exclaimed Joanna. The group dispersed.

The next week—Indian restaurant this time—Joanna was first out of the starting gate. Her essay was entitled "Pie of Death." She was so wound up, she was practically raving. "Ms. Squashlife is grotesquely obese because she keeps trying to fill a huge void in her life with food. It doesn't work, but since she is basically a retard, she keeps stuffing herself. For the sake of the school, she needs to be expunged."

"Expunged?" said Ralph.

"Yes. Wiped off the map. And the way to do this is to place a pie on her doorstep early every morning. Within three months she'll have a heart attack, or perhaps explode, and Jefferson High will be rid of this greasy, overstuffed moron."

Everybody laughed. "Tell us how you really feel," said Aline.

"Listen, Joanna," said Jack, "the school board will just replace her with someone equally incompetent. In order to really change the school, you'd hafta change the student population, from anti-Caulfields to pro-Caulfields. They'd hafta put down their cell phones and start reading books. I just don't see that happening."

"Aline," said Ralph; "you give it a shot." She sat up straight, very controlled in comparison to Joanna.

"Ms. Squashlife has no one in her life to love or value her. She got her present job by working her way up the administrative hierarchy. She feels she is a fraud, an imposter, for she has no real interest in education, and is just marking time until she can retire. When she does retire, not a single person will come to visit her. Her conversations with the teachers are like prerecorded messages. She knows that their politeness is phony, and that they would just as soon she drowned in her bathtub. Eating like a pig gives her some short-term comfort; it's a substitute for love. Although I personally find her disgusting, I also feel sorry for her."

"First-rate," said Ralph; "I think you pegged her very well.

But let me suggest something to you guys: What do you say we invite her to one of our meetings?"

"Omigod," exclaimed Joanna. "Not to worry," Hip told her; "she'd never accept. What we're doing here is reality, and Squashlife doesn't do reality." Ralph decided to try anyway. The next day, he called her on the phone.

"Ms. Squashlife," he said, "this is Ralph Ramírez calling. The students and I would like to invite you to our next meeting. They want you to see that nothing evil or illegal is going on."

"Mr. Ramírez, I never said evil. I—" "Will you come?" Ralph interrupted her. "What do you say? Thursday evening, 6 p.m., at the All You Can Eat Buffet on Eighth Avenue."

"Perhaps," she replied; "I'll have to think about it." "That's all we ask," Ralph told her.

The assignment for that week was to write one or two paragraphs on "Can anyone really know another person?" Much to everyone's surprise, Ms. Squashlife showed up. "I can't tell you how happy all of us are to see you," said Ralph. He explained that discussion topics varied from week to week, and gave her the title of this week's assignment. She smiled weakly. "Let me go to the food bar first," she said. She came back to the table with about five pounds of fatty foods piled high on her plate.

"OK," said Ralph; "who wants to start?" Joanna raised her hand and began reading from her paper.

"One of the definitions of 'persona'," she read, "which is the root of our word 'personality', is 'mask'. All of us have a hidden self, which we cover up by presenting a personality to the world —a mask. We are afraid to expose our real selves, so we offer up a false self for others to deal with. Of course, they are also offering up false selves, so the whole effect is shadows talking to other shadows."

"Pretty good," Ralph interjected. "Let's hear more."

"When we were asked, a few weeks ago, to write down the

things we loved, Aline had masturbation on her list." (At this point, Ms. Squashlife's face turned a deep red, and she began to sweat profusely.) "This was very courageous, because it's a secret we all share. After that meeting, Aline and I compared notes, talked about how we did it. I told her that I had a vibrator, and inserted it into my vagina every night before I went to sleep." (Ms. Squashlife went into a choking fit, upon hearing this. Jack got up, got her a glass of water.) "I have a particular fantasy to go with it, a boy in school I'd love to sleep with. He's dumb as a stick, but he's so good looking I don't care. So I imagine myself in bed with him, and I climax pretty quickly.

"Of course, sexual secrets are only one type of secret that we have. I am passionate about the poetry we have heard in this group. But if I revealed that to the girls at school, they would ridicule me. Meanwhile, many of them have serious eating disorders. They are anorexic or bulimic or obese—which gives the game away, because it shows how miserable they are. The final point is that you are only as healthy as your secrets. If you've got a lot of them, all you can do is relate to others in an unreal way."

"I'm sorry," burst out Ms. Squashlife; "I just remembered I have to be somewhere else." She got up noisily, knocking over her chair, and ran out the door. When the students came to school the next day, they learned that Ms. Squashlife had tried to hang herself, but that the attempt failed because the rope broke. She was now in the hospital, and had been put on indefinite paid leave. The school board was in the process of looking for a replacement for her.

"Jesus H. Christ," exclaimed Joanna at their next meeting. "I was joking about 'Pie of Death', and now it looks like I nearly killed her. I feel really bad about this, maybe even a little crazy."

"Why do you think she tried to kill herself?" Ralph asked her.

"Oh Ralph," Joanna replied, "that's a slam dunk. I talked

about phony relationships and eating disorders—I pushed her over the edge."

"Maybe," said Ralph, "but she had been moving toward that edge for a long time. All you did was tip her over it. After all, there were a lot of things she could have done besides attempting suicide. Set up an appointment with a therapist, for example."

"Yeah…" said Joanna. "Although all that talk about masturbation and vibrators and sexual fantasies, it was much more than she could handle. Honestly, I feel like I'm a terrible person."

"Joanna," countered Aline, "what you wrote was not pointed at Squashlife. You didn't even know she was coming, right? So let's lighten up on the self-flagellation, OK?"

"You're a terrific person, Joanna," said Ralph; "and you have nothing to feel guilty about. Aline is right about not beating yourself up." He paused for breath. "Hopefully Ms. Squashlife will recover, retire, and maybe think about her life. Which brings me to our next assignment. I want you to imagine that you're a therapist, and that you have a patient who is slowly edging toward a crisis, of realizing that his or her life has been a mask, a charade. They are on the verge of revealing their secrets, but you are afraid that this degree of self-awareness could push them to suicide or a nervous breakdown. What do you do?"

"Why don't we invite the Vice Principal in for that one?" Jack suggested. "We might be able to knock off the whole administration, one at a time—just kidding."

"You guys are something else," said Ralph. "See you next time."

"AMY, YOU GO FIRST THIS TIME," said Ralph.

"I had a hard time with this," she responded, "because I think the correct solution depends on a person's age. So I wrote two scenarios. Can I read both?" "Fire away," said Ralph.

"OK. So this is a woman of about thirty-three. Her drama is about men, what else. She has had a number of relationships that didn't work out, and is worried that she'll never have a husband or children, which she very much wants. In therapy, she got to the point that she realized that all of this was connected to her father. She had a very close relationship with him, idolized him, and when he died when she was thirteen, her entire world imploded. She has not been able to let go of him, emotionally speaking, as a result. She has photos of him all over her house, including a large one in a kind of 'shrine room'.

"When we explored some of her failed relationships, she admitted to having been very possessive, of adoring the men and wanting them to be her reason for existing. The pressure was understandably too great, and they split. Recently she had a sexual dream about her father, and woke up feeling scared. 'I know I have to let go of my father', she told me, 'but I just can't. He was the only person in my life who really cared for me. I'm terrified that if I let go, I'll fall apart. I'll have nothing to hang onto.'

"In this case, I believe the correct solution would be to slowly wean her away from her father. Get her to take down the photographs, and write a goodbye letter to him in her journal. This will generate an ongoing crisis for her, which she can work through in further therapy.

"My second case study is an investment banker, seventy-five years old, a hard and driven man, who has no interest in therapy, but came to see me at the insistence of his wife. She wrote me that his whole life has been about making money; that he has no friends or outside interests; and that all he knows is ruthless competition. She begged me to help.

"In our first session I suggested he keep a dream notebook,

127

which he grudgingly agreed to do. What then followed was a series of dreams that were pretty grim: he commits suicide, is tortured, is thrown in a dungeon, and so on. I began to feel that if we were to unpack those dreams, he might go psychotic. I finally told him that the dreams were saying that he was badly overworked, and that he needed to book a cruise and go on an extended vacation with his wife. He was happy with the diagnosis, and never returned to therapy."

"Wow! Thank you, Amy. This is a lot to think about. Anyone have anything to say on Amy's case studies, and her solutions?"

"I think the therapist did the right thing," offered Aline. "The girl was young enough to endure the anxiety of change, whereas with the old guy, it was simply too late to switch gears."

"I dunno," countered Hip. "I don't think it's ever too late to opt for a better life."

"But Hip," Joanna put in, "he thinks he already *has* the best life possible. He has no motivation to opt for something else. He doesn't even want to be in therapy."

And so the argument went. The Half Brains debated the issue until nearly midnight, when the restaurant tossed them out. They stood out in front, breathing in the cold night air. Amy threw her arms around Ralph. "I love you," she said. He smiled, hugged her back. Later, lying in bed, he thought about his attraction to the girls. Of the three, he found Joanna the most attractive. He imagined having sex with her, but then stopped himself. This was dangerous ground. What he needed, quite obviously, was a girlfriend. The possibility emerged two days later in the form of a phone call from the Jefferson High art teacher, Ms. Novak.

"Mr. Ramírez," she said, "could we meet for coffee sometime? The school has some concerns about the group you've been running, and wants me to discuss it with you."

"What concerns?" he asked her.

"Well, some of us have been wondering about the zero time

gap between Ms. Squashlife visiting your group, and her suicide attempt. No one is saying that the group caused it, but they do want me to talk with you about it."

"Ms. Novak, the group is hardly responsible for Ms. Squashlife trying to kill herself. But OK, why don't I meet you at the Higher Grounds Coffee House on Jackson Street tomorrow at four, when you get out of work?" "See you then," she said, "and thank you for being so cooperative."

Ralph was very worried about all this. He was not going to tell the group about the meeting; he also felt strongly that he had to protect Joanna, whose little essay may well have driven the ex-principal over the edge. It would be necessary to talk with Ms. Novak in very general terms.

Ralph got to Higher Grounds around 3:45 p.m., ordered a cappuccino, and took a seat facing the door. He was not prepared for the woman who came through the door at precisely four o'clock. She was a knockout. Ms. Novak was statuesque, with long blond hair, a beautiful face, and a figure that would cause any heterosexual male to weep. She looked like she had just stepped out of the pages of *Vogue*. She was not wearing a wedding ring. Ralph tried not to gape.

Barbara—that was her Christian name—extended her hand. "Once again," she said, "it was very kind of you to agree to this. There are a lot of rumors floating around about Ms. Squashlife's suicide attempt, and it would be good to put them to rest." Ralph realized that he didn't want to lie to this woman, especially if he might eventually muster the nerve to ask her out. At the same time, he wasn't going to throw Joanna under the bus. He decided to take the initiative.

"Ms. Novak—" he began. "Barbara," she interrupted him. "May I call you Ralph?" "Of course," he replied. "Look, let's start by my asking *you* a question. Why do you think this group exists at all?" She looked at him through her lovely blue eyes.

"That's easy," she told him. "These five kids are the school's misfits. They actually fit into my art class somewhat—the guy who calls himself Hip is very talented, in fact—but they don't fit in anywhere else. The one teacher they were simpatico with was Ruth Olivetti, and Squashlife fired her. Once she was gone, their radar was probably out for a substitute, and I guess that was when they met you. Or perhaps two or three months after that. Ruth was not as far gone as Robin Williams in *Dead Poets Society*— well, she wasn't far gone at all, in my opinion—but she packed her course with a lot of extracurricular stuff that made Squashlife nervous."

"Like *The Catcher in the Rye*," put in Ralph.

"Exactly," said Barbara. "These kids are the school iconoclasts, Ralph; the Steppenwolves, if you will. They are always insisting on 'the real', as they like to put it. They are very smart, but a bit too out there; and the school rumors have it that they somehow drove Squashlife crazy."

"Barbara," Ralph replied, "may I be frank? I'm no psychiatrist, but it really didn't take much to see that Ms. Squashlife was already crazy, in her own way. She weighed— weighs—something like 240 pounds. When I went to see her, at her request, she accused me of being unethical, and when I asked her to tell me how, exactly, she became incoherent, began to wave her arms and choke."

"If you considered her a basket case, why did you invite her to sit in on the group? What good could possibly have come from it?"

"Well, I wanted her to see that nothing unethical or illegal was going on," Ralph replied. Barbara leaned into him; her perfume made him a bit dizzy. He wanted to kiss her, but figured it was probably not a good idea at this point. "Ralph, you and I know there's more to it than that. Tell me what it is. Off the record, I promise."

"Can I really trust you?" Ralph asked her. "It goes no further than me, you have my word," she said.

"OK, then. The other part is that given how miserable and unhappy Squashlife obviously was, I had some thoughts about saving her soul, if you'll permit me the expression. I'm an engineer, or was, but I read a lot in the psychological literature, and there is some debate in psychological circles about the importance of dismantling a patient's abysmal ego structure, and then putting them back together on a sounder footing, versus just letting them be, as it were, on the theory that what they presented was the best they could do. Now, I had no intention of therapizing Squashlife, let alone breaking her down; but somehow, that's what happened."

"What was the group discussing, on that particular evening?" Barbara asked him.

"The topic was whether one could truly know another person. Martin Buber, if you will. This is typical of the group. As you indicated, these kids are very focused on 'reality', and this topic overlapped with that. There was nothing out of the ordinary here; it's only a guess on my part, but I think what might have pushed Squashlife over the edge was the general ambience of the group, the open way in which they discussed things, rather than any particular issue. Perhaps I should have figured out that *I and Thou* would be as threatening to someone like Squashlife as *The Catcher in the Rye*. But I say this in complete honesty: in no way did I imagine a suicidal reaction, and such a thing was never my intent. If I had any hopes for Squashlife in a healing direction, it might have been that she could relax a bit, become a little bit more human. That's it."

Barbara was silent for a moment. "It's nevertheless strange, don't you think, that a grown man is hanging out with teenagers. That I don't get."

"That's a different matter altogether," Ralph replied. "You

wanted to know if the group caused Squashlife's suicide attempt, and I'm telling you that it didn't. If you want to know more about me, perhaps we could have dinner sometime." Barbara's eyes widened. "Here's a question for you, in any case," Ralph went on; "do *you* believe one can truly know another person?" Barbara smiled. "You're a smooth operator, Mr. Ramírez," she responded. "Like in the song."

"Sade?" he said. She ignored this. "Ralph, you are also a good guy. I have this feeling you're protecting individuals in the group, but I'm going to tell the school board that there isn't any connection between the group meeting and Squashlife's suicide attempt. That the close timing between the two is just coincidence, nothing more."

"I appreciate that," said Ralph, "but you still haven't answered my question."

"Ralph, I don't think we can even know ourselves, let alone another person. *I and Thou* is an ideal, and perhaps one to strive for. But human beings are far too fucked up, if you'll pardon my French, to operate with much clarity. Squashlife is at the far end of the spectrum, to be sure; but in a kind of scary way, she's really all of us. As for dinner: yes, Ralph, I would like to get to know you."

I love this woman, Ralph said to himself. I would climb Everest for her.

(Just to jump ahead for a minute, three weeks later the group —i.e., Joanna—asked him, "Are you boning the art teacher?" "Boning?" Ralph replied. "*Boning?*" In any case, he never revealed to them the contents of his conversation with Barbara.)

He picked a small Italian restaurant famous for its cannelloni and its atmosphere. Barbara was dressed to kill: short skirt, low-cut blouse, revealing a bit of black lace brassiere. How I'm going to get through this dinner, Ralph said to himself, I have no idea. He ordered a bottle of Chianti, and offered a toast: "To knowing each other," he said. "Even if it's impossible," Barbara added. They both laughed.

"So what kind of art do you do?" he asked her. "Oil paintings and sculpture," she said. "Nothing abstract. For me, art has to emerge from an emotional base, from the gut, and reach people on that level. Van Gogh, Giacometti, not Picasso."

"It's important to know what you want, what turns you on," said Ralph.

"So what turns you on?" Barbara asked him. "Chemistry?"

"Yeah," he replied; "chemistry and English lit. I did a double major in college. I can still recite a few poems by heart."

"Show me," she said. He looked directly into her eyes.

"'Shall I compare thee to a summer's day?
Thou art more lovely and more temperate.'"

"Jesus, Ralph, you really are a smooth operator. Let's try something less charged."

"'That's my last duchess painted on the wall,
Looking as if she were alive.'"

"Robert Browning," said Barbara. "That's one of my favorites." Ralph leaned over and kissed her. "Part of getting to know you," he explained.

"I don't mind a smooth operator as long as he's honest," she replied. "Listen, Ralph: no sex tonight, OK? I need a few more dates."

"Sounds good," he said. He kissed her again. "How about a movie next week?"

"DVD at your house," she suggested. "You pick the film."

Ralph chose *La Strada*, the 1954 film by Fellini. He and Barbara sat side by side on the couch, facing the screen. At the point where Zampanò accidentally kills the Fool, and Gelsomina starts to go mad, Barbara started crying. He held her for a long time, and then they kissed for a long time. Finally, she got up, undressed completely, and led him to the bedroom. Ralph was very excited, didn't last that long, but Barbara was happy nonetheless.

"Smooth Operator," she said in the afterglow. "That's your real name."

"What should I call you?" he asked. "Whatever you like," she told him. "Anything but Kim."

He laughed. "How about No Ordinary Love?"

"Too long," she said. "Then how about My Love?" he offered.

"Much too forward," she replied, smiling broadly, "but I'll take it."

They were rarely apart after that night, except for Thursdays, when he met with the group. It was about three weeks later that Joanna asked him about "boning." "Joanna, I'm not 'boning' anybody. But I am in love with Ms. Novak." Everybody applauded. "Go for it, dude!" Jack exclaimed, "with ah! bright wings."

"Does she love *you*?" asked Joanna.

"Jesus, Joanna, you are the most —"

"Come on, Ralph; we're about reality here, as you well know."

"OK, fair enough. Honestly, I really don't know. Time will tell," he told her. Joanna lifted her glass of Coke: "Here's to Ralph, Ms. Novak, and true love."

"Hear! Hear!" It was a fun night.

———

WELL, no one could accuse Joanna of being shy. At their next meeting, she put the following question to Ralph:

"Have you thought of doing anything postmodern with all this? I mean, there's no real conflict here, no place to go. You're all lovey-dovey with Ms. Novak, we keep having these great meetings, the school has decided not to hold an Inquisition over the Squashlife affair, and Squashlife herself is now living in the

Happy Valley Rest Home. You need to introduce some dynamic elements at this point, or else end the story altogether."

"OK," said Ralph; "any of you have any thoughts on the subject, or should I just type 'The End' and try to publish the damn thing?"

"Ms. Novak could get pregnant," Jack ventured.

"How about the school decides to interrogate each of us," said Amy, "and Joanna spills the beans about obesity and masturbation, and they pack her off to some teenage delinquent facility? Then maybe she breaks out, contacts the four of us, and together we burn the school down to the ground."

"Then," Hip put in, "you, Ralph, get us all passports, and we flee to Budapest."

"Why Budapest?" Ralph asked him. Hip shrugged. "I hear it's a groovy place. Then we could all become spies and pass classified information on to the Russians."

"All this is rather exhausting," Ralph declared. "This has been a successful story, more or less. Why don't we just call it a day?"

"Because your readers want to know more about us," said Joanna. "They want to know if I get it on with Rick; if Hip becomes a famous poet, and Ms. Novak a famous artist; if Ms. Novak wears those high heels of hers in bed —"

"*Joanna —*"

"OK, OK, but I do have an image in my head. The point is, we're not really done yet. Are we?"

"Joanna, why don't we just let our readers continue the story on their own?" Ralph suggested. "We've done our job: we launched the tale. Our readers are smart enough to take it from there, don't you think? Here's the assignment for our next meeting: just for the fun of it, outline what you think might be a logical sequel to this story, OK? See you all next week."

## 7

---

# SWEET HONEY IN THE ROCK

G ood evening, my friends. I hope I am not intruding. I promise to take only a minute of your time. My name is Jean-François Champollion. I died in Paris in 1832, at the age of forty-one, from a stroke. I am writing to you from beyond the grave. To you, who might want to listen.

Do you know me? I am the decipherer of the Rosetta Stone. Yes, the one that has been sitting in the British Museum for more than 200 years now; that one. I cracked the code of Egyptian hieroglyphics. I made the Egyptian language, and Egyptian civilization, accessible to the West. Me, *le jeune*, as my friends used to call me, in contrast to my older brother, Jacques-Joseph.

But this was not some exercise in "Orientalism"—not at all. First, because I regarded Egypt as a great civilization. Not, as the British believed, some boring slave civilization centered around a death cult. Now *that* was Orientalism. No, I saw Egyptian civilization as a vibrant, complex, and long-lasting culture, with values and purposes different from our own, but no less superior for that.

And second, because my real goal was to demonstrate the

opposite of Orientalism, which is empathic understanding. It is not difficult to see that the great curse of mankind is a failure of empathy. Everything has to be viewed through the lens of our Self; the Other is merely an (inferior) other. We can never seem to grasp that the Other is a Self all its own. We do not seek to understand or explore that other Self—not at all. All we want to do is paste labels on it. Why? I wish I knew.

So know that I am an Orientalist in the positive sense: my goal was to understand Egypt from the inside, as well as to demonstrate the principle, and the benefits, of empathy. I hope I succeeded.

There is one thing, however, that I am not proud of; it haunts me to this day. In terms of the Stone, and cracking the hieroglyphic code, I wanted all the credit—*la gloire*—for myself. And so rather than talking about "standing on the shoulders of giants," I deliberately played down or ignored the contributions of those who preceded me, in particular the British doctor and physicist Thomas Young. Looking back now, I realize that this is just another form of denying the Other; which means that it too is a form of oppression. I just said that I didn't know why we typically seek to denigrate the Other, or impose the Self on it, but maybe the phenomenon of plagiarism makes it clear: if I am insecure about my Self, then it is very tempting to try to obliterate the Other; and grabbing all the credit for one's Self is one way to do this. Human insecurity, in short, is ultimately at the root of violence.

I confess, that really depresses me.

The content of the Stone itself is not very important. It's just a pharaonic administrative decree, fairly banal. So the translation of this text is not my legacy. My legacy was to make translation of Egyptian hieroglyphics possible in general, which then allowed scholars to find out what Egyptian civilization was actually about. Equipped with the key in the lock, which I had provided for them, they translated one carving, one papyrus, and one wall inscription after another. Thus we learned about Egyptian history, mythology, burial customs, and belief systems. We discovered that these people had a sophisticated knowledge of astronomy, mathematics, and architecture. All of this would have been a closed book if not for me. And for me, this was the "honey in the rock," so to speak, what Nicholas of Cusa called "the sweetness of truth."

Shall I go on, my friends? Shall I tell you how I did it? As with Young's formulation of the wave theory of light—*mon dieu*, what a genius that man was—these "aha!" experiences are a combination of sweat and spark, of deep background information plus some inexplicable click in the brain, when everything falls into place. Roughly twenty years after I died, my fellow countryman Louis Pasteur declared, "chance favors the prepared mind." *Et voilà, mesdames et messieurs!* There you go.

The Stone was discovered when I was nine years old, in the course of Napoleon's expedition into Egypt. The expedition, as is well known, touched off an "Egyptomania" among the educated classes in France, and I got caught up in it. When I was sixteen, I wrote to my parents: "Of all the peoples that I love the most, I will confess that no one equals the Egyptians in my heart." *Zut alors!* You have to be an adolescent to say things like that. In fact, I didn't get to Egypt until 1828.

My great breakthrough occurred in 1822. For starters: What, exactly, does the Rosetta Stone contain? For those of you who haven't been to the British Museum, let me spell it out. It consists of three texts, all of which say the same thing. The upper part is written in hieroglyphics, and the bottom part in Greek. The middle text is written in what is called the demotic script of the Egyptian language, and is related to Coptic, a modern language— one which I had studied extensively (it's the latest stage of the Egyptian language, and written in the Greek alphabet). So the trick became to match the bottom two texts against the top one, eventually yielding a translation of the latter.

My friends, I don't wish to bore you with the technical details, but let me just summarize by saying that the point I discovered that ran through all three languages was the verb "to give birth." This broke open the hieroglyphic text. In my own imitation of Archimedes (albeit fully clothed), I ran down the street to my brother's office at the Institut de France, and yelled *"Je tiens l'affaire!"* — I've got it! Subsequently, I was able to establish an alphabet that applied to all epochs, and I deciphered grammatical words along with the names of kings and private persons. This opened the door to Egyptian civilization. This was my legacy. Ten years later, due to poor health, and probably the stress of unrelenting work, I was dead.

What did I do in the interim? I worked on other hieroglyphic texts, and published several books on my discoveries. I traveled to Italy, visiting collections and monuments there. I met the pope, who helped me obtain funds for an expedition to Egypt. In 1826, the king appointed me curator of the Egyptian collections of the Louvre; in 1831 I was made chair of Egyptian history and archaeology at the Collège de France. The next year, I was buried in Père Lachaise Cemetery, a kind of national hero. I am, to this day, regarded as a major figure in modern French history, the "Father of Egyptology." Recently I learned that a lunar crater on the far side of the moon was named after me. It all seems like a dream.

I don't know why the Fates chose me for this purpose, this opening up of the richness of Egyptian civilization to the West. I don't know why they gave me the gift of languages, and I don't know why they took me from the earth at so young an age. I was married, and had a beautiful daughter, Zoraïde, whom I loved dearly. That I had to leave her prematurely was the hardest part of dying. You'd think there would be a code book somewhere, something like the Rosetta Stone, that could be deciphered to explain all of this; that could explain the workings of the human heart. But there isn't.

Reflecting on my life now, I have to ask myself why Egypt in particular was my "laboratory" for exploring otherness. Part of it was the national "Egyptomania" already referred to. But it went deeper than that. If Egypt was the oldest human civilization (or one of them), then it promised to tell us the most basic things about human beings; or so I believed. The other factor was the sheer unfamiliarity, the opaqueness, of the script. It made Egypt the most Other of Others. What I was really exploring, I can see now, was myself. Egypt is my mirror; is me.

It has been said that we can never truly know another person, but some psychologists have added that we can never truly know ourselves, as well. I tell myself that in the grand scheme of things, it doesn't matter. That I don't count for anything, despite all of the national tributes. What counts is a rock sitting on display in the British Museum. And yet, what is it all for, if not for human beings? What is a rock, compared to a beating heart—*my* beating heart? On cold winter nights, here in the spirit world, I think about these things, and wonder.

8
———

# LIFE: THE CLIFFSNOTES

I have lived in San Francisco for many years now, and like many other local writers, I treat the Caffe Trieste in North Beach as a kind of second home. The café has a painting on the back wall, of a small fishing boat on a beach, somewhere in Italy (I'm guessing). It feels like Sicily, but it it's hard to tell. It evokes for me a fantastic land, a Sicily of the mind, one might say. Occasionally I close my eyes, and imagine being transported to that quiet, dreamy coastline.

I often wonder what qualifies a place as exotic. Distance, of course; but then Moscow is far away, and does not feel exotic—at least, not to me. No, there has to be a magical element to it, something mysterious that conjures up infinite possibilities. That painting has it, whatever "it" is.

It was on one of my forays into North Beach, a little more than two years ago, that I met Vanessa, at the Trieste. It was not clear to me why she sat down next to me. I am a guy of only average looks; attracting women never came easy for me. I remember having a friend in college who was extremely good looking; women were always coming on to him. If only, I would say to myself. Steve wasn't particularly good for my ego: if the two of us were sitting in a bar, attractive women would sit down at the next table and chat him up, while ignoring me completely. For better or worse, my genes were intellectual rather than physical.

In any case, Vanessa sat down next to me. As the college expression goes, she was built like a brick shithouse. Large breasts, low-cut blouse, and gorgeous legs emerging from a very short skirt. I tried not to gape or otherwise act like a jackass. She looked over at my notebook. "What are you working on?" she asked me. "Oh," I replied, trying to act nonchalant, "a collection of short stories. It's not flowing very well today, unfortunately."

"That's too bad," she said. "Are you a writer, then?"

"Trying to be," I replied. "I've published a bit of nonfiction, but this is my first venture into storytelling. It ain't easy. Thank God I've got a day job. How about you?"

"I model for art classes," she said. "And occasionally I wait tables at Vesuvio's, down the street. If I dress like this, the tips are pretty good."

"Gee, I can't imagine why," I replied. We both laughed. "Look," I went on, "I'm sorry, but I have to ask. I'm a very ordinary looking guy; I would hardly describe myself as handsome. So I can't figure out why you would sit down next to me. I mean, you're clearly outta my league."

She smiled. "Well, I do like a guy who's modest. But OK, to answer your question: I could tell you, but you'd think I was a flakey New Age nut case."

"That's OK," I told her; "be a nut case."

"God," she said; "this is embarrassing. But here's the story. I have a psychic adviser; she works with Tarot cards. I've had a pretty dry spell for the last six months, which Annie had actually predicted. That gal is never wrong. Anyway, two days ago, when I went to see her, she told me the dry spell was over. She said that within a day or two, I would meet an average-looking guy who had a powerful mind; that we would become lovers; and that he would help me to open my heart, which has been closed for most of my life." She was blushing a bit, by now.

"I guess it's my lucky day," I responded. "But why is your heart closed?"

"I don't trust very easily," she replied. "But never mind that, at least for now. The point is, you're the guy; or at least, you could be. Are you interested?"

"Very," I told her. (No surprise there.) We made love that afternoon, at her place. I was surprised at how compatible we were. "How was it?" she wanted to know, when we were done. "Do you really have to ask?" I answered. "Good," she said. "That's a good start." As for me, I had to come to terms with the fact that there really might be a God.

We hung out a lot together after that, when neither of us was working. I started taking one of the art classes she modeled for; she read my stories and gave me feedback. We also spent a lot of time sitting in the Caffe Trieste, getting high on cappuccino.

"You're always looking at that painting," she said to me one day. "What's the attraction?"

"It's exotic, because it's distant, unavailable," I told her.

"Am I not exotic, then, because I slept with you two hours after we met?"

"You didn't give it all," I told her. "Both of us are emotionally holding back from each other." She nodded. "Yeah, I know. Is that good or bad?"

"Let's find out," I suggested. "Tell me your darkest secret." A shadow came over her face. "Aaron, I can't do it. Once I tell you, you won't want to be with me."

"I doubt that," I replied. "But if you need time on this, that's OK." She heaved a sigh of relief. "How about *your* darkest secret?" she asked me.

"Oh, it's really rather tame. Deep down, I don't think I'm a very good writer. It haunts me. I worry that I'm wasting my time. A few years ago I had a writing instructor who told me I was a decent writer, but that I lacked a certain magical or irrational quality that was essential to being a great writer. I think that's why I keep looking at that painting. It contains a mystery that I apparently lack."

"Why don't the two of us take a trip to Sicily?" she suggested. "Maybe that will do the trick for you. And something else: if we do that, I'll tell you my dark secret." Two weeks later we flew to Rome, and then down to Palermo. I rented a car, and we drove around the island. And yes, some of the beaches were similar to the one in the Caffe Trieste painting, although that obviously didn't prove anything. I didn't do any writing, but I did feel something stirring.

A week into the trip, while we were lying in bed together, Vanessa turned her back to me. "OK, I'm ready to tell you my secret," she said. I waited, didn't say anything. "It happened when I was in high school. I had a friend, Irene, with whom I was close for two or three years. Irene suddenly came out of the closet: she told me she was gay. She swore me to secrecy, because in those days homosexuality was still a bit of a stigma. Well, I don't know why, but I told several of our friends about it, and two days later Irene hung herself from a beam in her parents' attic. Her friends wouldn't speak to me, except to say that I had killed her. I had to transfer schools; I was also too cowardly to apologize to her parents. It's a stain on my soul I can't seem to erase." She wept quietly, while I held her.

"Say something," she finally said. "Have you thought of writing her parents a letter?" I suggested.

"I've started one fifty times, and can never get it done." She rolled onto her other side, turning towards me. "What do you think of me now?"

"I think teenagers often make mistakes, including very bad ones. I think you probably need to write that letter, but I also think you need to forgive yourself. After all, Irene didn't *have* to commit suicide."

"That's it?" she asked me. "That's it," I said. "It might help you to open your heart," I added.

Vanessa continued to struggle with writing the letter, but other than that, something had definitely changed. It seemed that the act of confessing her secret to someone came as a great relief. She became much more easygoing with me, both in and out of bed. "I'd like to help you with your writer's block, or whatever it is you have," she said to me a couple of weeks later. "Tell me what it feels like."

"This may surprise you," I replied, "but when I was in college, I majored in mathematics. It was way over my head. I struggled just to understand the theorems and proofs, while there was a guy in my classes who was actually *formulating* theorems. I saw I could never be a great mathematician, and since I wanted to be great at something, I didn't continue with math after I graduated. Instead, I began to take writing workshops. But then I hit the same brick wall: the fear that I could never be great at it."

"Why is it so important to be great?" she challenged me. "Aaron, there are very few Homers, or Prousts, in this world. Why isn't good, good enough?"

"Good question," I replied. "I don't know. Well, yes I do. I want to be immortal. A hundred years later, anyone with half a brain knows who Proust was, and what he wrote. So he's not immortal in body, of course, but he is in our minds. That's what I want.

"You know," I went on, "some time ago I read a short story about a writer who is obsessed with this question. So he finds a time machine and travels one hundred years into the future. There is a World Digital Library there, so he inputs his name to see if he is in the data base. None of his books are there. All he can find is a footnote in some book of literary criticism referring to him. He is crushed. He returns to his own time frame, and finds that he is unable to write another word. He dies with a permanent case of writer's block."

"And the moral of the story for you is — ?"

"Be great or be nothing, I suppose," I answered.

"So life is a zero-sum game? Kinda depressing, I'm thinking," she said.

Two days later, the block mysteriously lifted. I wrote a semi-autobiographical story about a roommate I had decades ago, who went from being a stockbroker to a chicken farmer. Vanessa was dazzled by it. "Aaron," she said, "this is world class. I mean it. This is a *great* short story."

"OK," I said; "I have another anecdote for you. Many years ago I was living in New York, and I took a class in painting and drawing. Not nude models; mostly still lifes, with charcoal. In one of these collections of objects there was a brass candlestick. I picked up the charcoal and in thirty seconds I reproduced the candlestick with just a few strokes. I saw that it was impressionistic and yet very realistic. Without thinking, I had captured the play of light and shadows on the object; got the essence of it, like Cézanne's apples. The instructor, Lucinda, looked at it, and then at me, wide-eyed. 'So you're going to give up your career as a writer to become the next Van Gogh?' she exclaimed. She was only half joking.

"'Lucinda,' I replied, 'the difference between me and Van Gogh is that I can do something like this once every ten years, if I'm lucky, while Van Gogh was able to do it every day.'

"'Which drove him crazy,' she countered. 'He was staring into the sun all the time. Better once every ten years, don't you think?' When the class was over, she asked me to stay behind for a moment. Then she closed the door, and kissed me on the mouth for a long time; after which she said, 'It's enough to know that you have Van Gogh inside you.'

"We never did become lovers. As sexual as it was, it was more of a spiritual kiss—like being annointed. We never kissed again, and I never produced another 'Van Gogh'. But I never forgot Lucinda, my sketch, or the kiss."

Vanessa was quiet for a minute or two. "I have to tell you that this story makes me terribly jealous. I wish *I* could do that for you. But I'll try to put my emotions aside for the moment. The real issue, at least for you, is that your chicken farmer story is the same thing as your candlestick sketch, but in a different medium. Aaron, you badly need to take Lucinda's advice: it's enough to know that you have Van Gogh inside you. Your story is absolutely transcendent. It's honest, transparent, brilliant, and ephemeral. It's a true slice of life, and it will leave your readers thinking about it for days. Anyway, Lucinda got your tongue; I get to have all of you."

We made love all afternoon. "I'm still jealous of Lucinda," she confessed. "After all, she got to be your muse. I'd like that as well."

"I think that's already happening," I told her.

---

OUR RELATIONSHIP CHANGED DRAMATICALLY after that. Vanessa began to dress conservatively at Vesuvio's; she also started wearing a wedding ring and an ankle bracelet. The ring, she explained, was there to discourage men from hitting on her, and the ankle bracelet signaled that her body was taken, belonged to someone else. "We are a power couple," she told me, "but not in the Wall Street or Washington sense. In a psychological sense. Our fates are intertwined. My goal in life is to be happy, and you're a big part of that. As for you, you may have to wait ten years for another chicken farmer story, but at least you know it's within you."

The days passed in a kind of haze. Vanessa continued to model and wait tables (for sharply reduced tips); I continued to write less-than-great stories. Together, we continued to frequent the Caffe Trieste, and continued to make love every day, after dinner.

"Have you ever thought of contacting Lucinda?" Vanessa asked me one day. Uh-oh; dangerous ground. "We stayed in touch for a year or so after the class ended," I replied, "but eventually that petered out. I don't feel any great need to contact her at this point."

"That kiss you told me about: it just seems so unusual. How long did it last, anyway?"

"Van, what is this? You're torturing yourself over a kiss that happened more than twenty years before you and I even met."

"I know, but I keep wondering if our kisses are spiritual as well as sexual."

"They are probably two sides of the same coin," I suggested. "I can't tell you why I didn't sleep with Lucinda, except that it didn't feel right. Our minds were meeting on the level of art. There was something pure about that, and going beyond the kiss would have spoiled it. I'm sure Lucinda felt the same way."

"Where do *our* minds meet?" Vanessa asked me. "Is there some pure point where you and I touch?"

"Let me show you something," I responded. "This will seem strange, but just indulge me. I want you to stick out your tongue, so that the tip is in contact with the tip of my tongue. You can close your eyes if you want, but the important thing is to maintain contact, tip to tip. OK?"

Vanessa shrugged, but closed her eyes and stuck out her tongue. I extended mine, until the two tips were in contact. We held each other, tongue to tongue, for about twenty minutes, at which point Vanessa broke contact. "That was incredible," she said.

"What were you thinking about while our tongues were touching?" I asked her.

"I felt a lot of emotions going through me. I felt that by obeying you, I was giving up my power to you, and so at first I was angry at you. And then I felt a sense of excitement at being dominated by you, and wanted to say, 'fuck me, take all of me'. At the end, I experienced that pure point you referred to. Not the pure point of art that you had with Lucinda, but the purity of being known by you completely. It was almost as if you had touched and squeezed my internal organs: heart, lungs, liver, kidneys, intestines, ovaries—the works. And I thought that this must be the greatest purity that exists. That was when I withdrew my tongue, because it seemed to me that the exercise had achieved its goal, of a knowing beyond all knowing. I feel like I could die now, and it wouldn't matter. My heart is open. I forgive myself for Irene. And I want to be with you forever."

"Sort of like staring into the sun," I responded, "like Van Gogh."

"More like looking into the center of the universe, and feeling you understand how it all works," she replied. We made love, and then fell asleep.

Ours was the strangest relationship either of us had ever had. There seemed to be an unending series of layers, which we were peeling back week by week. And with each layer, our connection became deeper. The sad truth is that most relationships eventually go sour. As the layers are peeled away, couples become increasingly disenchanted, until they finally break up. In fact, this is the stuff of absorbing romance stories. I remember reading an interview with Haruki Murakami—a successful short story writer if there ever was one—in which he said that no short story can be successful unless the protagonist was unhappy, or became unhappy. But here we were, Vanessa and I, creating our own story and defying gravity.

The layers seemed to present themselves all on their own. One morning, Vanessa awoke from a dream, crying. "What is it?" I asked her. She shook her head. "I can't tell you; you'll be angry with me."

"Tell me anyway," I encouraged her. She turned her back to me. "OK," she said. "I dreamt that you were kissing Lucinda for a long time, while I was watching. I couldn't speak; I was broken hearted. When you finished, I asked you: 'Don't you love me anymore?' Then I woke up."

"Van, do you really believe I don't love you?" She shook her head. "I know you do, but I feel like Lucinda is the ghost at the banquet. It's crazy, but I can't seem to get her out of my head."

"Have you seen Annie recently?" I asked her. "Last week," she replied. "I talked to her about this. Her recommendation is that you and I go to New York and track Lucinda down, take her to dinner. Annie said that this would deflate the charge that I had built up around you and her. I told Annie that I was scared it might *increase* the charge; which is what this dream was about."

"Well," I said, "I could try tracking her down on the Internet, if you want. Just say the word." Vanessa agreed to it, and I located Lucinda fairly easily. She was running a school in the West Village called Art & Soul, and was also a successful artist on her own, from the look of things. I showed her website to Vanessa.

"Up to you, hon," I told her. "Let me know if you want me to contact her." Vanessa said nothing about it for two weeks, during which time her lovemaking was more passionate than usual. Finally she said, "OK, write her. I can't live with all this uncertainty."

"Dear Lucinda," I wrote; "A voice from the past. Do you remember me, Aaron Singer? I took an art class from you, sketched a candlestick in charcoal that you said put me in a class with Van Gogh. I happened to look you up on the Net—a walk down memory lane, I guess—to discover that you were doing very well. Which makes me really happy. As for me, I'm still plugging away at writing, although the Great American Novel continues to elude me. Anyway, drop me a line, if you feel like it. I'd like to be in touch once again."

Lucinda wrote back a day later. "Dear Aaron, Of course I remember you. How could I forget the famous Van Gogh candlestick? It's nice to be back in touch. Yes, things are good here. My school, Art & Soul, is oversubscribed, and I've had a couple of shows at a gallery on West 57th Street. Major sales— I'm almost well-to-do! Sorry to show off. Anything of yours you'd like me to read, just send it along. Also let me know if you're planning to come East any time soon. It would be great to see you again."

I showed the correspondence to Vanessa. "Sounds friendly enough," she remarked. "No mention of any kissing, in any case."

"Can you let it go now?" I asked her.

"I wish I could say yes, but no, I still want to meet her."

"OK," I told her, "we'll go to New York for a few days, and take her out to dinner. But you have to promise me that you will not mention the infamous kiss, or even hint at it. It would embarrass her, put her on the spot, which would be unfair and unkind. Agreed?"

"Word of honor," she replied. So I wrote Lucinda that my girlfriend and I were planning a trip to New York, would like to see some of her work, if she didn't mind, and would also like to take her out to dinner. "Sounds great," was the response. I booked a hotel room and plane flights the next day.

Vanessa's lovemaking became extra-passionate once again; she also became increasingly nervous as the departure date drew near. "Honestly," she said, "I don't know how you manage to put up with me. I'm little more than a neurotic moron." I hugged her.

"Maybe a little more than just that," I grinned. We arrived at LaGuardia, took a taxi to our hotel, which was not far from Art & Soul, showered, made love, and found a Japanese restaurant a few blocks away. Before we set out, I phoned Lucinda and arranged for dinner the following night. "Meet me at Art & Soul at 7:30," she said.

How shall I describe her, after all these years? "Elegant" is the word that comes to mind, along with "gracious." Now in her early fifties, tall and slender, with slightly graying hair and bright brown eyes, full of life. I hugged her, then introduced her to Vanessa.

"My God, Aaron; what a beauty! I'm so happy for you. And for you too, Vanessa; Aaron is one of kindest and most talented men I've ever had the pleasure to teach." Vanessa smiled from ear to ear. "Don't I know it," she replied.

"OK, then," said Lucinda; "there is a nice little Italian place just about ten minutes' walk from here. *Va bene?*"

Salad, spaghetti, olive oil, garlic bread, parmesano, Montepulciano, gelato—it was all fabulous. "How did you manage to snag this guy?" Lucinda asked Vanessa. "It wasn't hard," Vanessa replied; "I just took off my shirt." We all laughed. "Actually," she went on, "it was almost that aggressive. I went after Aaron like a shark, on instructions from my psychic adviser. Yes, I know, very California, but Annie is never wrong. Two years now, and I'm still crazy about him." She put her arm around me.

"Lucinda," I said, changing the subject, "tell me if I'm out of line here, but I take it you're still single?" She nodded. "Honestly, you look so refined, so elegant, I can't imagine why you would be on your own. What guy wouldn't want you?"

"Oh, Aaron, plenty have wanted me, but the truth is that I'm married to my art. Sure, I've had a number of affairs over the years; I'm hardly a virgin. But in some ways I'm like a medieval nun, committed to the life of the spirit. Some women find God in a relationship, marriage especially; I found it in art. Vanessa, I hope what I'm about to say won't upset you—it was so long ago—but after Aaron sketched the candlestick, we made out. It was great: as you know, he's no mean kisser. But for me it was as much spiritual as it was sexual. Which is why it never went any further." Vanessa's face had turned beet red.

"And to tell you the truth, when Aaron wrote me that he was coming to New York with a girlfriend, I knew it was about that kiss. I don't know how I knew it, since I don't employ a psychic, but I did. I knew that for whatever reason, Aaron had told you about the kiss, and that it stuck in your craw. But Vanessa, my dear, you can relax. We were not destined to become lovers. And when I look at the two of you now, it's obvious that you were."

Vanessa was crying by now, reaching into her purse for Kleenex. "It's a crazy jealousy, I know," she said, blowing her nose, "but I felt you were his muse, and I wanted to play that role exclusively."

"But honey, Aaron did not pursue a career in art; the candlestick inspiration was short-lived. What he did do was continue to work on his writing, and apparently as a result of a conversation with you, he turned out the chicken farmer story. Yes, I read it; Aaron sent it to me as an attachment. It's a masterpiece, as you well know, and you were a major factor in its genesis. You're the muse now, honey; that's the God's honest truth."

Vanessa turned toward me, buried her face in my neck, and cried once again. Then she got up without saying anything, went to the ladies' room, and washed her face. "Jesus, Luce, you sure know how to pack a wallop," I said. "Just as well."

Vanessa came back and sat down in her chair. "How did you become so wise?" she asked Lucinda. "Wise I doubt," Lucinda replied, "but art is definitely about intuition. Anyway, as I told you, you're the muse now. You've got what Aaron needs."

It was a remarkable trip. We spent the next day with Lucinda, looking at some of her canvasses, and Vanessa also served as a model in one of her life-drawing classes. "Good Christ," Lucinda whispered to me; "what a body. Were you a saint in a former life, and this gal is your karma in this one?" I laughed. "As good an explanation as any," I replied.

———

WE DRIFTED for a while after that. Both of us needed a break from peeling layers. The Lucinda episode had been rather exhausting, and in addition, Vanessa accepted that she and she alone was my muse. These were happy days for her; she felt fulfilled.

The next layer appeared about two months later. Vanessa read a book on Vipassana meditation, and decided she wanted to start practicing it. She located a meditation center on the outskirts of town, and went off to investigate. As it turned out, admission to the sessions was not automatic; an interview with the abbot was a prerequisite. As she later described this to me, the abbot was a man of about sixty, with a round face and a kind of angelic expression. He asked her why she was interested in Vipassana, what she hoped to achieve, and so on. Vanessa gave him stock answers—she wanted to become more spiritual, attain inner peace, etc.—which seemed to satisfy him. If he thought she was bullshitting him, he didn't show it. So he gave her her first lesson, concentrating on the breath. It lasted an hour; he didn't charge her for it. She returned home, feeling serene.

"Meditation," he told her, "is designed to slow everything down. Most of us rush through life, live in a blur, and then die. We don't *savor* life, aren't really present in our experiences. If you have a partner, you want to import meditation into your lovemaking. When you cook, cook slowly and deliberately. Same thing when you eat. The next time you pose for an art class, try watching your breath; it will make holding the position a lot easier. Meditation will change your life, I promise you." So Vanessa began going to the ashram twice a week, and finally persuaded me to accompany her. I went through the same interview that she did, and apparently passed the test. After which we began going together, when our schedules allowed it.

Things took a kind of weird turn when the abbot asked Vanessa if it would be OK if he took an art class for which she modeled. She told him that he would have to speak to the instructor, but that as far as she knew it was an open door policy.

"I'm sorry," she said to me; "I can't figure out why the abbot suddenly wants to study art. Although he told me he had done some drawing many years ago."

"That's easy," I said; "he wants to see you naked. These monks are celibate; drawing you in the nude is a form of vicarious sex." Vanessa shook her head.

"I don't believe it. The abbot has never shown the slightest bit of sexual interest in me or any of the other women in the center. I know there have been numerous scandals regarding gurus sleeping with female disciples, but this guy seems like the real thing. Above that."

"Well," I said, "let's see what happens. This could be loads of fun." Vanessa threw me a dirty look.

So the abbot showed up at Vanessa's next class, newsprint and charcoal in hand. Vanessa always made an effort not to strike provocative poses, but with a body like hers it was hard to avoid it. Breasts, thighs, vagina, rear end—all were there to be seen and sketched. And the abbot's sketches were, surprisingly enough, not half bad. But the striking thing about them was that they were decidedly erotic. They weren't lewd, or anything like that, but they gave off a definite sexual vibe—as though he were her lover. Vanessa didn't comment on them, but she felt a bit uncomfortable. This went on for a few more weeks, until Vanessa decided to ask him for a private consultation.

"Why are you interested in drawing me?" she asked him. "Aaron says it's vicarious or sublimated sexual experience. Is he right? I'm just finding posing in front of you a bit creepy. It's also creepy that you've posted a few of your drawings on the walls of this room."

"Yes," he replied, "Aaron is right, but not quite for the reason he thinks. You know, in my particular branch of Vipassana there is a practice called 'enlightened seeing'. In this practice, the student doesn't merely observe his breath; he also watches an object, like a flower or a rock. After an hour of this, he is then asked to sketch the object while maintaining continuity with his breath. Done carefully, the drawing will have a heightened charge. The idea is that Aaron's candlestick experience, which he told me about during his interview, not be a flash of accidental illumination, or a Van Gogh-type staring into the sun, but something in between. Enlightened seeing is prolonged sensual observation of an object. Check out this drawing of a lotus blossom"—he pointed to a sketch posted on the left wall—"which I did after my first year of apprenticeship. You can feel the texture of the petals, you can almost smell the fragrance. Do you understand what I am saying?"

"Why not stick to flowers and rocks, then?" Vanessa confronted him. She pointed to the opposite wall, on which he had posted a drawing of her seated in a chair, with her legs spread apart. "How did you manage to graduate from flowers to vaginas?" The abbot smiled.

"Try to see past your indignation, which is a rather childish emotion. First look at the lotus, then at your vagina. Anything in common here?" Vanessa remained silent. "The petals of the lotus are very much like your labia," he went on. "Enlightened seeing is an esthetic response, not a sexual one. What I see in both petals and labia is a quality of silkiness. I have no more interest in having sex with your vagina than I do in having it with a lotus flower. The art of enlightened seeing can be applied, and should be applied, to literally everything: rocks, vaginas, a slice of pizza, Christ on the cross. Your insistence on my supposedly being prurient is blinding you to the larger picture. Sensuality is much larger than sexuality, my dear. Aaron brought a candlestick to life. If you or he were interested, I could show you how to sustain that vision."

Vanessa sat in front of him, taking it all in. Her spiritual crap detector was normally pretty good, but in this case it was failing her. Was he conning her? Was it really about sex? Or was he onto something similar to the tongue-touching exercise she did with Aaron? Was this man a genius, or a charlatan? "Let me think about it," she said, then got up and left.

Back home, she gave me a detailed report of her meeting. "I'm at a loss, babe," I told her. "Forced to choose, I'd say it was about sex, and that he was a con artist. But I really can't be sure. Was his reference to the candlestick enlightenment, or manipulation?"

"OK," said Vanessa; "here's what I think. It's both. Remember what you were telling me a while back, about Jacques Lacan being a bullshit artist who was nevertheless in touch with a great truth? That's the abbot: both genius and charlatan."

"What do you want to do, then? Should we quit the center? Ask him not to attend art class? Or would that be a big mistake? And besides," I added, "he might eventually get tired of sketching your pussy, and move on to frogs or beat-up old cars. You're probably right that he has mixed motives. I'm tempted to stay with it, myself, because maybe enlightened seeing could expand my abilities as a writer. Maybe I could write another chicken farmer story."

"But what if it's at the cost of a mindfuck?" said Vanessa. "That's supposedly what Lacan did to his devotees."

"That's because they—many or most of them—only saw through him very late in the game. But we can see through the abbot right now. He's drawing your cunt because he's horny. He imagines fucking you. But he also views your labia like lotus petals, and this leads him to an enlightened place. I say we stay in, at least for the present."

"OK," she said. "I'm in it for the time being. But in the interim, why don't you talk with him about applying enlightened seeing to your writiing?"

"Done," I told her.

"TEACHER," I asked him, "from what Vanessa told me, I think I understand the technique of enlightened seeing applied to art. But how can I apply it to my writing? That remains unclear to me."

"Aaron," he responded, "enlightened seeing applies to everything, or can be so applied. Is it a lotus blossom, or a vagina? Are they distinct, or interchangeable? Do you love Vanessa, or do you dominate her? Or is there true love in the domination, and vice versa? What if she were to dominate you? Was Socrates a liberator or a disruptor of Greek traditions and values—or both at the same time? In a sense, everything is a kind of optical illusion, like the famous vase/faces diagram of Gestalt psychology. The technique of enlightened seeing involves holding opposites in a dynamic equilibrium. This is well-known in the East. In the West, only Hegel came close to it. So pick a concrete starting point and ride out the dualistic tension. Now you see it, now you don't."

My head was spinning. I went home, sat down at my desk, and in less than an hour knocked out one of my best stories,

"Murder, He Wrote." It was exactly in the *trompe l'oeil* mode, leaving the reader to wonder whether the author of the story was in fact the murderer of two men who lived across the street from him.

"Oh my God, Aaron," cried Vanessa, when she read it. "This is almost as good as 'The Chicken Farmer', maybe better. If the abbot wants to be your muse, I'll gladly step aside. Fiction doesn't get much better than this. He can sketch my pussy till the cows come home, for all I care, if he's going to make stuff like this possible."

So we kept attending the meditation center, at least for a while. As I predicted, the abbot eventually got tired of Vanessa's genitals and stopped coming to art class. In addition, Vanessa and I became so adept at seeing "dialectics" everywhere that we finally felt we could leave the center behind. She told me she was angry at me for dominating her, but that she also loved me for it. I contemplated various topics for short stories, and "rotated" them in my mind, seeing the dark in the light, the yin in the yang, and vice versa.

Which is where this story has to end. Vanessa and I continue to defy gravity, and disprove Murakami. The Japanese master deserves a Nobel; no question about it. But I find his unhappy protagonists rather tedious, predictable. Surely, there is more than one way to skin a cat.

"The spirit of our days," wrote William Morris, "has to be delight in the life of the world." Sounds right to me.

9
———

# THE GANDHI EXPERIMENT

I saac was eighty-five years old, and spent most of his time thinking about death. He tried not to, because he knew he was wasting precious time in the present. And yet, he just couldn't help it. The moment of death seemed terrifying to him. One minute you were alive and fully conscious (ideally); the next minute there was no "you" to experience anything. Just a blank screen. Not even that. He couldn't imagine the transition, and couldn't stop being scared about it.

He identified strongly with a poem by Edna St. Vincent Millay called "Dirge Without Music." In it she says she is not resigned to the notion of bodily death; that she simply cannot accept it. This was Isaac's view as well. The notion that one could "defeat" death or "cheat" it by having children, or by leaving some great legacy behind, some body of work, so that one "lived on" through one's progeny or posthumous reputation—that struck him as being completely phony, a variant of sour grapes. Bottom line: death sucked, and that was all there was to it.

He did, however, meditate every day, trying to appreciate the present moment. Sometimes, out for a walk, he would suddenly stop and look at the world around him: light filtering through the trees, or an old car parked on a street corner. This did help, a bit, but ultimately he just couldn't get over the fact that one day, he would wink out; that his consciousness would be obliterated.

Isaac had retired from teaching at age seventy. His field was mathematics, and he actually made it into the textbooks on complex variables with a theorem all his own, one that bore his name. The problem was that once he retired, he lost all interest in math. Why, he had no idea, as so much of his life had been devoted to puzzles: mathematical ones, but also chess games, Go, and crossword puzzles. But his wife died shortly after he retired, and all of that faded. And after that, his grown children rarely visited. Well, the boy worked for an engineering firm in Germany, and the girl, married with children, lived in New Mexico, and was busy being a wife and mother. Both of the "kids" called once in a while, but the truth was that he and they had very little to say to each other. Had he failed them? They didn't seem to care about him, one way or the other. As for friends, they were more on the order of acquaintances. Not much in common, really.

Other options presented themselves besides just sitting around. He enjoyed the movie *The Intern*, in which Robert De Niro plays a retiree who finds meaning in life by becoming an intern at a small online clothing business, run by a woman played by Anne Hathaway. Isaac supposed he could have tried something like that when he retired, but it really wasn't his thing. He also had a colleague, George, a chemical engineer, who retired at age sixty-six and then spent the next thirty-five years—he was now 101—making violins. It was heroic, really: George never played the violin and certainly had never built one. But between 66 and 101, George had made nineteen of them. Again, this was not really something Isaac would emulate; it would seem like he was just filling time. His problem was not only fear of death; it was also lack of purpose.

His day typically began with a cappuccino at an Italian café down the street. He would order his coffee and a croissant, and spend an hour or so reading the *Times*. He hated to leave, to go home, because he didn't know how he was going to fill the rest of the day. Also, for reasons he couldn't fathom, the barista, Lydia, was always very friendly towards him, giving him some motivation to dawdle. This was a real pick-me-up, because she was absolutely gorgeous, and Isaac still had enough of a flicker of libido left to make the interaction interesting. For some reason, Lydia was interested in him — not romantically, of course, but as an older person. He was the only old geezer she knew.

One day, on a whim, he returned to the café around 5 p.m., which is when she got off work. "Sit with me for five minutes," he said. "Let's talk." "Sure," she replied. "Do you want anything to eat or drink?" "Maybe a decaf," he said. She got herself a caffè latte and brought him his decaf.

"How old are you?" he asked her, rather brusquely. "Twenty-four," she told him. "Did you go to college?" he continued. "Yes, I graduated two years ago. I was an English major." "And now what?" Isaac asked her. "I mean, I doubt you're going to be a barista all your life. You seem too smart for that."

"Well, I might," she replied. "I'm not really clear about what I want to do. I guess I'm waiting for inspiration to strike. In the meantime, I serve people coffee. It's OK, I don't mind."

"So there's nothing that captures your imagination?" he went on.

"It's a bit deeper than that. This might be a depressing thing to say, but I don't see the point of doing anything. Did you ever read that Russian novel, *Oblomov*?"

"Indeed I did," said Isaac.

"Well, I'm like Oblomov. He never got out of bed because he

never saw why he should. How old are *you*? if you don't mind my asking."

"Eighty-five."

"You're kidding. Jesus, you certainly are well preserved. I would have said seventy at the most. What did you do with your life? Were you a businessman?"

"A math professor," he told her. "And now?" she asked him.

"Now, I'm sort of like you. I also don't have any particular motivation. Maybe I should get a job as a barista." He smiled.

"Hey, I could put in a word for you, if you want," she suggested. "Just kidding."

"What do you think about during the day, while you're serving coffee?" he asked her.

"Sometimes I think about the novels I read in school, ones that I can't forget—like *Middlemarch*, for example. Or occasionally I think about guys I might be dating. I'm currently between boyfriends, and can never seem to attract the kind of guy I want: sexy, but dependable. Most guys just want to have sex and then move on. Not my thing."

"Anything else?"

"Yeah...traveling. I've talked with a girlfriend about going to India together, but right now I can't afford it. But what about you? When you finish your coffee and newspaper and return home, what do *you* think about?"

"Death, mostly," he said. He told her about the transition point, and his fear of just disappearing into the ether. "God," she said, "I never thought of it that way. I guess if you lived in India, at least you'd have the consolation of reincarnation."

"You seem to have some kind of interest in India," he said. "Any particular reason?"

"Yeah...Gandhi is sort of my guru. I read a number of biographies of him, as well as his own writings, and I keep a notebook of his sayings. He was a great soul—never lost his appetite for life. Unlike you and me, I guess." She put her arm around him, affectionately.

"I keep wondering how to get it back. Do you?"

Lydia looked away, was quiet for a couple of minutes. "I have a Gandhi-ish idea that might help both of us, but I'm edgy about telling you what it is. It's kinda crazy. I'm afraid it will offend you," she added. He looked at her with raised eyebrows. "Try me," he suggested. She took a deep breath.

"OK, here goes. In later life, to test his ability to resist temptation, Gandhi would lie naked with attractive young girls, who were also naked, but not engage in any sexual activity. He said that this exercise helped him overcome desire, which according to Buddhism is the cause of all our troubles."

"You're saying you wanna lie like that with me?" Isaac gasped, incredulous. "Yes," she said, "but not for helping you to defeat desire. If we do this, there's a good chance it will *increase* your desire, by which I mean your appetite for life. I personally believe that libido is connected to meaning and purpose. So we wouldn't have sex, but you might experience a renewed energy. What do you think?"

"What do you get out of it?" he asked her.

"I'm not sure," she replied. "Possibly nothing at all. But this is so far from anything I've ever done, that maybe it will shake me up. A kind of shock therapy. I mean, I'm not really going anywhere in this coffee shop, as I admitted earlier. Plus, over the past year you and I have become pretty friendly. You're a nice guy, and I like you."

"Lydia," he told her, "this may be the strangest conversation I've had in my entire life, and I've had some pretty strange ones. Your proposal is, like, from Mars. But hey, I don't have to justify myself to anyone. Why the hell not? I could drop dead tomorrow."

"Let's go to your place," she suggested. And so the two of

them left the café and walked over to Isaac's apartment. He let her in, and closed the door. "Now what?" he asked her.

"We get undressed, and get into bed. No bodily contact whatsoever. I just lie next to you. First in a spoon position, and then face to face. Then we get dressed and discuss the experience."

Which is what they did. Isaac marveled at her beautiful body: the firm breasts and buttocks, the triangle of light brown hair. Oh to be sixty years younger, he thought. Life is so unfair.

They lay in the spoon position for thirty minutes, then she turned over and faced him for another thirty. He badly wanted to take her in his arms, but he knew that was a no-no. Finally they got up and got dressed.

"Hot chocolate?" he suggested. She nodded yes. They sat at his kitchen table, sipping the chocolate. "OK," she said; "you go first. How was it for you?"

"Well, I didn't get much of an erection, but I was definitely aroused. Your body is so beautiful. I badly wanted to hold you. In any case, I'm still tingling, a little. How about you?"

"It was pretty amazing," she replied. "You may be old, but you are still a very good-looking guy. So for a while I felt waves of desire; then they would recede and I would feel a sense of peace. The two waves kept alternating. They still are."

"What would you say the experience did for you?" he asked her.

"Not sure," she replied, "but I definitely want to do it again. Like you, I do feel more alive."

"Jesus," Isaac exclaimed; "this is some weird shit. I can hardly believe we are doing this. But I guess Gandhi knew what he was up to." Lydia gave him a long hug, and then left. "Tomorrow at five?" she asked him, as she stepped out the door.

"It's a date," he told her.

ISAAC DIDN'T GO to the café the next morning. Instead he stayed home, made himself some Assam tea with milk and sugar, and spent hours on his computer, researching Gandhi's life and tantric sex practice. The hours flew by. At 4:50 he was out the door, walking down the street to the café. Lydia smiled at him as he walked in. "Looking for something, mister?" she winked at him. "Not some *thing*," he replied; "some *one*." He felt like a teenager. What was it Sir Laurence Olivier had said? "We are all seventeen, with red lips." No shit, Sherlock.

"Good answer," said Lydia. "Give me a few minutes to clean up."

"Today," she informed him, "we're going to have bodily contact, but not of erogenous zones. We can hold each other around the waist and shoulders; that's about it. Let's start again with the spoon position."

It was like eggs over easy (or hard): thirty minutes on one side, thirty on the other. Both times he held her around the waist. She wrapped a towel around her hips, so as to prevent any direct contact down there. Then once again, they got up, got dressed, and did a postmortem, so to speak.

"OK, Isaac: how was it?"

"I had a hard on, on and off," he told her. "It felt so good to have my arms around you. When you were facing me, it was hard for me not to kiss you. I'm still very aroused. I have a feeling that *not* having sexual contact is the source of my excitement. My libido is definitely up," he concluded.

"If you had to say what the purpose of your life is, right now, what would you say?" she asked him.

"Pleasure. Pure unadulterated pleasure," he replied. She smiled.

"So eros defeats morbid musings on death," she offered.

"Apparently," he admitted. "How about you?"

"This is gonna sound crazy, but I feel like I'm a little bit in love with you. Not enough to make love, but there's definitely something there. I suppose it's an unresolved daddy issue, but I don't care. This feels healthy. I wanna keep doing it."

So they did. After a few more sessions, it got slightly sexual, but Lydia didn't object. In the spoon position, he kissed her back, and touched her breasts. He also gently squeezed her thighs. But that was it; the towel remained in place.

"Isaac," she said after one session, "why don't we take a trip together? I mean, you'd hafta pay for it, since I don't have any money; but if that wouldn't bother you, let's go on a kind of nonsexual honeymoon."

"India?" he asked her.

"Well, that would really be expensive. It doesn't have to be India. France, maybe, or Italy. What do you say?"

"I like it," he replied. "Let's do it."

"When was the last time you thought about death?" she asked him. "Can't remember," he told her. The next day, he ordered plane tickets to Rome for two, booked a hotel room for a week, reserved seats on a train to Naples, and arranged for a car rental so that they could tour the Amalfi coast. Was this really happening?

The night before they left, she let him go a bit further in his touching: lightly pinching her nipples, gently licking her back, and putting his hand on the part of the towel that covered her vulva. She moaned softly, which was music to his ears.

As for Rome: what a delight. Isaac had been there many years before, but remembered very little from that trip, so it all seemed new to him. Their hotel room was overlooking Piazza Navona, and they would start the day at Tre Scalini, with omelettes and grossly overpriced cappuccino, looking at Bernini's fountains. It helped that Lydia spoke a bit of Italian; she had an Italian grandparent. This made it much easier to get around.

One day they visited the Borghese Gallery, and when they came upon Bernini's famous sculpture, *Apollo and Daphne*, Isaac turned to Lydia and said, "You see? That's us. He is pursuing her, and to enable her to escape him, her father, a river god, turns her into a laurel tree, at her request."

"Isaac, I hardly think I'm turning into a tree. Besides, as you well know, I haven't been denying you access to certain sensitive parts of my body." He laughed.

"Fair enough. And you do seem to enjoy it." She blushed a deep red. "Guilty as charged," she admitted. That night, during the spoon practice, he removed the towel and spent most of the time gently squeezing her buttocks. When she turned to face him, her face was again flushed.

The week went by very fast. They took the train to Naples, picked up their rental car, and drove along the Amalfi coast, to Sorrento, Positano, and other (heavily touristed) lovely towns. They also stopped at Ravello, where Gore Vidal had lived for thirty years. It was pretty blissful.

"Why couldn't you be sixty years younger?" Lydia complained, somewhat angrily. "Isaac, you're everything I want in a man. You're sexy; your touch is perfect; and I can talk to you about literally anything. You always understand me."

"My dear," he responded, "if I were sixty years younger I'd probably be a jerk, like most of the guys you've dated; at least, according to you."

"Are we in love, Isaac? Is that what has happened to us? We both have renewed purpose in life, and that purpose seems to be love. The truth now: Do you love me?" He nodded. "You know I do." They kissed for the first time.

"Isaac," she continued, "I know this is classic neurotic female behavior, but I'm wondering what we are doing together, where all this is going."

"Where do you want it to go?" he responded.

"I'm not sure," she said, "but we seem to have reached a transition point, and it's hardly into death. I've never felt this alive in my entire life, and maybe you haven't either. All I can tell you is, I don't want it to end. I can't imagine being without you."

"Lydia, I'll probably be gone in ten years or less. It's going to happen sooner or later."

"Then let's make it ten years of love," she replied. "That's more than most people get in an entire lifetime."

Lydia moved in with Isaac upon their return from Italy. They made love the first night back home; the Gandhi experiment, which had been a roaring success, was over. She cut her hours at the café in half, so that she could spend more time with him, and also return to reading the classics of English literature. She even tried her hand at writing poetry.

Isaac, much to his surprise, experienced a revival of interest in mathematics, and began working on a second theorem, thirty years after he had formulated the first one. Yes, the Gandhi experiment had certainly been a success. The two of them were awash in creative energy.

Two months later Isaac died in his sleep from a cerebral embolism. He was completely unconscious; he never had to witness the transition point he had so greatly feared. Lydia fell completely apart. Financially, she was taken care of, because unbeknownst to her, Isaac had made her his sole heir in his will. But emotionally, she was a total wreck. "My partner in life is gone," was all she could say. Truly, the age difference had been no difference. Spiritually speaking, she and Isaac were the same age, and had lived on the same plane of existence. What else did two people need, to be lovers in the most meaningful sense?

Slowly, Lydia emerged from her depression, and began to

function again. She even went back to her part-time job at the café, donating her salary and tips to a hospital research unit on the cerebral causes of death. She also ordered a headstone for Isaac's grave, and held the unveiling on the first anniversary of his death. The epitaph said it all:

MY LIFE IS MY MESSAGE

## 10

## ANAXIMENES!

If Jean-François Champollion, as a teenager, had fallen in love with the Egyptians, something similar happened to Jason Anscombe with respect to the Greeks. Seeing his strong interest in Greek civilization, Jason's father hired a tutor for him, such that by the time he entered university he was a fluent reader of both Homeric and Attic Greek. Awards followed upon awards, until age thirty-nine, when he was appointed head of the Greek Antiquities Department of the Metropolitan Museum of Art.

Jason was a decent-looking sort of fellow, in a scholarly way. He was a little over six feet, rather slender, with dark brown hair that was only just starting to thin out. His horn-rimmed glasses gave him a rather owlish appearance; he wore tweed jackets with suede patches on the elbows. Women had occasionally been interested in him over the years, but he was not interested in them. Jason was more or less asexual. Any libido he had he poured into ancient Greece. He had a very respectable job, good relations with his family (who had given up on trying to marry him off), and a fairly wide circle of friends. Despite his inherent shyness, Jason could be witty and charming, and found himself invited to many fashionable New York parties. All was well in his world, in short.

The calm surface of his existence, however, was suddenly shattered by an incredible e-mail. Someone identifying himself only as "Spiros" wrote to say that he was in possession of an original manuscript by Anaximenes of Miletus, who flourished in Ionia during 586-526 B.C. As Jason knew, Anaximenes, a pre-Socratic philosopher, had left no surviving texts. Everything we knew about him came via commentaries such as Aristotle. He believed that air was the substance of which all things were made, and his most famous quote was, "Just as our soul, being air, holds us together, so air encompasses the entire world." It was very unlikely that an original text by Anaximenes would suddenly surface 2,500 years after his death.

However, this Spiros was no fool, and didn't intend to be dismissed as one. He added an attachment to his e-mail, a scan of the first page of the alleged manuscript, on which the author identified himself and gave the title of his work: *Light and Shadows*. "Mr. Anscombe," wrote Spiros, "I am a book dealer, not an academic. I accidentally discovered this manuscript, which is fifteen pages long, in the National Library of Greece. I needn't tell you that a discovery of this magnitude is nothing less than earth-shaking, and I am willing to sell it to the Met for 250,000 USD. Please do not dismiss me as a crank. That would be a grave error on your part. Your purchase of the manuscript for the Met would very likely establish you as the greatest scholar of Greek antiquity who ever lived. Think hard before you hit 'Delete'."

No mention was made of how he got the manuscript out of the National Library of Greece, but it was obviously a case of theft — of an item the NLG apparently didn't even know it had. If the provenance were ever made public, they would of course want it returned; but if Jason kept mum on the subject, no one would be the wiser. Already, he was thinking like a crook, but this was Anaximenes, for fuck's sake.

Spiros added a ps: "If you want access to the manuscript, you will need to meet me in London. I am sending a plane ticket to your office address. I expect to meet you at the café in Russell Square at noon, one week from today. Lunch is on me."

It was all too much for Jason. He took a taxi home, popped an Ambien, and slept for ten hours. The next day he returned to his office, where he found the promised plane ticket in a FedEx envelope in his mailbox. What the hell? he thought; I'm going to London. He booked a room at the Russell Square Hotel for two nights, and cleared his calendar for the week in question. He also informed his secretary that he would be out of the country during those days, "chasing some ancient manuscript, if anybody asks."

Five days later, Jason checked into the hotel, and then walked over to Russell Square, just to scope out the café. He ordered lunch at surreal prices, and sat at an outside table, enjoying autumn in London. The next day, as arranged, he went back there at noon.

It would be hard to miss Spiros. Not only did he look very Greek; he was also wearing a Greek sailor's cap, so as to avoid any confusion. A small man with a small moustache, he was sitting at one of the outside tables, upon which he had placed a beat-up leather briefcase. He got up as Jason approached. "Mr. Anscombe?" he asked, extending his hand. Jason shook it. "This is all rather cloak-and-dagger," Jason observed.

"Well, with material like this, one can't be too careful. Let me get you a coffee, and you can read the manuscript—or rather, a copy of it—while I read this book I brought along. After which we can have lunch and discuss how to proceed. *Ça va?*" he said in French.

And that's what they did. Much to Jason's relief, Anaximenes —if this manuscript was indeed real—had written in Attic rather than Ionic Greek; it took Jason only forty-five minutes to read the entire text, after which he looked up at Spiros in amazement.

"I assume you've read this," he said. Spiros nodded in the affirmative, with a broad smile on his face. "But this is none other than Book VII of the *Republic*," exclaimed Jason, "which dates from around 375 B.C. The Parable of the Cave. I can't believe this. If this manuscript is authentic, Plato emerges as the first great plagiarist in history!"

"Indeed," replied Spiros. "250,000 USD is rather a bargain, don't you think?"

"Sure," said Jason, "if the thing is authentic. I don't want to repeat the debacle of the *Hitler Diaries*, quite obviously. But there is hardly any way to check if it's Anaximenes' handwriting, since no sample of such exists."

"True," said Spiros, "but there *is* a way of checking the age of the thing. Athens happens to have one of the world's leading experts in radiocarbon dating. I can return to Athens, cut three centimeters off of the original papyrus, and he can determine the age of the manuscript to within a few decades. If it dates from the sixth century B.C., he'll be able to tell us. Or if you prefer, as a matter of caution, you can come with me to Athens and we can go to his workshop together. What do you say?"

The next day, the two of them were in Athens, and Spiros took Jason to the studio of Stratis Papadopoulos, not far from the Parthenon, together with three square centimeters of the original text, which Spiros now showed Jason. Stratis asked them to come back the next day.

"It's genuine," he told them; "it dates to the sixth century B.C. Congratulations. This is the greatest discovery since King Tut." Jason and Spiros repaired to a nearby café, where Jason ordered feta, olives, spanakopita, dolmades, keftedes, horiatiki, and a bottle of retsina. He raised his glass. "O Anaximenes!" he exclaimed. "Opa!"

"Opa!" cried Spiros. They had two bottles of wine, and got quite drunk. Jason then returned to his hotel, took out his computer, and wrote the director of the Met, explaining the situation, and urging him to buy the manuscript. "If you agree to this," he wrote, "please wire me the money asap, or come over with a check. That Plato plagiarized the Parable of the Cave from Anaximenes is the biggest find in Greek scholarship in the last 500 years. The holder of the manuscript, Spiros, has agreed to sign a waiver of any claim to it, and to give the Met permission to reproduce it, in the original Greek and in translation (which I'll be glad to execute), in print, online, or in any media form it chooses."

The director flew out to Athens the next day. He himself didn't read Greek, but he examined the manuscript, interviewed Spiros (the subject of theft/smuggling was carefully avoided), and also talked with Stratis about the radiocarbon dating. After which, he presented Spiros with a cashier's check for 250,000 USD, and took possession of the manuscript. He and Jason returned to New York the following day. A copy was made of the original; this latter was deposited in the Met vault. Jason set to work translating the text, which took him about a week to accomplish to his satisfaction. The discovery was then announced to the world, and the full English translation was published as a special supplement by the *New York Times*. At that point, the shit hit the fan.

The mob of reporters that descended on the Met was greater than if the Met had been hosting after-hour orgies in the entrance hall. PLATO PLAGIARIST screamed the headlines of every major newspaper in the world. Scholars of Greek also descended on the Met, demanding to see the original manuscript. It was bedlam, and it lasted for weeks. Jason, shy guy that he was, was on TV for much of that time, explaining the Parable of the Cave, and how it said that human beings mistakenly took phenomenal events (the "shadows") for reality, missing the truth (the "light") that was casting these shadows. But then, at the height of the frenzy, an unexpected development occurred. One of the scholars allowed access to the manuscript sneaked a razor blade into the Greek Antiquities Department, cut off a square inch of the manuscript, and took it to a radiocarbon dating service in Brooklyn. The verdict: the so-called papyrus dated from the late twentieth century.

"What they hey?" cried Jason, when the professor showed him the radiocarbon report. The two of them ran down the hall to the director's office, and gave him the bad news. "I may have to kill myself," mused the director. He then searched for Spiros and Stratis on the Net—which obviously all of them should have done earlier—and turned up nothing. "Jason, get yourself over to Athens asap, and to Stratis' workshop with a copy of the Brooklyn report. Also ask him to locate Spiros for you."

Jason was in Athens twenty-four hours later; but when he went to Stratis' workshop, he found it was abandoned. There was a lock on the door; when the police forced it, all they found were two empty rooms. And no one in the neighborhood knew of any Spiros or Stratis, who had vanished into thin air. With a heavy heart, the director fired Jason and informed the *New York Times* of the hoax. ANAXIMENES HOAX EXPOSED screamed the headlines this time around. It was not the Met's finest hour.

Jason was essentially unemployable. Although he did have some money put away, it wouldn't last forever. He took a job chopping vegetables at a Greek restaurant on the Upper West Side, occasionally crying out, "i zoí eínai angoúri!" which means, "Life is a cucumber!" The rest of the proverb goes, "Some taste it and are refreshed; others have to stretch." Jason had definitely taken a cucumber up the ass. He finally moved to the island of Sifnos, where he grew his own food and wandered the streets, lost in a daze. One day, he thought he saw Spiros, wearing his captain's hat, piloting a yacht out of the harbor. He ran down toward the dock, about to shout "pusti malaka!"; but by the time he got there, the boat had pulled away.

It wasn't a total disaster, however. Jason switched his interest from ancient to modern Greek; he also learned Greek dancing, à la Zorba. He met, courted, and married a pretty Greek widow, which enabled him, for the first time, to experience the joys of the nonvirgin life. There was only one hitch, one fly in the ointment: Phronesis was unable to help herself (or so she claimed): she cried out "O Anaximenes!" when she climaxed. It did bother him, but Jason decided it was a small price to pay for marital bliss.

# 11

# THE POLITICALLY INCORRECT
# COMEDY HOUR

There is a widespread feeling many people have that by some strange fluke, they wound up in the wrong life. Sarah McLeod was one of those people, and the life she felt she was *supposed* to have had was that of an actress on *Seinfeld*. It was far too male-dominated, in her opinion; it could have benefited from having another woman in the cast besides Elaine. But it went deeper than this: Sarah had a great sense of humor. In high school she regularly contributed a humor column to the school newspaper, and this carried over into college. Sarah was funny, and people told her so. In the late eighties, when *Seinfeld* was on the table at NBC, she could have applied for a part on the show—sent in her credentials and hopefully obtained an audition. Instead, thanks to pressure from her mother, she applied for a job with Estée Lauder and was now head of their East Coast division. All these years later, she was in her early fifties, single, rolling in money, and dissatisfied with her life.

Sarah dated, and slept with, a variety of men. The problem inevitably arose when she revealed her *Seinfeld* fantasy, which— let's face it—had an obsessive quality to it. She just couldn't stop talking about it: how she was perfect for the show, how she missed the boat, etc. The guys would listen, and then not call her for a second (or sixth) date. As soon as *Seinfeld* was out of the bag, the men concluded that she was just a bit too odd. But then something completely unexpected happened. She met Arnold, who happened to be a producer for NBC, and who told her to forget about *Seinfeld*.

"That ship sailed years ago," he said. "If you want to realize your ambition of being an actress, you need to start your own show. I'll help you, if you want." Thus was born a call-up TV show known as "The Politically Incorrect Comedy Hour." "The humor," Arnold told her, "will come more from the callers than from you. In case you hadn't noticed, Americans are quite dumb. It's almost as though they had shit in their heads instead of brains. They are also absurdly self-righteous; they think they are virtuous, and are doing something effective."

"Won't I get into a lot of trouble?" Sarah asked him.

"You'll avoid racial slurs, of course. I think the only reaction you'll get is hate mail, and who cares about that?" Arnold coached her on presenting the pilot to the executives at NBC, who were persuaded to take a chance on this controversial show. "Our ratings are so low," one of them mused, "that we might as well try something outrageous."

So "The Politically Incorrect Comedy Hour" aired on a Thursday evening at 8 p.m. Sarah sat in a chair behind a desk, as the president might do from the Oval Office, and addressed the viewers. "Good evening," she began. "My name is Sarah McLeod, and this is The Politically Incorrect Comedy Hour. The premise of this show is that most Americans are stupid, and that by provoking them we can provide a few laughs for the small number of citizens who aren't. It takes very little to get Americans all wound up," she continued. "They like to get all self-righteous, beat their chests. All of you are going to hear a lot of that during the next hour. Let me start off by getting the Jews all riled up. Can anyone tell me why Jews have big noses? The answer is, because the air is free."

The call board lit up immediately. The first caller, obviously Jewish, ranted and raved about the historical oppression of the Jews, the Holocaust, and so on. Finally Sarah told him, "You know what you are? You are a Jewish turkey. Did you ever hear the expression, 'Lighten up'? Listening to you, my kishkas ache."

The next caller, it turned out, also Jewish, was on Sarah's side. "That's exactly right," he said. "That guy is a real shmuck. You'd think you had denied the Holocaust, or something like that. Jews are supposed to be smarter than other people. That guy is about as smart as week-old chopped liver."

"Thank you, caller. Our goal here is to insult every ethnic group, so I'd like to move on to blacks; or as they pompously call themselves, African Americans. What a farce. Should I start referring to myself as a Scottish American? Anyway, what I'd like to say to our black viewers is this: you are running around with signs saying 'Black Lives Matter'. Are you kidding me? Only an idiot could fail to see that precisely the opposite is true: black lives *don't* matter. The proof of that is that across the nation, white cops are gunning you guys down in the street like dogs. So how could black lives matter, in the US?"

Once again, the phone lines went crazy, and the first (black) caller, like the previous Jewish caller, played the victim card, ranted and raved about slavery, called Sarah a racist, and so on — the usual nine yards. "Sir," said Sarah, "my previous caller was a Jewish turkey. You are simply a black turkey, and all turkeys of whatever stripe can do is gobble. None of your tirade addresses what I said. You're dumb as a stick."

And so it went. By the end of the hour, Sarah had insulted Koreans, the Chinese, Native Americans, Latinos, etc. Only the Native Americans had the intelligence, and the self-respect, not to take the bait. Meanwhile, the Nielsen ratings went through the roof, and dozens of companies called NBC, wanting to advertise on the show.

"Wow!" she said to Arnold the next day; "you certainly pegged that one correctly. Your colleagues e-mailed me a very generous contract for five more programs. But I confess, I'm worried that I'll get stale. I don't wanna turn into Rush Limbaugh, for God's sake. Maybe we could brainstorm some ideas for the next show."

When the next Thursday rolled around, Sarah started out on a very different note. "I'd like to apologize for last week's show," she began. "Not that I said anything wrong, or that most of the callers weren't morons; it's rather that I left out a key ethnic group, namely white Christian Americans. Talk about dumb! These people take the cake. Most of them reject evolution, think we all lived among the dinosaurs, agree with whatever the government says or does, especially when it leads us into stupid wars, and so on. I urge the people I ridiculed last week to stop any white Christian person on the street, at random, and ask him or her why we are in Afghanistan, and see what they say. Or ask them who won the war in Viet Nam. They'll tell you we did, when the truth is that we suffered a humiliating defeat. You wanna see a collection of bozos? White Christian Americans are at the top of the list."

Once again, a very successful show. White Christian Americans called up and made fools of themselves, while the other ethnic groups called up to make fun of them. As one NBC exec put it, "A splendid time was had by all."

"Arnie," she said to her now-boyfriend, "I've got a great idea for the next show. Just wait and see."

It was the third Thursday in the series. Sarah sat at her desk, with a sheet of paper in her hands. "I'd like to start tonight's show by reading a poem. It's by a famous Greek poet—well, famous everywhere but in the US—named Constantine Cavafy. It's called 'Waiting for the Barbarians'."

"What are we waiting for, assembled in the forum?

The barbarians are due here today.

Why isn't anything going on in the senate?
Why are the senators sitting there without legislating?

Because the barbarians are coming today.
What's the point of senators making laws now?
Once the barbarians are here, they'll do the legislating.

Why did our emperor get up so early,
and why is he sitting enthroned at the city's main gate,
in state, wearing the crown?

Because the barbarians are coming today
and the emperor's waiting to receive their leader.
He's even got a scroll to give him,
loaded with titles, with imposing names.

Why have our two consuls and praetors come out today
wearing their embroidered, their scarlet togas?
Why have they put on bracelets with so many amethysts,
rings sparkling with magnificent emeralds?
Why are they carrying elegant canes
beautifully worked in silver and gold?

Because the barbarians are coming today
and things like that dazzle the barbarians.

Why don't our distinguished orators turn up as usual
to make their speeches, say what they have to say?

   Because the barbarians are coming today
   and they're bored by rhetoric and public speaking.

Why this sudden bewilderment, this confusion?
(How serious people's faces have become.)
Why are the streets and squares emptying so rapidly,
everyone going home lost in thought?

   Because night has fallen and the barbarians haven't
   come.
   And some of our men just in from the border say
   there are no barbarians any longer.

Now what's going to happen to us without barbarians?
Those people were a kind of solution."

"What is Cavafy saying here? He is, of course, not talking about Americans in particular, but what he says certainly applies to us, it seems to me. When a person has no real substance, when he or she is empty inside—like most Americans—they have two choices. They can confront the reality of their condition, and attempt to deal with it, or they can blame the Other—some group or nation outside of themselves—and thus not have to undergo the pain of self-examination. That's why he says, at the end, that these Others, whom we like to refer to as barbarians or savages or whatever, are a *kind* of solution. They are not a real solution; they are a convenient, invented solution. Think over the ranting and raving we heard during the last two shows, with everyone playing the victim card, or needing to have someone to blame, someone to fight with. The very few intelligent viewers out there correctly regard these people as stupid, but it cuts deeper than that: these people are *sad*. They need opposition, illusory barbarians, to make themselves feel OK. It's a charade, but since they can't think of what else to do, the charade goes on.

"I have received tons of hate mail from these sad people. Given what Cavafy says, this was to be expected. These folks are now demonstrating in front of the NBC studios, and once I start taking calls, you'll see: their rage and pain will be directed against me, their personal 'barbarian'. Only the tiniest percentage of the nation could hear this poem and really understand its implications. So now let's take some calls, and you'll see what I'm talking about."

But the first call was in a very different vein. "Hi Sarah. Thank you for reading that poem. I'm not calling to berate you. Instead, I have a question. I'm sixteen years old, and I'm in high school. I love poetry, and read it all the time. But my classmates make fun of me. They spend all their time on their cell phones, and say poetry is for wimps. My question for you: Why is that so? Why do 99 percent of my fellow-students hate poetry?"

"A very good question, dear; thank you for calling. Why do *you* think they hate poetry?"

"Well, I guess it's not practical, and for Americans everything has to be practical. But I feel there must be more to it than that."

"I'm sure there is," Sarah told her. "Look, can you say what poetry does for you?"

"I guess it helps me to know myself better," the girl replied.

"Do you think that most people in this country, whether kids or adults, want to get to know themselves better?"

"No," said the girl; "probably not."

"So they distract themselves with toys, right?" said Sarah. "Listen, dear: thank you for calling, and keep reading poetry. You're on the right track."

The phones went silent after that, for a minute or two. "Well,"

Sarah finally said, "there's a sixteen-year-old girl who got the rest of us thinking, like Cavafy should have. You know, in 1979 Jimmy Carter sat a a desk like this one, in front of viewers very much like you, and told them that we could not keep blaming the Soviet Union for all of our problems. That that was the easy way out—the 'barbarian' solution, to quote Cavafy. That we would do better to examine our own behavior instead. This was not, of course, what his viewers wanted to hear, and the following year they voted him out of office.

"Friends, when I started this show, my goal was pretty simple: I just wanted to have some fun, have a few laughs. But you and I are not bound to any particular format. We can make the show be whatever we want. If I tell those of you who are stuck in the blame-the-barbarians mode to go elsewhere, ratings will drop, NBC will be very unhappy, and they will probably not renew my contract. But really, if you just want to keep howling at each other, what's the point? Better you should go elsewhere, and leave the field to the few intelligent Americans who are left. In that spirit, I'd like to read another Cavafy poem, and dedicate it to the high school girl who called up earlier; whom I should call a woman, not a girl, because she is as mature as they come. This poem is called 'Growing in Spirit':

"He who hopes to grow in spirit
will have to transcend obedience and respect.
He'll hold to some laws
but he'll mostly violate
both law and custom, and go beyond
the established, inadequate norm.
Sensual pleasures will have much to teach him.
He won't be afraid of the destructive act:
half the house will have to come down.
This way he'll grow virtuously into wisdom."

"Anyway, that's all for tonight. For those of you stuck in the 'barbarian' mode, let me say this: there is a better way."

The executives at NBC, Arnold included, were stunned by this development, but even more stunned by the ratings, which remained high. Sarah expected viewers to switch channels, or turn off their TV sets, but they didn't.

"Hell's bells!" exclaimed Arnold. "What are you planning to do for your fourth show?" he asked her. "The last one is going to be a hard act to follow."

"I'll think of something," she told him. "For now, let's make love."

----

WHAT SARAH DID in the interim was post a question on the show's website. "Friends of the show," it said, "what would you like the fourth program to be about?"

A number of respondents suggested she commit suicide on the show; each ethnic group demanded an apology; there were numerous death threats, and so on. But a few fans of the show suggested more poetry readings; some believed she was doing therapy, and wanted her continue with it; many men wrote in to ask her out, and many women wrote in asking her advice on how to "land" a man, as though they were fish. All of this was fodder for show No. 4.

"OK, gang," she started off, "it's show time once again. I'm going to take my own advice about lightening up, because we got way serious last time around, if you remember, and this is supposed to be a comedy hour. So let me read you some of the mail that wound up on the program website this past week. I'm going to change the names to protect the innocent. Here's a letter from Madeleine in Madison, Wisconsin:

"Dear Sarah,
Is your show intended to be sexually stimulating? I ask because
my boyfriend and I watch it every week, and as soon as the hour
is up we are both so horny that we copulate like rabbits for the
rest of the night. I think he's going to ask me to marry him, as a
result, and I owe it all to you. My concern is: what happens if the
show gets cancelled?
Sincerely,
Madeleine"

Sarah's reply:

"Dear Madeleine,
That's funny; the show has the same effect on me and *my*
boyfriend! We go directly home from the show and can't get
enough of each other. However, I don't know why that is. As for
what you, and I, will do if my contract is not renewed, all I can
suggest is porn videos. If you find a better solution, please let me
know.
Love,
Sarah"

At this point, the phone lines once again lit up. It turned out
that hundreds of viewers were experiencing the same sexual
arousal from the show, and they wanted to talk about it. They also
wanted Sarah to do the show three nights a week, and some
women asked her if she had any tips on how to drive a man wild
in bed. Did she wear a garter belt and black stockings? Was there
any particular position she especially enjoyed? Etc.

Sarah stopped the calls for a minute. "Ladies, ladies; I don't
want to turn into Dr. Ruth. I have no particular sexual advice to
give you; you might want to read *Cosmo* instead. Let me switch to
a nonsexual topic. This letter is from Brad in Queens:"

"Dear Sarah,
I'm possibly your biggest fan; I live for Thursday nights. The problem is that my family will no longer speak to me. They say that you're a communist. What should I tell them?
Sincerely,
Brad"

"Dear Brad,
I think by now you've figured out that talking to your parents is fairly pointless, so I suggest you have some fun with them. Tell them that not only am I a communist, but that I'm also a satanic devil worshipper and host orgies in my house, during which we roast and eat human flesh. Please let me know their response.
Love,
Sarah"

All of this easily filled up the hour, and again, everyone had a good time. NBC was making piles of money, and offered Sarah a contract for shows 7-12, doubling her salary.

"You're on a roll," Arnold told her. "Any ideas for show No. 5 yet?"

What Sarah did was go online and compile a list of names of people who had called 911 when McDonald's failed to get their order right. She invited several of them to come on the show and explain why, in their minds, an incorrect food order had warranted an emergency call to the police (who had arrested all of them). For this, she would pay airfare, hotel expenses, plus an "honorarium" of $1,000. Three of the seven contacted agree to come on the show.

"Good evening," she began show No. 5. "We have a real treat in store for you tonight." After giving the audience the background information, she introduced her first guest, Tracey Fandangle, who purchased two bacon cheeseburgers at her drive-in McDonald's, and got home only to discover that the bacon was missing.

"Tracey," said Sarah, "I'm curious as to why you chose to dial 911 instead of going back to McDonald's. Could you explain that to our viewers?"

"Well, Sarah," Tracey replied, "I was very tired, and didn't really want to get back in my car and drive back there; it's two miles away. Calling 911 seemed a lot easier. Plus, for me it really was an emergency. What else do you call a bacon cheeseburger without bacon?"

"The thing is," responded Sarah, "that the police set up the 911 number for things like rape, murder, physical assault, arson, burglary—that sort of thing. Do you know why they arrested you?"

"Sure; they claimed it wasn't an emergency."

"Do you feel that missing bacon falls into the category of a violent crime?" Sarah asked her.

"Well, to me the missing bacon was *emotionally* violent. I tried to explain that to the officers, but they were stubborn—just turned a deaf ear."

"I see," said Sarah. "We have a number of calls coming in, so let's see what our viewers think about all this."

"Hi Sarah, Tracey; this is Bob from Omaha. I'm wondering if Tracey could explain to us more clearly what constitutes emotional violence, and how missing bacon qualifies to be in that category."

"Sure," said Tracey; "be glad to. I was tired and hungry. I had paid for that bacon, and never received it. It hit me like an assault."

"Hmm," said Bob. "Wouldn't it have made more sense just to eat the burgers as is, since you were tired and hungry, and write the missing bacon off as inconvenient, but hardly a crisis?"

"But it *was* a crisis, Bob, for reasons I already stated."

"Tracey, do you know what narcissism is?" Bob asked her.

"Uh, no," she replied.

"It's a condition in which the person is narrowly focused on themselves, and is unable to see the larger picture. Do you think your making a big deal over four missing strips of bacon might put you in that category?"

Tracey began to shout. "But can't you see? It *was* a big deal!"

"Have you ever taken an IQ test?" he went on. "There is a category called Moron, and I'm thinking you fit it pretty closely."

"I'm not a moron!" she shouted. "I—" But Bob had already hung up.

Subsequent callers suggested that Bob was right, that Tracey was both moronic and narcissistic. One caller called her a buffoon; another said she was little more than a joke. Tracey remained defiant to the end.

"I want to thank you, Tracey," Sarah concluded the session, "for sharing your valuable insights with us."

There were two more interviewees, but they followed the same pattern: McDonald's failure to deliver the goods was a crisis —one of the interviewees actually called it a "horror"—and the cops were "cruel" in their failure to understand. Sarah thanked them both, and referred to their "valuable insights" in these cases as "wisdom." Another viewer called in.

"Hi Sarah. This is Bonnie in Miami. Great program, thank you, and a good profile of much of the American public. I am not only impressed by how stupid these three people are, but also how stubborn. Frankly, the president behaves in the same way, and so does our military. They screw up badly, deny that any mistakes were made, and then engage in a cover up. What Americans do on an individual level, the government does on the national level. You could have called this particular show 'Morons on Parade'."

"You nailed it, Bonnie. To that, I have nothing to add. See you all next week. Be thinking about what you want to discuss."

---

GIVEN HER CONTRACT RENEWAL, show No. 6 would not be her last. But Sarah was at a loss as to how to fill it. Show No. 5 was comical, but also tragic and depressing, really: a terrifying look at the American psyche. We need to have a session on straight comedy, she thought. But what?

So again, she just put it out on the website, that we needed a show that was funny without also being a downer. "What," she wrote, "was the funniest thing that ever happened to you? Please share it with us." And so, show No. 6 was quickly upon them. Sarah decided to start out with a funny story of her own.

"OK, you guys; this is so embarrassing that once I tell it, I'm guessing none of you will have any inhibitions about revealing your own funny stories. I was in the fourth grade, and I badly had to make poopoo. But Mrs. Ryan, our teacher, wouldn't let me go. 'Sarah', she said, 'you're always running to the bathroom, probably just to get out of class. Well, this time you're just going to have to hold it in for a bit'.

"Unfortunately, I wasn't kidding, and finally just pooped in my pants. I was horrified that Eric Johnson, a boy I had a crush on, would find out and be disgusted. As luck would have it, I was sitting next to Gavin, a nerd whom I didn't feel any need to impress, so I leaned over and said to him, 'Gavin, I just pooped in my pants'. He said, 'Sarah, give me your panties with the poop in them'. So when Mrs. Ryan's back was turned, I slid my panties down, careful not to spill any of the poop, and handed them to Gavin. He got some of it on his hands, but didn't care. Shortly after, Mrs. Ryan said she had to make a quick phone call, and would be back in a minute. As soon as she was out the door,

Gavin walked up to her desk with my wet, brown panties, opened the center drawer, placed the panties inside, and shut the drawer. The other students didn't notice, as they were too busy making out.

"Anyway, Mrs. Ryan returned from her phone call—I'm guessing she really had to go to the bathroom—and smelled the stench coming from her desk. She opened the drawer and screamed, then ran out of the room and soon returned with the principal, who looked at the contents of the drawer with horror and disgust.

"'Who put their feces in Mrs. Ryan's desk?' he demanded.

"'What are feces?' asked one of the students.

"'Your poop', said the principal; 'number two'.

"'Ugh, gross', several students exclaimed. Gavin and I sat there poker-faced, saying nothing. Later he walked me home. As a reward for rescuing me, I pulled up my skirt and showed him my pussy. End of story."

Lights across the call-in board. The first caller was actually laughing as she began to talk. "Sarah, that was wonderful! I nearly pooped in my own pants listening to you tell that story."

"Any stories of your own, my dear?" Sarah asked her.

"No, but thank you for yours. Honestly, this is the greatest show on earth. Your viewers never know what to expect. I'm so happy they renewed your contract." Two other callers shared embarrassing or ridiculous incidents in their lives, and then Sarah called it a night.

"So you pooped in your pants in school at age nine!" exclaimed Arnold later that night. "I actually got a hard on listening to you tell that tale."

"Arnie," Sarah responded, "if this is a bid for anal sex, forget it. You're not getting in there. I already told you that."

"So you won't let me go boldly where no man has gone before?" he raised his eyebrows.

"No way, José. And you can forget the Star Dreck, amigo. Pick a different orifice, and I promise to make you happy." Arnold did as he was told, but he kept thinking about her wonderfully round behind.

SHOWS 7-12 went off pretty easily; Sarah had clearly found her groove. Thanks to Arnold, she had actually fulfilled her ambition of being a TV star, if not on the *Seinfeld* show. Tapes of the programs sold like hotcakes; they were even sold abroad, translated into several languages. But it had its down side: on a holiday with Arnold in Japan, a middle-aged man pointed at her on the street and said, "Sarah poopoo!" "That's how I'm probably known around the world," she said to Arnold: "Sarah poopoo."

They sat on tatami mats in a teahouse in Kyoto. It was beautiful, tranquil, like a scene in a Japanese print. Finally, Arnold asked her, "OK, babe, what now? You accomplished what you set out to do. What's the next step, do you think?"

"I think I may give up the show. NBC hasn't approached me about programs 13-18, and I haven't asked them for a contract renewal. I could easily retire, if I wanted to. But I'm not sure what I would do with myself. I may live forty more years, and I don't know how I would fill them. I actually feel depleted. I wanted to prove something to myself, and I did. I don't need to prove anything else, but I'm not sure where that leaves me.

"You know," she went on, "Americans are raised to climb mountains: to achieve, aspire, stand out. Which is fine, but it's only one model of how to live, and it may not be the best one. I need a different model, but I don't know what that would be. I'm not going to move to a condo in Florida and play shuffleboard."

"What's the role of a relationship in your life?" he asked her.

"Arnie, I knew you were going to ask me that, and I was

dreading the moment. I like you, I like hanging out with you, I enjoy the sex, but I don't feel I really love you. I feel terrible saying this. But I think that what we really had was a working partnership, a business relationship of sorts. Now, I feel like we probably need to go our separate ways. I think I've been infected with the Japanese notion of impermanence: everything passes. My alternative to the driven American way of life, I think, is just to drift, and see what happens. It won't be easy."

"Will you stay in Japan, do you think?" he asked her.

"Maybe, for a while. Sit *zazen* every day, take up *ikebana*. I think I need to just be."

"I'll miss you," was all he said. They went back to their hotel, and made love one last time. Arnold flew back to New York the following day.

---

THE TRUTH WAS that Sarah had entered some sort of existential crisis. She was unable to say what life consisted of; what it should be. Everything seemed programmed, whether it was Estée Lauder or NBC. She thought of another poem by Cavafy, one she never aired on the show, called "Ithaka." The point of it was that as far as life was concerned, the going was the goal. Ultimately, we didn't know who we were, or why we did what we did. All we had was the journey, and while on it, its purpose was unclear. This too seemed very Japanese.

She wondered if she was in the midst of a nervous breakdown. She ate very little, slept a lot during the day, and had no motivation to leave Kyoto because somehow, everywhere seemed the same. An old Zen saying: "Wherever you go, there you are." She wanted, Buddhist style, to just disappear; but in fact, she was very self-preoccupied. She felt her relationship with Arnold had been shallow, a failure. She had traded sex for professional guidance; she hadn't really loved him, and she doubted that he had loved her. If love was the most important thing in life, then she never really experienced it. Or maybe an acting career was the most important thing, but at the present time she had no feelings for it; it had just come and gone, and left her feeling blank. Stardom was an illusion.

Oddly enough, she found herself thinking about the incident with Gavin, almost forty years ago now. She realized he must have been in love with her, to gather up her panties full of shit, so that no one would know she had crapped in her pants. As a reward, she showed him her pussy, when what she should have done was kiss him. That was probably what he really wanted.

Sarah suddenly felt a terrible ache in her chest. She wanted to go back in time, and do it right. The exchange with Gavin was the template, one that she had repeated with Arnold. It was always an exchange: sex for favors. Were the feminists right, that marriage was just legalized prostitution? Did all male-female relations boil down to exchange?

She walked over to a Zen garden, sat and watched as a beautiful butterfly slowly opened and closed its wings. She saw that she had dispensed wisdom on her TV show, but that she herself was not wise. She thought of seeking out a Zen master to help her, but she knew that he would say, "The answer is within you." Which was true, but *where* was it within her?

Virgil: *Sunt lacrimae rerum*: "Are the tears of things." More freely translated: "The pain of the world." Was this what she was feeling? She thought of Gavin again, and suddenly started to weep, right in the garden.

"I'm sorry, Gavin," she cried aloud; "I'm so sorry." But this was a bit like her longing to be an actress on *Seinfeld*. Arnie had been right: that ship had sailed. The trick was to become an actress *now*, not in 1989. Gavin too was long gone. So what, then, was the universe asking of her now? She saw it clearly: to love, unconditionally, without "exchange." This is what the Gavin incident had been trying to teach her, if in a reverse way.

Where had she heard this saying? She couldn't remember. "Life is to be understood backward, but lived forward." If there were another Gavin out there, she thought to herself, she would start with a kiss.

## 12

# OPERATIO SEQUITUR ESSE

J ill had always looked askance at online dating, but her friend Barbara's recent success gave her moment to pause. "It was a total shot in the dark," said Barbara, "or almost. Rick had posted his name, picture, and profession on Couples.com, and I was immediately drawn to him. He's very good looking, thirty-four years old, and runs his own architectural firm. I was actually a little hesitant to write him: Why would someone like that be interested in a mere secretary? I thought. But I picked up my courage and dropped him a line. That was two months ago. He proposed on our third date. Can you believe it?"

"How's the sexual chemistry?" Jill asked her.

"Jesus, don't get me started. Rick practices tantric sex. He comes, but he doesn't ejaculate. It's not unusual for me to have six or seven orgasms a night—every night. Listen, Jill," she went on, "I'm not saying you'll strike gold on the first try, and I agree with you that most men are jerks; but there *is* gold out there, and you really need to go panning for it."

"Yeah...what the heck. I've got nothing to lose, unless I hook up with a mental patient who chops my head off with a machete."

"Just don't date any Mexicans," said Barbara. "You know what Ann Coulter says: they're all rapists."

"Ann Coulter is fucked in the head," countered Jill.

"Well, sure; just kidding. Besides, some of them have very large penises."

"Barbara—"

"OK, I'll stop. Rick has got me cultivating my sense of humor," she said. "*Bad* sense of humor, you mean," offered Jill.

"Guilty as charged," said Barbara. "Listen, let's go over to your house and search Couples.com on your computer right now. What do you say?"

Ten minutes later the two of them were checking out the postings online. "How about this guy?" Barbara pointed to a man listed as forty years old, divorced, with one son. "Too much baggage," said Jill.

"OK, then, this one."

"Barb, he lists his hobbies as collecting butterflies. He's probably gay."

"More likely metrosexual," said Barbara.

"What?"

"Metro—Oh, forget it. OK, no butterflies. But he's hardly Vladimir Nabokov."

"Who?"

"Jesus, Jill: *Lolita*? Don't you know anything at all?"

"So I should date a pedophile?" she said.

"It's hard talking to someone who has scrambled eggs in her head," Barbara observed.

"What do you want from me?" exclaimed Jill. "I'm just a dumb secretary. I admit it."

"Which means you can never read a book?"

"Barb, I think we're getting off track here. Here, this guy might be OK."

"Wow!" cried Barbara. "Dave Smith, thirty-two, trained for the Olympic swimming team. I'll bet his body is hot. And since you're just a dumb secretary, it won't matter that he doesn't read either."

"And we know this how?" Jill asked her.

"Who has time for books, if you're in a swimming pool all day long?"

"OK, then, Dave Smith. Let me send him a message."

"Dear Dave,

I would like to meet you. My name is Jill, I'm thirty-four years old, and I'm looking for a serious relationship." She broke off, turned to Barbara. "Should I list my measurements, do you think?" (Jill had a great figure.)

"Are you nuts, girl? You say you want a serious relationship and then you dangle sexual bait? Honestly, Jill, I think you must have rocks in your head. Anyway, once he sees you, that will be advertisement enough. Me, I'd kill to have your tits."

"OK," said Jill; "no measurements. What else?"

"Tell him you have shit for brains and that the only thing you ever read is your cell phone. At least it's true."

"Very funny," said Jill. "I'm also not going to add that I'm a great lay, and hope he's into tantric sex."

The date took place in a public, neutral place. Jill wore an outfit that was halfway between a librarian and a slut. Dave wore a suit, sans tie. "Wow!" he said, taking her in: "this is a nice surprise. You didn't write that you were a bombshell."

Jill blushed. "Hardly," she said, trying to be modest.

"So," he went on, "how long have you lived here?"

"All my life," she replied. "I'm not a very adventurous person. How about you?"

"I was born in Belgium, actually. My parents moved to the US when I was nine years old. That was when I began taking swimming lessons."

"So you speak French," she said.

"And Flemish," he added. Jill had no idea what Flemish was, and whether it had anything to do with phlegm, in which case it would be disgusting; so she didn't say anything. There was an awkward pause. "Jill, can I be frank?" She nodded. "I know this is terribly forward, but the reality is that if two people aren't sexually compatible, there's no point in pursing a relationship. Would you be willing for us to go to my place or yours, and sleep together?"

"I—I—"

"I know," he said; "I'm being terribly aggressive. But I still think that what I just said holds true."

What would Barb tell her to do? she wondered. Run! Of course. "OK," she said. "Let's go." Dave was not adept at tantric sex, but his body was gorgeous and he lasted a long time. Jill was not accustomed to having multiple orgasms the first time she slept with someone.

"Well, Olympic man; what's the verdict?" she asked him.

"Compatible!" he declared.

---

SHE MET with Barb the next day. "How did it go?" her best friend asked her.

"Fabulous. I fucked him, and it was spectacular," said Jill.

"Oh, no," said Barbara. "That was a dumb move, kid. You'll never hear from him again." Which proved to be the case. Jill was really depressed.

"OK," said Barbara; "back to the computer. Maybe butterfly man will look better this time around."

They settled on a cop. "Reliable, responsible," said Barbara. "What if he wears his gun to bed?" Jill asked her.

"Jill, you haven't even met him and already you're thinking about bed. Don't you think it might be time to stop being an adolescent?"

The date went fairly well. Jill especially liked the fact that Mark didn't know what a metrosexual was, and had never heard of Flemish or Vladimir Nabokov. He was into baseball, and took her to a couple of games. But the relationship, such as it was, went south when an annoying little dog kept barking at them one afternoon, and Mark took out his gun and shot it. Obviously, that was a deal-breaker.

Another coffee klatch with Barb. "He shot a dog?!" she practically screamed. "Right on the sidewalk," said Jill. "I guess guys don't list that sort of thing on Couples.com."

The next guy she dated wanted to choke her while he was fucking her. The fourth guy wanted to video themselves having sex. "I'm not having a lot of luck," she informed Barb. "Keep looking," Barb advised her. "They can't all be nut cases."

And the fifth guy, Bill, was...perfect. He was in his early forties, slim and very handsome, and a gentle lover. No guns, dogs, strangulation, or video cameras. A straight arrow. He told her he had a government job—"pretty boring, you don't wanna hear about it." But on their fifth date, he came clean.

"Oh no," Jill said to herself; "here it comes. He has some weird shoe fetish, or whatever. Well, I can probably live with that."

"Jill, I told you my government job was boring. It's not. I'm a spy. I work for the CIA. This poses two problems for you. One, I could get killed. It's not likely, but it's at least possible. Two, it means the Agency will be tracking on you. They've already compiled a profile—I refused to look at it. But the reality is that as long as we are together, they'll be watching you, because they are concerned that our intimacy might lead to my getting careless about state secrets. If you want to pull out, now is the time."

She stared at him. "That's a lot to take in. Give me some time to think about it."

"What should I do?" she asked Barb at their next coffee date. "It's your decision," Barb replied; "I can't make it for you."

"What would *you* do?" she asked Barb. "Except for the CIA thing, he's perfect."

"That's a rather large 'except'," said Barb. Jill sighed. "The gods hate me," she said. "I'm doomed."

Jill decided to stick it out with Bill, although she wondered if that was even his real name. And then life threw her a curve ball: Bill told her he had to go down to South America, "on business," and would be gone for about a month. Two weeks later, Francisco González, the democratically elected president of Parador, was overthrown and murdered in a military coup. These events were splashed across the front pages of every major newspaper; even Jill would have to know about it. The problem was, she didn't know what it meant, and she didn't know if Bill was involved.

"What it means," Barbara fairly shouted at her, "is that the government is up to its dirty tricks again. Francisco González was a popular socialist, and the thugs in Washington weren't about to allow that. Look, Jill, I know you don't know shit about politics, but take it from me: this is pure evil, and there's some chance that Bill was part of it. These coups typically involve atrocities— torture and massacres. Bill may be innocent of all this, but even if so, he's not allowed to tell you about it. So you will never know the reality of the situation, and you should end this relationship now."

"What if I fly down to Parador?" she suggested.

"A good idea, if you want to get your head blown off. You stay put, girl. Just see what information you can drag out of Bill when he returns."

Which he did, and Jill invited him over to dinner. The first thing she asked him (this on Barb's advice) was whether her apartment was bugged. "I can't say 100 percent," he replied, "but it's not likely. That would be a case of overkill. After that initial report on you, they probably continue to monitor you, but not that closely. *My* apartment is bugged," he concluded; "of that, I'm quite sure."

"OK, then. Next question, and I want a straight answer. Is your name really Bill Evans?"

"Jill, I'm going to give you a straight answer, but in doing so I'm violating my contract with the CIA. You must never, ever, reveal this information to Barb, your family, or anyone else. Do I have your word on this?" She nodded.

"It's Theo van Aken. Dutch descent. But everyone outside the Agency calls me Bill, and you can continue to do the same if you want."

"I'm used to Bill," she replied, "so I guess I'll stick with that for now. Finally: Were you involved in the campaign against Francisco González?"

"Jill, as you well know, my answer to that would have to be 'no' whether I was involved or not. If I were to say 'yes', and it ever got out that I told you that, I'd wind up in a military prison overnight, and my career with the US government would be over."

"So you just happened to be in Parador at the same time that he was murdered? It's just pure coincidence?" (Barb told her to ask this one.)

"I never was in Parador," he replied; "I was in Argentina. Here, here's my passport; look for yourself."

(This Barbara had not been prepared for, but she subsequently said to Jill, "That proves nothing; the CIA could have easily arranged what got stamped in his passport and what didn't.")

Jill was stuck. She realized that his contract with the CIA did not permit him to come clean with anybody. He was leading a double life—like all spies do. But she didn't kick him out, or end the relationship. She slept with him that night, but didn't climax. She was too wary, too confused. Meanwhile, since his place was probably bugged and hers probably not, they took to sleeping at her apartment most of the time.

It was about a week later that he began talking in his sleep. Apparently—something she didn't know—Bill/Theo spoke Spanish. She couldn't make out exactly what he was saying, but it sounded like "No! Parale! No lo mates!" When she fed these words (as best as she could duplicate them) into a Google translator function, what came back was "No! Stop! Don't kill him!"

This time, she said nothing to Barbara or anyone else; certainly not to Bill. Two days later, he moaned loudly in his sleep, and cried out, "Que estamos haciendo? Quinientos muertos! Para que?" Google gave her: "What are we doing? Five hundred dead! For what?" So apparently Bill *was* involved in the coup, but was trying to head off atrocities. Why hadn't the CIA pulled him off the job, then? Apparently, he was only getting in the way. She mulled this over, and a few days later, after dinner, confronted him with the information.

"Bill, Theo, I know you were involved in the coup. Don't ask me how; I just know. I also know that it got pretty vicious, and that you tried to block its worst excesses. If you were getting in the way, why didn't the CIA ship you back to the States?"

"Jill, I wasn't in Parador, I—"

"Cut it, Bill; you've been talking in your sleep and you spilled the beans. So answer me: Why weren't you sent back?"

His shoulders dropped; he suddenly looked very tired. "I *was* sent back," he admitted, in a low voice. "The coup was still in progress when they put me on a plane. We were torturing innocent people to protect our economic interests, and I wasn't having it. So the Agency wasn't having me."

"Why haven't they swept you up, then?" she asked him.

"They still might, for all I know. But they also know that I'm a professional and will keep my mouth shut. Which I'm obviously not doing now."

"Theo, what are you worth right now, in liquid cash reserves?" she asked him. "A little over half a million dollars," he replied; "why?"

"Because maybe both of us should fly the coop. Am I being too paranoid here? Your life isn't safe here, and I doubt mine is either. They could easily arrange an 'accident', if they wanted to. We could stay with your family in Haarlem, or perhaps disappear into Eastern Europe. Make it hard, at least, for them to find us." He stared at her.

"You're serious about this?" he said.

"I just don't want to die for nothing," she replied.

---

TO KEEP UP APPEARANCES, Theo put in for an extended leave from the Agency, for reasons of "mental exhaustion" (true enough). Jill, on the other hand, quit her job with no explanation. Barbara was the only one she told about what was going on, and asked her not to try to contact her for at least a year. She said nothing about Holland. Jill and Theo took the train to a small town up the Hudson Valley, where they were married by the Justice of the Peace, and flew to Amsterdam the next day. Haarlem was only a short train ride away. They decided it might be too risky to stay with his family, so they rented a house on the outskirts of town. Jill found Dutch incomprehensible, but much to her relief, most people spoke some English.

Jill also discovered that she was in love with Theo. He was, after all, a hero, one who stood up to gross injustice at great personal risk. She became more loving in bed. It came naturally, required no effort. She said "I love you" to him frequently, and saw that he was happy. Six months later, nothing had been heard from the CIA, and they concluded that they were probably off the radar screen. Theo took up landscape painting, while she enrolled in classes in the Dutch language. Eventually, she thought, I might be able to get a secretarial job here or in Amsterdam.

So this bizarre story seems to have had a happy ending, except for Theo's conscience. He began to consult with lawyers at the World Court, in The Hague. He told them that the coup in Parador was a war crime; he gave them the names of CIA agents and Army personnel. They began investigating, to see if charges of genocide or atrocities could be brought against the United States.

"Theo, darling, why did you do this? We were off the map. Now, we are back on it, and may wind up in the CIA's crosshairs."

"Don't worry," he told her; "the World Court lawyers promised to leave my name out of their investigation."

"So what?" she exclaimed. "The CIA isn't stupid; they'll know where the info came from. And what if, at some point, there is a trial, and the lawyers ask you to testify? Then what?"

"That's way down the line, Jill, and besides, it may never come to that."

Jill had briefly met Theo's parents a while back, shortly after they arrived in Haarlem. "Theo, I think it's time we told your parents the whole story. They have a right to know. Happily, they were never contacted by the CIA, so I think this will be safe. I also want their opinion on this World Court thing. Do they speak English?"

"A little," he said, "but I can speak with them in Dutch, and translate for you."

"Fine. Dinner at their house this Friday, OK?" He told her yes.

———

THEY REALLY WERE WONDERFUL PEOPLE, the van Akens, warm and friendly. Theo's uncle, Joop, who spoke English, also joined them. Dinner was excellent; lots of wine flowed. After which, Theo prepared to do a dual translation.

"Mom, Pop, Uncle Joop," he began, "Jill and I have something to tell you." He gave them the whole story, in particular what he had witnessed in Parador, and his current dealings with the World Court. "What do you think I should do?" he asked them.

"Looks like you've already done it," said his father. "What should your mother and I say if the CIA comes knocking?"

"Tell them that of course you're in contact with me, but that you have no knowledge of my actions while I lived in the United States. And that you're happy that I got married and returned to live in Holland. That's it. How do you feel about my contacting the World Court?" he added.

"It's a considerable risk," his father replied, "but your mother and I always told you to live your conscience, which is what you seem to be doing. My concern is that this could put Jill at risk. The poor thing innocently went out on a date with you and got her life turned upside down. It was obviously much more than she had bargained for. If the CIA comes knocking, you need to have a safe house available where she can stay. I suggest you make these arrangements now. I have a friend in Rotterdam who can help you with that."

Jill lay in bed that night, after they made love, staring at the ceiling. She wished she had Barbara with her here. What her father-in-law said about going out on a date, just anticipating a nice evening, and then a few months later hiding out from the CIA in some safe house in Holland—how do these things happen? What crazy god is up there, in heaven, rolling the dice? Life simply made no sense to her. Although if this god's goal was to get her to grow up very fast, he certainly succeeded.

She decided she wanted to talk to her father-in-law about these things. He was nearly eighty, a wise old bird. She also didn't want Theo present, so would need Joop to do the translating — although she did understand a lot of Dutch by now. She asked Theo to set it up.

Mr. van Aken hugged her at the door, and asked her to come in. He poured her a large glass of sherry, and the two of them sat on opposite sides of the kitchen table, with Joop at the end of it, between them. And suddenly, she began to cry. She didn't know why, really, except for having wound up in a life that was incomprehensible. Mr. van Aken got up, sat in the chair next to her, and took her in his arms. "My child," he kept repeating in Dutch; "my daughter." She understood it, and it made it cry even more.

"What is it, my child, what is it?" he asked her. "I don't know," she answered in Dutch, then switched to English, with Joop translating for his brother. "It's exactly like you said. One day you're a flighty American airhead, going out on innocent, or even silly, computer-generated dates, and a few months later you're hiding from the CIA. Oh, have no doubt: I love your son. I hope to give you a grandchild someday. But my confusion is larger than all of that. Father (she used the Dutch term, Vader), who is throwing the dice of our lives? Is he a mad demon? I was just a naive secretary living in America. I basically had a boring life. My best friend told me I was a moron. And now all this. It's not merely that I can't make sense of my life. It's that I can't make any sense of life in general."

Joop translated all through her confession, if that's what it was. By the end, his eyes were wet. The Dutch were not used to this degree of emotional honesty.

"Tell me, my daughter," said van Aken: "if you could turn back the clock and not have that first date with Theo, would you do it? Say what's in your heart."

"To be honest," she replied, "yes and no. Part of me wants that, I guess. The problem is the extremes. In that life, nothing was happening. In this new life, too much is happening."

"My dear, when I was a boy, we all had to study Latin in school. I still remember a lot of it. Here is a famous line, I think from Aquinas: *operatio sequitur esse*. It means, 'as one is, one does'. I don't believe in accidents, and I don't believe you were ever boring or moronic. Naive, maybe, but there's no shame in that. Life, or the universe, if you will, came along and offered you this new life because *it was already who you were*. Do you understand me? As one is, one does. Don't fear life, child; embrace it. And if I may get practical for a moment, if Theo's activity in The Hague puts the two of you in danger, here in Holland we too have a witness protection program, and can get you out of harm's way."

Jill cried some more, and hugged him, and then Joop. That night, Theo lay inside her for a long time, and she got pregnant. Somehow, she knew it, and her fear of the CIA, and her confusion over the meaning of life, began to recede.

The lawyers at the World Court finally wrapped up their case, and released it: the names of those officers who committed the crimes, and what they did. Of course the US government denied it, and in any case said that they didn't recognize the jurisdiction of the World Court. But public opinion began to mount, worldwide; other countries saw the US as a rogue state, especially in the wake of the fascist junta that now ruled Parador. And for what? asked newspapers from Boston to Bangkok. So that the US could obtain favorable trade arrangements with Parador, on behalf of wealthy American businessmen? "It all stinks," declared one editorial.

As luck would have it, Theo was called upon to testify, and felt he could not refuse. He began his testimony with a statement that came to be regularly quoted in textbooks on human rights:

"If it please the court, I need to preface my testimony regarding atrocities committed by the US military in Parador with a few personal remarks. It's June now; because of this testimony, I may not live to see the end of the year. America is a rogue state, and the CIA and the US Army are criminal organizations. They would have no more regrets about rubbing me out than they would about swatting a fly. My wife and child are hidden now, so hopefully they will escape American criminal wrath. I suspect that I won't. But the operation in Parador, which has now left its citizens under the cruel yoke of fascist dictatorship, was carried out for no other reason than to make a few wealthy businessmen wealthier. When Lyndon Johnson took office in the wake of President Kennedy's assassination, he remarked that the CIA had apparently been 'running a goddamn Murder, Inc.' That was an accurate statement; the problem is that nothing changed as a result, as coups like the ones in Chile and Parador demonstrate.

"At the risk of our lives, we must bear witness to these crimes, ones that involve the torture and mass murder of innocent people. If I don't live to see December, I'm sure that my wife and son will continue this tradition. I ask all of you here today to join in that effort."

Two weeks later, Theo was run off the road and killed in a highway "accident." Jill selected the headstone. The epitaph was in Latin:

OPERATIO SEQUITUR ESSE

## 13

---

# CIRCUS DAYS

There was an annual fair that came to our town, which included circus acts, magic demonstrations, and all kinds of other shows. One year, when I was seven, my parents took me to it, and bought me a large cone of cotton candy. It was pink, and tasted of sugar. I ate the whole thing, then threw up in a nearby garbage can. When I finished, I looked around, but my parents were nowhere to be seen. You'd think that I would be afraid, start crying or whatever, but instead I had a heady sense of freedom. Ours was not a happy home; my parents were always fighting. I often dreamed of running away, and now, suddenly, the opportunity had presented itself, like a prison break.

I began making my way among all the tents and displays. In one, there was a fat lady with a moustache; in another, a man riding around on a bicycle with only one wheel. Finally, I stopped at the magician's booth. The magician was tall and handsome, wearing a tuxedo and a top hat, and sporting an elegant moustache. His assistant was a very pretty lady in a bathing suit. He did things like pull a rabbit out of a hat, or "saw" his assistant in two—which she miraculously survived. I had by now pushed myself up to the front row of the crowd. Mr. Miraculo, as he was called, was holding a balloon in one hand and a long, thick needle in the other. He announced that he was going to pierce the balloon, but that the balloon wouldn't pop. He leaned over to me and asked me to touch the point of the needle with my finger.

"Is it sharp, sonny?" he asked me. I nodded. "Tell everyone here," he said. I turned to the crowd behind me. "It's sharp!" I declared. Then his assistant, who was called Miss Yvette, held the balloon in her hands, while Mr. Miraculo pushed the needle into it. The balloon didn't explode; instead, the needle went through it like butter and came out the other side. Mr. Miraculo took a bow, and the audience applauded.

I was dumbfounded. How in the world could a sharp needle not pop a balloon? Mr. Miraculo and Miss Yvette did a few more tricks with cards and coins and handkerchiefs, but I wasn't interested. All I cared about was learning the secret of the balloon trick.

It was late afternoon by now; all the stands were packing up, including Mr. Miraculo's. I approached the stage, looked up at him. "How did you do that?" I asked him. "Do what, sonny?" "Put a needle through a balloon," I answered. "Oh, that's a trade secret," he said; "a magician never gives away his secrets. But maybe someday *you'll* become a magician, and then you'll know all the secrets." He smiled broadly.

"Why not right now?" I asked him. "You could teach me."

"Shouldn't you be getting on home?" he suggested. "It's getting late."

"I have no home," I told him. "My parents disappeared the other day, and I've been sleeping on the street." I faked crying. I guess that was *my* magic trick.

"There, there, sonny." He bent down, put his arms around me. "We should probably go to the police."

"No police!" I shouted; "no police! Let me live with you!" He and Yvette lived in a large covered wagon. "Let me stay in your wagon. Look how big it is."

Mr. Miraculo looked over at Yvette; she just shrugged. "Why not?" she said; "we might even be able to use him in one of our acts. Come on up here, sonny; we can fix a bed for you right below ours." And so began my apprenticeship with Mr. Miraculo —and Yvette.

The three of us toured the countryside, performing tricks in various towns. Mr. M. showed me the secret of the balloon: you coated it with oil. Then, when the needle pricked it, the oil moved in to seal the spot before any air could escape. Oil was also poured into the inside, so that the same thing happened when the needle emerged from the balloon. I was really excited by this, and Mr. M. let me practice with it until I got it right.

He and Yvette were really kind to me; I never figured out why. Mr. M. used me to "test" the needle for the audience, and gave me pocket money for this. They shared their food with me, took care of me. I was finally free from my parents, and I was in heaven. This was my idea of a real family.

As we tended to get up very early, we all usually went to sleep around 9 p.m. Every night, for some reason, he and Yvette would wrestle on their bed, and she would moan and groan. Should I say anything? I worried that he was hurting her. But the next day, she always emerged with a big smile on her face. She apparently enjoyed these wrestling matches, so I decided it was OK.

I began to pester Mr. M. to teach me some magic tricks. And slowly, he did. I learned the rabbit-in-the-hat trick, and the saw-Yvette-in-half trick. Meanwhile, Yvette introduced me to the Tarot. "These cards," she said, "tell the person for whom you are reading what is happening in his life, or her life. Sometimes, they can foretell the future. But you have to know how to read them correctly. I'll teach you, and then we'll set you up with a table next to the stage. You'll read for people, and charge them fifty cents. You get twenty-five, and Mr. M. and I get twenty-five. OK?" I nodded happily.

"People want to know that their lives are on track, that things are going well. Or if not, they want some idea as to how to fix things. Women always want to hear that they are going to meet a tall dark stranger. Men want to hear that they will soon be rich. You understand what I am saying?" Again, I nodded.

"Now take this card, for example. Death. It's part of what we call the Major Arcana. It could, of course, represent death, but it could also stand for a major change in a person's life—which could be a good thing. So when you're doing a reading, instead of telling your customer that he or she is about to die, tell them that some big change is going to occur in their life, and that they should be ready for it. Get the idea?" I said yes.

"Why do you and Mr. M. wrestle every night, when we go to bed?" I asked her. Her face turned as pink as that cone of cotton candy I had eaten long ago.

"To keep fit!" she said. "It's really good exercise."

"I was afraid he was hurting you," I said.

"Oh, no, not at all; it feels really good."

"Could I try it?" I asked her. Her eyes widened. "What, with me?" she exclaimed. I nodded.

"No, sonny. In order to wrestle properly, you need a girl your own age. You'll do it when you get older, you'll see." I was deeply disapointed, but I didn't say anything. Meanwhile, I started running "Oscar's Tarot Table" next to the stage, charging fifty cents per customer. It got easier as I got more practice with the cards. Yvette was absolutely correct: the women wanted to meet a man and fall in love, and the men wanted to make lots of money. So I tried, when I could, to steer the readings in these directions. But what my customers wanted, above all, was that things come out "all right" for them, whatever that meant. I discovered that all of them were worried about their lives; often, very worried. What they most wanted from the readings was reassurance, and I did my best to provide it. This often led to generous tips.

One evening, instead of the usual wrestling match, Mr. M. and Yvette had a big fight. I was sitting outside the wagon at the time. I wasn't sure what the fight was about, but I heard her cry, "Look at all the years I've put in! Look at all the loving I gave you! Don't you think it's about time?" She jumped out of the wagon, ran into me, put her arms around me, and cried like a baby.

"Yvette," I said; "what's wrong? Tell me."

"He won't marry me," she said, angrily. "After all these years of being together, all these years of being his faithful assistant, he says he doesn't want to get married. Jesus, what else does a girl want, anyway? I have half a mind to leave him."

"Why doesn't he want to marry you?" I asked her.

"Oh, the usual male nonsense about wanting to be free, needing space, and so on. I think he might be interested in another girl."

"No one could replace you, Yvette; no one," I told her.

"Thank you, honey; you're such a doll. Can I sleep in your bed tonight? I don't want to sleep with Guido right now."

It was kind of a strange arrangement, that night. I curled up in Yvette's arms, and smelled the fragrance of her body. She was still wearing her bathing suit, and I pressed against her. "You're such a great kid," she kept saying. "I wish I could have a kid just like you."

The fight with Guido blew over for a while. Yvette was still angry, but she wasn't ready to go off on her own. After all, what could she do? Read Tarot, probably, but that was all. She was an assistant, not a magician.

Then a dark cloud suddenly appeared. The next town we got to, there were posters with my face on them, stuck on walls and telephone poles. MISSING they said; REWARD OFFERED.

"OK, Oscar, no Tarot this time around," said Guido. "You need to stay in the wagon, out of sight." At one point a cop even came by, carrying a poster. "You haven't seen this kid by any chance?" he said to Guido and Yvette. "Apparently he ran away from home."

"Sorry, officer," said Guido; "haven't seen any sign of him." The policeman laughed. "Kid probably ran off to join the circus," he said jokingly.

That night Yvette, Guido, and I had a "family meeting." "Listen, kid, we're in a bit of a bind here," Yvette explained. "If you get caught, we could go to jail for kidnapping, even though we didn't kidnap you. Do you want to go back home?"

"This is my home," I told her. Yvette shot a look at Guido. "What do you think?" she asked him. He shrugged. "Let's take the chance and keep him," he said. "He just hasta stay outta sight in those towns where the posters are up. Meanwhile, he can keep earning money from Tarot readings, and I'm going to continue to train him in the magical arts. That way, when he gets older, he'll have a craft." Talk about kindness.

So I stayed. The sleeping arrangements continued to be kind of weird. Two or three nights a week Yvette would wrestle with Guido; the other nights she slept in my bed, hugging me tightly. Guido didn't seem to mind. As for me, I loved her body, loved the smell of it, the sensation of it. "You're going to make some girl very happy some day," she told me. I was now eight years old; I had been with her and Guido for over a year, and was not to learn the joys of "wrestling" for another seven. (More on that in a moment.)

In any case, we finally got caught. Someone had identified me from a poster, and turned me in to get the reward. Guido and Yvette were arrested. At their trial, I testified that coercion had never been involved; that I was never kidnapped, and had in fact imposed myself on *them*. The judge accepted this, but jailed the two of them for a year for harboring a minor and failing to report it to the police. I went back to my parents, who were still fighting all the time, and pretty much suffered in silence. I was not allowed to visit Guido and Yvette in jail, but I wrote her two or three times a week (she saved all my letters). When she was released, I met her outside the jail, and we hugged and cried. I also got together with Guido, and thanked him for teaching me to do magic, which I practice to this day.

I go by the name of Mr. Fabuloso, and have a lovely assistant named Peggy. As for Yvette, she finally left Guido and married a prosperous wheat farmer. She and I kept in touch, and she also acted as my "wrestling" coach, told me what to do and how to do it. Let's just say that her instructions were very precise; clinical, really. For this, Peggy has always been her biggest fan, and we wrestle quite often.

Yvette also joined a dance troupe, and Peggy and I would go to see her when she was in town. "How is the farmer at wrestling?" I got bold enough to ask her, one time. She pinched my cheek. "Like a tractor, kid."

# 14
## SUOMI

It was at the age of fifteen that Ricky Franklin discovered that he had some sort of spiritual power. His parents, veterans of the hippie generation, had enrolled him in a "creative" alternative school, which included classes in dance, art, and meditation. The meditation teacher, Linda Sokol, explained that very few people in America meditated, and the majority of those who did saw it only as a form of relaxation. But, she told the class, almost all non-Western cultures believed in the existence of an invisible "energy," and that this energy could be "accumulated" by means of meditation. It gave its practitioners power, she said. When Ricky asked her about it after class, Linda said she would lend him a book on the subject.

*Pathways to Power* discussed the beliefs of numerous cultures with respect to the existence of an invisible force that was believed to pervade the world. The Hindus called it *prana*; the Chinese called it *chi*; in Melanesia it was known as *mana*, and for the followers of Islam, *baraka*. The Iroquois term for it was *orenda*. And so on. In the West, it was mostly regarded as quackery or superstition. The "magic" of the West was, in fact, technology. Ricky wasn't particularly interested in that.

Ricky was attracted to the idea of an invisible force because he felt he had no power in his own life, or over it. He was an only child, and not very healthy. He tired easily, for one thing. His home life was a wasteland, with his father frequently absent, and his mother putting in long hours in a nail salon. The subject of energy easily began to fill the emptiness in his life.

When he finished *Pathways to Power* he asked Linda if he could study meditation with her outside of class. She told him that the school would not be happy with such an arrangement, but that she could introduce him to her own meditation teacher, who was a Tibetan shaman. "You'll have to pay for the lessons, though," she warned him. "Can you get a part-time job after school?"

"I already have a paper route," he replied, "and some money saved from that." And so, the instruction began.

In the center of a noisy city, the Tibetan master's meditation room was a haven of silence. It was lush, filled with exotic rugs and wall hangings, and Ricky and the master sat cross-legged on cushions, facing each other. "I am called Tulku," he told Ricky, "but you can address me as Teacher. Linda—Ms. Sokol—tells me you are a very good student, committed to meditation and eager to learn more about it. Tell me, Ricky, what do you hope to gain from studying with me?"

"Power," Ricky blurted out. "I am alone in the world. I have no family life, and no real friends. I feel I need to protect myself." Tulku nodded.

"It will take a lot of discipline and training to acquire such power," he said, "and what I am going to teach you is not necessarily from the Tibetan tradition. As you know from your reading, many non-Western traditions speak of an all-pervading energy—the Chinese call it *chi*—that can be captured and directed. But you should know that it has great dangers attached to it. Many years ago, I had an enemy, and I directed this energy against him. It didn't kill him, thank God, but he was paralyzed for life. You can imagine how I felt, still feel. This was an excessive, if somewhat accidental, use of power, and I have regretted it ever since. I need to know that you will use this power to protect yourself, but not to hurt anyone. Agreed?" Ricky nodded.

"There is also the category of parlor tricks, things like levitation, or being able to move solid objects across a table. These things are valuable as training exercises, but otherwise are beneath the serious practitioner of directed *chi*. You must not flaunt your power, or use it to amuse or impress others. Agreed?" Again, Ricky nodded.

"Good," said Tulku. "As you become a practitioner, you will feel more protected, and less lonely. These are good uses of directed *chi*. So let's begin."

Lessons were twice a week, each session lasting two hours. Tulku charged Ricky a nominal fee. He saw that the boy was kind of a lost soul, and wanted to help him find his way in the world. Step by step, he taught him to concentrate, to accumulate energy, and to direct that energy. Ricky asked Linda about it, one day after meditation class.

"Did you learn to direct *chi* from Tulku?" he questioned her. She nodded. "How have you used it?"

"Mostly for peace of mind," she told him, "although once in self-defense."

"What happened?" Ricky asked her.

"Someone tried to rape me," she said. "I focused my *chi* on his chest, and it disabled him."

"Heart attack?" Ricky suggested.

"Happily, no. It just took the wind out of him. He fell backwards, struggling to catch his breath, and I was able to escape."

"Wow!" said Ricky; "that's awesome."

"True," she replied; "but as Tulku says, you need to be careful with it."

---

AFTER WEEKS OF CONCENTRATED MEDITATION, Tulku had Ricky start to practice with a pencil. "You can do this at home as well," he told him, "if no one else is around. If you can successfully direct your *chi* toward the pencil, you should be able to get it to move along the table an inch or two." It took Ricky three months, but he finally did it—and was amazed. "This is a miracle," he said to Tulku. Tulki shrugged.

"It's just an illustration of what the mind can do," Tulku replied. "Remember not to get hung up on tricks. The importance, the purpose, of directed *chi* is to do good in the world."

As luck would have it, the very next day Ricky had an opportunity to do just that, along the lines of what happened to Linda. It was on the school playground, where an older boy was bullying a younger one, a kid often ridiculed as a nerd. Ricky marched over to the two of them and said to the bullyer, Bobby Ackerman, "You leave him alone." Bobby gave Ricky a shove. "Mind your own business, asshole." Ricky concentrated his energy on Bobby's chest; he then fell down, gasping for breath.

"Take off," Ricky said to the younger boy; which he did. But it didn't end there. Bobby told one of his teachers that Ricky was practicing "witchcraft," who then told Mr. Carlisle, the principal; who then called Ricky into his office.

"What's this I hear about you practicing witchcraft?" he asked Ricky.

"What's witchcraft?" Ricky responded.

"You knocked Bobby Ackerman down without touching

him?" said Mr. Carlisle. Ricky shrugged. "I just looked at him. He must have tripped, or had an upset stomach."

"Hmm," said Carlisle. Meanwhile, news of the incident reached Linda Sokol, and she took Ricky aside. "Ricky, I know what happened. Another incident like that and you could get expelled, and they might suspect that I had something to do with it. You need to lay low with this sort of stuff."

"But Bobby was bullying a little kid," Ricky objected. "I couldn't let it go on."

"I understand," Linda told him; "but pick your fights very sparingly. You do know what happened to witches in New England in the seventeenth century, right?" Ricky shook his head.

"They got burned at the stake. Point is, if a rumor arises that you've got some kind of supernatural power, you could wind up in a lot of trouble—draw a lot of unwanted attention to yourself. You read me?" Ricky ignored the question.

"Besides that rape incident," Ricky asked her, "how do you use *chi* in your own life?" Linda got a bit red in the face.

"Ricky, what I'm about to tell you is just between us, OK?" He nodded. "Last year, I was very attracted to a man who was in a yoga class I attended. I finally got up the nerve to ask him out for coffee, and he accepted. While we were on the date, I gently directed *chi* at his heart, to make him fall in love with me. Tulku cautioned me against it, but I couldn't stop myself, because I had such a crush on this guy. Peter, his name was.

"Well," she went on, "it worked. He did fall in love with me, and we were together for six months. But all the time it felt unreal, because I knew I had in effect cast a spell over him. Without that spell, he probably wouldn't have fallen in love. Well, who knows, really. Anyway, the guilt was killing me, so I finally confessed to him what had happened, what I had done. He left me after that; I never saw him again. I don't know if it was because he thought I was a kook, or because he believed me and was angry at being manipulated. Either way, he disappeared from my life. I'm still hurting from the whole thing."

It was a lot for Ricky to take in. That night, he lay in bed, trying to think of "safe" uses of *chi*. The next day, at lunch time, he left the school and went over to a nearby KFC. He went up to the order counter and said to the woman behind it, "Could you please give me a piece of chicken? I'm very hungry, and I have no money."

She shook her head. "Sorry, kid. You know what they say: in America, there is no free lunch."

Ricky tried the same experiment the next day, when yesterday's server was not on duty. It was a guy this time. He approached the counter, and focused his *chi* on the man's heart, repeating the same plea he had uttered the day before.

"Sure, kid," the guy whispered; "here's a little box of chicken for you. But don't tell anyone; I could get fired." Ricky made away with the box, exhilarated. He couldn't wait to tell Tulku.

"My son," Tulku said to him, "you really need to be careful with your use of *chi*. Suppose this man had gotten caught, as a result of what you made him do?"

"He's still working there," said Ricky.

"Not the point," Tulku replied. "You got lucky, is all, and so did he."

"So tell me then," Ricky went on, "how can I use my *chi* for good in the world?"

"The key," Tulku told him, "is to achieve expansion, or what I call vibrancy. People know when a person is vibrant, or alive, and they are attracted to that energy. Sometimes it's called charisma. Which also means deep self-confidence. Once you have it, you can get people to do what's best for you, for themselves, and for society, just by being who you are—i.e., without manipulation. If you have enough *chi* flowing through you, and you want to own a restaurant, it will be a great restaurant, very popular. If you want to be a mathematician, and you have the talent for it, you'll become a great mathematician. The idea is to use your *chi* to benefit society as well as yourself. Right now, your job is to be a great student—if that's what you truly want for yourself. If not, drop out of school next year, pick a craft, and become great at that. Understood?" Ricky said yes.

However, he wasn't really satisfied with this formula. He really did want power over others, like he had in that incident with Bobby Ackerman. He even wanted other people to fear him. He said nothing to Linda about any of this, because he knew she would disapprove. But he didn't know where that left him. He figured he should start slow.

The next afternoon, at recess, he watched the guys on the playground playing basketball. They never let him join in, calling him "weak" and "a loser." So he concentrated on each boy, as he was about to make a shot, and caused the kid to miss. And then the ball accidentally came his way, and he made the shot from a moderately long distance. Everyone stopped to look.

"Hey, the loser gets lucky!" said one of them.

"I'll be glad to do it again," Ricky offered. They passed him the ball, and—slam dunk. "Who wants me on their team?" he cried. Needless to say, Ricky's team won by a wide margin. After that day, everyone wanted him on their team.

What next? he thought to himself. Get girls to have sex with him? But then he remembered Linda's experience with Peter. Bad idea, he concluded. Still, what Tulku said about charisma was true. Hence previously shunned by the girls in school, he now was beginning to attract them. His favorite was Abigail, who wore her hair in pigtails and had budding breasts.

"How is it I didn't notice you before?" she asked him.

"Well, I'm a quiet type," he told her. They began hanging out after school, kissing a little bit. But he was determined not to use his *chi* on her; it all had to be real.

Ricky suddenly began to excel in school. Teachers asked him to read his essays in front of the class, for example, and he joined the debating society. But the issue of power continued to nag at him, along with the glamor of the American Dream. He didn't care about school. What he wanted was money, a swanky car, a driver, servants, and a house of his own—all this at age fifteen.

One day, Linda asked him to stay after meditation class. "So what's going on in that feverish little brain of yours?" she queried. Ricky couldn't look her in the eye.

"You won't like it," he said. "I've let you down, and I've let Tulku down."

"Let us down how?" So he told her the whole story, about his desire for money and power. She listened sympathetically. "Ricky, we can't escape the issue of power. Your parents' generation tried, and they failed. Most of them abandoned their ideals and became entrepreneurs, or tried to be. But the choice is not limited to being a hippie or being a corporate shark. There are lots of possibilities in between.

"Furthermore, although the path you want to be on is ultimately an empty one, you may have to pursue it for a while in order to really see that. There is also the additional danger that armed with a knowledge of *chi*, you could turn into a monster, hurt a lot of people. And then, it's really a very lonely path, to boot.

"But *chi* is not only about power, it's also about self-awareness, self-transparency. That relationship I told you about, with Peter? What I learned about myself was my extreme neediness. I was willing to do practically anything to be loved, to have a partner, to not be alone. This was not a happy thing to learn, but I'm better off now, having that information. Do you understand?"

"I think so," said Ricky. "Look, Ms. Sokol: I feel a similar need in the direction of wealth and power. Right now, it's what I need to do. And I think I'm going to drop out of school after this semester ends, so I can go and do it. I just want to ask you if I can check in with you from time to time, to keep me sane. Would that be OK?"

"Of course, Ricky," she said; "but you need to keep studying with Tulku as well." He nodded. "Yes, I'll do that."

----

COULD he influence the stock market? he wondered. Could he, at age sixteen, land a job in a law office, or a brokerage firm? Once again, Linda—multifaceted Linda—came to his aid. It turned out that she had a cousin who worked in an investment firm, and she put in a word for Ricky, who had dropped out of school in the meantime. "This is a very smart kid," she told him. "Teach him the trade. Don't just have him fetching you and the boys coffee."

Her cousin, David Orloff, took her at her word, and lent Ricky books on business management and investment banking. Ricky put in long hours after work, studying how the economy worked, and during the day he followed the market online. And then, one day, his big break came. How he knew, he never understood, but he had an intuition that a small aluminum manufacturing company was about to hit it big, and he urged the firm to invest in it. David put in 10K for himself, and 100K for the firm. Within twenty-four hours, he had become quite wealthy, and the firm cleared $24 million. Ricky, at age sixteen and a half, was the *wunderkind* of Kingston Enterprises. They closed up for the day and went across the street to the neighborhood bar. David stood up, glass of champagne in hand. "A toast, to my dear cousin, Linda Sokol, who sent us a genius, Ricky Franklin. To Linda! And of course, to Ricky!" ("Hear! Hear!")

In the generosity department, David was no slouch. With his newfound wealth, he bought Linda a space in midtown, so that she could be independent and have her own meditation center. Ricky went to visit her in her new digs.

"And this is all because of you!" she cried. "I now have my own classes, my own private students. Ricky, how can I ever repay you?" He looked her straight in the eye.

"You can become my girlfriend," he said, smiling broadly.

"Wha? Ricky, I'm nearly fifteen years older than you. Besides, you're under age. I'd go to jail. And what's going on with Abigail, by the way? Aren't you sleeping with her by now?"

"Yes," he replied, "but I'm not in love with her." Linda gasped. "And you are with me?"

"For a long time now. Will you wait for me? I'll be eighteen in sixteen months. You admit you need love in your life. Well, here it is." Linda began laughing hysterically, threw her arms around him.

"Oh my darling boy, my darling boy! A lot can happen in sixteen months."

"So don't let it," he told her. "You concentrate on your new career, and I'll concentrate on mine. The time will go by faster than you think." Linda's shoulders sank; she gave in.

"OK, hon, but no steamy e-mails or phone calls. We'll just have dinner once a month."

"I'll see you in a month, then. I love you." He left.

---

WITH HIS SHARE of the cash, Ricky—who had just gotten his learner's permit—bought a Mercedes, and enabled his mother to go part-time at the nail salon. An apartment of his own was still out of his reach, but meanwhile he was made a broker at Kingston Enterprises. The next few months brought no great bonanzas like the aluminum manufacturing company, but he gave steady advice and the firm got steadily richer. These were heady days.

He still studied with Tulku twice a week. He told his teacher what had happened in his life, omitting the part about Linda. As always, Tulku urged caution. "My son," he said, "learn the Japanese philosophy of impermanence. It could all vanish in a moment."

But things remained more or less permanent, or at least stable, over the next sixteen months. On his eighteenth birthday, Ricky did two memorable things: he bought a large apartment near Linda's studio, and he made love to her four times. "Ah, the wonders of an eighteen year-old penis," she exclaimed, after the fourth session. She had remained celibate for those sixteen months, and now couldn't get enough of him. As for Ricky, he was finally living the life he always coveted: private jet, expensive cigars, wine that went for 20K a bottle. A limo with a driver, a cook, a valet. Linda moved in with him, and they were a glamorous couple, often appearing in the society pages of the newspapers. They went on holidays to Monte Carlo and St. Tropez, and their sex life remained as passionate as ever. The next step came when Ricky and David left Kingston Enterprises to set up their own brokerage firm, Orloff & Franklin, with business connections in forty-five countries. Ricky was labeled "the witch of Wall Street," for his uncanny ability to pick winners. It didn't take very long for the new firm to have more than a billion in assets.

As Christmas approached, Ricky and Linda took to spending every evening in front of their fireplace, drinking cognac, before making love on the thick rug beneath their feet. "The only problem I'm having," he said to her one evening, "is that I can't square this lifestyle with the values of Tulku, of *chi*, and of meditation. They seem completely opposite to one another, and yet if I've sold out, if I've really betrayed my original ideals, then I should feel guilty—and I don't. I'm wondering what you think about all this."

"Rick, honey, Tulku would say that it's a matter of attachment. You know how he goes on about impermanence. Suppose this were the fall of 2008 instead of 2018. In a month, Orloff & Franklin, as well as my meditation studio, would shut down; we would be broke; we'd hafta sell this apartment, the limo, the plane, let go of the servants, and so on. And as Tulku will tell you, all of that could happen again; it could be gone in the blink of an eye. So the real questions are: Would we care, and what would remain, after such a massive loss?" He looked at her, questioningly.

"I can only speak for myself," she said, "but I need to know what you think as well. None of this stuff matters to me, if there is one thing remaining, namely our love. I think for a lot of wealthy couples, if you subtract the houses and cars and so on, it's the end of the relationship. I enjoy all the frufru—holidays on the French Riviera and so on—but I can live without it because for me none of it really matters. But the one thing I cannot live without is you." Tears covered her cheeks.

Ricky didn't reply. Or rather, his reply was nonverbal. He undressed her, and made love to her in front of the fireplace.

---

"LIFE IS LIKE THE *SAKURA*, the Japanese cherry blossom," said Tulku. "It lasts but a moment in time. And this can be true for *chi* as well. Now you have it, now you don't." Ricky had lost his magic touch; his financial intuition had suddenly deserted him. He had made a number of bad calls for the firm, and their resources were beginning to hemorrhage. "My *chi* is gone," he told Tulku, "and I'm getting very nervous."

"Let me give you an analogy from creative writing," Tulku suggested. "I have a friend who is a very talented novelist. He has studied *chi* direction with me for twenty years. During that time he produced a number of novels, two of which became best-sellers. But periodically, the energy deserted him. This is popularly known as writer's block. In one case, it lasted for eleven months. It was all I could do to keep him from killing himself. "Keep on meditating," I told him; "just trust the universe. You don't know what's best for you." And suddenly, without warning, the block lifted, without rhyme or reason. He proceeded to write *Dust and Memory*—maybe you've heard of it (I shook my head)—which went on to sell 3 million copies and get translated into thirty languages. My point is that if you think you can, or should, control *chi*, you've got the world upside down. You don't control *chi*; it's *chi* that controls *you*. You can only 'win' if you surrender to the flow of life, my son. This is how Fellini made *8½*, and how Proust wrote *In Search of Lost Time*."

"How do I do that?" Ricky asked him.

"Back to basics. Do you remember what I told you, very early on in our studies together, was the purpose of *chi* direction?"

"I—"

"It's to do good in the world. Can you say that you have been doing that?" Ricky sighed. "No," he answered.

"This, and complete surrender to the universe, are the keys to your recovery. Think about it, and talk it over with Linda. I don't have to tell you how wise that woman is. Then come back next week, and we'll see if anything has changed."

"Thank you, Teacher," said Ricky. He closed the door quietly as he left.

Ricky didn't want to go home right away. He walked for a while, crossed into a nearby park, and sat down on a park bench —and fell asleep. Ten minutes later, he awoke, startled, from a dream. In the dream, he had gone on a meditation retreat. It was led by a vibrant, handsome young man, of about thirty-five, who looked happy and healthy. At the end of the retreat, he poked

Ricky gently in the chest and said, "You look great. What we have here is a whole new way of life. Not force, but expansion."

Not force, but expansion, Ricky said to himself as he came to. A whole new way of life. He got up, hailed a taxi, and went home.

Ricky related the conversation he had with Tulku to Linda, and also told her about his dream. "Rick," she said, "you've just had two serious inputs of wisdom. The question is, what do you intend to do with this information?"

"Lin," he replied, "the truth is that the age difference between us is a real difference, and I'm really scared that it could pull us apart. The fact is that you are not attached to all this frufru, as you call it, and I am. You're committed to the life of the spirit, which is one reason I'm so in love with you. But I'm committed to material goods; somehow, I need all that stuff to feel OK. It leaves me wondering why you love me."

"Are you asking me?" He nodded. "OK, then: I'm drawn to you, and was even when you were a student in my meditation class, because I see that you are driven by an intense fire. I mean, I dated a lot of men in the past, and the persona they all projected —or actually had—was a cool sort of irony. I guess a lot of women are attracted by that, but it always rubbed me the wrong way. Even Peter was like that, to some extent. It's what's considered culturally acceptable. The problem for me is that it typically involves wearing a mask of some sort; it's rare, under those conditions, that you get the real person. But with you, there is no mask. You aren't posing. From the first, I saw a boy with raw, desperate energy, and I liked it. It's why I lent you that book, and why I put you on to Tulku. I suppose I shouldn't admit this, but these were substitutes for having sex with you, which I wanted to do, but obviously couldn't. Anyway, I figured that if anyone could teach you how to direct that energy, Tulku could. But your class background was stronger than his counsel, especially at your age; you really did need to go out there and chase money and power, and you may not be done with it yet. But this loss of *chi* that you're going through right now is a sign that something must change—which is what both Tulku and this dream are saying to you. As far as my love, I intend to stay with you through thick and thin, regardless of what choice you make; you can put that worry out of your head."

Ricky moved over to her, and let her hold him, head on chest, as though he were a baby. They sat like that for a long while. Finally she said: "Ricky, I want to give you an example of force versus expansion, so you can really understand what they look like in practice. OK?" He nodded, but kept clinging to her.

"My use of *chi* to get Peter to fall in love with me was force. The use of force emerged out of my own desperation. I didn't trust the universe to give me what I needed. Rather, *I* decided what I needed and then manipulated the situation so that I could get it. Finally, it all blew up in my face; which is what typically happens when one goes around operating by force.

"Expansion is what occurred, what I allowed, when you told me two years ago that you loved me. It made no rational sense, a boy of sixteen and a woman of twenty-nine; it was going to require that I not have sex with anyone for sixteen months; and it would get me labeled a cradle-robber or whatever. And yet, I knew this was the right life for me, a life that would expand me, and at that moment, I surrendered to you, and to my fate. That line from your dream—'a whole new way of life'—that was what I got."

Ricky didn't respond. Instead, he stretched out on the couch, with his head in Linda's lap, and closed his eyes. She stroked his hair, and he fell asleep. When he awoke, he kissed her. "Can you help me find my way back?" he asked her. "Back, and also forward," she replied.

This was his first serious surrender. He was resolved to just go with the flow. Whatever Linda would tell him to do, he would do.

He felt he had no choice. His present way of life, with the *chi* run out, was clearly a dead end.

First, she insisted that he attend two of her meditation classes a week, in addition to his work with Tulku. Second, he was to try and think of himself as a servant of *chi*, rather than a master of it. Third, the two of them were going to research the possibilities of using their wealth for the good of the community. And finally, for the time being, she was going to be dominant in the bedroom: she would tell him exactly what she wanted, and he would comply.

Ricky was uncomfortable with all of these "orders"; they seemed to be standing his life on its head. Taking classes with Linda drew him back to school days, when she was his teacher, not Linda but Ms. Sokol. Being a servant of *chi* meant his life was about trust, not about control. Giving away part of his wealth meant, obviously, that he would be less wealthy. And having Linda in command in the bedroom made him feel like he was at her mercy, even when he enjoyed it. All in all, it was the world turned upside down.

About three weeks into the new regime, however, Ricky noticed that a change was taking place: he made a correct call on the stock market. It didn't net the firm millions, only about 300K, but it was a hell of a lot better than *losing* 300K. Still, he intended to step gingerly in the investment area for the time being.

He and Linda also found an organization that was giving eleventh hour "happiness" to children dying of cancer. The kids would come out to their ranch for three weeks, where they would swim, ride ponies, play games, and generally have a great time. Ricky's heart was deeply moved by these helpless, dying children; the opportunity to afford them some joy while they were still alive became very important to him. He and Linda donated $10 million to the organization.

As for sex, Linda was now on top most of the time, but once in a while she allowed him to be in the superior position. This occasional "treat" made the lovemaking that much more intense.

Slowly, very slowly, the curve began to rise. Ricky was making more money. He and Linda donated another $10 million, this time to a medical organization in India that was operating on children to keep them from going blind. And their sex life was becoming more "egalitarian." Meanwhile, Ricky was starting to feel much more expanded. He wanted to direct his *chi* for political ends, he told Linda.

"I'm not following you," she said. "OK, let me give you an example," he responded. "I just read an article that reported that cities across the US are making it illegal to feed homeless people. Can you imagine it? Some people in Tampa were arrested for doing this. What if I were to go to one of these cities, buy a carton of fast food, and distribute it at a homeless shelter? Then when the cops come, I focus my *chi* and disable them."

"Actually," said Linda, "I like it. Just make sure no one gets you on video, or they'll be accusing you of witchcraft again."

Two days later, Ricky flew down to Tampa, bought $200 worth of food at McDonald's, put it all in a large carton, took a taxi over to the nearest homeless shelter, and began handing out Big Macs and fries. It took the cops—two of them—about three minutes to show up.

"Hey, pal," said one of them; "can't do that. It's illegal in this city."

"These folks are hungry," Ricky replied. "You are seriously going to prevent them from eating?"

"The law's the law," said cop #2. "Put away the food or we're going to hafta take you in."

"What if *you* were homeless and hungry?" Ricky suggested. "Wouldn't you want someone to feed *you*? The law may be the law, but it's a cruel law, don't you think? Is it so hard for you to put yourself in these people's shoes?" Cop #1 advanced toward him.

"OK," he said; "you're under arrest." Ricky pitched his *chi* at the man's chest, and he collapsed like a deflated balloon. Meanwhile, cop #2 was reaching for his gun, so Ricky brought him down as well. He then proceeded to collect their guns and their radio equipment, and put it all in the food carton. The two of them lay on the ground, breathless.

Ricky finished distributing the food, and then stood over the two cops. A small group of people from the homeless shelter had gathered near the three of them. "How the hell did you do that?" one of them asked.

"I didn't really do anything," Ricky replied. "They just suddenly collapsed. Maybe out of guilt," he added. Ricky looked down at the two of them, and felt a pool of hatred welling up inside of him. These guys are lower than dogs, he said to himself. They aren't fit to live. He had a great urge to direct a strong current of *chi* at their heads, to blow their brains out. Instead, he took a deep breath. Steady, Freddy, he told himself. He turned to the homeless folks.

"God bless you all," he said. He took the box with the guns and the radio equipment, and started walking. Eventually he came across a dumpster. He wiped the hardware clean with his T-shirt, and tossed it all into the garbage. A few minutes later he hailed a taxi, took it to his hotel, told the driver to wait, checked out, went to the airport, and flew home.

Lucky for Ricky, no one photographed or videoed the incident, but it got written up in the *Tampa Bay Times*, including interviews with the two debilitated policemen and two or three of the homeless people. "It was sort of like magic," one of the latter said. "The guy just looked at the cops and they collapsed." The cops themselves were bewildered, but also bitter. "I'm gonna find that son-of-a-bitch if it's the last thing I do," said one of them. "Who does he think he is? Robin Hood?"

Returning home, Ricky took a cab straight to Tulku's studio, and poured out the story in a big rush. "What scared me the most," he told Tulku, "was that there was a moment when I wanted to kill them. Somehow, I managed to pull back from the edge." Tulku regarded him sympathetically.

"My son," he said, "I understand your intentions, which are actually quite noble. But you are not ready for this. The man or woman who projects *chi* must always do it objectively, dispassionately. Otherwise, the remedy is usually worse than the disease. You are lucky that no one got a picture of you. For now, lay low; and if a similar urge should come over you, pay me a visit first. OK?" Ricky nodded.

"What if I could get close enough to the president to kill him?" he asked Tulku. "He's an evil man, after all."

"Yes, he is," Tulku agreed. "Only two problems: one, you'll surely get caught, and spend decades in jail; and two, he'll be replaced by the Vice President, who is also an evil man. Bad idea, in short." Ricky sighed.

"OK, I'll lay low for now. But at some point, we need to talk about the political uses of *chi*."

"You got lucky, babe," Linda said to him when he finally came home. "Just one photo and you would have wound up in the Tampa jail. Still, I can't help it: I'm proud of you. That city is sick."

"And it's not the only one. When did this country become so cruel, anyway?" Linda shrugged. "Just listen to what Tulku tells you," she advised.

---

ONE THING RICKY had discussed with Tulku was the positive use of *chi*, as he had done with the server at KFC a while back. He had softened the man's heart, caused it to expand, and the man had given him a bit of free chicken. But what about the clients of Orloff & Franklin? He had to face the fact that up to this point, the firm's only criterion for investment had been the bottom line. But some of these corporations abused and exploited their workers, and others did the same thing to the environment. He would have no trouble arranging appointments with the CEO's of these companies; but if he tried to project loving *chi* toward their hearts, would this change their behavior? Both Linda and Tulku were skeptical, but agreed with him that it was worth a try. David Orloff, on the other hand, was very nervous about this "experiment."

Two weeks later, Ricky found himself sitting across the desk of Firman J. Harkness, CEO of Big Mall Enterprises. BME had a chain of huge outlet stores around the world; their profits ran in the billions. But their labor policy was pretty much a disgrace: employees were paid minimum wage or less, when BME could get away with it, and were expected to carry out their duties like automatons. No union activity was allowed, and there was no medical coverage for employees. Pensions were effectively nonexistent. And so on. It was a clear case of corporate cruelty, as far as Ricky was concerned.

"Firman," he began, "let me start by saying that Orloff & Franklin has appreciated your business over the last couple of years, and your confidence in us." Firman smiled.

"It's been a relationship that has been beneficial to both of us," he replied.

"Indeed," said Ricky. "But I'm here today to talk with you about a sensitive subject, one which I feel it's necessary to broach." Firman's eyes narrowed; he was suddenly very wary. "OK, shoot," he said. Ricky stopped for a moment, and projected loving *chi* toward Firman's heart.

"Well, to get right down to it," Ricky went on, "you are in violation of the labor laws of a number of nations, including the United States. You are fighting numerous lawsuits. Employees have described working conditions at BME as 'barbaric'. I have here in this folder"—he held it up—"the results of investigations into BME, and it looks pretty bad." More projection of *chi*.

"Ricky," said Firman, "in spite of all the negative publicity, of which I am certainly aware, BME's profits continue to increase. Consumers don't care about any of that stuff; they just want cheap prices, and at BME, they get them. It's not clear why I should worry about these so-called humanitarian aspects of the business if the man in the street doesn't. Change him, and then I'll be open to change myself. You read me?

"Furthermore, Orloff & Franklin, no less than BME, is guided strictly by economic parameters. We make money for you, and that is surely your top priority. Giving thousands of employees medical coverage, for example, would sharply decrease our cash flow—and yours. I can't imagine you and David would be happy with that, right?" He looked earnestly at Ricky, while Ricky kept projecting *chi* into Firman's heart.

"Firman, why don't both of our companies take a financial hit, so to speak, so as to make the treatment of these people fair, and if I may say so, decent?"

"Rick, our employees are not slaves or serfs. They are free to quit BME and go elsewhere, if they want."

"Where, amigo?" Ricky replied. "To Wal-Mart? From what I hear, it's almost as bad. The truth is that the American worker is caught in a large, impersonal, and often cruel system. BME could lead the way in changing that." Firman stared at him for a moment.

"Ricky, tell me the truth. If my answer is no, would you then remove BME from your client list? Be honest now." Ricky realized that his loving *chi* approach was a bust. It was making no difference at all.

"At this point," he replied, "I really don't know. Let me think mull it over and get back to you. In the meantime, please think about what I've said." He shook hands with Firman and left.

The positive *chi* experiment was repeated with four other major CEO's, all with the same unhappy result. He and Linda and David got together one evening to discuss the matter.

"I have to take Firman's side in this," David began. "He's absolutely right: the ideology, so to speak, of his customers is the same as his own. He's no more cruel than the average American. Remember your homeless experiment? Americans don't care if the homeless can't get fed. They don't care in the least, unless it's *they* who can't get fed. In fact, I'll venture to say that if the US government decided to shoot all the homeless people and drop their bodies in the ocean, the rest of the population wouldn't bat an eye. Or if they got paid, would probably join in the operation."

Linda spoke up. "I hope you're wrong, David, but I worry that you not might be. Sometimes I think about the women— there are almost no men—in my meditation classes. They are largely there to relax. I've talked to them on occasion about the ethical basis of Buddhism, namely the interconnectedness of all living beings. They immediately zone out; their eyes just glaze over. The truth is that their only concern is No. 1, and their kids, if they have any."

"How did we come to this?" said Ricky. "You can't just dismiss it as human nature; that's a cop out. The Scandanavian countries work to keep the gap between rich and poor as small as possible. Their social services are quite extensive, and available to all. The individual Dane, for example, thinks of more than just No. 1. I'm beginning to wonder if that server at KFC who gave me free chicken was Danish.

"I'm also concerned that positive *chi* is mostly a waste of time, and that negative *chi*, like with those cops in Tampa, is the only realistic use of it. But in terms of changing the political landscape, where does that leave us?"

"Honey," Linda responded, "if you keep knocking down nasty cops, sooner or later you'll get caught."

"So what, then? Just sink into the general apathy of the rest of the population? I'm not quite ready for that."

---

RICKY SPENT the next few days sitting in his den, brooding. I'm living in the wrong country, he said to himself. America is organized around individual initiative; it's not organized around community, or caring for others. I've done the first; I proved that I could do it. Ultimately, it wasn't that hard, because I was moving with the grain. But now I want to do the second, and I don't know how to do that in an American context. Anything loving or supportive here goes *against* the grain. With that as a goal, *chi* would seem to be irrelevant. I'm in possession of a powerful, but useless, weapon. I need to talk to Tulku.

"My son," Tulku told him, "America works if you keep your head down. Of course, I see the difference between here and Tibet, and I hardly condone what goes on in this country. But America is a lot like a totalitarian regime: if you don't bother it, it won't bother you."

"Why not return to Tibet?" Ricky asked him.

"Oh, I'm too old," Tulku replied. "My family moved here when I was ten. I'm pretty assimilated by now. Tibet might feel a bit strange. And politically speaking, it's not an easy situation, with China in control of the country."

"OK, but what should *I* do?" said Ricky. "I see what America is, and now, with a different sensibility, I am not happy with it. I'd like to change things, but I don't know how to go about it."

"Massive change is not going to happen here based on an act

of will," said Tulku. "As you know, my solution, if so it can be called, is to fish one person at a time out of the drink. You could also take that path, but I suspect that would not be enough to satisfy you." (Ricky shook his head.) "The problem is that nations, civilizations, are what they are. America will change its values, and the way it operates in the world, only when it runs out of options. Which will probably happen in your lifetime, if that's any consolation. It won't be pretty; of that I'm quite sure. But if you feel that strongly about it, you might think about relocating to Denmark, or Finland. You've got the money to do it, after all." Ricky was struck dumb by all this; he never imagined this is what Tulku would tell him.

"Emigrate! I never thought about it. I need to talk to Linda." He bowed to Tulku and left.

"Denmark? Finland? Ricky, honey, you've got to be kidding!" was her response.

"Why is that so strange an idea?" he exclaimed. "You're teaching women who care for no one but themselves, I'm operating an investment firm whose clients don't give a damn who gets hurt, cities across the country have made it illegal to feed homeless people—I mean, what the fuck, babe? With the exception of our love for each other, our lives in America are pretty much pointless. The theme of American life is 'Me, Myself, and I'. I'd like to live in a place where the people gave a damn about one another. Maybe in Denmark or Finland we would feel our lives had a larger purpose. And maybe I'd be able to use my *chi* for the good of society."

"Maybe. But we don't speak Danish or Finnish, and those languages are not easy to learn. It might be two years before I could open up a meditation center—assuming I could even get a work permit—and what would *you* do?"

"Well, maybe I could write," he replied. "Or even get a work permit and start a whole new career. Teach *chi* to children, I dunno."

"Rick, honey, this seems rather harebrained, don't you think? Why doesn't Tulku emigrate? He could probably set up shop in France, if he wanted to."

"He says he's assimilated here, and too old to make that big a change. And he's OK with fishing one person at a time out of the drink, as he put it. But I'm not OK with that. Of course, I'm grateful to him for what he did for me, but in the larger scheme of things, it really makes no difference." Linda sighed.

"I just wanna be with you, babe. Go research those two countries, and when we have enough information to talk about this whole thing intelligently, we can come to a decision. Finland! Holy Mother of God!"

---

RICKY LEFT Denmark aside for the moment and turned his attention to Finland—*Suomi*, in Finnish. The online research took him less than a week. In the categories of justice and social services, the country ranked near the top of the list, worldwide. The police were trusted; feelings of safety were very high. The same went for the judicial system and the banking system. Relatively speaking, Ricky discovered, the gap between rich and poor was not very big, and the country did not suffer from any serious poverty. Corruption and organized crime were practically nonexistent. And the philosophy of life, in sharp contrast to that of the United States, was one of interconnectedness. Tarja Halonen, who was president of Finland from 2000 to 2012, put it this way: "Every person has to work hard for themselves. But that is not always enough. You have to help your neighbors." Bruce Oreck, who was US ambassador to Finland during 2009-2016, decided to remain there after his tenure was up, calling it "a highly cooperative society, where rules matter." Again, a sharp contrast to the US. In 2018, the country ranked No. 1 in the World Happiness Report issued by the United Nations. As the Finns themselves liked to say, "living in Finland is like winning the lottery."

Education, Ricky learned, was free in Finland, and of high quality—as opposed to the US, where it was expensive, and of poor quality. The same was true of health care. Only 9 percent of the population was unemployed, and those who were employed enjoyed a high standard of living. Life expectancy had increased, the suicide rate had decreased, and the mortality rate (of the under-five age group) had also decreased. The state offered not only generous maternity leave, but paternity leave as well.

There was, however, a down side; no place on earth is utopia, after all. This included high rates of alcoholism and depression. And the climate was possibly the worst in the world: very cold, with dark gray skies, short summers, and not much sun. The place was very uniform, homogeneous; the "cult of equality" rendered many Finns passive, bereft of ambition. For foreigners, the language was an enormous obstacle, a major hindrance to having an active social life. Plus, it was quite difficult for them to get jobs, and the cost of living was pretty high.

"So what do you think?" Ricky asked Linda, after finishing his Finland "report."

"Well, my love," she replied, "you've certainly done your homework. It would seem to be a tossup. Lots of positives, obviously, but the factors of climate and language are killers, don't you think? The place is also expensive, and our finding employment sounds like it would be a long shot. I vote to stay here." Ricky nodded.

"I agree that the down side would be, for us, very down. But you know what? There's no substitute for actually being there.

I'm going to spend a month in Helsinki, get the feel of the place. OK by you?" She hugged him. "Don't forget to write."

And he didn't. It was June, so the temperature was moderate, and the days were nearly nineteen hours long. Ricky went everywhere around the city, and loved it.

"My Dearest Linda,

"I've got good news for you. Two of the major obstacles we discussed two weeks ago are seriously reduced in Helsinki. First, the town is located on the southern coast of the country, so although—the Finns tell me—the climate does suck, it's not really that bad. Second, almost all of them speak English! What a relief. You could set up a meditation studio and run it entirely in English, and the Helsinkians (if that is the right word) would attend. (Of course there is still the problem of getting a work permit. And yes, everything is quite pricey here. A hamburger costs $15.)

"One unexpected plus: the city and its environs are gorgeous. I mean really beautiful. It's 'bright' (at least in June), and the architecture is superb. One place I wandered into is called the Chapel of Silence; you'd love it. It's located in the middle of town, and yet the interior is completely quiet. I sat there meditating for half an hour, and it was sublime. Helsinki is also the design capital of the world: you see great clothes, tableware, furniture, everywhere. A kind of visual orgasm.

"My tally sheet: much better than the US. I say move.

"Love you,

R."

THE NEXT TEN years were pretty happy ones for them, in contrast to the disaster that overtook the United States (more on that in a minute). Not everything was smooth sailing, of course; it took Linda two years of bureaucratic wrangling to get a permit to open a meditation center, but as Ricky had predicted, she was able to hold classes in English. Meanwhile, both of them signed up for Finnish language classes, and were making slow but steady progress. Ricky's life took an unexpected turn when he decided to start playing the violin. He hired a member of the Helsinki Philharmonic as his teacher, and applied *chi* to his practice. Within five years he had become a virtuoso, playing in the Finnish National Orchestra, and also giving solo concerts on a weekly basis—for free. He was once again a *wunderkind*, but this time in music rather than corporate investment. The Finns loved him, and often stopped him and Linda on the street to greet them, and occasionally invite them over for dinner. People would wave to them in cafés and coffee houses; they called them "Our Americans."

Across the pond, things didn't work out so well during those ten years. The economy, based as it was on greed and selfishness, imploded. Major banks and corporations went under. It was much worse than 2008; in fact, most Americans were out of work, and out in the street. Homelessness actually became the norm. There were mass migrations, and riots for food and water (which was heavily polluted). Donald Trump cancelled the election of 2024 and declared himself president-in-perpetuity. He also declared martial law, and the Army was empowered to randomly round up, or even shoot, dissidents (the exact definition of which was never made explicit). A large concentration camp was set up in Idaho, to house anyone the government or the police didn't like, under conditions even worse than the detention centers for migrants. Muslims were a particular target for these camps; these inmates were required to wear yellow stars. First they came for the Muslims...

There was also a large-scale failure of institutions. With no money and no staff, hospitals, schools, universities, the courts, shopping malls, supermarkets, airports, bus stations, newspapers, radio stations, and TV channels—all were shut down. The electrical grid functioned only sporadically; cell phones and the Internet were kaput. Criminals in prison were all released back into society; the hospitals tossed sick people out onto the sidewalks. A 6 p.m. curfew was imposed; anyone caught outside after that time was shot, no questions asked. The entire country finally made explicit what was previously semi-hidden: it was the war of all against all. Since most Americans were armed, they began mugging each other, as well as forcing people out of their homes—until they in turn were forced out. Piles of corpses littered the street corners of every major city, and the smell of rotting flesh was everywhere. There were even rumors of cannibalism, apparently necessary in order to survive. In summary, the curtain rang down on the American experiment.

Ricky held a public concert, at which he played "Taps" on the violin, and then gave a short talk in Finnish. "My friends," he announced, "America is no more. In reality, its fate was sealed from an early date, because its entire philosophy and value-system was based on greed and selfishness and uncontrolled individualism. It refused to consider humane alternatives—what we in Finland call 'Nordic love'; indeed, it was a nation steeped in hatred, antagonism, and ruthless competition. We all know Finland has problems, but its fundamentally healthy way of life means that it could never go the way of the United States. My wife and I have applied for Finnish citizenship, and we thank you for being our friends and supporters. *Suomi!*"

At this point the crowd surged forward, and lifted the two of them up in the air. "Our Americans!" they cried, in English. It was the high point of their lives.

## 15

---

# THE GARDEN OF EARTHLY DELIGHTS

I t was only four years ago that I was the secretary to the US ambassador to Spain, but it feels like another lifetime. Both his job and mine were sinecures: we pulled down lots of cash and did very little work. I think the ambassador, Rodrigo Gómez, chose me to be his secretary because I was bilingual and wore three-piece suits, and because he understood that I understood that the most taxing part of the job was showing up at official parties and spouting meaningless drivel. At the time that he picked me for the job, I was a junior partner in a small lawfirm in Madrid. Nothing very exciting.

It was the perfect assignment for another reason as well: I was, and am, a devotee of Hieronymus Bosch. I can't begin to tell you how many hours I put in at the Museo del Prado, staring at his famous triptych, *The Garden of Earthly Delights*. My own personal library contains a large number of biographies of the man in English and Spanish, including analyses of this particular painting. Indeed, it has fascinated many, many writers and art historians since it was painted more than 500 years ago. I suppose all of them believed it contained some secret about how to live, or whatever. I include myself among the ranks of the believers, although in the end, exactly what Bosch was trying to tell us remains a matter of speculation. It could all be modern projection, for all we know.

Of course, I spent time looking at the Goyas as well; he was such a fabulous painter. But there is only drama in Goya, rather than mystery: what you see (anguish) is what you get. With Bosch, there seems to be some eternal and universal mystery hiding in the wings. I suppose it's a natural tendency for human beings to look for pattern or meaning or secrets in anything, be it art or history or politics or religion or tea leaves. Perhaps we are all cabalists at heart, looking for that magic number, that key in the lock, that will, at a stroke, explain to us what the heck we are doing on this earth. Bosch also seduced me into his world because his images are so fantastic, so dreamlike. What he does, says one critic, is "depict man's life on earth as a repetition of eternal sensual desires." The truly religious life is what's called for, Bosch is saying, but we fail again and again to live up to it. The flesh always has the last word.

In any case, it was at one of those awful cocktail parties at the US embassy that I met Virginia. She was obviously bored, standing in a corner by herself and nursing a martini. (I never did find out what she was doing at the party, or who invited her, but I also didn't care.) I don't know what possessed me—her good looks, I suppose—but I sidled up to her and said, first in Spanish and then in English, "These embassy parties are truly horrific, don't you think?" She burst out laughing.

"A kindred spirit, I see," she replied. "I never imagined I'd find one here."

"Well," I told her, "if you close your eyes, you can easily imagine that this affair is an updated version of Hieronymus Bosch." She laughed again. "But nobody's fucking, or burning in hell," she observed.

"Give it time," I suggested. (More laughter) "I suppose you're right," she said. "But do you believe in hell?"

"Well, Bosch certainly did," I replied. "Have you been to the Prado yet?" She smiled, touched my arm. "Often, my dear. I take it you are a frequent visitor yourself."

And so the conversation went. Virginia had an unusual story. She had come over to Spain a year ago with her husband, a wealthy businessman who was a lot older than her. One month later, he had a heart attack and died, leaving her a wealthy widow. For several months, she drifted. She didn't want to return to the States, but other than that, was at a loss. She found herself drawn to the Prado, and to Bosch. "I finally decided to write a book called *Sex and Death in Spanish Art*. Obviously, Bosch is going to be a big part of it, because that's what his paintings deal with."

"Why did you pick those two themes?" I asked her.

"Because I believe that sex and death, beyond anything else, govern our lives, and I think Bosch was saying that these were the two things human beings can't avoid. Even before Freud, the connection between the two was recognized. Shakespeare uses the verb 'to die' as code for having an orgasm, and the French call it *la petite mort*."

"Well," I replied, "I've been trying to decode Bosch for ages now, and here you come up with the answer. Not that I necessarily agree with you, mind you; there are so many interpretations of his work." Despite the fact that I sounded like an academic windbag, it didn't take us long to become lovers, and experience the little death.

"I want you to help me write this book," she said to me one day. "In the course of which we can explore sex and death."

"Sex I understand. But death?"

"Maybe we can kill each other and come back to life," she winked at me. I didn't know whether to laugh or run. "Let's just do sex for now," I suggested. As part of the project, Virginia insisted that we keep a single dream notebook between us, so that we could explore the dreamlike quality of Bosch's work. Death, as it turned out, showed up pretty quickly.

"I dreamt you were dying," she said, "and that I was holding you in my arms. I took out my breasts and nursed you back to life. It was my milk, and my tits, that saved you. This is not an image that occurs in Bosch, but the overall flavor of the dream was like one of his paintings."

"What do you make of it?" I asked her.

"I'm not sure," she said, "but I think that the theme is that I give you the milk of life."

"Do you like playing that role?"

"I do...it's sexual, but perhaps more maternal. I like the idea of protecting you," she mused. "Does it bother you in any way?"

"Maybe; I'm not sure. What should we do, as a next step?" I wondered. "We could act the dream out in real life," she suggested. "Do you want to suck on my nipples?"

Which I did, for about ten minutes. "Maternal, or sexual?" she asked me. "More sexual," I told her. We wound up making love, but it actually felt maternal, like she was taking care of me. "Maybe that's not good," I suggested.

"Oh yes it is, hon. Sex moves around a lot; it's not just one thing. And that's what two lovers want: a kaleidoscope, one might call it. I really believe that sex and death are the great teachers."

So for Virginia, studying Bosch was a way of exploring sex and death. But what was it for me? As I already mentioned, I was looking for guidance. Bosch depicts people doing nothing more than chasing their desires, and winding up in hell as a result. Well, that was me, pretty much; I was like the protagonist of Fellini's film *La dolce vita*. I had become a lawyer not to get rich, but just to get by. Very little I did had much purpose to it. Why I believed that Bosch, in particular, could help me with this, I have no idea. I mean, why not Kierkegaard, or Kant? I couldn't explain it. I was just convinced that if I could crack the Boschian code, so to speak, I'd know what I was doing on this earth, or what I should be doing. It had to be more than pursuing "the good life."

Of course, what Bosch was doing on this earth was quite clear: being a good Christian, and showing his fellow man, and woman, the consequences of not staying on the straight and narrow path. That was his formula. But in order to buy into it, one had to believe in hell and eternal damnation, and I didn't. As Nietzsche said, once God is dead, everything is up for grabs. *La dolce vita* is the logical consequence.

"Do you believe in fate?" Virginia asked me, out of the blue. This caught me by surprise. "Sometimes I think I do. Why do you ask?"

"Because I have this feeling that fate brought us together, but I can't figure out why. What is it we're doing together, do you think?"

"Solving major puzzles?" I suggested, winking at her. She laughed. "Yeah, that sounds about right."

What did Fellini believe we were doing on this earth? I wondered. But it was no mystery, as he stated it on numerous occasions: to love (above all), to be open to experience, and to create. Not the Boschian path, to be sure, but it worked for him. Love meant more than just eros, of course; it was eros expanded to the entire world. The man was in love with life, just as it was.

"But we can't all be Fellini," Virginia objected, when I shared these thoughts with her. "As for love, why not start small? Love just one person."

"I already do," I told her. A few days later, she moved in with me.

---

ODDLY ENOUGH, it was shortly after this that Bosch sort of faded from our lives. For Virginia, it was as though our relationship had rendered the topics of sex and death irrelevant, although why this was so was unclear. As for me, I finally came to agree with the assessment of one art historian, "that Bosch's pictures are essentially not capable of being understood, and that what they are is, in the end, the story of their interpretations." Possibly more than any other artist, I concluded, his work was a Rorschach — you could find anything you wanted in it, but these "findings" were actually reflections or projections of your own psyche. In terms of figuring out the purpose of my life, then, I was thrown back on myself.

Yet one aspect of Bosch's work stuck with me, namely the same one found in *La dolce vita*: the utter folly of human life. How was anyone who saw this, really saw it for what it was, to orient him- or herself to it? For Bosch, as a medieval figure, there was only one possible response, and that was salvation. In our own age, it took on secular forms—typically, horribly misguided ones (Fascism, communism, consumerism, etc.). For Fellini, secular salvation meant creativity, and perhaps one might say that Bosch's artwork was a big part of his salvation as well. So I was left with the obvious question: What would my salvation be? Part of this was Virginia: her nursing me back to life, in her dream, suggested that this was so. In truth, neither of us had known love prior to meeting each other, and this knowledge, more than solving major puzzles, was very likely the purpose of our union. And yet for both of us, a larger world still beckoned.

"But this is why Existentialism exists at all," she said, when I told her about what I had been thinking. "Prior to the modern age, meaning was given; you didn't have to worry about it, or invent it. Now, inventing it is the great challenge. At the end of *Nausea*, Sartre concludes that the only way to escape existential nausea is to be engaged in something, be caught up in action, in present reality. Jazz is his metaphor for this. But of course, that's only one possible solution. However," she went on, "let me ask you this: How intolerable is it for you, to live without a purpose? After all, in the Zen tradition aimlessness is regarded as its own kind of wisdom."

"What would you say *your* purpose is?" I asked her.

"This relationship," she replied; "loving you is Numero Uno in my life. Giving you my milk, taking care of you. As for the rest: like you, I'm adrift, and like you, it doesn't bother me all that much. Honey, I've been aimless most of my life. Before I met Walter, I had random affairs and did the odd secretarial job, all of which meant nothing. When I met Walter, I made a decision: I would give him my body in exchange for living a secure, comfortable life. But this too was aimless, when you think about it. Then he died, very unexpectedly, and I met you. The point is that *things happen*. My aimlessness was so vast, and so vague, that when I met you I was ready for coherence, for deep meaning. The aimlessness ultimately proved to be productive, in other words."

"And as for the other part of your life, the part without me?"

"It's aimless," she replied, "but it probably won't be aimless forever. Which is probably true for you as well."

And sure enough, the next day, an idea popped into my head, seemingly out of nowhere. I never regarded myself as especially talented as a writer, but I had, in the past, published a couple of short stories, and thought that maybe I might give workshops in creative writing. I would do them in English, for the ex-pats, and in Spanish, for the *madrileños*. I posted the information on my website, and put up flyers in the neighborhood. My plan was to give a two-day workshop every weekend. Each of these would be independent, although if students wanted to keep coming back, that would be perfectly OK.

The first workshop, in English, took place three weeks later. Two people showed up, a man and a woman in their late twenties, both Americans. The advance instructions for all students was to bring a work in progress with them, even if it was only one page. We began with introductions, and then I asked them who wanted to go first. Madeleine, the young woman, raised her hand. She had about three pages; the story was called "The Date." Half a page into it, it became clear that the real title was "The Date Gone Wrong." A guy asked her out, took her to dinner, then walked her back to her apartment. She asked him up for "coffee." Once in her apartment, they undressed and moved to the bedroom. She then described the debacle in clinical detail: how she wasn't wet enough, didn't have any lubricant on hand, how it was painful, and how the poor guy ejaculated before he could get inside her. A disaster, in short. The other student, Brad, squirmed a bit, and was obviously uncomfortable.

"OK, Madeleine," I said; "if you were the teacher here, how would you critique your story?" She shook her head.

"I'm not sure. Too much information?" she offered.

"Yes," I replied, "that might be a reasonable criticism. But let me ask you this: What do you feel is the purpose of your story? I'm guessing it's autobiographical, right?" She reddened a bit. "Yeah, it is," she answered. "It happened only last week. I just wanted to write it up."

"I'll tell you," I responded, "most fiction has autobiographical elements in it; but if it is a straight report, so to speak, then it isn't fiction. You've got to give the reader a reason to *care* about your story--the events, the characters. Brad," I said, turning to him, "what was your take on Madeleine's story?"

"I guess I had a similar reaction," he said. "It just seemed more like a memo than a story." At this point, Madeleine flared up.

"These are just typical male reactions," she declared. "I'm guessing there would be a lot of women out there who could identify with this." At which point she gathered up her notebooks and stormed out of the class. "And I want my money back," she cried, as she made her exit.

"Well, Brad, I guess we're just a couple of male chauvinist pigs." He laughed. But the next day, to her credit, I received an e-mail apology from Madeleine. "I'm sorry I overreacted," she wrote. "You're right, it wasn't really fiction, and the purpose of the piece was catharsis—which hardly qualifies as literature. I'm going to try to rewrite it, and will be back next weekend, if that's OK."

This impressed me; I didn't think she had it in her. Next week, however, was the Spanish workshop, so I asked Madeleine to come back in two weeks.

The Spanish workshop—three people this time—was happily bereft of any drama. One man, about forty-five, came in with a poem instead of a story; the problem was that it was too close to the work of Antonio Machado. We discussed the problem of imitation, how to avoid it and so on, and in general it was a good class. A week after that, Madeleine was back, along with Brad and two new students, both female, around thirty-five. It turned out that they were sisters. Brad's stuff was rather pedestrian: how a fight broke out at a football match, and how he got a black eye while trying to break it up.

"Brad," I said, "I need to say to you what I said to Madeleine: this seems like straight autobiography. Can anyone tell me what the difference is between fiction and nonfiction?" The other two students perked up. Francesca raised her hand.

"This is just a guess," she proposed rather modestly, "but I think a real short story has to have a curve ball in it."

"Curve ball?" I enquired.

"Yes, you know: a twist, something unexpected. I mean, you can see this quite clearly in the work of O. Henry or Saki (H.H. Munro). I would kill to be able to write a story like 'Sredni Vashtar'." (A story by Saki in which a polecat ferret kills a boy's nasty caretaker)

Madeleine spoke up. "Mr. Perez, I changed my story so that

the guy, at the moment of truth, reveals that he's gay." I laughed. "Well, that would definitely qualify as a curve ball," I told her.

Amy, Francesca's sister, read her three-page story about a schoolgirl who was constantly ridiculed for being a nerd, and then as an adult became a popular clothing designer. This enabled her to make her way into the fashionable circle of her former abusers. She then invited them all to dinner at her house, and poisoned them. Meanwhile, her boyfriend rented a U-Haul van, and the two of them piled the six corpses into it, drove to the middle of the city's major bridge at 3 a.m., and dumped the bodies into the river. "I take it that's a curve ball, yes?" she asked me.

"More like wish-fulfillment," observed Madeleine. "I think I saw it coming." A heated discussion followed. All in all, it was a very successful class.

Meanwhile, a kind of curve ball arose in the class itself. I was attracted to Francesca, and she must have sensed this, because over time her outfits became increasingly revealing—along with her stories. In one, a young woman in her thirties is shipwrecked on an island, and starts dreaming about a man who shows up out of nowhere. His features are human, but he's actually an avatar. He impregnates her, and she gives birth to a baby who is half Martian. The story ends with her trying to decide whether to live on Earth or on Mars.

"It's just not believable," said Brad. "I couldn't identify with it."

"But no sci-fi is truly believable," Amy countered. "It's really a metaphor for something else. As in the work of Ursula Le Guin, for example."

" *Is* it a metaphor for something else?" I asked Francesca.

"Sure," she admitted. "I'm lonely. I'd like to have a man in my life. But I'm afraid something weird will happen--it always does, in relationships. I never had a relationship that didn't have a curve ball in it." Everybody laughed. I felt that Francesca's little speech might have been directed at me, but I showed no emotion. "Any other reactions?" I asked the class.

"This is a good story," said Madeleine. "It makes you think, about a lot of things."

"I agree," I said. "Francesca, see if you can't flesh it out a bit more. It's a tad too compressed right now, I'm thinking." She flashed me a big smile.

And then something weird started happening in the English workshops that got everyone spooked. Many years ago I had a college roommate who began to have prescient dreams. He would dream, for example, the outcome of a baseball game that was going to take place the next day, and guess what? The prediction was correct. The two of us began placing small bets on boxing matches, football games, tennis matches, and so on, and we always won. Finally, he had a dream about a winning racehorse, against whom the odds were 20:1. My whole life savings at that point was about $1,000, and I bet it all on that horse. The next day I went up to the ticket window and took away 20K in a paper bag. But that ended it, for me; I decided to quit while I was ahead. Roger, my roommate, continued betting, and currently lives in a mansion on Mallorca, with twelve servants, two Porsches, and four girlfriends, all of whom are ex-models. This was definitely the garden of earthly delights.

Anyway, the English workshop was joined by a British gentleman of about sixty-five, who had the ability to do the same thing in his stories. Except that the stories were not concerned with sports predictions, but with disasters. It started with a story about a seven-car crackup in downtown Madrid, for which he provided exact details, including the number of people who were killed. The accident took place the very next day. Thirteen days later, he not only predicted Trump's victory, but named all of the swing states that got him elected. As everyone, myself included, was getting nervous, I felt I had to confront him during the next class.

"Frank," I said, "you've got all of us a bit jumpy. I have to ask: How are you managing to predict the future?"

"The information actually comes to me in dreams," he replied. "Then I write it up as short stories. But I'll be damned if I know how or why I'm getting the info. Years ago, I went to a psychic who told me that I had a very rare condition of a split psyche, wherein half of it lived in this world and the other half inhabited the astral plane—the dream world, as it were. For example, I know what's going to happen to Francesca and Amy."

The two girls started, were suddenly very frightened. "Don't worry, my dears," he told them; "it's actually quite good. But I won't tell you if you prefer I didn't." Amy and Fran looked at each other. "Better not to know," said Amy. Francesca disagreed. They argued for about ten minutes, while the rest of us sat there as bewildered spectators. Amy finally gave in.

"OK," said Frank; "here goes. At some point during the next month, a man of about your ages will join the workshop. Both of you will want him for yourselves, and will fight bitterly over him. He will sleep with both of you, several times, until the two of you declare a truce and ask him to join you in a *ménage*. The three of you will be married, so to speak, for more than twenty years."

The two girls stared at him, starstruck. "You can't possibly know this," Fran finally said. "It's just not possible." Frank just shrugged.

"Well, sure, I could be wrong. After all, my previous predictions have all been about disasters. This one is just the opposite. But all the information I have says that you're going to be very happy gals."

"I bet he's right," interjected Madeleine. "Me too," said Brad. I kept quiet, but I thought the same.

And it all came to pass, more or less as Frank had predicted.

The man's name was John Baker, he swept the two girls off their feet, and within a month the three of them were living together. "I'm quitting the group," Francesca announced; "I got what I came for."

"Me too," said Frank; "my work here is done."

"Work?" I exclaimed. "What work?" But Frank just smiled, shook his head, and walked out the door. The workshop once again consisted of two people.

"Well knock me down with a feather," was Madeleine's response. There really wasn't much more to say.

I had, of course, kept Virginia up to date on what was happening all along. When the *ménage* finally took place, and Frank and the girls left with John, she hugged me and said, "Well, my workshop hero, how's your purpose doing these days?"

"Ginny," I replied, "this is no joking matter. My experience with Roger, as incredible as it was, was nothing compared to this. This is from fucking Mars. How am I supposed to go on, leading a quiet domestic life, after this?"

"What choice do you think you have, exactly?" she pointed out.

"Doesn't any of this faze you?" I asked her.

"Not really. It's no more fantastic than Bosch, when you get right down to it. Julio, I never believed that science had it all wrapped up. Our 'reality' has loopholes in it, and you've now run across this phenomenon twice. Why not just be happy for Fran and Amy?" I sighed.

"Oh well," I replied; "what's been going on with your aimlessness during this time?"

"*Nada,*" she said, "but that's OK. I've been enjoying your paranormal adventures vicariously, which is enough for now."

---

WE SETTLED INTO OUR ROUTINES. My workshops continued, without any supernatural interference; I occasionally suffered through a party at the embassy; Virginia started taking classes to improve her Spanish; and our love life continued to make us happy. For some reason, after the whole paranormal episode with Frank, I stopped feeling my life was aimless, though I was hard put to say what its purpose was, if indeed there was one. In fact, when I thought about it, ordinary daily life seemed like a miracle.

"My sister wants to come and stay with us for a month," Virginia suddenly announced one day.

"Your sister? How is it that you never told me you had a sister?" I was a bit angry.

"I dunno," she said; "I guess the subject never came up. Anyway, her name is Angeline, she's an artist, she lives in Chicago, and she says she misses me. She also wants to meet you." I was nonplussed.

"OK, sure," I replied. "I just think you could have told me earlier."

"I'm sorry, hon. She just wasn't a big part of my life until Walter died. She had been working as a paralegal; I sent her enough money so she could quit her job and devote herself to her art." I cooled off a little.

"What kind of art?" I asked.

"Oils, acrylic, watercolor," said Virginia. "She's not half bad, but she never managed to break into the galleries."

"Is she married?"

"Lived with a guy for five years. Arthur, an architect. I met him only once. That ended about six months ago. He left her for another woman. I don't think she's over it, yet."

Angeline arrived two weeks later. She was four years younger than Virginia, and just as attractive: long dark hair, large brown eyes, a pretty face with freckles, and a prominent chest. Not clear to me why any guy would leave her, but then looks aren't everything.

"I'm so happy to meet you, Julio," she said at the airport. "I think you've transformed Virginia's life."

"And she, mine," I replied. "We're happy you will be staying with us." Of course, we took her to the Prado to see the famous triptych, which she found fascinating, and then had lunch at an outdoor café near the museum. "You guys sure seem happy," she remarked. "I'd like to paint the two of you together, if you'd be up to it."

"I guess..." I said. "Sure," added Virginia.

"Don't agree too fast," said Angeline. "I'd like the two of you to pose in the nude." She smiled.

"Angie, are you nuts?" countered Virginia. "We're not going to pose for you in the nude. You can paint us with our clothes on." Angeline looked at me. "Julio, what do you think?" At this point, Virginia interrupted her.

"Julio, don't you dare say yes. My sister has flipped out."

"I'm just curious as to *why* you want to paint us in the nude," I asked her. "Is this something you've done with other couples?"

"Yeah, one time," said Angelina, "and it was at their request. They commissioned it. They were just married, and wanted something to celebrate the event. They weren't fucking or anything like that, when they posed, but what came out was a very sexual painting. I charged them two grand, and they were only too happy to pay it. Honestly, I wish I had kept the painting; it's one of the best things I've ever done."

"Well," I said, "I'll be happy to pay you two grand, but I'd prefer that we keep our clothes on. Angeline shook her head. "Virginia will probably be upset with me —"

"Angie, please stop!" Virginia exclaimed. "This is way over the line."

"Gin, just listen to me for a second. You wrote me, more than once, that sex with Julio was the deepest experience of your life. I'd like to capture that on canvas. The two of you would be standing side by side, just holding hands. There would be nothing salacious or prurient about it. I just feel this could be my best work, ever." The two of them argued for the next twenty minutes; I stayed out of it. Finally, Virginia looked directly at me.

"OK, hon, what's your vote on this?" I nodded slowly. "Your sister is onto something," I told her. "I can feel it. I say let's give her a chance."

The result was absolutely uncanny. The painting literally glowed. What Angie had captured, without realizing it, was the "milk" aspect of our love—the maternal angle of Virginia as my caretaker as well as my lover. At the same time, Ginny's face was radiant: a woman fulfilled. I was struck dumb.

"It's a masterpiece, Angie. This is exactly our relationship. I don't know how you did it, but you did." Virginia hugged her sister; she was practically weeping.

"The painting belongs to you," Angie said to us, "and I don't want you to pay me anything for it. But I'd like you to lend it to me for a while, so I can enter it in a gallery competition being held in Chicago next month." We agreed.

"What will you call it?" I asked her. She smiled.

"No Ordinary Love."

JUST TO FAST-FORWARD FOR A MOMENT: the painting became a chapter in the history of art. It won the gallery competition, and then was on display at the Art Institute of Chicago for six months; after which a wealthy collector offered Angie half a million dollars for it. The three of us agreed, on one condition: we could view the painting whenever we wanted to. The new owner, who lived in New York, was happy to oblige. Angie signed the contract, and he wired the money into her bank account. "It's yours," Virginia and I told her; "go take a holiday in the south of France."

To return to present time: one night Virginia went to bed early, and Angie and I stayed up, talking and drinking cognac. "Julio," she said, "I already love you like a brother. I have to tell you, I'm envious of what you and Ginny have. You guys are so lucky to have found each other."

"What happened with the architect, if you don't mind my asking?" She immediately got teary.

"Oh...I think I fucked up, really. I was a fool. I hope it's OK to tell you this. I don't know what Gin is like in bed, although I do know that she makes you happy. The problem with Arthur was that he was very experimental, or wanted to be, whereas I'm rather conservative in that department. I really don't know how we lasted five years. He would pressure me to do certain things, and I would resist. Finally, inevitably, he found a girl who gave him what he wanted. If only I had been just a bit more yielding, more flexible, we'd still be together." She started to cry.

"Angie, you're very pretty, very talented, and very smart. Sooner or later you'll find a guy with whom you're sexually compatible."

"Do you really think so?" she asked me, between the tears.

"I'm sure of it. Jesus, just look at you. You're gorgeous." She blushed.

"Nah..."

"No need for modesty, honey, and no need to envy your sister. The right guy is out there."

"You're terrific, Julio. I see why Ginny is mad about you." We talked some more. I was, indeed, attracted to her, but sleeping with your partner's sister was a good way to fuck up your life, so I kept it platonic. I told her the story of Frank, and how he wrote stories that predicted the future. And Virginia's reaction to it all.

"She's absolutely right," Angie remarked. "There's a quality of intuition in art, for example, that objective science can never capture. Just look at my painting of the two of you. You and Gin admit that I got to the essence of your relationship. Well, that wasn't the result of objectivity." I got up to go to bed; Angie came over and kissed me. "Better not, honey." I gave her a squeeze, then let her go. But the kiss lingered in my mind.

---

MY LIFE SEEMED to be one earthquake after another. Rodrigo Gómez called me into his office and announced that he was planning to retire. "I've had enough of the diplomacy game," he informed me. "I'm quite wealthy by now, and I want to move to Cadaqués, and sit on my porch and watch the sun set. I've written the State Department nominating you as my successor." I reacted as though he had hit me over the head with a wooden plank.

"Rodrigo, you can't be serious. I know very little about diplomacy. My appointment would be a disaster."

"What's to know?" he said. "You throw a lavish party once a month; you meet with the prime minister twice a year; and on the subject of Catalonian separatism, you keep your mouth shut. In return for that, you get to live in a mansion, have a limo and a driver and a cook and several other servants, and gradually become a millionaire. What do you say?"

"Let me talk it over with Virginia," I told him, "and I'll get back to you."

"Fine," he replied. "You've got three days."

"Ambassador?" she fairly shouted. "Are you kidding me?"

Angeline was still with us during this time. "I say do it!" she cried. "And I'll come live with you." (That, of course, made me nervous.)

"Julio," said Virginia, "our life is just fine as it is. It's a private life, and it suits us very well. This would be a public life, and as you're pretty much an introvert, you wouldn't be happy with it. Plus, I'm sure the US government has the place bugged, and would listen in on our lovemaking."

"There are technology companies that can sweep a place free of bugs," I told her. "I'd have them in once a month."

"Not the point. We don't need servants and a limo and a million dollars. Are you really sure you want to do this?"

I had to fly to Washington, interview with the State Department, and go through a Senate confirmation hearing. It wasn't hard: I knew more about Spain, and the job, than all of them put together. When I flew back to Madrid, Virginia and Angelina met me at the airport.

"Welcome home, Ambassador," said Ginny. "We read the news online." I hugged both of them. Over the next week, we moved out of our apartment and into a large, luxurious mansion. Angie came with us. Gin was only too happy to have her, and I couldn't possibly object, although the arrangement had me seriously worried. I remembered the kiss, and I was certain that Angie was in love with me. Fuck.

Meanwhile, to keep up appearances, Ginny and I got married. A small, quiet ceremony at the courthouse, with Angie and Rodrigo as witnesses. Gin was really happy. "I'm going to give you such a fucking tonight," she whispered in my ear.

And the job was largely pro forma, as Rodrigo had said. Sure, there were official duties, but they didn't take up that much time. As things heated up in Catalonia, I told reporters that the US government was taking a neutral position "at this time." In truth, my biggest worry was Angie. One afternoon, while Ginny was out shopping, I asked her to sit down with me in the living room.

"Angie, honey, I think you know that if I had met you first, I'd probably be married to you rather than Ginny. But things are as they are, and I love your sister very much. I don't want to hurt her, and I don't want to screw up our marriage." She nodded several times while I was talking.

"Julio, the problem for me is that I'm in love with you. Yes, I know I'm very needy, and that I'm still raw from Arthur and the whole sex thing. But that is neither here nor there. I see, very clearly, why Ginny loves you, and I love you for the same reasons. So what am I supposed to do?"

"For one thing," I replied, "you could move back to Chicago." She shook her head.

"No, this is where intuition comes into play. I'm sure that spiritually speaking, my home is now here."

"In that case," I said, "I want you to enroll in Spanish classes, and start socializing with the natives, so to speak. Mooning over me can only make you sick. If you become fairly fluent, you'll meet a nice guy and it will work out for you. And also, think about getting your own apartment. Ginny would certainly be willing to pay the rent on it, if you told her you needed to live by yourself." She was quiet for a moment, thinking it over.

"I know you're right," she finally said. "Your loyalty to Virginia only makes me love you more. I do want to remain here, but I'll do the other things you ask. I know I owe it to my sister."

We left it at that. I wanted to kiss her again, but I also didn't want to. In the days that followed, Angie selected a room to serve as her studio, and went into town to buy art supplies. As long as she's holed up there, I thought to myself, I won't have to interact with her; although breakfast and dinner as a threesome was a regular ritual. If Ginny suspected any kind of vibe was going on between Angie and myself, she didn't let on.

And so the days passed quite pleasantly. I rented a room in town to continue holding my writing workshops; now that I was an ambassador, it was typical to have thirty or more students in attendance. Some of them were outstanding, writing stories that were far better than anything I could produce. I used my connections to get the especially good ones published in literary journals.

The next "earthquake" that arose was when the State Department wanted me to get my portrait painted, and suggested that my sister-in-law be hired for the job. Nuts. I couldn't refuse—Gin would be upset if I hired anyone else. So I sat in Angie's studio, while she filled up the canvas with oil paint. There was only one problem with the result: no one who saw this painting would have any doubt that the artist was in love with her subject; and of course, Ginny was among the first to see it. She had a serious sit-down with her sister.

"Ange, I need to know the truth: Are you sleeping with Julio?"

"Gin, honestly, nothing ever happened between us, I swear. Julio is completely honorable; he would never betray you, and he hasn't."

"But *you* would betray me, right?" Angie started to cry, shake her head. "Gin, I can't help what I feel, any more than you can. But I can control my actions, and I have."

"For how long?" asked Virginia. "It's like we're sitting on a powder keg. The guy is only human, after all."

"But I rarely see him," Angie objected. "The portrait painting was a one-shot deal. There won't be any more."

"Angie, you see him at breakfast and dinner every day. Where does that leave us, really? And what does Julio say about all this?"

"He asked me to take Spanish classes, to mingle socially, and to trust that I'll find a man," she replied.

"Pretty good advice, I'd say," Ginny responded. "Have you taken it?"

"Yes," said Angie, "I've started the process."

"Well, keep it going. In the meantime, please don't fuck things up for us. I'm asking you as the sister who loves you. It would be a disaster that none of us would be able to recover from." Angie nodded her assent.

Now that things were out in the open, breakfast and dinner were a bit awkward, but we did the best we could. It was perhaps hardest on Ginny; I really admired her strength. One night, after making love, she said to me, "We've really got to get that girl laid." I chuckled. "Good idea," I said. "Do you know any guys at work you could fix her up with?" she asked me.

"A few," I replied, "but they are bureaucrats, would probably be kinda dull for Angie's taste. She needs more than a dick inside her; she needs to fall in love. This crush on me is just a rebound from Arthur. She needs to meet someone she can really admire." Ginny sighed.

"Julios don't grow on trees, my friend. She may be waiting a long time. Sweetheart, promise me you won't sleep with her. I think it would kill me." I kissed her, and we made love again.

Sad to say, the story didn't have a happy ending — at least, not in the immediate future. Months went by; Angie's Spanish got fairly good, and she went to various mixers and parties. The result was zero. "She can't meet anybody because she's in love with *you*," Ginny declared. I feared she was right. In the end, Angie decided to return to Chicago. She looked like a wounded bird, and my heart ached for her. Really, she was an innocent, she had done nothing wrong, and life had thwarted her search for happiness. I was depressed for weeks after she left. Ginny was relieved, of course, but she too felt bad for her sister. They didn't correspond much after that.

---

"HOW ARE we doing in the aimlessness department?" Ginny asked me sometime after that.

"You tell me, babe," I responded.

"I love it when you call me 'babe'," she said.

"You're dodging the question," I told her.

"Honey, I'm still in shell shock from the whole thing with Angie. I feel we came perilously close to a major disaster. It's very hard to resist an attractive woman who is madly in love with you, after all. My aim was to protect my marriage."

"And now?"

"Now...as an ambassador's wife, I guess I have no aims other than being an ambassador's wife. If I'm not a lot happier a year from now, I want you to seriously consider giving up the job."

"OK," I said; "that's a fair request."

But as it turned out, Virginia did find a purpose, and it was writing a book. Not the one she had originally planned, on sex and death, but rather a series of vignettes, many of them episodes from her own life. One was on marrying a man for his money, and how depressed she eventually became as a result. Another was a revealing one on how she learned to relax around sex, become less inhibited. Then there was a vignette on Bosch, and his importance in her life. A fourth was on Angie's painting of us, "No Ordinary Love," and on Angie's portrait of me. (In the case of this last vignette, she sent Angie the draft, for her permission. Angie agreed, but insisted that Virginia not say much beyond her discovery of Angie's love for me, and the fear it provoked in her (Virginia).) There were essays on the parks of Madrid, and the city's architecture, and two on her childhood—growing up in Chicago. Changing the names, she told the story of paranormal Frank, and how he upended my workshop. There was even one on aimlessness. I read through the entire manuscript.

"Wow!" I said when I finished with it. "Honey, these are beautiful. I can't believe how well you write, and how fascinating all these stories are." She smiled broadly.

"And it will be a best-seller," she added. "Know why? Because I'm the wife of the American ambassador." I shook my head.

"Only partly," I said. "The talent here speaks for itself. These essays are page-turners. I'm going to get Javier Mariano to review it for *El País*, and I myself am going to translate it into Spanish. It will definitely be the book of the season."

Which is how it turned out, especially when the Spanish edition was published. With myself acting as interpreter, Ginny appeared on all the popular radio and television shows. It was mostly women who called in:

-"How did you get out of your marriage to the rich guy?"

-"How can I learn to relax around sex, and please my boyfriend more?"

-"How did you deal with your sister's love for your husband?"

-"How was 'Bob' able to predict the future?"

-"I too am aimless; how can I find purpose in my life?"

Ginny was a hit, not so much because she was my wife, but because her essays spoke to the human condition. She struck responsive chords across the human spectrum, especially with women, and her audiences regarded her as a guru, of sorts. Her face was splashed across the front cover of popular Spanish magazines. It also helped that she spoke a decent Spanish by now, and often answered the questions directly, without myself acting as an intermediary. The country fell in love with her. They were proud of her admiration of parks, architecture, Bosch, and Goya. She even did an essay on George Orwell's *Homage to Catalonia*, and the Spanish civil war. For that book season, at any rate, she was the nation's darling.

Of course I hosted a "Virginia evening" at the embassy; the *haute monde* showed up in full force. Combined Spanish and English sales of the book exceeded one million copies during the first six months of publication. It took a while for the hullabaloo to die down, which it never did completely.

I think the funniest episode during "Virginia fever" times was a popular women's TV program on sexuality, "El poder de la vagina" (Vaginal Power). Prime time on Thursday nights; more than half the female population of Spain regularly tuned in. Virginia decided to field this one without me, which was just as well. Where she got the answers to the questions posed to her by Mariana Medina, the show's host, I have no idea. It went something like this:

MM: Virginia, since the publication of your book, have lots of men tried to sleep with you?

VP (Virginia Perez): Mariana, you have no idea. I need to walk around with a sign around my neck, with just one word on it: ¡OLVIDALO! (Forget it!). It's really all about conquest for men, and women know this. That's why they wear stiletto heels.

MM: I'm lost. Why do women wear stiletto heels?

VP: The heels signal sophistication, power. If a woman goes to bed with a man, especially wearing high heels, it means she has surrendered her power to him. He has his conquest, and this excites them both.

MM: Do you and the ambassador do that, then?

VP: On occasion. But what these women don't understand is that sex should be many things, like a kaleidoscope. There is lots to explore beyond games of dominance and submission. For example, there is also a maternal aspect to it, which is very tender. My marriage works because, among other things, both Julio and I are into psychological variety. Too many men and women tend to think one-dimensionally, which is why the relationship fails, in the long run. The whole thing gets boring, and the two of them start to look elsewhere, outside the bonds of matrimony. I recently read that in the United States, something like 50 percent of husbands and 40 percent of wives have committed adultery. It may be less in Spain, but I bet the percentages are still high.

MM: Tell us what happened with your sister.

VP: I really can't say too much. It was difficult for a while, because she fell in love with Julio, but what woman wouldn't?

Julio is not merely a talented diplomat; he's also a charismatic human being. My life turned completely upside down when I met him. The American expression is, "I hit the jackpot." And I think he feels he did as well.

MM: How does Bosch fit into all this? I understand you originally planned to write a book about him.

VP: Bosch understood what life was about, namely sex and death. Sex is not very far from most people's minds. Why do you think your show has the ratings it does? Because it's a no-holds-barred discussion of sex. High heels, dominance and submission, oral sex, anal sex, threesomes, sex in public places, garter belts—nothing is taboo on this show. One can say you too hit the jackpot. (Mariana laughed.)

MM: And death?

VP: Oh, Mariana, that would take hours to unpack. But let me just say this: death is, in addition to sex, the crucial fact of life, because it teaches us impermanence. Everything passes, including ourselves. To understand the significance of that—well, William Blake said the one who can do that "lives in eternity's sunrise."

MM: Let me give you a hug, Virginia. What a pleasure it's been, to have you on the show. By the way, what's next on your agenda?

VP: I haven't the faintest idea. (They both laugh.)

(Just a ps: As a result of the show, the sale of stiletto shoes went through the roof.)

I hugged her when she came through the door. "My God, Ginny; with your endorsement, I should probably run for political office. That was quite a show. How did you get to be so brilliant?"

"Easy, amigo: hanging out with you."

"Feel like slipping on your high heels?" I winked at her.

"I can't think of anything I'd rather do," she replied.

VIRGINIA and I were eventually offered a half-hour TV show called "Felicidad" (Happiness). It aired once a week, and was almost as popular as "Vaginal Power." It would start off with a ten-minute discussion between the two of us on some subject related to happiness—say, taking your kids to the zoo, or reading great poetry aloud—and then taking phone calls from the viewers. The show continued for a while even after I was relieved of my post. I suspect my self-sabotage was deliberate. First, I criticized the government's austerity program, which was a source of misery for millions, and led to rioting in the streets. Plus, Virginia and I donated half a million euros for hunger relief. The State Department was unhappy with both of these actions, and even more so when I, speaking as a private citizen, came out in support of the separatist movement in Catalonia. I was quickly replaced by a government lackey who toed the "correct" line. For my part, I couldn't care less, and Virginia was overjoyed. We moved out of the ambassadorial mansion, out of the limelight, and bought a house in Cadaqués. The era of fame and the "power couple" was over.

"Well. hon," I said, "we've had quite a run, don't you think? Frankly, aimlessness sounds pretty good right about now." Virginia nodded in agreement.

"CONGRATULATIONS you guys," wrote Angeline; "I'm really happy for you. Meanwhile, get this: I met a guy! Yes! And he's teaching me to be a lot more flexible." To this she appended a winking emoticon.

"I guess there *is* a God," was Ginny's only comment.

Like Rodrigo, the two of us sat on our porch every evening, and watched the sun set. "I finally figured out what happiness is," I remarked. "A pity we never discussed it on the show."

"OK," she said, "I'll bite. What is happiness?"

"A blank agenda book." She laughed, and gave me a long kiss.

# 16

## AUTHENTICITY

Every girl needs a heroine; for me, it was the Spanish artist Remedios Varo, when I was fifteen. One painting in particular caught my eye: *Breaking the Vicious Circle*. It showed the artist breaking out of a metal ring, or wire—an escape to freedom. Looking at her other paintings, which I found in library books, I realized that she was mapping her evolution to this point, starting from being trapped in a Catholic upbringing. She was living an inner rebellion against all that mindless conformity, which eventually became an outer rebellion. But her life was more than just iconoclasm; it was also the slow evolution toward an authentic self. All this to me was true womanhood; it was what I aspired to as well.

How did we do it? In my case, liberation came in the form of a boy in my class, Bobby Sullivan, who would walk me home from school and tell me that Catholicism was "a pack of lies." "Honestly, Joanne, who could believe in the virgin birth, stigmata, resurrection of the dead, and all that stuff? You'd hafta be a moron." My attraction to Bobby, at age sixteen, made all of this easier to accept, and the Church's hostility to sexuality was a further point against it, in my mind. As time went on, our after-school walks took a detour into a park, where we would neck for ten or fifteen minutes before resuming our walk. Eventually, I let Bobby finger me, and the pleasure was so intense that I knew that the Church had to be wrong. A pack of lies, as Bobby had said. Sometime later, I lost my virginity in the back seat of his car (borrowed from his parents).

Remedios, of course, had a number of lovers during her lifetime, and I was sure that for her, as for me, sexual fulfillment was tied to her search for authenticity. What could be more authentic than an orgasm? In any case, the nuns finally kicked me out of school, much to my parents' chagrin, telling them that I was "impure," and might corrupt the other students. ("Impure is good," was Bobby's reaction to this.)

As I got older, I began to realize that there was a larger issue hanging over all of this. Authenticity—which meant breaking away from group norms in favor of one's inner convictions—had a serious down side: isolation. Groups are generally hostile to mavericks, so the road to authenticity is inevitably a lonely one. The satisfaction comes from being courageous, and being right: after all, who in their right mind could believe in the virgin birth?

For many of those in a group, however, conformity means comfort rather than claustrophobia: safety in numbers, that sort of thing. But whether one chooses conformity or rebellion, the fact is that there is a price to be paid either way. For me, as for Remedios, the choice was clear: the price of group protection was the extinction of the self. She wasn't having it, and neither was I.

However, if you are going to be a rebel, it helps to have a goal you are moving toward, beyond "authenticity." For Remedios, it was to be an accomplished artist. I had no equivalent to this, and hence I was kind of lost. Trysts in Bobby's car were fine, but sex can hardly be a life goal. And so, as a young woman of seventeen or eighteen, I could see that there were limits to having Remedios as a role model.

My parents, of course, wanted to find another school for me, and wanted me to go to college; but I wasn't interested in formal education. They had a bit of cash stashed away in a crockery jar that I was not supposed to know about; on my eighteenth birthday, I stole the money and set out from home, leaving only a brief note of explanation and apology. My backpack was stuffed with clothing, toiletries, and a copy of *The Denial of Death*, by Ernest Becker. I knew it wasn't a good idea for a single girl to hitchhike, but I made it out to San Francisco without an incident.

A few days later, sitting in the Cafe Flore on Market Street, I asked one of the waitresses if they were looking to hire anybody. June was a friendly type, and thanks to her I was hired the very next day. June was also looking for a roommate, so I moved in with her, and we split the rent (or so I thought; it turned out she was actually paying 80 percent of it). Things were going much better than I expected.

But as time went on, I began to realize that the arrangement had certain drawbacks. The first of these was that the walls of the apartment were very thin, and June was visited by her boyfriend two or three times a week. At least she warned me in advance: she and Sam were into S&M, so I shouldn't get scared by what I heard coming from the adjoining room. It turned out that June had had a Catholic upbringing as well, but in her case she bought the propaganda: sex was a sin. Hence, she could only obtain sexual satisfaction by first being punished, which Sam provided for her in the form of a wooden paddle applied to her bare rear end. I once counted twenty strokes, after which June was sobbing. He then put her on her back and fucked her until she came, which was almost immediately. She did offer to "lend" me

Sam for a session, but I had no interest in acquiring a sore rear end.

"He can just fuck you, if you want," June offered, but I still turned it down. "Wouldn't you be jealous," I asked her, "listening to the sounds coming from my room?" She shook her head. "Sam and I aren't monogamous," she replied. "We both are free to hook up with other people." Still, it wasn't something I wanted to get involved in.

The second drawback was a bit more serious. It just so happened that Sam was part of San Fran's criminal underworld. He had done two years in prison for forging checks; after his release, he got into smuggling cocaine up from Mexico. June was his "mule"; she would insert packets of cocaine into her vagina, and bring them across the border. A tricky business, but so far she hadn't been caught.

"My work at the Flore," she explained to me, "is just a front. It pays peanuts, compared to selling coke, but it serves as a convenient cover for being in the drug business. The thing is, Joanne, I need you to help us out. My vagina is only so big; Sam and I could double our sales if you agreed to work as a mule as well. And in no time, I should add, you'd be sitting on a pile of dough."

"Too risky," I told her; "if I got caught, I'd wind up in jail."

"Joanne, what do you think the rent on this place is?" she asked me.

"$400, and I pay half. Why do you ask?"

"Because it's actually a thousand, and I'm paying $800. I could carry you for a month, but from now on we'll need to split it, and your wages and tips at the Flore are not going to cut it. I'm sorry to put it like this, but if you won't work for us, you're going to have to leave."

I was flabbergasted; the whole thing—job, apartment, "friendship"—had been a setup. "Let me think about it," I said.

While all this was going on, I was involved in an ongoing flirtation with a guy who dropped by the Flore almost every day. He was about thirty years old, a professor of music at San Francisco State, and terribly good looking. He was very soft-spoken, and had a way about him that was very engaging. On our first date he took me to a small Italian restaurant in North Beach, and it was all very romantic. He talked about his interest in music, and his own specialty—the Renaissance. David actually owned a lute, and knew how to play the harpsichord. I expected him to invite me over to his place to listen to some music, as a prelude to lovemaking, but he was very restrained—a real gentleman, not in a rush. After dinner, he drove me back to my apartment, walked me to the door, and kissed me. I gave him a deep French kiss; I wanted him to know that I was available.

Finally, the day of reckoning came with June, and I realized I had no choice. She and Sam put me on a bus to Tijuana, and gave me the address of their coke dealer, Juan Cortado (obviously an alias). Juan's girlfriend, "Ramona," showed me how to insert the packets of coke into my vagina, but insisted I stay over a couple of days; returning the very next day might look suspicious. So I went back to the US two days later, crossing the border without incident, and delivered the sticky packets of white powder to June. For this, she paid me $1,500 in cash, from which she subtracted $500 for the next month's rent. It was official: I was a criminal.

I was now leading a double life. Every three weeks I would make the run to Tijuana. Meanwhile, I was dating a college professor, who probably thought I was some version of Snow White. On our third date, David and I slept together, and while I didn't come, it was very pleasurable. The guy certainly knew how to use his hands and mouth. Renaissance music played in the background; I began to associate sex with John Dowland and William Byrd.

But I did have the sensation that I was playing with fire; that sooner or later, I would get strip-searched coming back to the US. And I didn't like the fact that I was hiding what I was doing from David, but I was sure he would dump me if I told him. I couldn't quit the mule business, because I needed the money to pay the rent, and in addition, San Fran was getting as expensive as Paris or Tokyo. And I was damned if I was going to give David up: he was a real find, and made me happy. I could only quit the mule business if I moved in with him; but his apartment was small, and I could tell he liked living alone. So for the time being, there was no escaping the double life.

One other thing nagged at me: my search for authenticity had gone by the boards. How did this happen? I started out with Ernest Becker in my backpack, and wound up as a dope smuggler, hiding my shady life from a guy who was, for all I knew, in love with me. Was I leading David on? I loved the dinners, the music, and the sex, but push come to shove, I wasn't really gaga. I hadn't been gaga over Bobby either, and I started to wonder what it was that made people fall in love. But the bottom line here was that no matter how you looked at it, I was not living an authentic life. In fact, my life seemed to me to be incoherent, a collection of fragments, without any clear meaning at all.

One afternoon, I found myself sitting inside an empty church. I had just wandered in, for some reason. I took in the stained glass, and the sculpture of Christ on the cross. Did you ever really exist? I asked him, in my mind. Or are you nothing more than the rest of the Catholic mythology, designed to give comfort and meaning in a comfortless and meaningless world? On the opposite wall was a small, exquisite sculpture of the Madonna (from the waist up), holding the Christ child in her arms. Who carved this? I wondered. And then suddenly, I started to weep. The Christ child had the Madonna to love and protect him; I had no one.

There wasn't a single person—well, maybe David, but I wasn't sure—who loved me, who had my back. Not my parents, not June, nobody. I was alone in the universe.

A priest walked down the nave of the church, nodded to me, and then disappeared behind the organ. A few minutes later the strains of "Ave Maria" filled the air, a song I must have heard dozens of times. It was painfully beautiful, and I started crying again.

Soon after that, David asked me to go away with him to Mendocino for the weekend. I said yes, although I was worried that he might propose. He had rented a lovely cottage with a fireplace, and after dinner we made love on the rug in front of it. It was really blissful.

"David," I asked him, "do you believe in anything, in particular?" He looked at me, a bit surprised.

"What, you mean like God?" I nodded.

"Well, you know that universities are pretty secular. Us professors tend to be atheists," he said.

"I'm not asking 'us professors'," I replied; "I'm asking *you*."

"Well," he said, "I like to think of it in terms of the best one can do, or the best one can be. What I believe is that we need to take our lives seriously. If we don't do that, then nothing has any meaning, really." He caught me by surprise; I wasn't expecting anything along those lines, and I had to think about it. I certainly wasn't being the best I could be; that much I knew.

"So you don't believe in God, or a Higher Power, or anything like that?" I asked him.

"Do *you*?" he came back at me. I told him about my Catholic upbringing, my rebellion against mythology and conformity, and my recent experience in the church. "It just left me confused, is all," I concluded.

"What's the confusion?"

"Why was I so moved by that statue of the Madonna and child? Why did I start crying?"

"Joanne, you know the answer to that. Like all of us, you want to be loved and protected. It's a cold world out there." I began to cry again. Finally I said, "Do you love me?" He nodded. "A little bit, I think," he answered.

"What's holding you back?" I asked him. He shook his head. "Joanne, this is going to sound weird, but I've always had the sensation that there was a whole other side to you that you weren't telling me about. I can't explain it; it's just a feeling. Are you dating anyone else?"

"No, just you," I said.

"Then what is it?" I looked away.

"David, I can't tell you at this time. I'm sorry. But I promise you, I will eventually talk about it. It's just that now is not a good time. But I can tell you that I need you in my life. Tell me you're not sleeping with anyone else."

"I'm not," he responded: "you're the woman I want. But all of this mystery bothers me. I'm hoping you won't take forever to let me know what's going on."

"I won't," I said; "I just need a little more time. Please don't break up with me."

"Joanne, it's my turn to ask: Are you in love with *me*?" And suddenly it hit me: I was. This was not a take-it-or-leave-it situation for me. How did this happen? I had no idea, but it had, in fact, happened.

"Yes," I said, "I do love you." He gathered me up in his arms, and we lay like that for a long time, before going off to sleep.

———

NEXT MORNING, we had breakfast on the deck outside the cottage. It was a brilliant, sunny day. The cottage was equipped with a coffee maker, along with cereal and milk. A nice, simple breakfast. "How did you sleep?" he asked me.

"Very well," I replied. "Admitting that I loved you, even to myself, somehow released a lot of tension." We were quiet for a while.

"Do you think people ever escape their upbringing, their backgrounds?" I finally asked him.

"Why do you ask?"

"Well, my crying in the church suggests to me that when all is said and done, I'm still a Catholic. I wish it weren't true, but apparently it is." I proceeded to tell him about how June still believed sex was a sin, and that in order to enjoy it she first had to be spanked—to "earn" her climax, as it were. "You'd think she could leave that fucked up belief behind, but no: she has to be paddled until she's crying her eyes out, and then she can have an orgasm. It's like penance. Actually, it *is* penance."

"Well," David offered, "at least that's an imprinting you managed to escape. In what way do you feel you're still a Catholic?"

"My father never told me much about himself," I replied, "but one Christmas eve, for some reason, he related a story from his past that was extremely important to him. I hasten to add that he wasn't drunk. In any case, the story also became important to me. I never forgot it.

"It was a Christmas Eve of many years ago, and he had gone to Paris the week before on business; after which the city pretty much shut down for the holidays. He was by himself; he hadn't yet met my mother. He was staying on the Left Bank, near the Sorbonne, and started walking as a light snow was falling. It was nearly midnight, and he walked into the church of Saint-Séverin. It was crowded; midnight mass was in progress. He stood at the back of the church; he didn't feel like taking communion. The interior of the place was gorgeous--all that art, that stained glass. I think Saint-Séverin dates from the thirteenth century. And the combination of the visual beauty, the music, and the incense, he said, took him back to the Middle Ages, and he thought that this must be God in physical form. He told me that this was the holiest moment of his life, and in that moment everything made sense to him. In fact, he met my mother two days later."

"Jesus, what a story," said David. "It almost makes *me* a believer."

"I guess I was feeling some of that when I sat in the church last week. I realized that while I didn't believe in God, I did believe in sacred experience. I guess that's what music does for you." David nodded.

It was a great weekend. I was able to let myself go completely. My body never felt so alive, so ecstatic. And yet, hanging over it all, was the shadow of my other life.

As it turned out, I didn't have to make a "confession" to David about my shadow life; I got caught at the border and called him to bail me out. I thought of calling June, but I was sure she would tell me, "You're on your own, honey." David posted bail, and a trial was set for six weeks hence.

"Now you know the mystery," I told him. "I've been working as a mule, smuggling cocaine." He took me in his arms. "Well, at least the mystery is finally solved," he said.

Back home (I was staying with David now), I told him the whole story, of how I met June, and for lack of money got caught up in the whole smuggling scene. "Honestly, David, I didn't know where else to turn, short of prostitution. You know what rents are like in this city, and I don't make very much as a waitress. The only other serious option I had was to return home, defeated, and I couldn't face the humiliation. So instead, I'm going to jail."

The trial came and went. I was sentenced to eighteen months in the women's prison in Chowchilla, 150 miles from San Fran. I hugged David goodbye, and told him I didn't expect him to wait for me. It turns out I really didn't mean it, but I guess I believed it at the time.

And what about the authentic life? Prison reduces everything to the lowest common denominator. I got beaten up a number of times; the other inmates labeled me "The Princess," and hated me. Their own stories were brutal: alcoholic fathers, prostitute mothers, rape, incest, you name it. Prison might be called a course in Reality–Reality 101. When I emerged fourteen months later (with four months off for good behavior), I was a different person. Possibly, a more authentic one.

David had come to see me once a week (it's more than a two-hour drive), but that faded away after a few months. He wrote that he had met someone else. That he was very sorry, and actually a bit ashamed, but that that was just how things had worked out. That he would meet me when I was released, put me up for a few days (sans his new girlfriend), and give—not loan— me two grand to enable me to get back on my feet. I was sad, but also grateful that he was being so kind to me, when he didn't have to be. But then, I thought, maybe he was feeling guilty. Of course, he hadn't promised me anything, but nevertheless I felt betrayed. I also wondered how I could get a job, with a prison record. Hopefully, the Cafe Flore wouldn't care.

I didn't have much to say to June, when I returned to the café. I just told her that I had gotten caught, and spent fourteen months in the slammer. For her part, June had little to say as well. I was just an object to her, someone to be used, and discarded when no longer useful.

David did drop into the café one time to check up on me, and I told him how grateful I was for his help, when I was released. "You're a very kind person, David. There aren't many like you." I also visited the church that I had wandered into two years before, but this time the Madonna and child didn't move me. What relevance did that statue, that image, have for all those women in

Chowchilla, whom life had beaten the shit out of? And yet, I clung to the memory of my father at Saint-Séverin, and felt that despite everything, life did have a sacred dimension, and that that epiphany was, in the end, a big part of authenticity. Another big part was honesty. I decided to give David a call.

"I need to talk to you," I told him. "Can I come over?"

"Of course," he said. "Is your girlfriend there?" I asked him. "I need to talk to you privately."

"No, she's not here," he assured me. David let me in, thirty minutes later. "It's good to see you, Joanne; what's this all about?"

"Look, David, I know you didn't promise me anything when I went to jail, but I need to come clean about how I feel, irrational though it may be: you betrayed me. I really loved you. If you would have asked me to marry you, I would have said yes. And then you destroyed it all by going off with someone else. Who is she, David? Is she really good in bed? Tell me." He looked directly at me.

"We broke up a month ago," he said. For a moment, I was speechless; this I hadn't anticipated.

"Why didn't you tell me? Why didn't you come by the Flore and let me know?" I demanded.

"Because I felt you would think I was using you. Of course I wanted you back, but I was afraid it would seem—I don't have the right word—opportunistic, maybe, or manipulative. Unfair, in any case."

"Do you still want me back?"

"Very much," he replied. I shook my head, almost groaned. "I hate you, David. I hate you for abandoning me when I needed you. It was a cruel thing to do, and it will take me a long time to forgive you. But as much as I hate you, I also love you. I want you to fuck me now, and while you're doing it, I want you to know that I hate you. When you come, I want you to realize that I really, really hate you."

The lovemaking was more powerful than anything we had previously experienced, and when I came, I nearly passed out. After, we lay side by side, breathing heavily. "Can we begin again?" he finally said. I was quiet for a moment. "Yes, I think so," I told him. "I think we can begin again."

# 17

---

# THE FREE SPIRIT

At thirty-six years of age, Peter Argyle was the youngest Associate Professor in Faircross University's Department of Sociology. His colleagues liked him, and admired both his work and his work ethic. He had generated a favorable reputation for Faircross, and the Department, with two major books on the sociology of religion, which became classics in the field. His current interest was urban communes, and he was using his sabbatical year to study one located forty miles north of the city, a group that called themselves The Free Spirit, or FS. Not quite urban, then, but close enough. One aspect that made it attractive to Peter was that it had lasted now for five years.

This longevity was atypical. Most of the "hippie" communes failed because unlike, say, the Amish, they had no religious or "transcendental" basis to hold them together. Rather, the desire to live in community was itself the glue, which was not very powerful. It was a lot like getting married to escape loneliness without paying much attention to whom you were marrying. In any case, the FS had a fairly stable membership of about twenty people. They were proud of their longevity, and their mode of organization, and as a result had no problem with Peter hanging out as a kind of anthropologist, doing a study of the "tribe."

The guru of the tribe was a tall, slender man of about sixty, with piercing blue eyes and a short, gray-white goatee, Walter Ascott. Walter had worked as a therapist in private practice, and was now retired. He purchased the three acres on which the commune stood, for that purpose. The membership was mostly white men and women in their mid- to late-twenties, folks who had dropped out of college and floated around for a few years before coming together to form the FS. Two of the members were black women; one was a Native American man.

An important factor in the group's longevity was Walter's personal commitment not to sleep with any of the female members. Some of them casually flirted with him from time to time, but he never took the bait. He had a girlfriend in the city, Cynthia, twenty years his junior, whom he visited once a week, and who came down to the commune once a week. She was a cellist, and a very easygoing person. Everyone liked her. Romantic pairings did occur, of course, among the members of the group, but given the "free spirit" nature of the FS, they tended to form, last a while, dissolve, and then regroup in new configurations. As a result, nearly everyone had, in the course of the five years, slept with everyone else, but amazingly enough, there was remarkably little friction or jealousy.

Peter's focus, however, was not on sexual relations, but on the matter of the social glue. The FS did have a religion, namely the FS itself. Again, Peter regarded this as pretty thin fare. He wondered to what extent Walter's ownership of the property, and his charisma, were the real glue holding the FS together. The members worked the land on which the commune sat, but they paid no rent; and almost all of them saw Walter as a kind of substitute father. Plus, everyone had a vote in the management of the FS. The organization purported to be a democracy, and held "town meetings" once a week, to take stock of how they were doing. Walter presided over these meetings, and what Peter noticed was that he was something of a Svengali. The whole thing *looked* democratic, but in reality Walter was a benevolent dictator. Somehow, in the case of any major conflict or decision, it was his view that prevailed. Almost no one in the group saw this, which was probably another factor in group stability. So far, so good.

The turning point for the FS, which occurred during Peter's tenure there, was the murder of one of the women, a gal of about twenty-eight named Carla Mellon. It was pretty sad: spontaneously, as it were, her heart stopped beating, and she died in her sleep. The problem was that Carla had been in excellent physical health (also confirmed in the autopsy), which led the police to suspect that there had been foul play at work. Within a couple of days, then, the place was swarming with cops, and everyone, Peter included, was a suspect. But it seemed to be a crime without a motive; there was really no reason for anyone to want to rub Carla out. The only thing that stood out in her case was that she was a bit of a maverick, someone who didn't fit in on a 100 percent basis. She was possibly the only member who was aware of the fact that the politics of the group was not really democratic. She had her own opinions about things, and while it occasionally led to some friction—which Walter claimed was good for the group ("she challenges us")—it never rose to the level of intractable conflict. It didn't seem likely that anyone in the FS would kill her over that, and yet, there she was, dead as a doornail.

Carla had had her share of sexual partners, but none of the other women seemed to hold it against her. Nor was there anyone with whom she had had a particular enmity. Like the police, Peter was completely baffled, although there was a potential "hook" here: Carla had been attracted to Peter and had made her sexual interest explicit. For his part, Peter let her down gently, as he didn't want to blow his credit rating, so to speak. Had Carla mentioned this to the other girls? Would this have occasioned any conflict? He had no way of knowing. But he decided not to say anything to the police about it. The real problem for the FS was that if the culprit could not be found, the stability of the group would be seriously threatened by a climate of paranoia.

The only thing Peter could think of was that someone who was zealously attached to the group found Carla's independent ways a source of deep rancor, and perceived her as a serious threat to group stability. Two members in particular came to mind: Victor Carey, who in fact had had a relationship with Carla for several months at one point, and Phyllis Roberts, one of the earliest members of the group. Phyllis was thirty-three, a bit older than the average, and a gal with something of a crush on Walter. But as far as Peter could make out, neither she nor Victor had any kind of psychotic or homicidal tendencies. He doubted that either of them was the guilty party.

Walter, for his part, was devastated. He had apparently liked Carla, actually admired her independent streak (up to a point), and was horrified that she was snuffed out at such a young age, with her whole life ahead of her. But Peter suspected something else was also at play: the FS was Walter's baby. It had become his whole reason for being, and now, with a death in the family, the entire organization was threatened. Even if the culprit was apprehended, it was possible that the commune would not be able to survive the event. This would be a very difficult cross for Walter to bear.

With the permission of the police, Peter was allowed to sit in on the interviews they conducted with the members of the commune. He was allowed to take notes, but not to ask any questions of the interviewees. He did suggest to the cops that they begin their investigation with Victor and Phyllis, if only to eliminate them from the list. Before that, however, they had a question for him.

"Why didn't you tell us that Carla had propositioned you?" asked the sergeant in charge. Peter was taken aback. So apparently Carla had mentioned it to someone, and this juicy bit of gossip had gotten around.

"I didn't think it was relevant," he replied, rather lamely. "She did do that, but I said no."

"Professor Argyle," said the officer, "you're not an idiot, so please don't play me for one. An event like that is potentially explosive, and therefore very relevant. Carla has the hots for you, you reject her, she's upset and tells a friend, and other women who might have had their eyes on you get jealous. After all, you're a college professor, well off, tolerably good looking, and not that much older than they are. Or perhaps they think Carla is lying, that you did not reject her, and that the two of you are lovers. Fertile ground for anger, no?"

"So the theory is that one of these girls snuffs Carla out because she is jealous? If so, you're looking for a pretty psychotic individual," he concluded.

"It would hardly be the most unusual event in the history of crime," the sergeant replied. "We have to pursue all possible leads."

"OK," said Peter, "sorry about that. I should have brought that information forward on my own initiative, obviously. Personally, I still think that Carla's maverick status is a more likely cause."

"That's for us to decide," the officer responded rather drily. In any case, they did begin their interviews with Victor Carey.

"Please sit down, Victor. I'm Sgt. Moynihan. You were involved with Carla for several months, were you not? At which point she moved on to someone else. Were you angry about that?" Victor chuckled.

"You'll get different opinions as to what actually happened," he answered, "depending on whom you talk to, but the fact is that I left *her*. We were like oil and water. Absent sexual attraction, we would have never gotten involved. I was a lost soul when I found the FS; Walter saved a drowning man, and I'll always be grateful to him. Carla never said it publicly, but she regarded him as a fraud, a kind of dictator who was using the group to inflate his ego. When she began to say these things to me during sex, I decided enough was enough. I told her we needed to go our separate ways. I suppose I was a little jealous when she took up with Alfred Manning a few days later, but for the most part I was relieved. In any event, I didn't kill her. What would have been the point?"

"Well," said Moynihan, "even if we believe you about not being very jealous regarding her new relationship, there was still a lot of potential anger at her severe criticism of someone you adored, no? Perhaps you saw her as a threat to him, or even to the entire group."

"Sergeant," replied Victor, "you're spinning theories out of thin air. Grasping at straws. The bottom line is that I'm just not wired up to kill. I'm not a violent type, and I didn't kill Carla Mellon." The cops let him go, with a warning about not leaving the state. Moynihan turned to Peter. "What do you think?" he asked him.

"It's not him," he replied. "He's telling the truth." Moynihan nodded. "That's what I thought as well."

Meanwhile, as might be expected, the newspapers were blowing the whole thing out of proportion. SNAKE IN THE LOVE NEST was a typical headline, and it hardly made Moynihan's work easier. He surrounded the property with yellow tape, to keep the paparazzi out. He was also set to interview Phyllis Roberts when a second murder occurred: Angela Lincoln, one of the black girls. The second death made it clear that these were homicides. Two heart attacks within ten days in two healthy individuals was out of the question.

The police talked to Peter about the possibility of a pattern. Angela was hardly a stereotypical young black rebel, crying "Black Power!" with upraised fist. And yet, like Carla, she had a few criticisms of the FS and didn't wholly fit into it. But her death eliminated the possibility of sexual jealousy as a factor. In her three years with the commune, she had slept with no one. Instead, she had a lover in the city, whom she would visit two or three times a month. So if any pattern were shaping up, it would be that the killer was hostile to dissenters, or even semi-dissenters. But it was only a theory, at best.

Much to Peter's surprise, Moynihan suggested that he hold a private discussion with Phyllis Roberts prior to any formal police interview. "I don't know why," he said, "but I have this feeling that a police uniform could get her back up, and that she might be uncooperative as a result. You, on the other hand, present a friendly, nonthreatening persona. Plus, you're almost the same age, which might help." So Peter suggested to Phyllis that the two of them raid the communal fridge, and have lunch together at one of the picnic tables that were set at a distance from the house.

"Is this a date?" was her opening statement, after they sat down to eat. Peter laughed. "A date requires wine, don't you think? No wine here, that I can see." He had to admit that she was quite sexy: long, dark brown hair, somewhat pouty lips, and a good figure, partly hidden under a hippie grass skirt that was nevertheless open at the sides, revealing long, beautiful legs.

"You're dodging the question, Peter," she said. "I need to know if you are interested in me." He shook his head.

"Phyllis, a good way to destroy my objectivity, and my research project, would be to move from observer to participant. If I start sleeping with any of the FS women, the whole thing would blow up in my face. It's just not worth it. This is not personal; I don't mean to offend. You're quite lovely, in fact."

"Walter tells me you're rather famous," she responded, in something of a nonsequitur. "Only in small academic circles," he told her. She made a face.

"Peter, I need to ask you some questions, and I want honest answers. If you're going to bullshit me like that, then this date, or whatever it is, is over. OK?" He nodded sheepishly.

"First question: Weren't you a guest on Letterman, discussing your work?" He admitted he was.

"Second question: Then why did you hand me a load of crap about small academic circles?" He sighed.

"I just didn't want to appear to be boasting, or promoting myself; to come off as superior," he replied.

"But you *are* superior, Peter. You are a professor and a famous author, whereas I'm just an ageing hippie who doesn't know what to do with herself. It doesn't mean I'd automatically sleep with you, assuming you were interested, but let's not pretend that there is no difference in status."

"Phyllis, I'm interested in who people really are, not in their status. In their hearts, in a word. And I'm absolutely sure that my heart is no better than yours." At this, she softened a bit, touched his hand. "OK, so you're not an asshole," she said. "Good to know." She continued:

"Question No. 3: If I asked you to make love to me, would you do it?"

"Phyl, I think I've already answered that. If we met in a bar or café in the city, as two independent strangers, of course I would say yes. But that's not our situation here, and as I said, I'm not willing to jeopardize my work for sex or romance. By the way, if you don't mind my asking: Isn't Walter the one you really love? At least, that's what several folks here have told me." She reddened a bit.

"OK, true enough," she replied. "Which doesn't mean I can't be interested in you. In any case, Walter rejects me for the same reason you have: it would wreck his larger commitment, in his case, the FS itself."

"Why do you stick around, then?" he asked her. "Are you hoping he'll change his mind, sooner or later?"

"I don't think he will. He's been involved with Cynthia, his cellist friend, for more than two years now, and will probably marry her."

"So again," Peter repeated, "why do you stay here?" She got a bit teary-eyed. "Peter, will you keep what I'm about to tell you to yourself?" He nodded yes. "I have very low self-esteem. Believe me, this is not a bid for pity, or an attempt at seduction. My parents loved my older brother—he's actually now head of cardiology at Connecticut University Hospital—and showered him with praise and encouragement. To me, for reasons I still don't understand, they were basically cruel, telling me I was useless. My mother even told me once that all I would ever be good for was fucking." She began to weep; he held her hand across the table.

"The problem is," she went on, "I believe it to this day. What could I offer Walter, or you, beyond sex?"

"Don't say that, Phyllis. You're obviously a kind and intelligent person. You would be loving and supportive, I'm sure of it. Any man would be lucky to have you."

"I wish I could believe that," she replied. "My parents shattered my confidence." They were silent for a while; she kept her hand in his. "Anyway," she continued, "—and I'm counting on you to be honest—if this is not a date, what is it?"

"Phyl, the police wanted me to determine if you had anything to do with the deaths of those two girls." He winced as he said this. She stared at him for a moment.

"What do *you* think?" she asked him. He continued holding

her hand. "I can't imagine it," he said. "What motive could you possibly have for killing two innocent young women?"

"Exactly," she answered. "Pete, I'm a bit angry that the cops used you to do their dirty work, so to speak. I wish you had refused to cooperate with them. And I'm angry at you, because I feel a bit tricked. I do like you, and I was actually hoping this *was* a date. I thought that was what was going on."

"Phyl," he said, "I'm really sorry. You're right to be angry. I was of course certain that you had nothing to do with these awful events, but I wanted to help the police in their process of elimination. I hope you can forgive me."

"You're a good guy, Pete; I know that," she said. "I've observed you for several months now. Can I ask you to consider something? This is rather forward, but I'll say it anyway. After your time here is up, and you return to the city, could I come with you? I think I could make you happy." She leaned over and kissed him; he didn't pull away. It went on for a minute or more.

"I'll definitely consider it," he replied. "You can be sure of that. When I said any man would be lucky to have you, I meant it." He told Moynihan that he thought she was innocent, hoping that the kiss hadn't clouded his judgment. In any case, the cops interviewed everyone else themselves, with Peter once again sitting in as an observer. The "maverick" theory didn't really pan out; both they and Peter were at a loss as to who the guilty party might be.

With the third murder, the FS fell completely apart. The frightened members scattered to the four winds. The only pattern Peter could discern at this point was that someone was out to destroy the entire commune, and had pretty much succeeded. The third victim—who could believe it?—was Victor Carey.

But if that was the motive—destruction of the commune—then no one in the FS fit the profile. Carla and Angela had been the only "opponents" of the organization, and they had been victims. But of whom? And Victor was a devotee of the FS, so why would he be a target? It all seemed random. The whole thing was falling into the category of Unsolved Mysteries. As for Peter's research project, he could obviously kiss that goodbye.

Walter never really recovered; he was a broken man. He moved down to the city and moved in with Cynthia. He was never heard from after that.

Phyllis also moved to the city, with Peter. She was certainly right about her ability to make him happy, and two months into the relationship they got married. Soon after that she was pregnant with twins. But something happened four months after the FS murders, as they came to be known, that turned his world upside down, and made it seemingly impossible for him to continue with his career. The FS never had much to do with a commune that was located ten miles down the road, called The Avenging Angels (AA). The place got busted for performing satanic rituals, and two of the members confessed: they had perfected a technique of killing at a distance, by stopping victims' hearts while they were asleep, which is what they had done to Carla, and Angela, and Victor. Peter phoned Sgt. Moynihan as soon as the news broke, and asked him to hold off on interviews until he could get down there—two hours later. Moynihan brought the two members of the AA into the examination room, and sat them down across of himself and Peter.

"So tell me and Professor Argyle exactly how you killed the three people over at the Free Spirit," he began. The two men, in their mid-thirties, wearing sport coats, were actually very relaxed and articulate. It was almost as if the whole thing were a game to them. Peter was surprised that they didn't ask to be provided with legal counsel.

"It's a medieval witchcraft practice," Perp. No. 1 replied. "It's actually all explained in the papers you confiscated from our house. It's known as 'focused incantation'. Sometimes it's called

'action-at-a-distance'. We weren't out to kill any particular individual, only members of the FS in general. So we aimed the incantation—which is in Latin, by the way—at the entire FS property—the house, that is—on three separate occasions, and on each occasion someone's heart stopped in the middle of the night."
Peter interrupted at this point.

"May I ask *why* you did this? Did you know people in the FS? Was there some revenge, or personal animosity, going on?" The two perps shook their heads.

"Not at all," replied Perp. No. 2. "Look, professor: medieval witchcraft, or black magic, is essentially a technology. Its similarity to science is quite remarkable, and in fact Isaac Newton made action-at-a-distance, which he learned about from his study of alchemy, the basis of his Law of Universal Gravitation. The thing about technology—any technology—is that once it's developed, it's only a matter of time before it's used. This is what happened with the atomic bomb, in fact. Read your history."

Thanks for the lecture, Peter thought to himself. "So you're telling me that you killed these people simply because it was do-able?" Perp. No. 2 nodded. "You got it," he replied. "Not really so different from why we dropped the atomic bomb on Hiroshima. You seriously believe that killing three people is worse than what we did to the Japanese?"

"We were at *war* with Japan, for Chrissakes," Peter fairly shouted. "Had the FS ever pulled a Pearl Harbor on you? And besides, what does one thing have to do with the other?" But Perp. No. 2 was one step ahead of him.

"Academic hairsplitting, professor. For one thing, the US bombed civilians, not the military—innocents who were hardly involved in Pearl Harbor. But more than that: it's about the use of technology that's the issue. Prior to Japan, the Manhattan Project had Germany in its crosshairs. The scientists involved didn't give a hoot about the target, they only cared about the technology—

which is all we, at AA, ever cared about. This is how the whole country operates, in case you hadn't noticed. So the cops will put us in jail, but they will be missing the point."

"Spare me your sophistry," Peter told him. "Those three people were younger than you are, did you no harm, and you snuffed them out for no reason at all. So don't give me a load of shit about Hiroshima." He got up and left the room. Outside, in the corridor, he sat down on a bench and wept. Maybe the fucker was right, he thought; maybe all of America *does* operate that way. But he wasn't prepared to condone the sacrifice of three innocent young lives for some abstract principle.

There were four men involved with the FS murders, and they all received life sentences without possibility of parole. Cold comfort, as far as Peter was concerned.

Professionally, the whole thing left him in a quandary. He was a child of the Enlightenment. When he wrote about religion, or witchcraft, or any belief system, he wrote as a sociologist, i.e., wrote about these things from the *outside*. He certainly didn't take these beliefs seriously, be they of the Yoruba or the Catholic Church (transubstantiation, for example). But here he had proof that things like witchcraft — heart-stopping at a distance — actually worked; which made a mockery of his books and his entire professional life. To make things worse, this magical practice was messily intertwined with Newtonian science and modern technology; the perps weren't wrong about that. All of which left him up the creek without a paddle. What in hell was he supposed to write about now, for fuck's sake? The sociology of religion was actually meaningless.

*The Free Spirit* appeared two years later. Peter just spilled his guts, told the whole story, and included all the confusion and unanswered questions in it. As a result, he was made full professor, was invited to give a series of lectures at Yale (title: "Is Sociology a Religion?"), and appeared on just about every radio and TV talk show in the land. As one of his colleagues put it, "Peter cracked open a can of worms, which is what real scholarship is all about."

On the domestic front, the twins were by now eighteen months old, and he and Phyllis remained very much in love. "I knew, way back then, when we had that date or nondate at the FS, that you were the guy for me," she declared. "There is another name for kismet," she continued; "it's called action-at-a-distance. *White* magic, in this case."

Who needed sociology to understand that?

## 18

---

## AFFINITY

Gerald Hawkins had been considered a number of times for the Nobel Prize in chemistry, but never quite made it over the top. It was, of course, frustrating for him, but he had to admit that the real joy in his life was the work itself. We all want to be recognized, however, and he couldn't deny that he had received numerous accolades: various plaques and citations dotted the wall of his den, and the university considered him one of their most important assets. He had been president of the American Chemical Society at one point, was often called upon by the courts for forensic testimony, and had been chair of the Chemistry Department now for ten years running. He was often asked by various universities to deliver the commencement address. But the Big Prize, the Nobel, eluded him.

Of course, he was aware that the Nobel committee had made egregious errors, more than once. Two war criminals, Henry Kissinger and Barack Obama, had ironically been awarded the Peace Prize, and the committee had passed over Philip Roth in favor of Bob Dylan. It doesn't get dumber than that. So no one could accuse the committee of fairness or objectivity. But Gerald was getting on in years, and began to think that he would never be more than a runner up.

Most of the time, however, he focused on his work, rather than on the Nobel. His particular area of chemical research was what is called valency, or bonding, the affinity that atoms have for other atoms, so as to form compounds or molecules. Building on previous researches, Gerald had sorted out which atoms were attracted to other atoms, and which were not. There were basically three categories: attraction, repulsion, and neutrality. He liked to use the analogy of *sexual* chemistry, which psychologists speculated about in terms of pheromones or genetic makeup — matching phenotypes, for example. Bonding in this arena happened as quickly as it did in chemical bonding (or nonbonding). You are sitting in a café, let's say, and a woman comes through the door. The assessment is almost instantaneous: you want her, you don't want her, or you don't really care. And of course, women often make the same rapid assessment of men.

One model of affinity that Gerald particularly liked was the one given by the character of Aristophanes in Plato's dialogue *Symposium*. In very rough terms, Aristophanes posited an original scenario in which the earth was populated by hermaphroditic "blobs" that were each both male and female, and which got cut in two by Zeus, and then got scattered to the winds. Each half-blob was then condemned to a quest to find his or her missing half, the union with which would make them whole again. Love was "the desire and the pursuit of the whole," he asserted. What each half-blob was seeking was his or her soul mate, and Aristophanes' speech was often cited thereafter as a model of romantic love. Gerald wondered if the phenomenon had a chemical, i.e. atomic, basis.

Of course, this sort of speculation was a hobby for Gerald; he hardly published papers on romantic love. But he thought about it a lot. He also wondered if there were a class of nonromantic affinities. For example, he had a best friend with whom he had "clicked" while in high school, and the friendship had lasted all these decades. The two of them lived on opposite sides of the country, but they made it their business to get together once a year. One could probably say that in such cases, the "force field" was weaker than in the case of romantic bonding, but that it was nonetheless real, and was certainly stronger than the neutral category (apathy), which characterized most human relations. He also wondered about communal ties, such as one found in the Israeli kibbutzim, or in intentional communities that were popular in some parts of the United States. And then of course there was affinity on a national level. During World War II, for example, the dominant Japanese slogan on the home front was "one hundred million hearts beating as one." All in all, from atoms to nations, affinity was not merely a fascinating subject; it may be, thought Gerald, the most important phenomenon on the planet.

The crucial factor in the field of chemical affinity was "bonding energy," because this ran the gamut from weak to strong —as in human relations. Gerald's contribution to the field was to classify levels and types of bonding energy, which led to predictions as to whether different materials would fuse, and to what degree. The industrial applications here were obvious, and Gerald had taken out several patents in materials science, all of which had made him quite wealthy. But he had no great affinity for money; it was the science, and its human applications, that turned him on.

Gerald's marriage of thirty years followed a typical bonding pattern. He and Gwen were "magically" drawn to each other in the early phase of their relationship, bonded very quickly, and for a while had sex on a daily basis. Slowly, this began to taper off; they were by now more or less affectionate friends, and the "glue" of the relationship was their shared history. He was aware that for many couples, marriage was entered into because of convenience, or because it was socially approved. Pairings like this fell into the category of apathy, he supposed. The saddest situation, perhaps, was unrequited love. In this case, one member of the dyad felt a strong affinity toward the other member, but the other member was repulsed, or just apathetic. Lots of love stories, Gerald realized, revolved around this sad, or even tragic, dynamic: Apollo and Daphne, for example, or the novels of Anthony Trollope.

Gerald also thought a lot about affinity to an idea or ideology. He read Arthur Koestler's description of discovering Marxism, how it explained (for him), in a single stroke, how the entire world worked, and how it felt like light pouring across his brain. Surely, Gerald thought, this was love, even though it didn't involve another person. What about addiction? he wondered. Clearly, it had a chemical basis, and if one was "in love" with alcohol, this too would have to be regarded as a bonding phenomenon. Gerald wondered if he himself had fallen in love with the idea of affinity, because he saw some variant of bonding everywhere he looked. Like Marxism for Koestler, it seemed to explain everything. He had fantasies of capturing bonding energy in test tubes, and then using it to create valent situations. Not much different from the idea of love potions supposedly concocted by gypsies, or in the magical practices of the Middle Ages, when he thought about it.

And what about the attraction of mutual repulsion? It was often the case that people enjoyed having an enemy, because it filled up their time, kept them busy, feeling "alive." Some historians had argued that this was the real (if hidden) history of the United States: it had to have an enemy in order to keep functioning. So it started with demonizing England as "decadent," Native Americans and later Mexicans as "savages," communists as "godless atheists" (the "evil empire"), Muslims as "Islamofascists," and so on. As Constantine Cavafy had written in his poem, "Waiting for the Barbarians," the endless threat of "barbarians" offered a pseudo-solution to the problems of the state. The attraction of repulsion was blind, unconscious, and seemingly endless.

All of this rumination came to a head one evening when he and Gwen were watching television, and some interview-type program had invited a sociology professor, Peter Argyle, on the show. Gerald was spellbound by Argyle's discussion of his new book, *The Free Spirit*, in which he described a commune that fell apart in the wake of three unexplained murders. Argyle was also interested in affinity, in this case the social glue that bound commune members together, at least for a time. He explained that the murders were committed by members of a nearby commune, The Avenging Angels, who had used a medieval witchcraft ritual of action-at-a-distance to cause these deaths. The man was modest; he confessed to his own bewilderment over the whole affair, and talked about the relations between magic, science, and technology—which he said he had yet to unravel. Gerald immediately ordered the book off of Amazon.

When the book finally arrived, and Gerald read through it, what he thought he saw in the case of the "hex" placed on the Free Spirit by the Avenging Angels was what might be called an anti-love potion (negative affinity). It was the opposite of E.M. Forster's famous line, "only connect." The goal of the Angels (for whatever reason) was to *dis*connect—to disrupt the bonds holding the FS together, to dissolve the affinities, and thereby destroy the commune. They were obviously a pretty sick bunch, and four of them were now in jail for life; but the whole event made Gerald wonder if affinity or anti-affinity could somehow be distilled and bottled, like perfume, or skunk oil (if the latter even existed). If that wouldn't win him the Nobel Prize, nothing would.

For example, Gerald thought to himself, suppose he could concoct a powerful perfume called Affinity, and sell it to Estée Lauder? Closer to home, suppose he could sprinkle it on Gwen's corn flakes? Would she suddenly have the hots for him, as in their early days of marriage? He became dizzy just thinking of the possibilities. Before experimenting on his wife, however, Gerald figured he should work with the general public. He imagined placing an ad in the local newspaper:

WANT TO GET HIM/HER
TO FALL IN LOVE WITH YOU?
Dr. Fallopio can make it happen!
[phone number]

First, however, he obviously needed to get to work in the lab, concocting "Affinity." Time to experiment with molecular bonding. It took him four months to create such a bonding situation in the lab, and then generate a potion based on it. However, there was a potentially fatal flaw here, an unwarranted "leap." For example: scientists might determine that some sugar substitute caused cancer in laboratory rats. Did that necessarily mean it would do so in humans? Often, the results in one area were not transferable to another. There was, in short, no alternative to trying out the love potion on human guinea pigs; which could get him into ethical and legal difficulties. That said, he finally decided to place the ad.

While Gerald waited for responses, he couldn't help wondering if he had gone mad. He remembered that old song, "Love Potion Number 9," in which the guy drinks it and then starts "kissing everything in sight." What was he about to unleash on the world? An erotic A-bomb? He had a few sleepless nights.

The first person who answered the ad was an unlikely candidate: a scrawny sixteen year-old high school kid, not particularly good looking, who had his eye on last year's prom queen, a voluptuous babe currently dating the captain of the football team. Gerald explained to the boy that the hardest part would be to put a few drops of Affinity into the girl's food or drink without being noticed. If he could pull that off, he told him, there was a good chance that she would fall in love with him. He charged the boy a nominal fee, and told him to come back when he had any results, whether positive or negative.

It turned out to be all Gerald could have wished for. Indeed, it was damn near miraculous. Francis, his guinea pig, sat at a table next to Melinda's table in the school cafeteria, where she was surrounded by a number of popular girls. Finally, they all got up to leave, which enabled Francis to put a few drops of the potion into the unfinished can of Coke she had left behind. It was a gamble: Would she come back to retrieve it? She did. The next day she called him up, asked him out, and they had sex in the back seat of her parents' car. After that, they were inseparable.

"Dr. Fallopio!" the boy cried, after relating this unbelievable tale. "How can I ever thank you?"

"Just keep the whole thing under your hat," said Gerald. "If this information gets out, I could be dealing with hundreds of customers, and I don't have time for that." Calls came in at a very slow trickle, in fact. Most people who saw the ad figured it was a scam, and the name "Fallopio" was sure to put them off. In any case, his next client was an overweight, middle-aged woman of about forty-five, Gertrude, with two kids and a husband who was no longer interested in her. He had taken a mistress as of late, and she was devastated. "Help me, Dr. Fallopio!" she cried. Gerald put his arm around her.

"Not to worry," he assured her. "A few drops in his morning coffee ought to do the trick." And it did. She came back to report the results, and was overjoyed. "It's more sex than I can handle!" she exclaimed. "Bill wants to do it twice a day. Honestly, Doctor, I'm all fucked out." Score No. 2, Gerald said to himself. What next? Try it on Gwen? Not just yet. Meanwhile, a fly in the ointment showed up: Melinda also, it seemed, had gone into high gear, sexually speaking, and she wanted a tryst with Francis nearly every night. "I can't get any homework done," he complained to Gerald. "Plus, even when we're not having sex, she wants to hang out with me, smell my T-shirts or whatever. Do you have anything I can use to tone her down?" Gerald would soon be asking the same thing.

Could he do it? After all, he had done all his professional work on variable binding energy. Could he come up with a tone-it-down antidote? Back to the lab. Unfortunately, for some reason, he wasn't able to do it. Meanwhile, Francis' dick was completely raw, and he transferred to a high school out of state. As for Gertrude, she met with Bill's mistress, a chorus girl named Lola, and begged her to start fucking Bill once again. Lola was glad to oblige; the problem was that Bill was interested only in Gertrude, who finally moved out of their house and sued for divorce. The case actually made legal history: there was now a new ground for divorce, called "Sexual Excess," or more informally, Overhumping. Gerald had to face the fact that his experiment was so successful that it failed. Affinity was powerful, but useless. Then it hit him: the solution was a time-release liquid. Could he create it?

By the time he had it in hand, "Dr. Fallopio" had a waiting list of fourteen people. He phoned the first person on the list, Frieda Marcus, and asked her to come in. She was an average-looking gal, thirty-eight years old, with a rather depressed affect.

"I work in a law office," she told Gerald, "with a lot of good-looking guys. In the year that I've been there, not one of them has asked me out. Am I so ugly?" She began to cry.

"Frieda," said Gerald, "I have a new experimental remedy that may resolve your difficulties. But it works on a time-release basis. In other words, you pick the guy you want to date, and when he's not looking, you put a few drops of this liquid in his coffee. He won't immediately go gaga over you; his interest will grow slowly.

But it will grow, and you should be sleeping with him in three to six weeks. I'm asking you to be patient, in other words. Once the sexual relationship begins, he may only want you twice a week. Can you live with that?"

"What if I put the drops into more than one guy's coffee?" she asked him. "Very bad idea," Gerald replied. "Your life will spin out of control. Everything in moderation, my dear. Do you have a dildo?" She nodded. "Then I suggest you use that on non-intercourse days, OK? And report back to me in three to six weeks." Frieda agreed to follow his instructions.

Much to Gerald's relief, it worked. Frieda was not victimized by Overhumping; the sexual activity followed a smooth curve. She was Gerald's first enduring success story. And yet, with this new version of Affinity, a new fly in the ointment showed up: the romantic effect wore off after about three months. All of the clients who were using it had to keep coming back for a new batch. Gerald was busier than he wanted to be.

To make things worse, one of his clients accidentally spilled the beans in a podcast, which then went viral. Gerald suddenly had 4,500 potential clients, and Estée Lauder contacted him about a business deal. Everyone wanted love, and it seemed like Affinity was the way to get it. And then, both he and Estée Lauder found themselves mired in lawsuits, as those who had been "love-targets" claimed that they had chemical partners, not true soulmates. It was starting to border on a national crisis. Gerald quit the business and went into hiding. To quote George Costanza, it was as though he had discovered plutonium by accident.

He had a sudden inspiration: he would contact Peter Argyle, ask him if he could pay him a visit at Faircross University. Argyle was very gracious, and suggested that Gerald come to his home. "I'd like you to meet my wife," he told him over the phone. Two days later, Gerald knocked on his door.

"Come in, come in," said Peter. He was exuberant. "I wanted you to meet Phyllis because I think she can explain things better than I can." Gerald was introduced to a tall, beautiful woman in a hippie grass skirt, who had a gorgeous smile. She sat opposite Gerald on the sofa, while Peter went off to make coffee.

"Gerald," she began, "—may I call you Gerald?"—he nodded. "It's sort of like this: the notion that there is something unkosher about a love potion strikes me as being rather dubious. I was out to 'capture' Peter and I was pretty aggressive about it. My own love potion was to give him an unexpected, long kiss, and tell him —practically out of the blue—that if he chose me as a partner, I'd make him very happy. This was a kind of hex, don't you think? I bewitched the poor guy, and he's been happy as a clam ever since. One friend of mine, on a first date with the guy who is now her husband, achieved the same result by taking off her shirt at the end of the date. Was this manipulation? Sure. So what? The guy isn't exactly complaining, last thing I heard. My point is that there are all kinds of love potions."

Peter came in with cake and coffee. "Are you telling Gerald how you sank your hooks into me?" he asked. "Yes, and how grateful you are that I did," Phyllis added. They all laughed.

"Small problem, Phyllis," Gerald interjected. "You and Peter already found each other attractive, and in this sense there really wasn't any manipulation involved. Your kiss, and your promise to him, just served to cement the deal. The reason I'm being sued by a number of people is that they claim that in their cases, there was no basis for mutual attraction. Worst example I can give you is my very first client, a high school kid named Francis, who hexed or potioned the most glamorous girl in the school. That match would never have happened without Affinity, and she's quite right in asserting that. I don't know what the courts will decide, but the truth is that she's way, way out of his league. What she'll argue in court, I'm fairly certain, is that Affinity colonized her brain."

"Yes, I see what you mean," said Phyllis. "I just think that practically everything is brainwashing. Look how well American propaganda works on American citizens, for example. Everything the government does, both at home and abroad, is soaking in lies and propaganda, and yet even so-called progressives buy into the dominant ideology, which is one of extreme individualism, unbridled competition, and mindless consumerism. Perhaps the government deserves to be sued, but who is going to sue them? And when you teach your students chemistry according to Western science, isn't that also brainwashing? What about alchemy, and action-at-a-distance, which both Isaac Newton and Peter discovered is fully real? I hope you're taking notes, Gerald, because this is what you will need to argue in court." Gerald laughed.

"Jesus, Phyllis, you're really something. Maybe you could come to court with me, be my coach."

"Gerald," she went on, "how did the German government manage to convince an entire population that the Jews were the cause of their suffering? It made no objective sense at all. But it was a meme that spread like a virus, and in a relatively short period of time the German people, actively or passively, murdered six million of them. I guess you might call this anti-affinity. Have some more cake."

They spent the afternoon talking, and then his hosts insisted that Gerald sleep over. His head was spinning; he had never considered things in this light. But he was not sure where all of this left him. The next morning, Phyllis made them eggs and toast, and Peter did another round of coffee. "Phyllis," said Gerald, "I think you put a hex on me yesterday. My brain is totally scrambled from that discussion, even more than these eggs."

"Gerald," she replied, "the minute you open your mouth, you're influencing the other person. Sexually or nonsexually, we're always seducing the person we are interacting with."

Gerald thanked them both, and caught a taxi to the airport. When his case came up in court, he used Phyllis' argument. The result was a hung jury. Some jurors felt that he had fucked with Melinda's head; others bought the argument that everything was propaganda. However, the judge issued an injunction, that (1) it was illegal to put anything in someone's food or drink without their knowledge (similar to using roofies for date rape, he said); and (2) Gerald, Estée Lauder, and everyone else was prohibited from manufacturing love potions. He also added, with a wry smile, that if a woman wanted to take off her shirt at the end of a date, she was completely free to do so. It violated no known law that he knew of. The court was convulsed with laughter for several minutes.

In a move that surprised himself, Gerald decided to quit the field of chemistry, with the exception of teaching undergraduates. He wrote Peter proposing that the two of them, along with Phyllis, write a book on propaganda, nationalism, and action-at-a-distance. Peter wrote back only two words: WE'RE IN! With the publication of *Affinity and Propaganda*, two years later, the two of them were back on the lecture circuit; Phyllis stayed home with the twins. "I'm busy turning them into noncompetitive, nonconsumerist, little Buddhists," she declared. "That's *my* propaganda." She also wrote a book of her own, entitled *Your Breasts Are a Love Potion*, in which she urged women to take off their shirts at the end of a date. It was a roaring success, and the trend of shirtless dates swept the country. The nation was a lot happier as a result, on the whole, as male-female relations improved dramatically.

The final development in this strange tale would have to be classified as a miracle: the three of them were awarded the Nobel Peace Prize. Gerald went to Oslo to accept the award. "I chased the Nobel in chemistry for many years," he told the assembled guests, "for my work on affinity, and was always rejected at the eleventh hour. I have no resentment about that, however, because my work with Phyllis and Peter Argyle, on social and political affinity, is far more important, in my opinion. Here is my message to all of you here, and to the world: ONLY CONNECT!"

Standing ovation; the applause was deafening. A thousand hearts beating as one.

# ABOUT THE AUTHOR

Morris Berman is a poet, novelist, essayist, social critic, and cultural historian. He has written sixteen books and nearly 200 articles, and has taught at a number of universities in Europe, North America, and Mexico. He won the Governor's Writers Award for Washington State in 1990, and was the first recipient of the annual Rollo May Center Grant for Humanistic Studies in 1992. In 2000, *The Twilight of American Culture* was named a "Notable Book" by the *New York Times Book Review*, and in 2013 he received the Neil Postman Award for Career Achievement in Public Intellectual Activity from the Media Ecology Association. Dr. Berman lives in Mexico.

www.ingramcontent.com/pod-product-compliance
Lightning Source LLC
Chambersburg PA
CBHW060946030726
47503CB00003B/745